TEMPT ME
WITH

Darkness

SHAYLA BLACK

D0210163

POCKET BOOKS

New York   London   Toronto   Sydney

Pocket Books
A Division of Simon & Schuster, Inc.
1230 Avenue of the Americas
New York, NY 10020

This book is a work of fiction. Names, characters, places, and incidents either are products of the author's imagination or are used fictitiously. Any resemblance to actual events or locales or persons, living or dead, is entirely coincidental.

First Pocket Books paperback edition September 2008

POCKET and colophon are registered trademarks of Simon & Schuster, Inc.

For information about special discounts for bulk purchases, please contact Simon & Schuster Special Sales at 1-800-456-6798 or business@simonandschuster.com

Illustration by Jonathan Barkat

Manufactured in the United States of America

10 9 8 7 6 5 4 3 2 1

ISBN-13: 978-1-4165-5858-3
ISBN-10: 1-4165-5858-6

To the readers who've bought my books and contacted me through the years. Your kindness, support, and encouragement have kept me going during some dark times. You all have inspired me to tackle one of my most ambitious ideas and make my fantasy of publishing books in this series a reality. Words cannot express how much you mean to me. I treasure your letters and e-mails, and hope that you find this book deserving of your anticipation and wait.

Acknowledgments

With much thanks to my wonderful advance readers, who offered amazing encouragement and feedback, propped me up, hugged me or kicked my butt, whenever and whatever needed—not to mention catching my typos: Jennifer Ray, Natalie Sickles, Denise McClain, Rhyannon Byrd, Melissa Schroeder, and Alice Miller.

With more gratitude than you can possibly imagine, amazing technical wizards and damn fine friends Sylvia Day and Nikki Duncan. Without the two of you, there would be no www.doomsdaybrethren.com or new www.shaylablack.com sites. I'd still be on the phone with GoDaddy trying to figure out why I needed a Linux server while banging my head against my monitor, wishing I knew how to meld multiple images into something cool. Syl, you're a WordPress goddess and one of the best people to talk to ever. Nikki, I bow to your Photoshop abilities, organizational skills, and utter goldness. Can I be like you when I grow up?

To my brainstorming partner, standing lunch date, head cheerleader, and all-around great guy Lee Swift...a million thanks for letting me prattle on and finishing my sentences for me and tolerating my long pauses while I tried to rub two words together to articulate my plot problems so you could help me solve them. Your day is coming, and I can't wait!

I must thank Abby Zidle, my wonderful editor at Pocket. Thanks for helping me hone and distill this into the book we have today. I know it took a lot of hard work and insight on your part. It wasn't painless for either of us, but it was worth it. I'm grateful for your support and your belief in me...and our shared love of *So You Think You Can Dance*.

And to my family for their unfailing love and hand holding through a decade in publishing, and especially during the difficult summer in which I began writing this book. You've always been there, always done your best to understand... and didn't complain too loudly about the four-month diet of takeout. You're amazing people! Love you bunches!

CHAPTER ONE

BESIDE THE LUSH BANKS of a pond, a woman beckoned, familiar. Yet Marrok of Cadbury had never seen her face in his life.

Vivid grass and multicolored flowers rioted around her. A cityscape towered in the background. None of that held his gaze rapt. Her bare-to-the-skin nakedness and dangerous beauty did.

The woman's sable hair swept over one pale shoulder, curling under the swell of a generous breast topped by a berry nipple—and framing a birthmark he knew well.

She no longer possessed the platinum tresses into which he'd once thrust his hands. Her new face was delicate—higher cheekbones, pert nose, pillowy mouth—but the siren could not disguise herself from him. Black lashes fluttered over violet eyes that had long haunted his nightmares.

Morganna.

Lust crashed into him, a battering ram to the gut. Need stiffened his cock. He wanted her as he never had, with a frightening desperation. Bollocks! Was he daft enough to let her lure him to further doom?

Acid hatred mixed with clawing desire. He tried to look away, but his gaze caressed her small waist, her curved hips, the moist flesh between her thighs glistening. Luminous, her smile coaxed him to touch her, challenged him to walk away.

Marrok didn't—couldn't—do either.

Morganna bewitched him more now than she had on their wind-drenched night of shared pleasure an eon ago. The strawberry mark low between her breasts brought back memories of pale moonlight surrounding them as he'd succumbed to temptation and tupped her senseless. For that mistake, he'd paid dearly.

With the last fifteen centuries.

Mist swirled around her like the mystical fog of legend, as if caressing her. Though she was deadly, Morganna in this new form captivated him. Today, society had clinical terms for his obsession. He cared not. Getting the treacherous bitch to release him from his hell . . . nothing else mattered.

With an alluring curl of her fingers, she summoned him. Marrok gritted his teeth. To yield would only mean further torture. But his body betrayed him, inching closer, his cock swelling painfully. Cursing, he closed his eyes.

If he must resist her to be free, he feared he was doomed.

Marrok opened his eyes as a fresh rush of desire slammed him. Want was a luxury; this woman he *needed*. The feeling was as new as a baby's first breath . . . and as welcome as the plague. And likely illusory, merely one of Morganna's tricks.

Though he dug his fingers into his thighs, her haunting eyes pleaded with him. Marrok very nearly surrendered to the urge to touch her.

Then she waved her hand. Suddenly, she clutched to her naked breasts the ornate red book he knew meant the difference between his life and death, and she backed away.

Nay!

Marrok launched himself at her. They fell to the ground in a tangle of breaths, arms, and legs. The book fell beside them, its maddening lock still firmly closed.

Before he could grab it, she latched slender arms around his neck and arched, distracting him with her lush curves.

"Marrok, love me."

Her plea spiked his fevered lust. He ached to sink deep into her. But he had to resist this fatal woman. Somehow.

"Release me," he growled.

She clung tighter, then writhed against his erection. By God, she was wet. He was on fire for her. A heartbeat from explosion. A mere moment from forgetting how treacherous she was.

"Open the book!"

"You want me." Her whisper made him shiver.

Why deny that? A waste of time and breath.

As she wriggled under him, lightning chased across his skin. Like a fool, he thrust against her and groaned. The need to utterly possess her screamed through him. Later, he'd remember all the reasons he could not.

Marrok dropped his hands to her thighs and pried them wider. "If you tempt me thus, you will take what I give you. All I give you."

"Anything."

Morganna's nipples burned his chest as he lifted her legs over his arms. From one instant to the next, his clothes melted away and he poised himself at her entrance.

Groaning, he buried his face in her fragrant neck. Incredible. Inevitable. More intoxicating than ever. Marrok had sworn never to touch Morganna again—a promise he had kept for centuries—but now . . . he *had* to be inside her.

"Everything . . ." she encouraged.

As he surged forward, Morganna grabbed the book. Desire chained him; he could not move, not even to snatch it from her grasp.

With a wave of her pale hand, Morganna unlocked the

volume. The cover fell open, revealing a hint of its pages, as she faded away.

"Give it to me!"

He shouted at fog. She—and the book—were gone.

Again, she'd used her power against him. Desire sizzled deep but he was, as ever, cursed. Desolation slashed him, leaving his soul to bleed.

His anguish made no sense. He'd never mourn Morganna's loss. He would, in fact, spit on her grave if she had one.

"I am the key." Her soft entreaty swept through the wind. "Find me."

Marrok dragged himself to his feet, suppressing a primal scream. He must hunt her. That cityscape behind the pond he recognized as London. There, he could find her. His torment would never end without that book—and without a taste of her flesh.

Around him, something rattled. Marrok sat up with a startled gasp, his bed rumpled, eyes wide. Panting, he scanned his surroundings. Bare walls, carved bed. A sword beside his hand. Glock under his pillow.

His cottage, not a mist-draped clearing. No Morganna.

The book! Marrok whipped his gaze around. On his bed-side table rested the leather-bound tome. The vehicle of his never-ending torment, the key to his freedom, was still here and still locked.

It had been but a dream.

Or perhaps a message? Though it had been centuries, Morganna had once enjoyed reaching from her exile to taunt him in sleep. He dared not disregard the message—she had returned to this mortal realm as an ethereal brunette, able to unlock the volume and intent on thieving it.

He rose, determined to find the sorceress in her new disguise. She alone could end the torture of his ages-old existence. Shadow and torment her he would, until she granted him what he wanted most in life.

Death.

A sharp rap against the cottage's front window startled Marrok—the same sound that had awakened him. He hadn't had a visitor in a decade, and preferred it that way. Guests were both unexpected and unwelcome.

Marrok slid the book into the safe hidden beneath loose floorboards in his bedroom, then took up his sword and stalked down the hall. As he slid around the corner, his heart raced with the anticipation of impending battle. Morning sunlight seeped through the window, illuminating dust motes and casting a human shadow onto the gleaming wooden floor.

If someone had come to take the book from him, he would greet them with bloodshed.

Marrok crept forward, crouched for attack. The shadow disappeared. A faint crunch of footsteps outside replaced the silhouette. He slipped toward the door silently, weapon in hand.

"Hey, freak of nature," a familiar male voice called from outside, punctuated by another knock. "Are you in there?"

Heaving an annoyed sigh, Marrok yanked the door open to find a nightmare nearly as bad as the one that had awakened him. Golden hair spiked above sleek brows and wicked blue eyes. A glittery Hollywood smile belied the gifted wizard's immense power. Bram Rion. Marrok groaned. Now he would never have any peace.

"Are you calling *me* a freak of nature? Coming from you, that is rich."

"If today is your day to conduct beheadings, count me out." Bram flashed the million-dollar smile that had seduced magickind into seeing things his way for four hundred years.

Marrok frowned and propped his sword against a nearby wall.

Bram paused outside. "Are you going to invite me past the magic circle guarding your place, or must I continue to stand on the mat?"

"If I do not?" Marrok challenged, raising a dark brow. He was heartily tempted not to. The magical coxcomb amused him at times . . . but Marrok didn't dare trust him.

"If you don't let me past, I can't tell you something juicy . . ."

Bram would not go away until he spilled his secret, though Marrok cared little what the wizard had to say. He must find Morganna in her new guise, then force, coerce, or beg her into unlocking that accursed book and setting him free.

"Enter," he huffed.

Bram stepped inside and shut the door behind him. "You look like hell. Did you sleep in yesterday's trousers?"

Marrok stared at his rumpled chinos. "Did you come all this way to be my mum?"

"If you need one . . . " Bram shrugged, mischief lurking in his eyes.

"What the hell do you want? Say it and be gone," Marrok demanded, striding to his room to snatch a fresh T-shirt and old jeans out of a drawer. Then he trekked across the hall to his bathroom.

Bram followed, lingering outside after Marrok slammed the door in his face.

After donning fresh clothes, he turned to a mirror and slid a brush through his dark hair. Ancient eyes stared back at him, filled with misery, anger, and thwarted lust. He *did* look like hell.

"To talk to you," Bram said through the door. "You know that only something gravely important could bring me to the Creepified Forest."

"Important to magickind." Not necessarily important to him.

"Since I'm the only friend you have, it's important to you, as well."

"I have no friends." Marrok pictured Bram gritting his teeth. He smiled.

"All right, then. I am the only living being who knows of your immortality and still speaks to you."

Marrok grunted and reached for his toothbrush. "I am not interested. I must hunt."

"The local market too civilized for your Dark Ages up-bringing?"

Marrok wrenched open the bathroom door, staring at Bram as if he were a bloodsucking insect. "Is magickind so starved for a comedian that you suffice?"

Bram sighed. "I really have come for a reason."

Though the wizard loved to antagonize him, Marrok knew the darling of magickind would not visit without cause.

"You will only pester me until I give in. Why are you here?"

"Because I've had a vision."

Vision. Being in the same room with anything or anyone magical was enough to give him hives. Having Bram around was like a permanent case of leprosy. "Why tell me? You must have a magical healer for this sort of thing."

"Because when it comes true, it will involve you."

"I involve myself in nothing." He shouldered past Bram and headed for the kitchen.

"And all of magickind knows it. Ever heard of the Book of Doomsday?"

"Nay."

"It's also called the Doomsday Diary."

His uninvited guest placed his hand on Marrok's shoulder. Immediately, he sensed a tightening under his forehead, then between the temples. Bloody hell, the bastard was trying to sneak into his thoughts. Marrok jerked away and slammed a mental door between them.

Bram reared back in surprise, speculation on his face. Clearly, humans were often unable to block him from their minds. But Marrok hadn't survived half of forever without learning a few tricks.

"Never have I heard of the accursed book by either name. Do not touch me or attempt to invade my head again, or I will slice you in two."

"It would be amusing for you to try, human." The wizard snorted. "You've never seen the book? It's red with gilt inlays, and is small, ornate, and very old."

That sounded like . . . Marrok shoved the thought away, lest Bram read it. No reason to add fuel to his fire.

"You *do* know something." Excitement revved up Bram's face. "All magickind knows of the Book of Doomsday. It's part of our folklore. I thought you might know of the book because it was created by my grandfather's nemesis."

"I did not know Merlin well. Why should I know of his enemies?"

"Well, Morganna *was* your lover."

Marrok grimaced. "You have confused a one-time sating of lust with a real bond."

"She's the reason you're immortal. She cursed you with the book, didn't she?"

By hell's fire, how could Bram know that? "I know naught of it."

"You're lying."

"Shove off!" Marrok stomped to the door, opened it, and gestured with a wave.

"A moment more . . ." The wizard sent him a sober stare. "I want to share my vision with you."

"Of?"

"The future. Watch."

"Keep your visions to yourself, you droning codpiece."

Bram ignored him, grabbed his arm, and waved a hand in front of his face. A picture appeared before Marrok's eyes. He fell into it, unable to back away.

Nighttime. A darkened home, once sprawling and lovely, now decayed. A small mass of people walked toward it. Some were clad in gray robes trimmed in red. Others wore normal dress and oddly vacant stares.

Intrigued against his will, Marrok peered closer, then reeled back in shock. The people in robes dragged the others toward the house with ropes about their necks. The air of excitement surrounding the berobed was palpable.

"Who are the people dressed like friars?" he asked.

"Definitely not clergy. They're part of the Anarki."

Marrok flinched. Even in his isolation, he'd known of the chaos and fear they created in their rise to power two centuries ago.

Once inside the run-down manor, a man in robes waited in an empty room, surrounded by a circle of flickering candles. His face obscured, he hovered over the still body of a naked man who, if human, looked to be about thirty.

"Who lies there?" Marrok asked Bram.

"Mathias d'Arc."

Even a seasoned warrior like Marrok shuddered at the name. Mathias was the magical equivalent of Genghis Khan, Caligula, Vlad Dracula, and Hannibal Lecter rolled into one. Cruel, clever, hedonistic, rapacious. Brilliantly evil. A wizard of great power and no conscience, Mathias wouldn't be happy until everyone in his path was either enslaved or dead.

"What are the Anarki about?" Marrok hissed.

"Watch."

As the group entered the shadowed room, they formed a circle around the candles, pushing some of the entranced people inside, closer to Mathias, who lay still as death.

The robed wizard who had been waiting stood at Mathias's head and raised his arms. "We, the Deprived, have waited centuries for this night. The Privileged will hear our thunder and feel only terror until they give us all they've denied our kind. Until the 'Social Order' laws prohibiting any with 'undesirable' traits and bloodlines from holding vital positions are dissolved, they will know war and pain and death. They do not know that we, the faithful, have waited for salvation. Tonight, our patience will be rewarded."

A cheer went up from those in robes. The others were silent.

From a distant part of the house, a clock chimed low and loud, *gong, gong, gong* . . . Twelve times. The room seemed to hold its collective breath. Then silence.

Mathias's eyes opened wide.

Around him, the candles flickered. His followers gasped. The ceremony leader knelt, then whispered reverently, "You've returned!"

"My faithful Anarki . . ." Mathias's voice was thin and strained. "My sleeping draught fooled the Brethren but you believed in me. They thought me dead?"

"Very much so," the first replied.

"Excellent. Did they all pass into their nextlife?"

"Within days of your sleep."

"Your name?"

"Zain Denzell."

"Your father served me well." Mathias smiled. "You have brought me what I need?"

Zain nodded eagerly, then stepped around the circle, wending through the unresponsive bodies in street clothes. Finally, he grabbed a paunchy, middle-aged man and a young woman with blond ringlets in a cotton dressing gown and thrust them forward.

"Lovely. MacKinnetts?" Mathias asked.

"Yes. The Council member's brother and his untransitioned daughter. You must be starved."

Mathias nodded. "Indeed. Take the woman to my chamber. I will see to her very soon."

A robed servant did so. Marrok, watching, held his breath.

Groaning and straining, Mathias rolled to one side, facing the older man. Reaching for the center of his chest, Mathias snapped. The man blinked and gasped, then opened alert eyes.

"Oh good God!" He tried to scramble back. "You!"

"Me." Mathias smiled weakly.

Two others in robes caught the old man.

"Shall we hold him?" one asked, his voice shaking with enthusiasm to serve.

"Yes. We must prove that the order of magickind is changing."

The MacKinnett continued to resist as Mathias struggled to his feet, then gripped the man's throat.

"No. No!" The man scratched out. "Please . . ."

"Shut up! Were I not so starved for energy, I would draw out your punishment. Your anger and fear will provide me a bit. Your niece, with her young, ripe body, will provide me *much* more. Delicious."

"Please, no," MacKinnett babbled. "Auropha is a sweet

girl with her whole life ahead of her. She knows nothing of peril or pain—"

"Then I'd best see to her education."

Beside him, Mathias peered at the MacKinnett lord. With a feral grin, he laid a hand across the man's chest.

Immediately, MacKinnett started screaming. A film of blood oozed from his pores, seeping through his yellow shirt. He turned white, kicking and flailing. Then his eyes rolled to the back of his head. He slumped over, dead.

With a wave, Zain removed the older man's shirt, and Mathias's mark spread across his entire chest like a series of infected boils.

"A job well done," Mathias said to Zain. Now I will adjourn upstairs and restore myself fully with the girl. Her fear and rage will intoxicate me with power."

"Dear God, he's going to kill the girl as he did her uncle?" Marrok asked, appalled.

"A death like her uncle's would be kindness. What she will endure will be worse. Much worse."

Marrok looked at all the berobed followers standing about. "Will no one help her?"

"Who? The Deprived of magickind are 'punishing her' because she is Privileged. Mathias will use her to re-energize his magic and make an example of her."

Recoiling, Marrok reached for his sword. He had never condoned the rape and torture of innocents in battle. Mathias must be stopped. But when he rose to his feet, Bram pulled him back down.

"You can't race into my vision. It hasn't happened yet. Watch. There's more to see."

"The MacKinnett chit is a spitfire," Zain said to Mathias. "She will give you a great deal of energy."

"Excellent. Tomorrow, send the dead to their family. It's time for the Privileged to know their worst nightmare has returned."

"I will see to it."

"And the other matter?"

"We're still looking."

"I must have that book. With it, what I can do is nearly limitless."

"The Anarki will do whatever it takes. I vow it."

The vision turned black. Bram released Marrok slowly. He blinked, returning to the here and now.

Then he glared at Bram. "Bloody hell! You say that has not yet come to pass?"

"Not yet."

Marrok released a relieved breath. "Then it may not. You have no proof."

"Except the fact I've never been wrong in my life."

Marrok prayed that was an overconfident boast and resented the horror Bram had made him feel for the brutalized MacKinnetts. "Why do you imagine I care?"

"This problem is going to knock on your door. Soon."

"Because Mathias seeks this Doomsday Diary, which you think I possess?"

"Yes. No other book would give him half so much power. With it, all he must do is write his destructive wishes on a blank page to bring about any tragedy he wants—even Doomsday itself."

Perhaps Bram told the truth . . . and perhaps he'd created the horrific scene to manipulate Marrok into releasing the book so he could use it for his own ends. Everyone knew Bram was an ambitious knave. Mathias would first have to unlock the book to be able to use it . . . but as magical as he was, maybe he could.

"Certainly you can see that finding and safeguarding the book is imperative," Bram went on. "Will you help me?"

"Mathias is magical, as are you. Cast a spell to ensure he can do no harm."

"Nice thought, but magic doesn't work like that. Mathias is born of a powerful bloodline with a strong tendency to produce sociopaths. As you saw, he gorges on others' pain and terror—even forced pleasure. Those facts make him very strong. And if he returns, he has magical defenses we can only guess at. Please. Give me the book."

Marrok grabbed him by his prissy Ralph Lauren collar and shoved him against the wall.

He did not trust the wizard for an instant. As Merlin's grandson, he was packed with powerfully magical genes. Marrok did not subscribe to the theory that his enemy's enemy was his friend. "Speak no more of the book to me or you will feel my blade in your belly!"

Bram shrugged out of his hold and straightened his shirt, clearly undeterred.

"I'll take that as a no. Pity. A lot of people are going to die. But then, you see death as a blessing, don't you?"

"Even if the book were within my grasp, why would I give it to you?"

"Because it will save you pain. Mathias *will* come for you once he realizes you possess it." Bram crossed into the living area, where he sank into an overstuffed chair, propping booted feet on the table.

Marrok clenched his jaw. "I know naught."

"Play dumb if you want, then." Bram flashed a brittle smile. "But I have another reason for coming here. There's someone I want you to meet, the owner of a new art gallery."

Socializing was the last thing he had time for with Morganna returned from exile. "Nay."

"This is a stellar opportunity. The place is called A Touch of Magic." Swinging his feet to the ground, he leaned forward, bracing his elbows on his knees. "It's very fresh, and recently opened—"

"Naught you say of that interests me. I need a ride to London."

"You? Facing civilization? Willingly?" Bram's jaw hit his chest.

"I seek a woman."

"Planning to test the limits of your curse again?"

How did Bram know of *that*? Nosy coxcomb. Marrok resisted the urge to tear the wizard's head off—barely. "Shut your mouth before I shut it for you."

Bram laughed. "The last woman you took to your bed disappeared for two days. That was a decade ago, wasn't it?"

"Not another word."

Crossing his arms over his chest again, Bram smiled. "I hear you astound humans and put even magical men to shame. But you're never quite . . . satisfied, are you?"

Marrok refused to admit to Bram that he could not find satisfaction in sex, no matter how many women he bedded, how many orgasms he gave, or how close he came to achieving his own release. It would only give the wizard something new with which to torment him.

"When you meet the gallery's owner, you may want to try your luck again. Olivia Gray already loves your carvings and she is quite dishy. Her magical signature is . . . interesting."

"She's one of your kind? Absolutely not! I seek one woman in particular."

"Oh, this is intriguing. You actually know a woman? You

haven't left this place in years. Did you meet her in a 'hot babes' chat room?"

Again, Bram clapped him on the shoulder, and Marrok felt the wizard trying to steal into his thoughts. Wrenching away, he marched to the sword, lifted the weapon and whipped it through the air with a menacing *whoosh*. "Cease your infernal invasion!"

Bram inched back. "Tell me about this woman. Maybe I can help."

The only help Bram would ever give him was a push into hell. "I know what she looks like, if not the name she uses now. I *will* find her."

"Hmm. Old flame?"

Old flame, old enemy. "Take me to London."

"I'll take you wherever you wish to go." Bram paused. "After you meet Olivia. She's very interested in your art, and I promised her an introduction."

Marrok reined in his frustration, wishing Bram would choose another day to be difficult. Or better yet, another target. His dream, the omen that could set him free, had finally arrived. Morganna was running loose somewhere in London. He would make the witch release him from hell.

"Antagonizing me amuses you, but I will not play today."

"That's my offer. Take it or leave it." Bram shrugged, looking totally unapologetic. "Unless you want to hand over the book?"

Gripping the sword tighter, Marrok arched a brow. The damn Book of Doomsday wasn't leaving his possession until he discerned exactly how he must use it to end his curse. There was just one way, according to Morganna, and he *would* find it.

Besides, putting the bloody thing in the hands of someone magical was putting the fox in charge of the henhouse.

"Guess not." Bram smiled tightly. "In that case, I hope you enjoy meeting Ms. Gray. I've shown her a few pictures of the pieces you sold in the past. She's very impressed. I've already arranged a meeting for you two this morning. Won't take long. Then the rest of the day is yours." When Marrok resisted, Bram added, "Come now, you must have pieces to sell."

Aye. In the last three months, he'd carved his best work ever. Marrok's gaze cut across the room to rest on a three-foot rendering of King Arthur and his enemy Mordred locked in mortal combat. Merlin and Morganna each hovered behind their champions, spinning magic to help their knights win.

Crossing the floor to the sculpture, Marrok stared at the angles of Morganna's wooden likeness. Fear, fury, and a flash of desire tightened his gut. How could he have been so foolish as to tangle with that magical bitch?

Soon it would end. Today, he would hunt her down and demand answers, even if he had to wring them from her pretty neck. He was unsure where to begin the search, but somehow he knew this feeling, her looming presence, would guide him.

Prying his gaze from the carving, he turned to the door. "Fifteen minutes. No more."

"Smashing. But until you give me the Doomsday Diary . . ." Bram grinned, "I'm your new best friend."

As soon as Bram parked three blocks off of Oxford Street, Marrok bolted from the hated automobile's small confines. Warriors did not travel in motorized death traps, by God.

They trekked through the gloom of London's gray morning to a narrow little shop, where a purple sign flashed A Touch of Magic. With a cynical grunt, Marrok stared through the picture window. A clay rendering of Pegasus took up most of the display space. He studied the piece critically. The sculpture had symmetry, but lacked life and movement.

As Bram opened the door, an electronic chime heralded their arrival. Two steps later, a wave of musky incense slammed his senses. That and the strains of a passionate ballad surged through him. Across his skin awarness burned and tingled.

A woman had recently stood here. An enticing mix of light perfume over natural scent told him thus. He inhaled peaches and vanilla.

The clatter of beads in a doorway at the back of the store brought his gaze across the room. A woman emerged, carrying an armload of boxes. He caught a glimpse of windswept dark hair and a fragile profile before she turned to deposit the load on the counter along the back wall.

Familiar movements seized his breath.

Marrok willed the woman to face him. Instead, she unpacked, swaying in time with the Celtic tune piping through the room. A dangerous slash of desire sliced his gut.

"Olivia?" Bram called above the music.

She turned and smiled at the wizard.

The sight was an invisible fist slamming into Marrok.

"Bram, thanks for coming by." Her distinctly American voice rang in Marrok's head as she shut off the music. "I know you're busy. Did you get my message last week?"

"I did. Sorry. I haven't heard anything more about your father. I'll ask again. Nothing new from the investigator?"

Her shoulders slumped. "No, just an address for a crazy man who claims to be nearly five hundred years old. I'll keep looking. I moved here to find him, and I'm not giving up."

As if just realizing they weren't alone, Olivia peeked

around Bram at Marrok. The welcome on her face faltered, fell. She covered lush lips with her hand and stared as if the sight of him shocked her.

He could hardly be more shocked himself. Delicate cheeks, a slightly pointed chin, and those bloody haunting eyes.

Morganna's eyes in the face from this morning's dream. Recognition jolted his every nerve.

She looked back at Bram. "Is this . . . ?"

"Of course. I told you I'd deliver."

Bram shoved him toward her. Normally, he'd growl at the wizard for touching him. Today, his attention was fixed on Olivia.

Or rather, Morganna. The one woman who could end his curse.

He had not believed she could make herself as beautiful as the woman in his dream. He had underestimated his opponent. That alone made her more deadly, to say nothing of the power she had surely gathered over the centuries. She looked so young, barely twenty. Though her youth was an illusion, she made him feel ancient.

Bram turned to him. "Marrok, this is Olivia Gray."

She paused. Her hand dropped from her mouth, and she bit her bottom lip. For such calculated hesitation, the gesture looked natural. But Morganna never displayed vulnerability without a trap looming close behind.

Finally, she extended her hand to him. Marrok stared, wanting nothing less than to touch her—and nothing more. A film of sweat broke out across his skin. Oh, how she must be laughing.

But the centuries had taught Marrok to play her game.

Pasting on a shark's smile, he enfolded her hand in his. Electricity shot across his palm, up his arm, rocking him to his soul. In that instant, his cock hardened. Blast it all, with one small touch she bewitched him, exactly like his dream . . .

Only stronger.

Olivia's eyes widened. Grim satisfaction seeped through him.

"Ms. Gray."

She quickly withdrew her hand. "I—it's nice to meet you. Bram has told me about you. Actually, about your talent," she clarified. "The pictures I've seen are very impressive."

Morganna had never cared about his carving, only for his reputation on the battlefield and in the bedroom. This pretense of interest infuriated him. What game did the witch play?

Looking flustered, she glanced Bram's way.

"Where is that piece you brought?" Bram asked him.

He'd been so focused on Morganna, he had forgotten it. "In your car."

Bram's gaze bounced from Marrok to Olivia, then back again.

"Well, then, I'll . . . go get it. You two get acquainted."

The door chime signaling Bram's departure sounded loudly in the room's silence. But Olivia never looked away from Marrok. Her heart zoomed into hyperspeed.

He stared as if he knew her, could see inside her. As if he were utterly aware that, just that morning, she had dreamed of being naked and wet for him, begging for his touch.

When his sharp perusal swept down her body, she had the distinct impression Marrok knew he'd starred in her erotic fantasy. His scrutiny didn't seem sexual . . . exactly. Still, she flushed and tingled in some interesting places.

He didn't return the interest, of course. Most men

weren't aroused by an odd-looking woman with nearly-black hair and purple eyes who resembled an extra from an Elvira Halloween spectacular. Doutful that a prime male like Marrok would be enticed by her.

He stood at least six feet four. His door-frame-wide shoulders bulged, straining the seams of his black T-shirt. The fists bunched at his sides were huge. A shaggy mane of dark hair framed his haunted, hollow-cheeked face, accented by a neatly-trimmed goatee and unfathomable blue-gray eyes. His mouth twisted in a mysterious smile, as if he knew he made her nervous.

Olivia restrained the urge to toy with the bangles on her wrist. Marrok was a temperamental artist. Period. She owned an art gallery, her dream since she'd been a moody teenager living a nomadic life with her cold, overprotective mother. If she wanted to keep this place afloat, she'd better stop mooning and do business.

"I'd like to carry your carvings here," she said. "I think you have a great deal of talent. I could help you make a tidy sum."

He raised a dark, disquieting brow. "Money does not interest me."

Really? "Prestige, then? Recognition. Is that what you want?"

He stepped closer, loomed above her. If his aim was to intimidate her with his sheer size . . . score. One of his biceps was as thick as her thigh.

"I do not seek recognition." His tone was dangerous and rough.

She'd never been so aware of being alone with a man. Of course, she'd never dreamed of being naked and aching for a major hunk, then meeting him in the flesh. But they were here for business; she had to concentrate.

Suppressing a shiver, she squared her shoulders. "You must want something in exchange for your work. Tell me what, and I'll—"

"You know what I want."

He clamped large, heated fingers around her hips. An unexpected rush of energy burst through her, like she'd been jolted with a live wire. Scary. Sexual. He couldn't mean it to be.

Her head snapped back. Those pale eyes, framed by thick black lashes, drew her without mercy. His scent, woodsy and wild, went straight to her knees.

Damn it, she didn't know him, and he was touching her. Why wasn't she afraid? Or at least annoyed by the one-sided lust she felt?

"No, I don't."

"You lie."

His fingers tightened, and he brought her closer. Their bodies brushed, his heat crashing into her. Was he . . . ? Yes, erect. *Oh God.*

Maybe the lust wasn't one-sided . . . Shocked to her toes, she raised a shaking hand to his chest to ward him off. He was like living, breathing stone. Everywhere.

"Stop," she breathed.

His mouth sharpened into a dangerous slash. "Stop what?"

"Touching me." *Confusing me.* "Don't."

Marrok released her. Almost magically, the spell over her senses lifted. Energy seeped from her body in a rush. Common sense and anger returned.

"We're discussing business." She tried for hard-nosed professional, not trembling virgin. "I'm offering to sell your work and give you half the profits. But that does *not* give you the right to put your hands on me."

Frankly, she was stunned that he wanted to.

Crossing his arms over his massive chest, Marrok sent her a contemplative stare. "Touching you was a mistake."

Of course it had been.

The door chime sounded, startling Olivia. She jerked her gaze around as Bram entered, silently damning the fact he'd returned sixty seconds too late.

"Found the carving," Bram called victoriously, gripping a wooden statue Olivia couldn't see around his big hands. "Looked all over the car, forgetting we'd stashed it in the boot."

Neither responded to Bram. Olivia knew she should reach for the carving, but she watched Marrok warily. His eyes were riveted on her, blazing. Anger, and something else— lust?—bled from him. The combination was bleak, powerful, inexplicable, impossible . . . She stepped back.

"Now that you've heard my offer, shall we do business?" Olivia asked.

Marrok leaned close once more. "I would rather bed down with the devil. I trust him more."

Turning on one heel, he crossed the room and flung the door open. The chime sounded, drowned out by the door crashing against the wall. Olivia jumped as Marrok stalked outside.

She frowned. Had he been shafted by a gallery owner before? Or did he resent the fact that, for a moment he'd found the unusal woman arousing? That possibility shouldn't hurt anymore . . . but it did.

"That's bloody odd," Bram exclaimed. "What did you argue about?"

"I don't know."

Bram frowned, handing her the carving. "Here, take this. I'll have a chat with him. No worries."

Olivia started to tell Bram not to bother. Then she looked

at the carving in her hand. A fawn. She could swear that, at any moment, she would see its legs wobble as it learned to walk. Its soulful eyes amazed her. Marrok's talent . . . wow. And this was just a tiny slice of it. She closed her mouth.

He would thrill art lovers. It didn't matter if she disquieted him. Thankfully, she was used to artists' quirks. She'd place his work on her shelves . . . or her business would soon go under. She needed that money to stay in England, to pay the detective and find the father she'd never met. Once she discovered what motivated Marrok, she'd work with him—no matter how difficult.

"Perfect. I want to see him again, as soon as possible."

CHAPTER TWO

"WHAT THE HELL is the matter with you?" Bram barked, chasing at Marrok's heels.

Marrok turned on him. Where was his damn sword when he needed to skewer a devious wizard?

"You knew. You bloody *knew*."

"That Olivia is a le Fay? Yes."

"Not just any le Fay. Morganna in a different package."

Bram paused. "That, I can't say. Morganna predated me, so I've no idea what she looked like. At the moment, Olivia's magical signature tells me only her bloodline."

"Magical signature?"

"It's like . . . her aura, but specific to her magic. Most fully transitioned witches and wizards can see them. Olivia's signature is weak. She looks under twenty-five, the age a witch comes into her power. If that's the case, I can't read what I normally would."

"Pry into her mind as you did mine. Learn who she is."

Bram shook his head. "With that method, I can read only her passing thoughts. Unless she happens to be thinking about the fact she isn't Morganna, it would do no good. I could only read deeper if I were . . . intimately touching her."

"Meaning?"

"The deeper the touch, the deeper I can delve into her mind."

In other words, if Bram was buried to the hilt in a woman, he could discern her life story. It should have been tempting to let Bram tumble with evil. Instead, the thought made him want to smash the wizard's face. Though Marrok hated Morganna in her new form, he couldn't lie; he wanted her all for himself.

"Do *not* lay a finger on her," Marrok growled.

"I hadn't planned to. Lovely girl . . . not interested. But if I pry into a woman's mind, I can also read the means to unravel her, sexually speaking."

Was he serious? He could figure out how to persuade any woman into carnal surrender? No wonder he was the Lothario of the magical world.

"If a woman's first thoughts fail to tell you what you wish to know, you simply listen to her fantasies and she turns wanton for you?"

"Absolutely." Bram flashed his signature grin. "I spent a great deal of time developing that skill."

"Stay out of Morganna's head."

"Marrok, I don't think she *is* Morganna. Why would her signature be so weak? My grandfather told me you could see her coming a mile away, all molten purple and iridescent."

"Rubbish. When was the last time you saw *any* le Fay alive and walking?"

Bram nodded, conceding the point. "It's been several hundred years, yes. But her son took human lovers by the hundreds who bore children. It's possible—"

"But equally probable that she disguises herself. There have long been rumors that Morganna could shape-shift. Perhaps she made herself into a young witch and muted her signature."

"Normally, I'd say not, but with Morganna, anything's possible." Bram sighed. "If she *is* back and luring you into her life, she can want only one thing."

The Book of Doomsday. It had once been her greatest source of power. When Merlin banished her centuries ago, the book had mysteriously locked itself. It remained closed to this day.

"The Doomsday Diary has extraordinary powers."

Marrok knew that personally. In the past centuries, he had been unable to open the book, shred it, deface it, or destroy it. Within moments, the little volume would regenerate, humming with power again. How could an object retain so much magic so long after its mistress had left this earthly realm?

"You have it. Save yourself whatever agony is headed your way and give it to me. I will protect it."

"Piss off." His long strides ate up the sidewalk.

Bram followed. "I popped in this morning because I want to help. Not that I believed you'd ask for or accept it."

"Wise man."

Bram jumped in front of him. Marrok was forced to stop or collide with the bastard.

"The book must be guarded by magickind. If it falls into

the wrong hands, it could mean the destruction of every witch, wizard, and youngling. You don't have the ability to protect it."

Fifteen centuries as the book's guardian said otherwise.

Marrok *needed* the book—and the le Fay woman to unlock it—to end his curse. Then he'd consider giving it to Bram . . . right after a blue moon on the twelfth of never.

"If Morganna reacquires the book," Bram said, "she could begin centuries of suffering and torture. And if my vision comes true and Mathias gets it, whatever Morganna would do will seem pleasant."

Bram headed for the car again. Marrok followed and slid inside, clenching his fists. He hated these contraptions. Where was a good horse when you wanted to go from point A to point B? Worse, Bram's driving would give even the stoutest warrior a heart attack. He buckled his seat belt.

Bram raised a golden brow. "You can't die. Why bother?"

"You do not drive a great deal, do you?"

"No," Bram admitted wryly. "I prefer teleporting."

"It shows."

Bram threw back his golden head and laughed. "Two jokes from you in one day. I might pass out from the shock."

"Unfortunately, you will recover."

After the engine roared to life, the strains of a harsh alternative rock song shook the car. A raspy-voiced male ground out a chorus about the animal he had become. Marrok winced. Bram ignored him and revved the car away from the curb. Not just any car, but a red Ferrari 599 GTB Fiorano. Nothing subtle about Bram.

"Nice vehicle for someone who dislikes driving."

"When you must, why not do so in style?"

"You can appear and disappear at your leisure. Why have a car?"

Bram smiled. "When I need to take a taciturn immortal warrior to London, does he want me teleporting him?"

"By God's blood, nay!"

"Exactly. The humans also get agitated when we pop in and out. Not a great way to keep magickind a secret . . ."

"Can you turn that racket down?" He gestured to the sleek car stereo.

"The music? It rocks, old man."

"It makes my head pound. How can you think with that shouting rattling about your ears?"

Bram turned it down. A little. Very little.

Stopping the car at a red light, Bram leveled Marrok a stare of such gravity, he was taken aback. "Mathias will be back soon, and we must take action. I've already warned the MacKinnetts. Fools. They're certain being Privileged means no one would dare harm them."

Marrok shuddered as images from the wizard's vision pelted him again, haunted him.

Gunning the sleek red vehicle, Bram screeched away from the red light. "Our most important task is protecting the book. Magickind, perhaps even mankind, is at stake."

Of course, throw in his race, too, so he had a personal reason to care. Tricky sod . . .

"The possibility of Mathias returning is troubling. However, if you seek information about the book, Ms. Gray knows far more than I." Marrok paused. "Perhaps you should let me talk to her."

"You just stormed out on her."

"Temporary insanity," Marrok pleaded with a shrug.

"All right, then. Talk to her. If she is Morganna, you must be careful. Her magic—"

"Is significant, aye. But so is yours."

"Not enough to thwart millennia-old power. Besides, I'd

rather not tangle with Morganna. My grandfather's dealings with her would predispose her to dislike me. And as his writings point out, she is one scary bitch."

It was not a good omen that Bram had a healthy respect for Morganna's powers. Marrok cursed his randy nature for ever inducing him to lie with the she-devil.

"To talk to her, I need some means of neutralizing her. I cannot endure her hexing me again. As much as I abhor immortality, spending the rest of eternity as a toad or something equally loathsome appeals even less."

Watching the traffic intently, Bram tapped the steering wheel with his thumb in time to another head-banging alternative rock song.

"My grandfather left a few things in my possession. One in particular he designed just for Morganna. Something with a *laggagh* stone. You can make use of it."

"What does that mean?"

"I'm not as good with the old language as I should be. Short attention span for dull subjects." Bram sighed. "According to Merlin's notes, it weakens her. The minute it touches her, it will block her magic. But there are side effects."

"Are they unpleasant for her?"

He frowned. "I should say so."

"Perfect." What did he care if he caused Morganna a little pain after the centuries of hell she had put him through?

Bram slanted him a harsh stare. "Be careful. If Olivia is, in fact, Morganna, she will be a dangerous adversary. And since I know she cursed you with the diary, I have no doubt you'll refuse to hand it over until you've exhausted all hope of ending her charming little hex."

"I never said I have the book."

Bram shot him a tight smile and shoved something into

his hand. "Pretend you don't, then. If you change your mind or need my help, toss this in the air and call my name."

"This is a rock," Marrok pointed out, staring at it. "Are you mad?"

"Don't wait long to call on me. We're running out of time."

Cursing, Olivia struggled with the keys that locked A Touch of Magic's front door. Her whole day—hell, her whole life—had been one mess after another.

She jammed her cell phone against her ear with a wry smile. "I'm fine, Bram. Just tired. I woke up at two this morning and couldn't go back to sleep. I never ate lunch, either."

Now exhaustion plagued her, its claws sinking deep.

"Sorry to hear that," Bram murmured. "Still worried about your father?"

"Yes."

All her life, she'd been told her father died before her birth. After her estranged mother's recent death, she'd combed through Barbara's belongings and learned that was a lie. Armed with her father's name, last known address, and a picture that proved she'd inherited her unusual eyes, she'd been determined to find the truth. Others found long-lost relatives with less. Her search, even with Bram and the hired detective, had turned up nothing. It was as if he'd disappeared.

That worried her. Among her mother's hidden effects had been an unopened letter her father had written nearly twenty years ago, mailed from London. Her mother hadn't cared what it said, damn her. Not surprising. Barbara had perfected the art of cold and unresponsive.

You have a roof over your head, young lady, because I do my duty. Do yours. Make better grades. Clean your room. Don't touch me.

Good ol' Mom had concealed every trace of her father. Then again, if there'd been a way to isolate Olivia or make her miserable, Barbara had pounced on it. Her suicide put an exclamation point on that fact.

In the letter, Richard Gray had begged Barbara to come back to him and bring their daughter. The poignant longing in his words had brought tears to her eyes. He'd wanted to meet Olivia, know her, love her. *Her*. She wasn't a burden to him.

He'd vowed to protect them. From what? Did whatever he feared have anything to do with her inability to find him now? Meeting him would, at least, satisfy her curiosity. At best, he might help her get beyond her fear of letting people close. Please God, don't let her be too late.

"My search is nearly at a dead end," she went on. "I've got one more address I can follow up on, but if that doesn't pan out . . . I'll have to think of something else. I'm so frustrated."

To make matters worse, business hadn't been great, so she feared losing this little dream shop. A Touch of Magic was her one place, her center, when everything else was crap. It was her greatest achievement to date. But she lacked the money to keep paying the detective. If she went broke, she'd have to decide: Stay here or go back to the States.

Go back to what? asked the voice in her head. Here, she had made herself some roots. No more moving to a new city every three months and being the new kid in town, as she had with Mom. In England, she felt more . . . at home. Her flat was small. She wasn't looking forward to the upcoming cold winter. And she hated the food. Didn't Brits believe in good enchiladas? But the sense of history, of permanency, was to die for.

"I have a feeling he'll turn up soon. Don't give up."

"Not as long as there's still a chance I'll find him."

"That's the spirit." Bram's warmth reached through the phone. "You tenacious American girls never fail to impress."

He was a good friend. A little flirtatious, but flirting was like breathing for him. She never took his smiles and charm seriously. Besides, men typically weren't interested in her that way.

Except, perhaps, for the broodingly sexy artist she'd met this morning.

Broodingly sexy? Marrok had been rude. An ass.

But for a brief moment, she'd sworn he wanted her. Jerk or not, knowing that had made her feel giddy and unleashed a hot tumble of desire inside her. One touch from him, and her body had lit up like a Christmas tree. Pathetic.

Ever since Marrok slammed out of A Touch of Magic that morning, a weird ache had nagged her body. Exhaustion dragged her down. Damn it, she needed sleep or caffeine— something.

"Olivia," Bram said. "I called about Marrok. Don't be surprised if you hear from him. I think he feels ghastly about whatever row you had today."

"Good. I'd planned on hunting him down tomorrow." And keeping her libido out of the conversation. "Temperamental, but wow, his talent . . ."

"I thought you'd be thrilled. He's difficult and odd. But give him a chance."

Olivia jerked on the door handle and tried to turn the key. Nothing. Some days, the old thing took an active dislike to her. Like today. Then a stutter beep in her ear made her sigh.

"Will do. I've got to run. My battery is dying, and I can't get the damn door locked."

They agreed to touch base in a few days and hung up. She tried the lock again. Jammed.

"Argh!" She pushed a strand of dark hair from her eyes. "Obstinate door."

"Does talking to it help?"

Olivia whirled at the deep, unexpected voice. Through the darkness, a male figure towered near.

Marrok.

Though the shadows held most of his face in mystery, shards of desire needled her. He stood unmoving as pale glimmers of light splashed across his wolfish eyes. His tight black T-shirt clung to broad shoulders, worn denim to long, hard thighs. He was like an action figure come to life.

"You startled me." A hint of accusation laced her voice.

With him near, exhaustion wasn't a problem. Suddenly, her body pinged with life.

"Not for the first time, I think." He stepped out of the shadows. Light from the half-moon bathed his hard face in silvery tones. "I startled you this morning as well. I apologize."

He closed the distance between them, so quietly she understood how he'd sneaked up on her. Then he withdrew the keys from her tense grip.

With a quick flick of his wrist, he locked the shop's door. Olivia couldn't look away from the planes of his broad back, the ripple of his shoulders.

What would they feel like under her hands as he thrust deep inside her?

The question blindsided her. Totally inappropriate. Completely ridiculous. Sure, he'd been erect earlier, but it was probably an involuntary reaction. Sex between them was unlikely to ever happen. Her brain was clearly in her panties.

He turned and deposited her keys back in her hand. Could he see the flush climbing up her hot cheeks?

"I've reconsidered your offer," he said suddenly.

Olivia's gaze snapped to his face. No explanation of his earlier behavior, no assurances it wouldn't happen again.

Though Marrok set off her personal danger sensors and lit her fire all at once, he was her best shot at success, at scraping together the money to keep searching for her father. After working at an art gallery during college, she was a pro with the high-maintenance ones. He had difficult written all over him. She'd deal with whatever he threw her way.

"So I'm no longer on par with the devil?"

He had the good grace to look sheepish. "Nay."

Nay? What was with his archaic shtick?

"Fine. We can talk." She glanced at her watch. "I have time for a cup of coffee."

Marrok shook his head. "I want to show you my entire collection, work no one has ever seen."

His intimate whisper sent a medley of tingles through her. The intimation that he wanted to show her something he'd never shared with anyone hit her bull's eye as a business owner—and a woman.

"All right," her trembling voice answered. "Where to?"

Marrok paused. Olivia had the impression he was studying her, monitoring her every reaction. "My flat."

Just then, a cab screeched around a corner and halted at the curb. Marrok opened the door and gestured her inside.

"I hired a taxi in advance, hoping you would come with me."

Logic warned her that only a fool would climb inside and follow a virtual stranger to his place. After all, what did she know about him? He'd grabbed and insulted her mere hours ago.

She bit her lip. Bram had just asked her to give him a

chance. And in her dreams, she knew intimately the feel of his hands spreading her thighs . . .

Stop there.

The taxi door gaped open. Olivia hesitated.

If Marrok wanted to hurt her, he wouldn't lure her back to his home in a taxi, with its driver as a witness, right? Odds were he lived in a crowded flat with three other starving artists.

She climbed into the taxi and scooted to the far edge, wrinkling her nose at the odor of stale smoke pervading the car's interior.

Marrok climbed in beside her. His presence absorbed three-quarters of the backseat. The scents of wood, earth, and male replaced smoke. He put off the kind of smell she could breathe in forever. It wasn't smart, but she leaned closer and drew in a deep breath. A buzz of energy wound through her, like a morning Starbucks run.

Marrok's blue-gray eyes glowed hot with lust. Then he looked away, clenching and unclenching his fists.

Something agitated him. Did he feel the pull between them? Her body responded, flowering with a tug of desire.

Forget it. Stay professional.

"How long have you lived in London?" He broke the quiet as the taxi sped off.

"Six months. Almost seven now," she replied. "You?"

"Seems like forever."

His conversation should have set Olivia at ease. Instead, she felt more edgy.

"Did you open the shop on your own?" He rolled down the window and sucked in crisp autumn air.

"Yes. I'm convinced your work would make an excellent addition to my shelves."

"After you've seen the rest of my collection, we will talk."

"I'm sure I'll love it. You're very talented."

He shrugged away her remark.

"Are you displaying elsewhere?"

"No." He unclenched his fists, then clenched them again. "Why an art gallery? Why do something as difficult as open your own shop, rather than take a job elsewhere?"

"I love art." She smiled. "When it's well done, it takes you to another place, evokes emotions you didn't know you had. When your life sucks, it allows you to escape into a whole new world. I mean, is there any woman who's looked at Botticelli's *The Birth of Venus* and hasn't imagined herself rising out of the sea, reborn into something . . . spectacular? Or looked at Renoir's *Bal au Moulin de la Galette, Montmartre* and couldn't picture themselves laughing and dancing with the beautiful crowd, being free and alive? Art is like . . . cleansing to the soul. An office job . . ." She wrinkled her nose. "I did that one summer in college. I got fired for falling asleep, and I wasn't good at taking direction. I'd rather have a few little shops like this that sell great art about real life to people who need its beauty. Like your fawn. That was stunning."

"I heard you tell Bram that you moved here to find your father. By yourself?"

Olivia hesitated. She understood him asking for her philosophy about art, since they were discussing her displaying his work. She had no idea why he'd be interested in her personal life. He'd touched her earlier, seemingly been aroused by her—just before he insulted her and stormed out. Was it possible he was interested in *her*?

Regardless, the subject of her father was a deeply personal one. It went beyond matters of flesh and blood, straight to her heart. Bonds between fathers and daughters should be special, and Olivia couldn't help but wish that to be true for her as well. She wasn't going to share more than the basic facts with a stranger.

"Yes. He and my mother were estranged. I've never met him." More than anything, she yearned to.

"So you live alone?"

She cast him a wary stare. This was more than chitchat to kill time. Was he fishing for her marital status? No, that couldn't be it . . . But the way he watched her, awaited her response, he seemed far more interested than she'd previously imagined.

"How much farther?" she asked instead as they headed south, past London's boundaries.

"Close now."

"I assumed you lived in a flat in London. Why move out here?"

He turned to her with another probing stare that made her feel like she should protect her very soul. "Long story."

Better to keep their conversation on business anyway. "I meant what I said before. I really think your work will be a hit in my shop. You'll bring people all kinds of joy. I'm glad you've changed your mind."

"After we have talked, I feel certain I will be, as well."

His answer did nothing to reassure her. She couldn't shake the thought they were carrying on two different conversations.

"I've been pleased with the other pieces I carry at the gallery. What do you think?"

With lifted brows, he replied, "I would rather not say."

His answer stopped a hair short of egotism. It needled her, though he was probably right.

Silence gnawed at her nerves as the taxi sped away from the dim streetlights of the residential districts and suburbs.

When they passed the last of the quaint homes, anxiety reared its claws. Where on earth was he taking her?

"Is it much longer?" she asked, pulling her gaze from the empty countryside whizzing past and peered up at his sharp profile.

"Ten minutes."

Okay . . . Olivia looked out the window again. The eerie night fog and Marrok's odd demeanor were making her paranoid. She took a fortifying breath, reached into her purse, and gripped her can of Mace.

Finally, agonizing minutes later, Marrok told the driver to stop at the mouth of a narrow dirt road. The drum of disquiet beat double-time inside her.

After paying the driver, Marrok exited and turned to her, holding his hand out expectantly. A shiver of uncertainty rattled her. What did she *really* know about him?

"Well, out you go," the driver barked, stained teeth large in his thin face.

"Take my hand," Marrok prompted.

"I've got other fares, so be gone wit' you."

"Give me a minute!" Olivia glanced at the taxi's meter. Marrok had negotiated a good fare at thirty pounds, but being flat broke, she didn't have that much cash with her . . . or in the bank. She didn't carry credit cards. Even if she wanted to return to London, the cost of the taxi decided her dilemma.

"Go on!" The cabbie shooed her.

"Come with me." Marrok's calm voice soothed the ball of tension in her belly.

If she wanted to see his carvings in person, she was going to have to get brave. Slowly, she reached out and placed her palm in his.

A flux of fire, hot and lightning fast, struck her fingers

and burned clear to her chest. The sensation was so intense, she nearly stumbled as she rose from the cab.

Before she could withdraw her hand, he jerked his away.

The taxi sped off in a cloud of dust.

Olivia shot Marrok a questioning glance. Why did he recoil from her every touch? At times he seemed to want her. At others . . . he couldn't stand her.

Focus. Do business. Get the hell out of here.

"Where are you taking me?" she demanded.

"To my home."

She looked around at the nearly-dead trees, their spindly branches devoid of leaves. Eerie. Silent. Foreboding bit into her belly.

"It doesn't look like anyone lives out here."

"I do, in the forest."

In other words, he lived where no one would hear her scream. The taxi's taillights faded away. Too late to turn back.

"Are you some sort of madman who's going to chop me into little pieces?"

He paused. "In this day, I see why you might believe thus, but nay. I require quiet and privacy to carve properly. There is none to be had in London."

Without another word, he stalked down the deserted dirt road, clearly expecting her to follow.

Through the glow provided by the waxing half-moon, Olivia glanced at Marrok's enormous, retreating back and set off after him. She couldn't decide whether he was just another odd artist or a total loon. She didn't get a murderous vibe from him, but something was . . . off.

Premonition, something she often ignored, told her he was about to change her life forever.

Darting after him, she matched his long steps until she

reached his shoulder. "I'm uncomfortable with this. Take me home."

He didn't look at her, didn't pause as he strode down the road that narrowed to a rarely used path. "I have no car."

"*What?*" she screeched. "How did you expect me to get back to the city?"

"Bram will be 'round soon."

That calmed her. Bram Rion, despite his outrageous charisma, had proven reliable in the few months she'd known him. Her father's letter mentioned him as someone he'd called on for help. So she'd hunted Bram down after reaching London, and they'd been friends ever since.

The dirt path before her was etched with a recent set of tire tracks. Surely if Marrok expected his friend back, he couldn't have anything terribly chilling planned for her, right?

Ancient, awe-inspiring sycamores lined the road, stretching endlessly on either side into a seemingly unbreachable forest. With apprehension, she stared up at the weather-ravaged branches that reached for her with spindly fingers.

Five silent minutes later, they broke through a clearing. A small cottage appeared. Its sloping roof bore Tudor-style markings and charming mullioned windows. Out front rested a rocking chair illuminated by a small porch light. The rocker's lines had been lovingly carved with engravings down its arms, while a plethora of ivy leaves was etched into the backrest.

Marrok hadn't been lying. Every notch in the wood demonstrated another facet of his talent. The depth of his ability thrilled her. No matter how strange he was, Olivia knew he could make them both a fortune.

Almost giddy, she rushed up the steps and trailed her fingers across the back of the rocker. "Wow. It's beautiful."

"It is but a chair, placed there for watching the sun rise."

Olivia could easily picture him, thoughtful as the sun burst over the horizon, its golden light pouring over the angled strength of his features.

Marrok stepped toward her and wrapped his fingers about her elbow. Tingles swarmed as she turned to him. He focused straight ahead, opening the door.

"There are many more carvings inside. Come."

Taking a deep breath, Olivia crossed the threshold and found herself stunned mute.

Rustic. Bare wooden floors with the merest hint of wax were the same natural oak color as the naked walls. Clearly, he didn't believe in bric-a-brac, as the tables displayed only an occasional lamp.

And his carvings.

Marrok had been underestimating when he'd said there were more. There were hundreds. The wooden masterpieces surrounded her, filling every corner of her vision. Here a hawk prepared for flight, there a mare and her colts played in a meadow. From the smallest creatures, like a bouncing kitten, to a five-foot rearing centaur, each amazing piece occupied space on the floor, on shelves, on tables—and rendered her speechless.

Even his furniture had been made with the skill of a master craftsman, with exquisite legs and lines. Bookcases, some trimmed with flowing scrolls and arches, others with straight Mission-style lines, delighted her. More wooden chairs, all with breathtaking etchings, constructed in every style from Renaissance to modern—truly beautiful and all of his making.

He had the hands of a master . . . and the heart of a poet.

Taking in his amazing talent, and the expression of his emotions, her eyes watered. "My God, this is unbelievable. Every piece . . . They're so real. I've never seen talent so—"

"Enough!" He slammed the door, then his fingers snaked around her arms. His mouth thinned to a hard line. "Drop the bloody pretense, Morganna. We are alone now, and I tire of your game."

Olivia pulled one arm free from his grasp, only to have him recapture it. Dread stabbed her. "I—I'm not Morganna. Remember? My name is Olivia."

His eyes glinted with ice and hatred. "Did you think I would be daft enough to believe that? I know who you truly are."

"Let go! I don't know anyone named Morganna. I don't know what you mean."

"I had a dream," he growled. "Of you. Naked. Inviting me into your body, then unlocking your accursed book as you stole it and disappeared. Cease the pretense."

Oh my God. The dream. *Her* dream. He'd seen it? Had it? Impossible. But Marrok had described everything perfectly.

God, she was going to be sick.

"Let me go! You're scaring me. I swear, I have no idea what you're talking about."

"Liar."

He grabbed her wrists and shackled them together at the small of her back with one of his huge hands. Then he anchored his free hand in the V-neck of her blouse. She twisted and lurched in his grasp, but despite her struggles, he ripped open the garment with a harsh yank, exposing the cups of her pink lace bra. Terror hit her like icy water.

"*No!* Don't touch me, you bastard!"

Olivia writhed in his grasp, straining to escape. His burning stare fixated on her cleavage. He ignited her fear and fury as his gaze roved over the lacy cups supporting her breasts and the front clasp of her underwire bra. The pained yearning she'd glimpsed in the cab returned.

Lowering her lashes, Olivia glimpsed the front of his jeans. Oh God, he was aroused again! Was it the thought of having power over her? He could rape her. God knew he had the strength.

"Are you pleased to know I react to your body?" he growled.

"No." But in a weird way, she was. That wasn't smart, she knew—but she couldn't help herself.

Be smart. Remain calm, she instructed herself and shifted her weight to her left foot. She watched his dark face. He never moved—and his stare never left her breasts. Mentally, she counted to three and raised her knee to his groin.

Marrok moved faster, catching her knee in his palm. As he swung her leg over his hip, doom crashed to the pit of her stomach. Now his erection pressed against her sex. Shockingly, she felt herself become damp. Drenched, even as she reeled with fury.

Frantically, she glanced around for a nearby weapon. He released her wrists and wrapped his fingers around her chin, forcing her to meet his stare.

"I remember you, Morganna. Your tricks. Your teasing. Every bit of your body, including the strawberry mark between your breasts."

With a single jerk, he flipped open the front clasp of her bra, exposing the mark she'd possessed all her life.

Shock reverberated inside her. How had he known exactly where it was and what it looked like? From the dream?

His gaze took an angry sweep of her face and breasts again, then released her so abruptly she nearly stumbled. "You cannot lie to me."

With shaking hands, she righted her bra and tugged the edges of her blouse together protectively. "How did you know about . . . ?"

His brows made an ominous V above his thunderous frown. "I touched every inch of your body. More than fifteen hundred years ago, aye, but I remember."

More than fifteen hundred years ago? As in the what, fifth or sixth century?

"I'm only twenty-three." She paused, grasping for a logical explanation. "Are you into past lives or something?"

"I wish. But you made certain there would be no death for me. You and the Book of Doomsday ensured I would live this hellish existence forever."

Clearly, he was both dangerous and delusional. And she was trapped with him in the middle of nowhere.

Olivia retreated. "I—I don't know about any doomsday book. You have me confused with whoever this Morganna is. We might have the same birthmark, but—"

"Because of you, I lost my knighthood." He stalked closer, his eyes shooting rage. "Arthur banished me for touching you. Still, your lust for revenge was not satisfied until you cursed me with immortality and never-ending solitude."

He thought he was immortal? Well, anyone who believed he'd been alive for fifteen centuries would think so. He also believed he'd been one of King Arthur's knights, and that she was someone called Morganna. As in Morgan le Fay, Arthur's half sister? And after becoming his lover, she had somehow made him immortal? Not even in her most fertile imaginings could she ever conjure up anything that fantastic. Olivia swallowed. How did one calm a raving madman?

"And what was my great sin? Insulting your vanity because I moved on before you decided you'd had enough of me in your bed?"

"Marrok, honestly. I obviously have some resemblance to this woman, but I never met you before this morning. I don't know anything—"

His fingers curled around her wrist like five fiery clamps, cutting off her speech. He dragged her closer. "You know everything, including how to release me from this blasted curse."

He dug into the pocket of his jeans. Olivia didn't wait to see what he had planned; she whirled and darted for the door.

Only to find it locked and the key to open it missing.

Marrok ran up behind her, trapping her against the door, his enormous chest covered her back, trapping her against the wood. His erection pressed hot and hard against her.

He grabbed her arm and clasped a medieval-looking bracelet around her wrist, securing it with a tiny silver padlock. He stepped back and stared in triumph.

"Amethysts the color of your eyes set in pure silver. Your weakening combination. Merlin made it for you. As long as you wear it, you cannot do magic. I have locked it snug around your wrist. There it will stay."

Magic? Olivia stared at the heavy, ornate silver bangle lined with huge purple gemstones. Discreetly, she tugged on it. Nope, it wasn't moving an inch.

"Marrok, I'm not this Morganna person." She trembled, hit by a wave of sudden dizziness. "Let me go, damn it!"

He pinned her with a furious glare. "The bracelet remains, as will you, until you set me free."

He crossed the room and disappeared down a hall. Olivia raced for the glass doors at the back of the cottage. Before she could reach them, he returned, grabbing her with one hand, clutching something red and square against his massive chest with the other.

"You never had a shred of decency, but find one now." He held up a red leather book, his eyes burning. "Open this and write the reversal of my curse, so I can finally die."

CHAPTER THREE

"You *want* to die?" He was both suicidal and delusional. Oh, this was bad. "Look, I don't know anything about that book. Just call Bram and let me go home."

Fury spiked across his face. He loomed closer. She retreated, heart pounding, wishing it was purely terror revving her up. But some invisible connection, along with the power of the book, resounded in her head, pulsed in her belly.

"You know *exactly* how the book works."

"I've never seen the damn thing. Get it through your head that you've got me mixed up with someone else. I'm not Morganna."

"Pretending amnesia, are you? No matter; I read your curse a thousand times before the bloody book locked. Mayhap you will remember these words: *'Under midnight's moon you loved me and made my body fly. By sun's harsh light you left me to ache, no matter what I try. Eternity is my curse on you, with nights of endless need. Find the key to free your black heart or live this hell, no matter how you plead.'*"

Oh my God. He'd made up the words to his own curse? This was really bad.

"With a few strokes of your pen, you condemned me to an eternity without companionship, sexual satisfaction, or end. Now open this book and end it."

Dear God, how was she ever going to leave this cottage without being carried out in a body bag on a two-minute segment of the news?

Marrok was straitjacket material. How could she find the man so . . . sexual? Why was she so attuned to him, wanting to cling to him? Her body ached. He actually made her dizzy, as if she'd had a bit too much wine.

Focus! she berated herself. "I'm sorry that Morganna . . . um, put a nasty curse on you. I'm sure it sucks. But I'm not her. Let me go."

"I cannot." His hand curled around the nape of her neck, bringing her so close, she felt him exhale against her lips. She tingled, trembled. His eyes glowed with ferocity—and hot desire.

What would it feel like to make love to a man so focused on her alone?

Sick thought. It went with the sick man. She should be concentrating on escape, not the wild sensation of Marrok's hands on her.

"Look, I don't know what delusion you live in, and I can see how the lack of sex would make you cranky, but I'm not Morganna or the answer to your problems."

Olivia scanned her surroundings for a weapon again, then remembered the Mace in her purse. Easing her hand into the bag dangling from her shoulder, she felt the can. As her fingers closed around it, relief spiked within her. This would bring him to his knees and give her an opportunity to escape this whole *Outer Limits* scene.

She withdrew it, aimed and sprayed in one fluid motion. But Marrok ducked, grabbed her arm and whirled her about, hauling her back against his chest.

Mace dissipated in the air, burning her eyes, as he ripped the can from her grasp. Swearing, he scanned the label and tossed it aside, sending it clattering across the floor.

"A modern potion, is it? Have you run out of your own or grown too lazy to make them?"

She struggled for release against the iron bands of his

arms. "For the hundredth time, I'm *not* Morganna. I'm Olivia Gray, we just met today, and you're insane. Let me out of here!"

As she twisted away, his arm tightened about her waist, enveloping her in hard flesh and body heat. Repressing her desire, she stomped her spiked heel on his toes. He swore, shaking the offended foot.

"Stop!" she cried. "I'm not the woman you want."

She struggled against him. The solid stone of his body slid across her hypersensitive skin. Languorous need wound through her bloodstream like an insidious drug. His arousal, large and heavy, wedged against the small of her back.

"We both know that is untrue," he spat bitterly. "Thanks to you, I cannot be satisfied by any woman. Would it be different with you, Morganna? Is that the thing I must discover?"

He thought taking her to bed would uncurse him? Crap, she was doomed. Especially since her body was pulsing in approval.

"Damn it, I'm *not* Morganna. Sex with me won't change your . . . state. Get that through your head!" *You make-my-knees-melt freak.*

Marrok wedged his hard body more tightly against hers. "Your curse says I left you to ache, no matter what you tried. It would be like you to punish me until I returned to give you what you need. Is it that simple?"

"No, no, no! Get your hands off me."

"If returning to your bed frees me, I will touch you how and where I wish. I avoided you for a century, until you . . . what, died after Merlin banished you from this realm? But no more. I will be on you, around you, inside you—"

"Not if I can help it!" He wanted freedom, orgasm.

She was merely convenient. As hot as she was for him, she couldn't lose sight of that. "No means no in any century, pal."

"After a hard ride, will you let me loose, Morganna? Surely, you have grown weary of toying with me. Or does it thrill you to know you affect me now more than ever?" He arched his hips, thrusting his steely erection against her. Liquid heat poured over her. Why? She should be terrified out of her mind.

"Have you naught to say? Or are you too busy gloating because I want you even as I hate you?"

Repeating the fact she was not Morganna would get her nowhere. She had to try something new.

Marrok's words and the carving of an angel right beside him gave her an idea. Logic rebelled against it . . . while her body applauded. The plot was hasty, insane, imperative.

He wanted her. Bad. The truth was getting her nowhere. Why not use his lust to her advantage?

No reason, except she was playing head games with a madman.

Olivia allowed her blouse to fall open. Fighting back a shiver, she turned in Marrok's grip, keeping the angel close. He towered over her, his cock nudging her belly. Oh God. Danger and desire pelted her in an unforgiving rain. The odd connection between them pulsated.

Get a grip!

Even with a sane man, she'd fear indulging this intense chemistry. She had almost no experience with sex . . . with touch at all. Her own mother had treated her as if she were diseased. Most everyone else had followed suit. Olivia had always felt like a freak, never expected a hunk like Marrok to want her. But as he pressed against her, she was dying to learn everything about sex, especially if having it with him would live up to the promise of the lightning charging through her blood.

No! She had to get away before she succumbed to this madness and he swallowed her up, body and soul.

Olivia shivered at the unbearable intimacy. Though this game was dangerous, if she wanted to escape, she didn't have much choice. She had to seduce him, then when he was distracted, incapacitate him with a whack to the head and escape. While ignoring her own clawing need.

"Is wanting me so terrible?" she said huskily, but her words quivered.

"Do not tease me," he warned, deadly quiet. "Tempt me, touch me once, and I will unleash all my unfulfilled desire on you. Consider that, in fifteen centuries, I learned a thousand different ways to fuck you."

Oh God. Olivia's head spun dizzily at his words. Her sex pulsed. Cramped. She swayed and grabbed Marrok's biceps for support. When fire shot up her arms, she ripped her hands away, but the sensation still burned her fingers. *What the hell is going on here?*

"Why did you go through the elaborate charade of arranging a meeting through Bram? You knew how to find me. What is your game?"

"What makes you think there is one?"

"From frightened maiden to seductress in the span of a heartbeat? You underestimate me, Morganna. Sorely."

"You're not intrigued?" She moved as close as she dared, so near he seared her. "Marrok, stop fighting what you want. I have."

His eyes narrowed to suspicious slits that mirrored the tight line of his mouth. Why didn't he believe her? She'd said all the right things, hadn't she?

"What you want is freedom. Your face says so."

And his face said that he was beyond furious. She winced, bracing herself, but he didn't do more than scowl. Despite that, she was drawn to him. What was happening here?

It didn't matter. Her freedom, maybe her life, depended upon it. She had to focus, to pretend that she desired him. Well . . . not really pretend, just focus on her bizarre connection to him, indulge in the inexplicable yearnings he aroused, the fantasy of making love with a man who needed her—and her alone.

"You're not reading me right." Her voice dropped to a purr as she tousled her hair with her fingers. Marrok's laser-focused gaze, burning her lips, her body. He clenched his jaw.

She had his attention.

Olivia placed her trembling hand against the width of his hot chest. Instantly he stiffened, as if he felt the same sexual jolt zigzagging through her body. The frightened part of her wanted to withdraw. She couldn't, not when she needed to escape, not when her body felt more alive than it ever had.

Marrok's heart beat furiously beneath her tingling palm. His wary, harsh stare told her that his head wasn't willing to give in just yet.

His erection said his body was already there.

"You see this desire I can't deny?" She pressed her breasts against his chest.

He drew in a sharp breath. A thrill rushed through Olivia.

"If you don't let me touch you, don't touch me back, this burning will consume me. I'm dying to know how good we can make each other feel."

Beneath her hands, he flexed with tension. His eyes slid shut. He swore softly.

"Do not do this." His words were gravelly and harsh. "Release me from this hell and leave me be."

Grab the carving. Hit him now! Yet . . . she couldn't. His anguish became hers. She actually hurt for him.

"Marrok, open your eyes. Look at me."

Reluctantly, he did. A spark sizzled between them, hot and bright. Olivia paused for a shaky breath.

A new misgiving assailed her, not for her safety, but her emotional health. She'd been much too vulnerable since her distant mother's death; her brittle shell had cracked. Loneliness and the pain of longing for someone to care about her tangled with anger. The weight of it felt crushing at times. Given how wildly she reacted to Marrok, if he treated her with an ounce of tenderness, he could strip her soul bare. Opening up to him was an invitation to her own destruction. But she had to move forward with her plan.

"I'm asking for a simple touch," she pressed on.

Pain haunted his face. "Nothing about you is simple."

Olivia hated to look into those troubled eyes and deceive him. A strange instinct, given her captivity. Then he leaned toward her, his lips closing in. Nerves battered her.

Then he placed his cheek against hers. His five o'clock shadow rasped against her skin—and disturbingly, he tugged on her heart. She laid her palm against the dark bristle on his other cheek, just as one of his large hands cupped the crown of her head, fingers tangling in her hair.

The carving of the angel was right there in her grasp—the perfect weapon. But against all logic, she melted against him. Breathing seemed impossible in the face of his surprising tenderness. She'd never imagined this imposing man could express such silent longing. She felt it in every stroke of his fingers, with every ragged breath.

"Kiss me," she blurted.

His fingers tensed in her hair. "I should make you wait for half an eternity, as I have for you."

"Is that what you really want, to keep waiting?"

He paused, backed away enough to stare into her eyes. The moment hung between them.

"God help me."

Olivia saw Marrok coming toward her, felt his breath and heat—and did nothing to stop him. She didn't want to.

He seized her lips in the next heartbeat. It felt . . . inevitable as his mouth took her own. The tangle of his hands in her hair, the stark lust hot in his touch, the scrape of his stubble against her face . . . everything about him was rough.

Except his lips on hers.

After a hesitant brush, Marrok covered her mouth again, deepening his possession, making her knees weak. She'd heard clichés about a kiss having that kind of power, but believed such descriptions were overblown.

Now, she knew better.

Marrok pulled her into him, urged her lips apart, and swept into her mouth, shifting the kiss from persuasive to demanding. Need slammed into her, and her world skewed like a Tilt-O-Whirl. With every brush of his lips, his unbearably male taste saturated her senses. Clutching his shoulders, she joined the untamed kiss, hungry for more.

He was like a mountain, durable and huge. Solid. Yet he hadn't used his superior size or strength to push her further.

He fisted his hand deeper in her hair, pulling her even closer. Olivia tried to absorb the surreal moment as another dizzying surge of desire crashed over her. Was this actually happening? The way he leaned into her, straining to be closer, flushed fresh heat all the way from her belly to her toes. The buzz in her brain picked up volume until it was like listening to a two-thousand-dollar stereo in a car the size of a Yugo.

"Your mouth . . ." He breathed hard against her lips before he sampled them again. "So bloody intoxicating."

Olivia moaned. Marrok was addicting. He tasted of sin, smelled like pleasure, wrapped in mysterious midnight. Even if she escaped tonight and never saw him again, she would never forget these sensations.

"Give me more," he murmured.

Yes!

She'd gone crazy. The man had abducted her. She had a case of vertigo that was about to knock her on her ass. The buzzing in her head was rivaled only by the *boom* of her heart.

So this is what desire feels like.

As if Marrok was tuned into her need, he slanted his mouth over hers once more, this possession his deepest yet.

Oh God, was she so lonely that she'd succumbed to some weird Stockholm syndrome?

No. Focus on escape. Don't feel anything, her mind screeched. *Don't let him affect you.*

Too late.

Instead of reaching for one of his nearby carvings to make it a weapon, her hands climbed from his biceps to curl around his neck, grasping at the thick column and the inky hair hanging there. Marrok's hands were in motion, too, sliding their way from her tangled curls, caressing down her arms, encircling her waist, until he grasped her hips. She writhed against him, his hold hot and unrelenting as he urged her closer, settling her right against the hard thrust of his sex.

Which proved he wasn't small anywhere.

"Madness," he growled. "I cannot taste you enough." He punctuated the sentence with a kiss even more voracious than the one before.

Olivia kissed him back, logical thought slipping away. But her body's desire was crystal clear. Every nerve and cell strained toward Marrok, melted into him.

She wanted Marrok. No, she *had* to have him. Did this

need to touch him stem from loneliness? Simple human need? Whatever. Giving herself to him felt necessary to her soul.

Marrok lifted his head. *Wonder. Desire. Determination.* The stare he sent her swam thick with each. Her dizziness returned in force. Olivia leaned against him for additional support as her knees collapsed. Even as her head screamed at her to stop acting like a nymphomaniac, her body knew he would be there to catch her.

"My God. You *do* want me." His growl vibrated inside her.

Then his restless hands journeyed from her hips to her waist again, farther up, resting just shy of her breasts. Anticipation for more launched through her body.

As if he understood, he covered her lips with his own and claimed her breast in his hot hand. Olivia arched as his thumb swiped her hard, eager nipple. Breath ragged and shallow, she clawed to get closer, feeling like she'd crawl out of her skin if he didn't give her more.

He had the same need, she realized, as he lifted her and carried her across the great room and down the hall.

To his bed.

He laid her on a mattress that smelled of cloves and moss. She craved the feel of his body enveloping her, driving deep. The glow in his silvery-blue eyes said he ached to give her that and more.

Marrok settled his body over hers and parted her legs with his own as he settled between. The heat of his body scorched her. The desperate grip of his hands on her face, along with the feel of him, seeped into her every pore.

Oh God. This was really happening.

At that moment, she couldn't imagine him *not* wanting her. They were on a collision course; she had dreamed of him. Maybe it was Fate.

Pleasure rolled through her body, and she didn't fight it.

His next toe-curling kiss had her meeting him halfway. He branded her neck with his lips, nuzzled her sensitive lobe, breathed fire across her skin.

Logic shouted, *He's insane! Dangerous. Maybe deadly.*

But longing whispered, *He wants you. You need him.*

For once in her solitary life, she was going for the fantasy. His touch was like drowning in champagne—heady, bubbly, smooth as it went down, difficult to stop imbibing.

Olivia yanked at his black T-shirt. "Marrok . . ."

He inched back and looked at her, framing her face in his hands. "Is this a hoax?"

She swallowed, shook her head. "I need this. I don't understand . . ."

"What you make me feel is truly madness."

"It is." In the real world, he'd never want her. Reality was hugely overrated.

The hot, hushed whispers stopped when he reached back, grabbed a fistful of his T-shirt at the nape and doffed it in one swift tug.

As he bared his torso, Olivia stared at every bronzed ripple. Marrok was intimidating enough when his shoulders strained the seams of his shirt, but with his upper body bare, he loomed much larger. A dusting of dark body hair, myriad scars, and raised veins accented his skin, from the firm swells of his pecs down, disappearing into the waistband of his jeans.

"Touch me," he murmured.

Olivia lifted her fingertips to his skin, bare palms to his shoulders. He was hard everywhere, back, arms, hips . . . the erection between her thighs, which got harder as her palms danced across his flesh. The more she felt of him, the more she wanted to take him all in at once.

Then Marrok was everywhere, his kiss dominating, his palm drifting to her thigh and lifting it around him again.

Olivia gasped as he pressed right against the spot guaranteed to ignite her.

Marrok reached for her lopsided shirt. His big hands, like the rest of him, were covered with scars and veins, showing evidence of a dangerous existence. He plucked at her shirt and pried the halves apart. Cool air and his hot gaze hit her at once. All that stood between Marrok and her breasts was a bit of lace.

In seconds, he conquered the bra's front clasp, then tore both it and her shirt away, flinging them across the room. His hungry stare fell on her. Her nipples beaded under his scrutiny.

For the first time, Olivia felt beautiful. And wanted. Whatever happened—or didn't—she'd be thankful for this moment.

She arched to him. "Please . . ."

The needy whimper had barely left her lips before he palmed her breast, caressing, fondling. His thumb stroked across the aching point. Olivia gasped. The sound hung between them as he manipulated the sensitive bud, then squeezed.

Her gasp became a moan when he laved that nipple and moved his fingers to the other, alternately grazing and tugging, driving her perfectly insane.

He kept on relentlessly until every nerve above her waist felt centered in her breasts. And still she wanted more. But Marrok moved on, gliding a rough palm across her abdomen, gripping her waist, sweeping over her hips, setting her ablaze. When she'd first kissed him, she'd expected anger, a brutal attack, a complete domination. Instead, he seduced— awakened.

Olivia encouraged him, hooking her calves around his, fisting her hands in his hair, pulling his mouth to hers.

The dizziness spun her world in a crazy tilt of colors. Fire and euphoria charged her veins. She felt almost drunk, but alive as never before, connected to a man who seemed desperate for her.

His breath rasped hot on her neck as he rained kisses there, making her shiver. "I must have all of you."

Desire pitched in her stomach as she worked her lips across his stubbled jaw. "Now."

He tore at the snap of her slacks and forced the zipper down, shoving the knit past her hips, over her thighs. She helped, kicking the pants off as he tugged.

The garment had barely cleared her legs when he gripped her panties. They shredded in his hands, and he tossed the scraps to the floor. Olivia didn't have an instant to think before he shoved her thighs wider and thrust two fingers inside her.

"Marrok!" A prickle of hot pleasure/pain shimmied down her senses. She arched in silent invitation.

"I dreamt of you," he whispered against her cheek. "I dreamt of you naked, and wanted you. But this . . . is so much more."

He stroked her bundle of nerves with his thumb. Her breath caught. She grabbed him, clawing to keep hold of her sanity as he made her world spin away.

Her thoughts slowly drowned. Logic faded, bleeding into pure, heated need. She moaned and spread her legs wider.

Words began to echo in her brain, words she didn't understand. These random, garbled, unfamiliar phrases buzzed through her mind, whispers at first. They grew louder and louder with Marrok's every touch, with each beat of her heart as pleasure screamed inside her skin.

Orgasm soared into a sweltering bliss she'd never experienced, but craved from him. It kept growing. Perspiration filmed her skin. The sensations swelled, congealed. She exploded, pleasure tearing through her like nothing she'd ever felt or imagined. Olivia screamed his name, clutching at Marrok as if he alone mattered.

As if, from this touch on, she had ceased to be alone in this world.

With a hushed curse, Marrok tore at his jeans, shoving them down and off. She watched in an unblinking stare as he loomed above her. Oh God, his broad shoulders packed power. His corrugated abs rippled when she dared to touch them. And his erection, tall, thick-veined. Ready.

The jumbled words swirling in her head suddenly took shape. Old. Odd. Ritualistic. But instinct forced her to hold her hand out to him. He clasped it, their gazes connecting. Marrok fell to the bed, covering her again, settling between her thighs.

"Become a part of me, as I become a part of you." The words fell from her lips.

"I look forward to it."

"And ever after, I promise myself to thee. Each day we share, I will be honest, good, and true. If this you seek, heed my Call. From this moment on, there is no other for me but you."

CHAPTER FOUR

The magical Mating Call?

Shock burned through Marrok's veins. He had read those words in magical texts when he'd researched Morganna's book. "Olivia" had spoken magic's equivalent of wedding vows.

Did she understand her words? Of course. No matter that she disguised herself as another woman. That birthmark, those eyes . . . Morganna could not hide from him.

But why issue the Mating Call to him when she already controlled his eternity? And why did she affect more than his body; how did she *compel* him to accept her?

"Marrok?" Something painful, vulnerable even, shone from her eyes.

He should not feel for her—not pity, not lust, not this mad desire to possess and protect; he could afford none of these, for her yearning could not possibly be real.

Was it possible that, after cursing him to an eternity alone, Morganna loved him in her own, twisted way? Could breaking his curse be as simple as saying aye to her Call?

Accepting was a gamble, but Morganna already held his destiny in her cruel fist. Staying the course for fifteen centuries had changed naught. Without playing her game, there would be no escape from this hell.

With her soft body under his, the urge to bury himself in her slick heat pounded him. The scent of her arousal drove him mad.

What would happen if he refused? Exactly what new horror would befall him if he rejected her again? He swallowed.

"As I become a part of you, you become a part of me." Marrok stared into her violet eyes, dragging the words from instinct and memory. "I will be honest, good, and true. I heed your Call. 'Tis you I seek. From this moment on, there is no other for me but you."

A smile wobbled across her face, then burst forth like the summer sun after a long, rainy spring. Blinding, beautiful.

For an unguarded moment, her happiness woke an answering joy in him, entwined with the need to sink deep inside her. When this night was done, he would either be mortal again—or Morganna's personal toy for eternity.

"Love me," she whispered, holding her arms open to him.

Heart thudding, Marrok kissed his way down her body, to her thigh. He dragged his lips across her soft skin and nibbled at her hipbone, brushing the back of his fingers across the curve of her waist. Goose pimples speckled her skin. Another chink in Morganna's armor.

His first night with her so many moons ago, she'd run him down like a parade of war horses, demanding he bed her repeatedly until he'd felt trampled. Never had she betrayed her own passion until climax hit her in a hard rush, finished and done before he could bask in her pleasure.

Curious about this new Morganna, Marrok explored her, dragging a thumb over the nub between her legs once more. Her breath hitched, back arched, skin flushed. She moaned his name.

If Morganna was willing to show her female susceptibility to his touch, he wanted to see how far he could push her.

Sliding smooth fingers across her pure ivory skin, Marrok laved his way closer to her wet heat, fighting down an urge to drive her up and over. As he cupped her breast, her sweet skin intoxicated him. The swollen folds of her flesh were a temptation he didn't resist.

He put his mouth to her, ravenous for her taste. Against his lips, she bucked, thrusting up to him. Her small fists clasped his sheets. She tensed as he swiped his tongue over the needy bud again. Try as she might not to verbalize her arousal, her body silently shouted it.

Marrok gloried as she swelled, thrashed on his bed, then cried his name as she convulsed in climax. Sliding up her body, he pulled her thighs wider still with his hands. He claimed her mouth with a kiss thick with urgency. He pressed his stiff cock at the entrance of her swollen sex.

Wet. Hot. Silky tight. Mind-boggling.

Mine.

He gave her one shallow thrust. She gasped, arched. Then he sank deeper.

And encountered something he never expected to find.

"You are untouched?" he choked.

How could Morganna alter her body to become virginal again? Her magic had grown to heights he could not fathom. *Bloody hell . . .*

Inky lashes lifted from her flushed cheeks and fluttered up. Violet eyes dilated, dreamy. The woman's beauty stole his breath; the witch's power disturbed his peace of mind. If he was not cautious, he would succumb to her enchantment and lose more than his mortality.

"Y—yes."

A virgin. Marrok wanted to disbelieve her, but the evidence blocking his entrance did not lie. He grimaced at the pressure and need inside him. Sweat poured off his skin. Want gnawed at his gut.

"Marrok." She swallowed, bit her lip. Lifted to him. "Please . . ."

Resisting her was impossible. He had answered her Mating Call. Not only must he claim her for strategy's sake, but he burned to make her his, no matter how daft it was.

Seeking her hand with his own, he tangled their fingers together. "Hold tight."

She blinked and fixed her gaze on his, shining with a sense of wonder he could not comprehend. But it touched him, damn her.

Marrok inhaled, drawing in her heady scent, then pushed

forward, tearing past her barrier, grunting over her sharp gasp as he slid deep down, down—to the hilt. At her jagged sigh, he squeezed her hand. "It is done."

Morganna nodded. "This feels . . . meant to be."

Perhaps.

Intense pleasure clawed up his spine. Zounds, he could not remember the last time the mere feel of a woman roused him so. He eased out, gritting his teeth at the unbearable tightness, the wild friction. As he pushed in again, she made a sound somewhere between a sigh and a moan. Everything inside him thrilled to the utter perfection of her, to be *claiming* her. Which made little sense. Morganna had enjoyed the centuries of torture she'd heaped on him. Why should he not wish to inflict the same?

Had to be the bond. Apparently, it affected humans. He had not anticipated such. Now that they were joined, he might even be mortal again. *If* he completed the joining. Deprived of an orgasm since his last days in Camelot, Marrok yet had doubts that he could.

Morganna arched to meet his next thrust. Gripping her hips, he set a fast pace and claimed her mouth as he took her body. Passion gushed up his spine; pleasure pooled in his balls. By God . . . The urge to release was overwhelming, and as he pressed into her again and again, she tightened, fluttered. Close . . .

Shifting his angle to graze her pleasure spot, Marrok filled her again. A shudder, a gasp. Her legs clasped him. She tensed under him . . . then screamed. Her body squeezed him tight. Pleasure spiraled inside him, taking him up, up, up. Sweet mercy! Climax was right . . . there.

There it stayed, so high that he felt delirious. Wildly, he pumped into her, sliding, falling deeper into her, reveling at the sensations. Closer to ecstasy than at any time in the past torturous centuries. The right touch would send him over.

Morganna clung to him, dusting kisses on his jaw, his neck. Sweat trickled down his back, his temples. As he lunged into her again, pleasure threatened to drown him. He welcomed the little death.

Seconds became minutes. Morganna moaned, tensed, came again. Marrok forged on, pumping hard, reaching for the satisfaction nearly at hand.

When she climaxed a third time and his legs turned numb, Marrok rolled away with a foul curse. Bitter defeat choked him.

Denied completion again . . . Why?

Was he now joined to the maker of his torment forever, unable to touch another woman, nor climax with his "wife"? If so, he had to give credit to Morganna for creating a new measure of horror. Pity he had not seen it coming.

"Marrok?"

He should hide his anger from her; she would only use it against him. But she wore a look of confusion that crawled under his defenses and made him boil inside.

"What the bloody hell are you about? Why keep me trapped in this immortal torture? What further amusement could I possibly hold for you?"

She blinked. "What do you mean?"

"Playing the innocent to the end, are you, Morganna? Stop."

"Morg— You still think I'm this woman?" she shrieked, grabbing the sheet and yanking it over her bare breasts. "I'm Olivia, you idiot!"

Her outrage looked real. This new Morganna . . . very subtle. Tricky. Too easy to believe. Fatal to trust.

"I will defeat you and free myself, Morganna. This I vow."

"You took my virginity, believing I was another woman?" She glared at him with angry tears trembling in her eyes. "All that need and passion . . . You lying snake! I can't believe I let you . . . Don't touch me again!"

He wished it was that simple, that his every touch had been a calculated ploy, rather than a surrender to her spell. "Do not act as if you are the one wronged. We both know better."

"No, one of us knows you're a delusional asshole. I felt . . . connected to you, and you were acting? Of course you were. God, I'm an idiot."

Marrok looked away. He had felt that bond between them. Had Morganna fallen prey to her own spells?

"I won't make the mistake of letting you touch me again," she promised. "Get the hell away from me!"

Morganna had spoken the Call, and he had answered. He possessed not a drop of magical blood, yet he knew those words were binding. Even if he left . . . he would return. But he must guard against falling deeper under her enchantment, despite its irresistible pull.

He donned his clothes in angry jerks. "Gladly. I have no use for a cranky witch, especially a treacherous le Fay."

Marrok slammed the bedroom door behind him, then sagged against it. His body regretted his departure instantly. He could *feel* Morganna on the other side, tempting him to further doom. With gritted teeth, he walked away and tried to call up his limited knowledge of magical mating bonds, looking for ways to ensure she was every bit as bewitched as he.

Jesu, was he doomed to obsess over an unforgettable witch who had given him naught but endless hell?

Marrok made his way to the sofa and sank down, cradling his forehead in his palm. The tightness in his chest and the recriminations screaming through his mind taunted him. He was doomed to want her. Eternally. With their bonding, she'd seen to that, and probably took perverse pleasure in knowing it.

He had announced his foolish lust, acted impulsively by answering her Mating Call and joining their bodies. It was only a matter of time before she used all that against him.

A memory tore through his head of this new Morganna crying out in pleasure, face flushed. Of her tears afterward. Such seeming emotional honesty. So unlike the Morganna he'd lain with centuries ago.

Was it possible she had been telling him the truth, that she wasn't Morganna, but a mortal woman named Olivia?

Ridiculous. With that birthmark and those velvet violet eyes, who else could she be? His dream of her had been too powerful. And her odd behavior was nothing more than a subtle form of combat, an attempt to pit her mind against his and rouse his self-doubts.

Peaceful death and release from this hell of her making; that was his goal. Revenge sounded sweet, but he could never repay Morganna for the pain she had inflicted, the centuries of chilling loneliness.

Still, he would try.

The dream of Morganna, in the guise of Olivia, came again that eve. This time she stood before him like temptation personified, all naked and exquisite. A vivid, erotic vision he suspected Morganna orchestrated for his torture.

But in this dream, instead of disappearing into the swirling mist after she lured him with the pale enticement of her body, Morganna curled her arms around his neck, pressed tight to him, kissed him with wild abandon. He held her, tasted her honeyed mouth and fevered responses, felt indomitable lust curl in his belly. Unable to resist her seduction, Marrok joined with her.

Once he was buried deep inside her, she opened the Doomsday Diary and disappeared. He awakened on his couch in a cold sweat, wrought by fear.

Calling himself every kind of fool, Marrok rose and paced down the hall to ensure Morganna had not escaped as he slept.

When he reached the threshold of his bedroom, he knew the rationalization was a lie. He wanted to watch her sleep in *his* bed, where he had claimed her.

On silent steps, he reached the bedside and pushed a stray lock of hair from her cheek. As his fingers lingered on her downy skin, he acknowledged that she looked innocent with those fragile ivory features and girlish lashes. He resisted the illusion. According to Merlin, Morganna had been born a witch in every sense of the word.

So why had she been a virgin? Why had Morganna seemed more . . . human last night?

Resisting a strong urge to touch her again, to slide between the rumpled sheets and sink deep into her, he left the room. Finding sanctuary on the sofa, Marrok picked up the carving he'd begun yesterday. In his mind, the piece had not yet taken shape. But he allowed his fingers to take him on an instinctual journey as his thoughts zeroed in on Morganna.

Bloody hell, he should be focused on learning the witch's secrets so he no longer endured her torment. To achieve freedom, he must stay focused, persuade her to set him free.

Thoughts of Morganna ignited a fresh bout of lust . . . and worry. If he could not suppress the bond growing between them, his chances of escaping the curse were bleak, indeed.

* * *

Olivia woke alone, heavy, aching, and exhausted. She should be grateful the sexy headcase had given her some breathing room. Instead, she felt hurt that Marrok had left her after . . . *Best not to think about it.*

The pain in her heart mocked her. What a foolish, simplistic plan, to lure Marrok close, strike him over the head with one of his carvings, and flee. Instead, he'd lifted her in his arms, carried her across the room, to his bed and— *Stop there.*

But she couldn't. The disturbing memory of his arms cradling her against that powerhouse chest as he sank into her, played over and over in her mind. He'd made her body—and soul—soar, seemingly at will.

Stupidly, she'd gorged on his touch. She'd never had so much human contact at once. The little unloved girl inside her had greedily lapped up his attention.

Talk about a mistake . . .

The weirdest part was the staggering sense of connection she felt after she'd uttered those mysterious words. Why had she said them? What did they mean? They seemed like something from a medieval wedding. Once he'd answered in kind, her link to Marrok had swelled, overtaking her.

It had apparently overtaken her good sense, too. She'd given her virginity to a stranger who believed he was immortal and she was the witch who'd cursed him.

Gotta get out of here, she thought, sitting up in bed.

Sunlight streamed through the windows, illuminating the room she hadn't seen last night. Her jaw dropped. *Wow* . . .

His headboard depicted a tale of two lovers romancing each other at the shadow of a hill. It alone must have taken years to carve in such sharp, perfect relief. And the four posts, in the form of wild wolves, so lifelike Olivia swore they would bite her if she touched them, surrounded the bed like snarling sentries.

Talent like his should be celebrated; he should be adored by the art world. If she could get his work on her shelves, he would be.

But Marrok not only lived in solitude, he prized it. Probably a good thing, since he was convinced he was immortal and cursed. Crazy, delusional man. But he'd touched her with such tender finesse that she'd begun to think . . . hope . . . but no. One night with one man could not undo years of her mother's rejection or make her whole. Wishing otherwise was pointless.

Once Marrok had—or rather hadn't—finished having sex with her, he had walked away. No surprise there. What kind of freak couldn't satisfy a horny man? Her, apparently. She winced.

Time to get the hell out of Dodge and haul ass back to A Touch Of Magic.

At the thought of leaving Marrok, an odd weakness slammed into Olivia. She hurt. Even her skin throbbed in agony. But wrapped in sheets that smelled faintly of his woodsy musk, she wanted him again. Burned for him.

Wasn't going to happen. Her libido needed an Ambien.

Grimacing with the effort it took to raise her wrist, Olivia glanced at her watch. Even her eyes hurt. 3:42 a.m. The numbers blared at her. Hopefully, he was sound asleep elsewhere in the house. She prayed that being "immortal" didn't mean he kept vampire hours.

Olivia braced herself against the pain as she scooted to the edge of the bed. Her legs burned, her stomach churned. Between her thighs, the throbbing need nearly drowned out all else. She forced herself to keep moving. If she wanted to escape, now was her best chance.

Crawling out of bed, Olivia gasped when cold air hit her skin. Damn, she was naked.

Because Marrok undressed you and had his wicked way with you, and you put up all the fight of a gnat.

What was done, was done. Dwelling on the past wouldn't change it. Yada, yada, yada.

Shuffling across the hardwood floor, Olivia tensed as each step stabbed needles of agony into the soles of her feet. The dizziness buzzed in her brain again. So not helpful.

Locating the bathroom was nearly cause for celebration, even if the short trip exhausted her. She shut the door, relieved herself, and noticed that the room had no window. A sink, yes. A shower, check. A toilet in the adjoining closet. But no means of escape.

Marrok's heavy navy blue bathrobe hung on the back of the door. His scent wafted from the garment. Incredibly yummy. She'd bet he looked great in it, too.

Stupid train of thought.

Slowly, gingerly, she rose from the toilet, only to realize her thighs were sticky with blood and her own juices. A shower would be nice . . .

Focus. Escape!

Olivia ambled on shaky legs and grabbed the robe, biting her lip to keep in a cry of pain. What the hell was the matter with her? This was like having the flu times ten. Had she come down with something?

Moving like an arthritic woman on a rainy day, Olivia donned the robe and tiptoed out of the bathroom and into the open space of the kitchen/living room.

There were two visible doors out of the cottage: one at the front, the other at the back. Thankfully, Marrok lay asleep on the couch in between. She knew from her earlier attempt that the front door required a key, which he undoubtedly possessed. The back door . . . worth checking, but she wasn't betting escape would be so easy.

As she hobbled to the door, Olivia scanned his cottage. Despite being isolated, it was decked out with high-tech security alarm, electricity, running water, every modern convenience available in both the bathroom and kitchen, right down to an electric shaver and a microwave.

But he owned no television. Worse, she saw no telephone. Even if she could find where her purse had fallen, the battery on her phone was undoubtedly dead now since the charge had been low yesterday. So much for calling 999.

Since Bram had not appeared, she assumed he wasn't coming, and Marrok's assurance otherwise had been a lie. God, how could she have been so reckless?

Resisting the urge to cry, then sleep for a decade, Olivia pressed on, watching Marrok doze on the couch. His head lay at an awkward angle. His face, even in repose, made her heart rattle in her chest. Her body ached so badly for him. The pain increased with every step she put between them.

Too bad. She couldn't stay.

Finally, the exit was in reach. French doors. Stained glass. Had he done that as well? Wouldn't surprise her.

Olivia braced herself. The damn dizziness returned, mingled with wretched pain. Her head . . . This was like a hangover, the flu, vertigo, food poisoning, and her period thrown in for good measure. She fell to her knees. God, she was going to throw up.

She had to get up, get out. Now!

Drawing in a fortifying breath, Olivia reached for the doorknob.

Her hand never made it.

CHAPTER FIVE

A FEMININE GASP AWAKENED Marrok in time to see Morganna crumple to the ground by the back door. He darted across the room and kneeled beside her. What the devil . . . ? She was pale, twenty shades lighter than white. Her breaths were shallow, her body so bloody still. Had he hurt her last night?

"Morganna?"

Not a muscle twitch, not a hint of a stir.

"Morganna!"

Was this some game? She was never passive or helpless. A new tactic perhaps? Did she punish him because he had not called her by her preferred name? In eons past, she had flown into a fury for less.

"Olivia? Open your eyes."

Marrok brushed the back of his fingers across her soft cheek. She was burning up with fever.

He lifted her into his arms and clasped her to his chest. She felt as if she'd spent all day under relentless summer sun, or was baking from the inside.

Cradling her, Marrok rose to his feet. She moaned.

"Can you hear me?" He could not mask the worry in his voice and prayed this was no hoax to gauge his concern so she could use it to drag him deeper into her muck.

Instead of a calculating laugh, she moaned again. "Burning . . . Need . . ."

"Need what?"

Silence.

He strode down the hall, trying not to jostle her. Lord, she could not weigh more than eight stone. And last night, he'd settled himself on top of her, pushed into her, insisted she take every inch of him . . .

Sweat beaded across Marrok's chest and back as he laid her on his bed. "Olivia, what do you need?"

"Touch . . ."

He did, gently putting his palm on her forehead. If anything, her skin had climbed another degree or two. Bloody hell, if this was an act, it was the best he had yet seen.

"I must cool you down."

Marrok raced to the kitchen. Ice. Loads of it in a bucket. Some towels soaked in cold water. Aspirin.

Hands full, he returned to see that she'd unbelted his dressing gown from about her waist and tried to open it. Dumping the supplies on the bed, he flung the garment wide, then drew it off until she lay bare.

"Better?"

She merely moaned and arched toward him, skin flushed. The woman was sick, and the sight of her bare, soft body had him unbearably hard. No doubt he was a scoundrel, but the pull he felt to her was undeniable, especially when she parted her legs restlessly and arched again.

Doing his utmost to ignore the tempting sight, Marrok draped one of the cool, wet cloths across her torso. Screeching, Morganna came up off the bed and tore at it as if it scalded her. Marrok held the cloth in place while she thrashed like a wild thing. What the hell was wrong?

"Morganna?"

"No!" Her wild violet stare leapt from her pale face. She shoved at the little towel again, baring her breasts and taut nipples.

Even in the midst of illness, not only did she ignite his desire, but she insisted she was not Morganna. Hellfire, she was taking this pretense far.

What if it were not a pretense at all? The possibility jolted him with horror.

Bollocks! The le Fay woman he would have killed for his freedom, he now tried to save. All he could think of was her suffering, her need . . . and the possibility that she was not Morganna. Regardless, letting her die was no option.

"Touch . . . me."

"With the ice?" He grabbed the bucket.

She clutched his shirt, dragging him against her, nearly spilling the frozen cubes. "Your. Hands."

She wished him to touch her sexually? Marrok stared at the hunger in her brilliant gaze. She wanted him? *Now*? He searched his memory for some side-effect of the magical mating words they had spoken. He recalled none.

"Relax."

He lifted the wet towel off her and fetched a fan he kept in the wardrobe. After frantically rummaging, he found the whirring device and plugged it in. As it stirred the still air, he looked again at the woman. Morganna? Olivia? Whoever she was, she was beyond ill, her fever spiraling out of control. The desire for sex must be delusion.

God, what had he done to her?

Had he, by chance, kidnapped the wrong woman and stolen her innocence? Morganna could not have been a virgin. Nor would she have ever shown this vulnerability. What if this truly was Olivia Gray?

She'd want to skewer him, and he would deserve it. But now, he must discern what ailed her. She was growing paler by the moment, her breathing more agitated, her body more restless.

She rubbed her hand across her belly, then slid it lower, between her thighs. Delicate fingers parted her folds and plunged inside. Dear God, she glistened, wet.

"Marrok . . ."

Her breathy plea went straight to his cock. He scowled. Maybe she would improve if he left the room and her sight. Perhaps his presence agitated her . . .

Marrok retrieved two aspirin and sloshed water in a cup, then approached. He fought her until she swallowed the tablets and half the water. The woman needed sleep, not sex. He paced to the living room, worried as hell, returning to the sofa and the carving he'd begun earlier. Still, he could not take his mind off the woman in his bed.

For the next hour, she screamed—his name, pleas for him, for sex. The screams became whimpers, then, as afternoon approached, those dimmed to occasional moans. Then silence, only a restless thrashing of her body breaking the eerie quiet.

For the hundredth time, Marrok crept down the hall and shoved the door wide, risking a peek at his magical "wife."

Now she lay as still and pale as death. He raced to her side and pressed his fingers to her carotid. Thin, erratic pulse. She scarcely breathed. At the thought of losing her, something inside him lurched in furious denial.

Who the bloody hell should he call? A doctor? Aspirin had done nothing, and he'd never seen anyone suffering from a flu-like fever crave sex.

This had to be a magical malady.

Who could he . . . ? Bram. Yes. He would summon the wizard, pray the man knew something useful.

Marrok darted across the room and yanked open a drawer. Inside, he found the small rock Bram had given him just yesterday. He ran to the back door, flung it open, and tossed the rock in the air. "Bram Rion."

Seconds later, there was a pop, then a screech as the rock became a large white bird and flew away.

Less than two minutes later, Marrok heard a knock on the door and pulled it open. There Bram stood.

"It worked." Marrok frowned.

He had been around magic for centuries, had suffered its cruelties. Yet some feats still amazed him.

"Of course. That is a simple spell. I bewitched my first rock at age four." He rolled his eyes. "You called—" Bram blinked. Then his jaw dropped. "You mated with her? You spoke the magical vow?"

Marrok stilled. "How did you know?"

"You have a magical signature now. It's fuzzy, but muted with her color." Bram paced a circle around him. "How did you know the actual words?"

"She spoke them and . . . the reply just came out." Marrok ignored Bram's surprise and raked a frustrated hand through his hair. "Will you help her or waste time asking questions?"

"Of course, I'll try. But this signature, something isn't quite right."

"Later," Marrok snarled. "Mor—Olivia . . ." he said, uncertain what he should call her. "She is barely alive."

Bram's expression tightened with concern. Storming down the hall, Marrok was relieved to hear the wizard directly behind. He rushed into the room, quickly covering her naked form. If possible, she had worsened in the past few minutes.

"Oh, dear God," Bram murmured.

"What ails her? Is it magical?"

Bram approached the bed, laid a palm over her forehead, the pulse at her neck. Even if she was ill, knowing that Bram touched her, that he stared at her body covered in nothing but a thin sheet, made him want to shove the wizard away with a growled threat.

When she kicked out, exposing a sleek hip and thigh,

Marrok blocked the wizard's view and covered her again, brushing a gentle palm over her shoulder.

She clasped surprisingly strong fingers around his wrist. "Need . . . Touch."

Marrok closed his eyes. He had touched her last night, and his body had reveled in every second. And he ached to do it again when she was not at death's door.

"What ails her is magical, is it not?" Marrok demanded as he gently extracted himself from her grip.

"I have my suspicions," Bram answered carefully.

"Listen, you spell-casting bastard, ponder later the fact I have likely bound myself to Morganna or some witch much like her for eternity. Now, you will tell me what the bloody hell sickens her. I refuse to watch her die."

"My aunt Millie should see Olivia. Her magic is of the heart. Millie is an expert in matters of mating and family. She can, no doubt, explain this. Then, I will do a bit of research of my own—"

"We cannot wait to locate people and look in old tomes. Do something now!"

With a nod, Bram left the room. Marrok knew he should follow and watch the impertinent weasel, but he could not bring himself to leave Morganna/Olivia.

Moments later, he heard a knock at the door and jogged down the hall.

"Invite my aunt in," Bram demanded.

Marrok opened his mouth, then thought better. Easy capitulation was unwise. No matter that Bram pretended to be a friend. He merely wanted the Book of Doomsday. If not for the little tome, the wizard might well have left Marrok's feverish mate to die.

Scowling, he looked at the woman standing just outside the door. She was a tiny, fey-looking female—small stature, dancing blue eyes, glowing skin. Her age . . . She could be anywhere between forty and four thousand.

"You have an ill mate?"

The witch had a sweet smile. Marrok saw clearly that her power came from her heart. She wore joy and goodwill like a fine coat.

"Come in, please."

Nodding crisply, the woman crossed the threshold. "In bed, dear?"

Marrok nodded and took hold of the woman's arm. "Follow me."

He urged her down the hall, barely short of a run. She neither struggled nor protested, as he prodded her to Morganna/Olivia's side.

"You spoke magical mating vows."

"Yesterday."

The woman's blue gaze danced around him, as if tracing his figure. "Clearly, you merged with her. And yet . . . not wholly."

Marrok did his best not to flush. Could they tell that he had not found his pleasure and released his seed inside her? "Aye."

"There is your problem. She is an underage witch, and it is unadvisable for anyone who has not yet attained their powers to mate. It creates a dependence that, unfulfilled, can be fatal. That you're nonmagical . . ." Bram's aunt shook her head. "It will take you twice the effort to keep her alive. Despite how virile you look, she may require care beyond your capability. It's tragic, but perhaps you're better off to make her comfortable before she passes to her nextlife."

Marrok heard her words and understood few of them. He glared at Bram. "I will be damned if I simply sit idle while she dies."

"You're already damned."

Resisting the ugly curse on the tip of his tongue, he took a menacing step toward Bram. "Give me the nonmagical translation for your aunt's prattling. Now."

"What's in it for me?" He raised a golden brow.

Mercenary varlet. "I might know something about that book you seek. But if she dies . . ."

"You and Olivia are mates. A vow was spoken and answered. Normally, consummating the union seals it and provides the energy exchange that keeps someone magical healthy and alive. It appears she gave her pleasure to you, and you did not give her yours in return. Magically speaking, she gave of her power and spirit, but you did not mingle it with your own and give it back. That leaves a power deficit in her, which makes her weaker by the moment. This," he reached for the *laggagh* stone about her wrist, "makes her even weaker. It was created to drain a witch of Morganna's immense, centuries-old power. Olivia is a witch who has not yet attained her abilities. She won't for a few years. So the bracelet is speeding up her rush to death."

"So . . . we are mated and I must bed her often to keep her alive? And the bracelet is draining and killing her?"

"Yes to all. No one has used the bracelet in centuries, so I'm guessing on that. But you missed the middle."

"The middle made no sense."

"I'll put this in small words." Heaving a sigh, Bram edged closer. "The fact you haven't orgasmed inside her means her body perceives that you haven't given her your vitality, only taken from her. Because you two are mated, she is now dependent on you for her energy. Because she hasn't reached transition, she needs more of your . . . um, vigor than a mature witch. Without you sharing your body—regularly—she will lose power until she loses her life."

Marrok felt the blood drain from his face. He pulled Bram aside, growling, "You mean if I fail to spill my seed inside her, something I have not achieved with any woman in fifteen centuries, she will die?"

"Yes. You are now the battery that powers her existence."

"Skin-to-skin contact will briefly provide her a boost, dear," Aunt Millie added, then winked. "But a rousing romp in the hay to mutual satisfaction will revive her for hours, perhaps days, depending on the pleasurable energy exchanged."

Staggering back, Marrok crashed into the wall. His mate was doomed. And while he'd sought Morganna's downfall for centuries, the thought of this woman's death filled him with panic. Damn, she might not be Morganna at all.

Bram leaned closer. "Magical matings have been known to break a curse or two. Maybe . . . in addition to the sex, a little remorse on your part for spurning Morganna centuries ago would help."

"If I had but known the risk of mating with her . . ." He raked a hand through long hair. It was one thing to kill in battle, fighting for one's country, chieftain, or king. But dying from absence of affection and pleasure seemed intolerably cruel.

"Don't give up yet."

Marrok knew he would not until she took her dying breath. He had no idea why the notion of saving her compelled him so, but the thought of living without her, even for a day, crushed him with grief.

"In the meantime," Bram went on, "we must get this *laggagh* stone off her wrist."

Bram leaned in to uncuff her. Marrok grabbed his arm to stay the man. "You are certain it's harmful?"

"Quite," his aunt answered. "Having the bracelet on her

is a bit like trying to use a simple power point to light up all of London. It's overwhelming her system."

"If she truly is not Morganna, I understand. But how can we know for certain?"

"If the woman in your bed was Morganna, she'd still have days, maybe weeks, of power under her skin. The *laggagh* stone blocks her from performing magic, but takes much longer to drain her. Your mate has been wearing this for less than a day," Bram pointed out.

Marrok couldn't concede that quickly. If the naked, unconscious woman on his bed was Olivia, not Morganna, that would mean he'd taken an innocent woman's virginity, bound himself to a stranger, and made a fatal mistake. "Perhaps she is Morganna reborn?"

The little witch scoffed. "Morganna has been in exile since I was a child. She's likely moved on to her nextlife. The only way she could return is through exceptionally powerful magic no one has seen in . . . well, since my uncle Merlin. But, given her signature, it's clear as the sky she's le Fay."

Aunt Millie pressed a hand to Olivia's forehead, then another to her heart. She frowned, then lifted one of Olivia's palms and stared. Another scan of Olivia's magical signature deepened Millie's scowl.

"She's a descendant through Morganna's son; she's not Morganna herself. In time, she will prove very powerful. But for now, she is a normal, underage witchling."

Marrok frowned. Did the little woman speak the truth? Her eyes, his gut, said yes. "Bloody hell."

"Perhaps a le Fay descendant will be able to undo your curse," Bram suggested.

And perhaps not.

Millie laid a soft hand on his arm. "Heart magic is my

specialty, not future telling. But this girl . . . I can feel that she's destined for importance. She must be kept alive at all costs."

But he could not guarantee that he could give her his seed at all, much less regularly.

Marrok whirled on Bram. "This is impossible. My curse . . . You know it has denied me for centuries."

Bram nodded. "There *is*, perhaps, another way of keeping Olivia alive."

"Aye?"

"To sever your connection to her would end her dependence on you."

Marrok frowned. "What do you mean?"

"Mate breaking," Aunt Millie answered. "It's rare, because we believe mates are fated. Once a pair mate-bonds, their lives become entwined. They need each other's pleasure to sustain their life, so their life spans become similar. Mated pairs often have many happy centuries together. A Call is rarely issued without knowing that the one they ask is their true love. And Calls are not answered unless—"

"Do you speak of magical . . . divorce?"

Bram nodded. "With . . . strings."

Naturally. "Such as?"

"Mate breaking is painful for both parties. Excruciating if the bond is deep. Afterward, Olivia will not remember you. A woman's mind is wiped clean so she can eventually take another mate and reproduce. But she will always feel the pain of loss without understanding why. The grief would linger unless you met again. Then her memories could return and endanger her once more. So if you break this bond, you must go far away and never return."

The entire idea sounded horrific. And inconvenient. Being le Fay, whether Morganna or not, she might be the only person who could help him break his curse. Leaving her was no option. But neither was watching her die.

"How would breaking our bond help her?" Marrok asked.

"If you separate, Olivia would no longer need your vitality to stay alive. She would come into her power naturally somewhere around twenty-five. If she survives the mate breaking—"

"*If* she survives?"

"Some witches and wizards don't. It's traumatic. Normally with a bond this new, the impact of breaking it would be minimal. The deeper the bond, the more dangerous it is to sever. The deeper the scar. Yours hasn't been fully formed. But Olivia is very weak . . ."

So a quick death, unless he and Olivia could discover the key to unlock his curse, or a probable death with a life of painful, illogical loss if she managed to survive. Neither option was acceptable.

What a bloody nightmare. Magic had once again shoved him into an untenable situation, and he'd rashly rushed in to his own peril—and Olivia's.

Was there any chance Bram had plotted this? Millie was his aunt, after all.

Much as he'd like to blame the cur, nay. Marrok knew he had heaped this situation on himself.

Or maybe . . .

Marrok whirled on Bram. "How much of this is the truth, and how much is you manipulating me to get that book you want so bloody bad?"

"*You* called *me*. Your mate is unwell. Do you think I cursed her into some 'illness' so I could maneuver you into this choice? How could I have known that you would enter a magical mating? I occasionally see the future, but you're giving me far too much credit, I assure you. And how would this get me any closer to the book?"

Before Marrok could reply, a little pop and a puff of white smoke appeared. Moments later, a bird circled, seeming to whisper in Bram's ear.

In the next instant, he blanched white and bounded for the door. "I must go."

Marrok followed him down the hall, grabbing at his arm. "But—"

"Later. The MacKinnetts have been attacked. It looks like the work of the Anarki. If that's true . . ." he grimaced. "Then my vision has come true. Mathias is back."

Four hours later, Bram returned to Marrok's cottage in the Creepified Forest. He knocked and waited long minutes.

Finally, Marrok opened the door, cradling Olivia's limp body against his chest. With the press of his strong hands, he tried to still her, but she writhed restlessly, wrapping her legs around him. Her tongue peeked out, lapping at his neck. The man's entire body was stiff.

"How is she faring?" Bram asked.

"Better now that your aunt removed the stone from her wrist."

"Need you. Inside me," Olivia moaned suggestively.

"Shh." He stroked her back.

The Olivia Bram knew would be mortified that she'd behaved this way around others. But after today's events, he could not spare a smile. And Marrok might hate magic and everything le Fay, but the way he cradled his mate, it was clear the bond was affecting him.

"Come in. You look as if you have been to hell." Marrok stepped back.

Bram supposed he did. He hadn't looked in a mirror lately, just into the sightless eyes of magical men and women slaughtered needlessly and viciously. The magical children who had vanished, never to be seen again until they'd been thoroughly inducted into the Anarki, haunted him. The fate he knew awaited Auropha twisted his gut.

"I have. And it will spread." Bram knew his hair was askew, his face smudged with dirt and caked with sweat. He didn't care. "Mathias is definitely back."

To say more now would just mean reliving the horror. He'd have plenty of time for that, when he presented information to the Council. "We're looking for the Anarki hideout in my vision and hope to save the captured MacKinnetts, but it's been hours."

"Sit," Marrok offered.

Exhausted, Bram stumbled to the nearest chair and fell into it. Marrok followed, folding his warrior's body on the sofa and cradling Olivia in his lap. She fell limp against him.

"How is Olivia?"

"Blessedly asleep, for now. But when she wakes . . ." He grimaced.

"What will you do about her? Keep the bond or break it?"

"I cannot afford to let her go, but if I release her and she dies anyway . . ."

"If she lives, I suspect that Mathias will seek her, just as he will seek the book."

Bram knew that saving magickind from Mathias might not be possible unless he got his hands on the Book of Doomsday. And until he found a way to thieve it or Marrok discovered how to end his curse, Bram could not touch it.

"By God, why?"

"If he obtains the Book of Doomsday, it's likely more

powerful if used by a le Fay. At least I believe so. Mathias probably does as well. I suspect he will want Olivia to further his evil cause."

Bram didn't think it was his imagination when Marrok cradled Olivia's slight body even tighter against him. The wizard reached across the space between them and grabbed Marrok's arm. "There are no easy answers, but magickind is resting on your decision."

"Mine?"

Bram was tired of talking. Tired, period. Marrok hated magic—with good reason. He would do whatever he wanted, never mind all the witches and wizards who would die trying to protect their children, never mind all the women Mathias would drain until death, or all the younglings who would vanish into the ranks of his disposable army once he'd forced them to commit atrocities and destroyed them.

"You need to decide quickly if you're going to break your mate bond. If you do nothing, Olivia will not live to see the sun rise."

CHAPTER SIX

"WELL?" THE FAMILIAR FEMALE VOICE prompted Bram the second he entered the manor.

Bram turned to his half sister. Sabelle was far more interested in magical politics than he liked. No longer were they limited to subtle intrigues and Machiavellian games; these were now officially dangerous times. Yet she stood nearby to jump into the treacherous waters headfirst. Good thing he was willing to act as his younger sister's life jacket. Sabelle had just celebrated her eighty-fourth birthday. Old by human standards . . . but still young in the magical world.

On the other hand, Sabelle was quick, clever, and understood magickind. Despite her youth, she provided surprisingly sage counsel.

"What did the Council decide about Mathias?"

"Nothing. Too busy squabbling." Bram rolled his eyes. "Ineffectual idiots. Why did I agree to take this post with all the elders?"

"Because you are the future of the Council. Their time is nearly past. Patience . . ."

"The elders fail to see that if they rescind the Social Order, Mathias will have no cause to hide behind and will be exposed as an evil power-grabber." Bram gritted his teeth. "But they fear Privileged backlash if they rescind it even more than they fear Mathias. So they argue between prudence and action. And they'll keep arguing while everyone around them is dying."

"You can't be surprised."

"No." He sighed. "But they're so bloody afraid of change! I'm annoyed."

"What about Marrok and the book?"

"Though he never admitted to having it, I'm convinced he does. I'd simply thieve it, but I have no notion where he's hidden it. He will not willingly part with it until he's broken his curse."

"Unfortunate, but you can hardly blame the man."

"I would like to."

Sabelle sent him a saucy smile. "In his shoes, you'd do much the same, I suspect."

"The good of magickind—"

"Means little to a man who has endured centuries of hell because of magic. Are you using your brain at all?"

"Whose side are you on?" Bram scowled.

Sabelle tossed a golden curl behind her shoulder. She looked like a cross between a faerie and a siren. Little wonder, since she had the blood of each running in her. If she ever found the right man, he'd stand virtually no chance of resisting her. But the bastard had better, unless he had Bram's blessing . . . or he wanted to die.

"What about Ms. Gray? Aunt Millie told me of her . . . illness."

"I think Marrok has realized she's not Morganna. I hope, anyway. If not, she's as good as in the grave."

"But they are mates."

Bram shrugged. "He hates Morganna. He'd cut off his right arm to destroy her. If she, Olivia, *is* Morganna in disguise and has duped us all, she's having quite a laugh at our expense. But she isn't our problem."

"Mathias is." Sabelle sank into a nearby chair. Distress and fortitude blended into a determined expression that, as an older brother, scared the hell out of Bram. "We must do something."

"Stay out of this, Sabelle."

The look in her blue eyes could have cut steel. "Don't be absurd. I may look fragile, but, like you, I have Merlin's magic in my veins. I won't sit about like some helpless princess while the rest of magickind fights. It's my cause, too. My people."

Bram couldn't fault her logic. Why couldn't she be totally selfish like her mother? Devanna would have happily sat back and watched others die for her.

"Sabelle . . ." he warned.

She grabbed his hand. As always, her touch soothed him.

Thanks to her siren blood and potent magic, she could put her hand on anyone and make them feel whatever she wished.

"Keep your tricks to yourself." He tried to shake free.

With a squeeze, she gripped him tight. "Take a deep breath."

Hell, there was no fighting her once she'd made up her mind.

After Bram had complied with her "request," she soothed him by rubbing a soft thumb across his knuckles. Resisting was a losing battle. Peace settled comfortably under his skin.

Finally, she released him. "Mathias has gathered the Anarki again and is—"

"Wreaking havoc," Bram replied. Grimness edged into Sabelle's artificial peace. "If the rest of the Council refuses to act, I must find people willing to put their differences aside and fight."

Sabelle opened her mouth, but three deep *gongs* interrupted her, announcing the fact they had company. From the sounds of the magical calling card, Lucan MacTavish had arrived. Saved by the bell.

Bram mentally opened a portal around the manor and his childhood friend Lucan appeared in the room, a large hand clasped in that of his mate, Anka.

Lucan stuck out his free hand. "Hello. Greetings to you. Peace be with you and yours. I'll even add live long and prosper if you'll tell me what's happened."

A grudging smile settled over Bram's face as he took in the well-mated couple. The match was a strong one. From good families, both of them. Powerful, magically compatible, well-educated, well-connected. Anka was light to Lucan's darkness, the laughter in his silence. Bram hoped to make such a match himself someday. First, said witch would have to appear.

Bram shook his friend's hand. "Peace be with you and yours. I plan to live long and prosper, thank you. Here's what happened." He scrubbed a hand over his tired eyes. "After the Council received a distress signal from the MacKinnetts in Surrey, I arrived to a bloodbath, despite my warning. All men and most women murdered—and branded with a certain symbol we all know. Every child missing—six of them, the youngest just four. The Council member's daughter has vanished. Sound familiar?"

Lucan scowled. "Your vision has come to pass? Mathias is back?"

With a grim nod, he said, "The MacKinnetts clearly weren't attacked by humans. Who but the Anarki would wield that symbol? And who but Mathias would be behind such atrocities?"

"Who, indeed? What can we do?"

The foursome drifted into a nearby sitting room.

"If the Council is going to flap its jaws, we must make plans, take action," Bram insisted. "I think we must find witches and wizards willing to work together for the greater good."

"Magickind banding together, without arguing?" Lucan's piercing blue eyes sharpened. "You're fantasizing. That's been impossible for . . . what, nearly four centuries?"

"More to the point," Sabelle added, "where would you find witches and wizards with the necessary strength and resolution to fight off Mathias—without so much hatred of their fellow warriors they spend all their time trying to kill one another?"

Anka smiled grimly. "A good question, that. My grandmother still talks about the old days, when magickind had a sense of community, not just jealousy and blind hatred."

"I never said it would be easy," Bram admitted. The rest

of the Council still can't see their Social Order has backed the Deprived into a corner they're willing to die—or kill—to escape."

Lucan cast a quick glance at his wife, so petite next to him. "Count me in, since Mathias seems to be up to his old tricks. We know from his last campaign that he's wily and powerful. Defeating him will require a unified effort."

"So now there are two of you." Sabelle conjured tea for everyone and poured herself a cup. "But you are friends. Now you must look at acquaintances, strangers . . . and enemies. Who will you call on?"

"I'll speak to Simon Northam. I suspect he would welcome such a conversation."

"The Duke of Hurstgrove?" Lucan clarified.

"Yes. Oh, quite." Sabelle smiled pertly. "He shall do. Very nicely."

Silently, Bram agreed. Best not to let on just yet. Sabelle may smile sweetly now, but rebellion was nearly her middle name. "For the cause, yes. For you? We'll see, little sister."

Sabelle crossed her arms over her chest and glared.

Anka laughed and reached up to plant a kiss on her husband's cheek. "Finding the perfect mate is worth the wait."

Lucan turned to his bonded female, and his hard eyes softened as he lifted her small hand to his mouth. The love between them was so clear, it was almost tangible. Bram envied his friend's good fortune.

"Who else would we approach?" Lucan asked a moment later.

Bram had thought hard on this. His choices were bound to be unpopular. "We could approach Isdernus Rykard."

Sabelle nearly choked on her tea. "Are you off your trolley?"

Lucan added, "With the bad blood between you, that idea is completely mental."

"He isn't insane." At least Bram hoped not.

With an arch of a blond brow, Sabelle added, "From the time I wore lace on my knickers, I've heard nothing about Ice, except that he's unhinged. And violent. He despises you."

"It's mutual."

"Whenever you're near him, you have the self-control of a rabid animal," Lucan pointed out. "That won't be good for the cause."

Bram rubbed the back of his neck. "I'll endeavor to deal with it. Ice is strong and has plenty of reason to want Mathias gone forever."

"The man won't welcome your overture."

"He's a powerful wizard. If there's one thing I know about him, he will do anything to protect his family from Mathias. And he won't wait on the Council."

With a nod, Sabelle conceded the possibility. "Who else?"

No one spoke for long moments. The *clink* of Anka setting down her fragile white teacup mingled with the sound of Lucan's sigh. Sabelle twirled a golden curl around her finger and looked at the carpet. Bram was pretty sure he knew what everyone was thinking.

"If matters grow as grim as I fear, there's no help for it. We must approach Shock Denzell."

Even though Bram felt sure Anka had been expecting his words, she started at the wizard's name. She faced him like a tigress, her amber eyes morphing from sweet to confrontational in an instant. "No. He'll do everything possible to kill Lucan."

Her mate reeled her back to sit at his side. "That's because I won the hot woman, love. He wound up alone."

"And you taunt him with that fact each time we see him. I feel terrible! Shock will spend the rest of his life without love because I rejected him."

"Don't feel sorry for him. He had to know you were not going to answer his Mating Call. He's tainted."

"His background is hardly his fault."

"His temper and reputation are." Steel underscored Lucan's voice.

Sabelle leaned forward and squeezed Anka's hand, then faced Lucan. "Perhaps, but Bram is right. Unless we can wrest the Doomsday Diary from Marrok of Cadbury, we may be relying on every witch and wizard, friend and foe alike, to come together as one to defeat Mathias."

The enormity of that task wasn't lost on anyone.

Bram nodded grimly. "Our nightmare has begun."

Daylight faded into night. Ominous shadows stabbed through the window, casting themselves over Marrok's bed, across Olivia's pale body now curled into a fetal position. He'd given her a cool bath but touching her skin was still like putting his hand in an open flame. She had not opened her eyes in hours or made a sound other than a pain-filled whimper that clawed at his gut.

He must either bed her or set her free—or she would die before morn.

Her death, for him, was unthinkable. He needed her in order to be released from his curse, which meant he must keep her safe from Mathias.

Olivia becoming his mate threw a twist in his plans. If he believed everything Bram and Millie said.

But why should he doubt? He'd met Olivia less than two days ago. Something had compelled him to speak magical vows with her. She'd induced him to actually *feel*, which he had not done in . . . decades? Centuries? They had shared scorching sex. She had tempted him closer to satisfaction than any woman since the Dark Ages.

But there was more.

An urge to keep her alive at all costs rode him hard. Because of the vows they had spoken, magic's way of ensuring the survival of the species? He sensed magic was not entirely to blame. Her bravado, sass, and mystery drew him. She had moved across an ocean—without guidance or assistance—to fulfill two dreams. Her shop was a reality. With her determination, he had no doubt she would find her father. She had a tenacity he admired.

Had he met Olivia under different circumstances, if he had not known from the first that she was a le Fay, he would have pursued her relentlessly. After all, he had time on his side.

Olivia did not. He must decide what to do. He had not the luxury of trying sex, then resorting to a mate breaking if unsuccessful. If he took her to his bed and his curse kept him from climax . . . Mate breaking was an hours-long process, and Olivia would not live that long. Already, she was alarmingly weak. If she died, his curse literally could stretch to eternity.

What the bloody hell was he going to do?

The bond affects you as it does any wizard. The thought of never touching Olivia again is beyond endurance, right? Bram had deduced. *Nor can you stomach the thought of her mating with another.*

Even the words had made him violent. Though nonsensical, Marrok could not deny the feelings for her existed.

How Morganna would laugh if she could see him now.

Beside him, Olivia whimpered again. Marrok grimaced and placed a comforting hand on her. She curled closer, seeking his touch. Her silent trust in him warmed him—and scared the piss out of him. He, who had stood alone for centuries, now had someone who depended on him. Someone who mattered to him.

Someone le Fay.

He was well and truly tied. It may be foolish and wrong and selfish, but Olivia had issued a Mating Call, and he had answered. Nothing, no one, would come between them now. For her, he would sweat and grind and thrust all night, focus, pray—whatever necessary to finalize this bond, his curse be damned.

She whimpered once more in her coma-like slumber. Tamping down panic, he smoothed a dark curl away from her hot brow. "Olivia?"

No response. He breathed through the terror. Giving in would accomplish naught. With methodical motions, he drew his shirt over his head. With a button and a lowering of his zip, his jeans came next. He rarely bothered with drawers, so the slide of denim down his hips and the removal of his socks bared him.

Then he climbed onto the bed beside Olivia, sliding his naked skin against hers. It was like cuddling up to an inferno. Marrok braced against the natural instinct to retreat and fitted her against his body.

Such soft skin. He brushed his fingers across her cheek, his thumb over the pillowy curve of her lower lip. Everything, from the arch of her raven brows to the tips of her red toenails, made his body scream out for sex. For satisfaction.

Closing his eyes, he focused on their bond. Inside him, it had grown since they had first shared words and bodies. Thin but sturdy, their connection wrapped itself around him. Mentally, he reached out for it. Every instinct inside him screamed at him to cover her, kiss her, touch her, mount her. This instant.

Once he made this decision, there was no going back.

But he could make no other choice.

With a nudge, he rolled her to her back and followed,

settling on top of her, resting his weight on his elbows. Her eyes drifted half open, and he rejoiced; that was the most alert she had been in hours.

Then her lips fell open a fraction, and she exhaled against his mouth. The sensation made him shiver. Made him harder than hell. Zounds, he was so aware of her naked body beneath him, the firm swell of her breasts, her flat belly, her thighs spread wide to him.

He drew in a sharp breath as impatient need stabbed him and demanded he slam inside her. But he restrained it. *Slow arousal. Desire. Build it. Feel her. This was for her.*

Focusing on Olivia was his only hope. Dwelling on his own frustration had denied him completion for more centuries than he cared to count. This time, he'd concentrate on each small detail, her scent, vanilla, peaches, and female, misting over her skin, softly tingeing every breath he took. Each inhalation a joy, a riot of luscious scents. Each exhalation a little bit of anticipation until he could smell her again.

Lured by her, Marrok lowered his head and brushed kisses across her jaw, then her neck. Her scent was strong here. Heavenly.

Inhaling her, he opened his mouth, tasting her with a slow lick. She was part salty, part sweet. The tang of her sat upon his tongue, made his mouth water. How had he missed all this sensory seduction the first time he'd been inside her? Too focused on their vows, on her identity, on the possibility of orgasm.

Not this time.

Under him, she moaned. The long, pleading sound went straight to his cock, as if she held him in her fist. God, the power this woman had over him. Never had he known its like.

"Marrok . . ."

"Aye, love." With his blood surging, need pumping, breathing rough, Marrok was fast losing the grip on his restraint.

"I ache. So bad. Need you inside me."

He closed his eyes. That was the wrong thing for her to say if she wanted him to take this slow and savor the experience of being with her.

"Soon," he promised, caressing her shoulder, down her arm, until her fingers tangled with his.

Olivia fixed her feet on the mattress and lifted her hips in blatant invitation. "Now."

Lord, the woman was killing him. His every muscle tensed. Sweat beaded on him.

He soothed her with a soft hand in her hair, across her cheek. "Let us not rush."

"Need. You. Now!" Olivia tore her hand from his grasp and planted it in his hair, her fingers curling around the strands all the way to his scalp, then using her grip to position him as she slanted her mouth across his own.

Instantly, her flavor burst across his tongue. Not minty like toothpaste. Not heavy like coffee. Not sweet with something she'd eaten. Just . . .Olivia, mysterious and irresistible.

On a groan, he dove into her mouth. From the moment their lips met, his goal became to taste, plunder, master. With fevered kisses, he took her mouth with unrelenting passion. Need roared inside him.

Olivia wrapped her legs around him, her nails digging into his shoulders, as she arched into the kiss. If he had ever lain with a more responsive woman, he did not recall it. Or maybe he had, and he'd simply forgotten every other woman. Olivia obliterated them with her white-hot responses and the little catches at the back of her throat.

He held her face, his thumbs brushing her cheeks, and kept

her still for his mouth's pleasure. He was starved for her, yet every taste did naught to assuage his hunger. He took the kiss deeper, overwhelmed by sensation. She clung tighter.

Her nipples stabbed into his chest. Blast it, he could scarcely take a good breath. Olivia seemed no better, her chest heaving, cheeks flushed, her ragged inhalations shouting that she was racing to the brink as quickly as he.

And they'd done little more than kiss.

His gaze touched the skeins of her dark hair framing a haunting face, those eyes so like Morganna's, but without the calculation and guile. He yearned to feel her, to take her.

"Tell me what you need."

Desire leapt in her vivid eyes as she placed his hand on the swell of her breast. Her nipples stood up, begging for his caress. He complied, grazing the sensitive tip. She keened, a sound of longing and frustration.

Marrok shifted to drop a kiss into the silky valley between her breasts. By hell's fire, her scent was strong here. Inhaling it deep made him harder.

He tongued the soft skin of her cleavage and tasted the spice of her desire. It mixed with her innocence and female strength to beguile him. One taste would never be enough. Nor would a million.

With a deep breath, Marrok switched to the untended nipple. It leapt to attention against his tongue, and a fresh burst of her spice spilled into his mouth. Never had he experienced a woman before with such sensory depth, but he was bloody ravenous over her softness and the desire he swore he could taste on her skin.

He dusted open-mouthed kisses to the underside of her breasts, where her heavenly smell loomed strong. As it filled his head, he could hardly think of aught but getting deep inside her.

Yet he could not pry his lips from her long enough to mount her. Soon. But first he wanted her slick heat under his fingers. Touching her pouting flesh, caressing her swelling clit, bringing her to the brink . . . Aye.

Trailing his fingers down her stomach and into her wet curls, the taste of her sex exploded across his memory.

Bring her to peak now!

In the part of his brain still capable of rational thought, Marrok knew he must arouse her only. Allowing her release would expend too much of her energy while she sat at death's door. The pleasure might cost her her life. But she must be well prepared, since Olivia had taken him deep but once. As hard as he felt now, he could inadvertently hurt her. He wanted to bask in her pleasure, but he must not wring it from her without sharing in the climax.

He slid his fingers through her hot, narrow channel. Already her flesh tried to suck him deeper. Zounds, how could he possibly outlast her lure?

"Marrok, please. Don't . . . don't stop. Oh my God!" she cried as he dragged his thumb across her nub of nerves. "I need you."

Her body tensed, her legs splayed wide. Marrok dared not arouse her more. He yearned to. Desperately. Violently. They were mated, and he should have the privilege of watching her come repeatedly, to see her face flush with pleasure and hear her scream his name.

First, he must seal this bond by giving her all the vitality he could expend from his body into hers. Somehow.

Marrok was not a man given to prayer, but at this moment, he would have gladly gotten on his knees for some Hail Marys.

Please God, do not let her die.

Marrok shoved the thought out of his mind as he pushed

another finger inside her, and she arched off the mattress, whimpering, wet, clutching his shoulders. She grabbed his head and held him still for a kiss that bewitched him—just as she did.

She loosed a tremulous gasp, then stiffened. Her sex rippled around his fingers. He pulled free of her scalding passage and rolled back on top of her. Instantly, she wrapped her legs around his hips and scattered wild kisses across his sensitive throat that made him shiver.

"I need you inside me."

He shuddered as she wriggled beneath him, shoved a hand between them, aligned the sensitive head of his cock to her opening and . . .

"Please . . ."

How the bloody hell was a man to say no to that?

Impossible, Marrok thought as he slammed into her, down, down, the tight squeeze of her sex boggling his mind and adding a new layer of torment to the pleasure.

She cried out and dug her fingernails into his back. He was glad for the signs of her desire and possession. As she arched to him and bit at the sensitive skin between his neck and shoulder, he thrilled that she wanted to mark him as hers.

Under him, she writhed, impaling herself on his stiff length with every thrust. Deep. Deeper. So perfect. He savored the clasp of her body and the little moans he wrenched from her.

Marrok withdrew inch by torturous inch. Then he filled her again. As he glided over her sensitive spot, Olivia's breath caught. When he pushed in once more and felt the mouth of her womb, she gasped and gripped him tighter.

He became lost in her, a prisoner to the rush of electric pleasure that arced up his shaft, straight into his gut. He hardened even more, though he had not thought such possible.

Gritting his teeth, he repeated the process, a slow thrill ride of mind-boggling pleasure that began to unravel him. Another thrust, and the sensations stacked on top of each other, staggering him. He began to sweat, tremble, letting the need build and build. But Olivia fluttered against his cock.

"Not yet, love," he growled. "Hold on."

"No," she panted. "I need—"

"Together. We both need it."

What he needed was more of her. Lacing his fingers through hers, he held her to the mattress for slow thrusts and drugging kisses. Under him, she stiffened, arched. The pulses of her channel pushed him to the brink. Desire loomed, coiling lower and tighter inside him. In centuries, he had not been this close to achieving climax! He must reach it.

Or . . . else.

Shoving aside the consequences of failure, Marrok slid inside Olivia again. Slowly. His breath came hard. So bloody close . . . but that meant nothing.

Damn it, this wasn't simply his pleasure at stake; it was Olivia's life. His forever.

Fate and magic had forced him into a terrible position. He channeled his fury into determination. It mingled with desire as Marrok glided into her with long, possessive thrusts, driving them both close to the edge.

"Look at me," he demanded, thickly.

Olivia opened heavy lids, looking slumberous and pleasure-drenched. Her violet gaze crashed into him. The connection of their bond surged.

"Want more . . ." She pressed her lips to his.

He wanted to give her everything, while he made her *his*. Need ate at the chains restraining his pleasure. Desire gathered and solidified. Her face glowed with yearning and joy. He felt her in a way he'd never experienced a woman, deeper than he'd ever imagined sex could be. It sank into his chest, penetrated his soul.

"Mine!" he growled, then captured her mouth.

With another thrust into her, she clutched him with her sheath, her arms, her kiss. Ecstasy ripped past centuries of desolation.

His world exploded. Everything inside him lit up, burning. Consuming. Gratification roared through him as if it would never end, as if it would shatter him into a million pieces.

Olivia sank her teeth into his shoulder. He groaned as ecstasy shook him. Robbed of breath and control, Marrok poured his seed into her.

Seemingly endless, the climax left him boneless and spent. He slumped against Olivia, his heart rate slowing from the wild rush. He'd given her every bit of vigor he could scrape together, every touch his screaming muscles could give. And he had surrendered a part of himself he'd never given another.

Had it been enough to help her?

CHAPTER SEVEN

HIS CHEST TIGHTENED with fear as he opened his eyes. Beneath him, Olivia's face glowed with vitality in the moonlight. Relief flooded in. The world had been lifted off his back.

She looked amazingly alert and well, though flushed and

slightly confused. As if the hours of life-threatening illness had never occurred. He didn't want to move, didn't want to separate from her.

Bloody odd sentiment. He had entered into and kept the bond merely to break his curse.

But even as he thought the words, Marrok knew he lied.

The woman beneath him made him feel vital again. Though he'd been alive for centuries, he'd been dead inside. She changed everything.

"Marrok?" she ventured.

"Aye."

Since running afoul of Morganna, Marrok had bedded hundreds, perhaps thousands of women. As often as he'd focused on achieving satisfaction, Morganna's curse had withheld orgasm every time. Until tonight. Why? Tonight, he had focused solely on Olivia and every sensation of being with her. Had that made the difference? What had released his black heart, as Morganna had accused him of having, so he might achieve satisfaction?

The bond. Mentally, he felt it now. Thicker and twice as dense as before. While he held her, it continued to grow. Such an odd sensation to *feel* the connection. Yet it was undeniable.

Had mere magic tied them together or was it something more?

He knew she had made her dream of an art studio a reality and that she longed to meet her father. But he sensed a much deeper woman beneath, unlike Morganna, who had cared only for beauty and power. Olivia's soul seemed purer. He thirsted to learn more.

But would it be wise?

She was likely the key to his curse. He must focus on that and not be distracted by murky emotions for a le Fay.

"How fare you?" he asked.

"What is going on?" She tensed. Her stare demanded answers. "How did we get . . . here?"

"You were so ill, I feared you would die."

"So you had sex with me? Damn, my head hurts. Wait!" She tensed. "Did you drug me?"

She struggled against him as shock and horror dawned inside her.

For years, even her own mother had refused to touch the "otherworldly" girl. Most men had jumped on that bandwagon. Yet Marrok had been determined enough to rape her?

"Drug?" He sounded puzzled.

"Oh God, somehow you slipped me something so you could—"

"Think you I tricked you into taking some substance to ensure your surrender to me?" Marrok held her down, not budging.

"Why else would I be naked with a man I barely know? I'm *so* calling the police." She tried again to escape his hold.

"I wanted you, wench, but never so much that I would use trickery. That is the work of knaves and scoundrels. When we came to this bed, you were very willing."

"Because you had me drugged by then."

"I gave you neither food nor drink."

"But you gave me that bracelet. Somehow that thing wiped out my inhibitions." She glanced at her wrist. "It's gone!"

"Before we first shared this bed, *you* came to *me*. 'You see this desire I can't deny'?" he quoted her.

"I said that when I tried to trick you to escape." At least that had been the biggest reason. The other . . . no denying the guy was sexy and affected her in a way she could barely comprehend. "You were foaming at the mouth about having sex with Morganna to break your curse. Oh God, is that why you drugged me? I really am stuck in a freak show!"

"I did not drug you and I know now that you are not her, but 'twas a simple mistake. You have her eyes and her birthmark. Our joining had naught to do with Morganna and everything to do with you."

Somehow, he made that sound romantic. The forlorn little girl inside her wanted to take him at face value. His stare lingered. He looked so damn sincere—and she'd be an idiot to fall for it. "Whatever. You're done with me now."

"Nay." He pressed a kiss to her mouth. "Not by half."

Sweet, like melted chocolate and caramel on her favorite ice cream. If his desire was remotely real . . . wow! Sign her up for more. But it couldn't be real. Which begged the question: why *had* he made love to her?

"Let me go." She squirmed against the intimate press of their bodies, and they separated. Olivia gasped. "You didn't use a condom? This just keeps getting worse. I swear, if I get a disease . . . Or pregnant. Crap!"

"There will be no barriers between us, ever."

He said that as if he meant it and was determined to have her again. The desire staining his cheeks confirmed that. She should be worrying about pregnancy and HIV. Instead, her body was fixated on the fact that a guy who was McDreamy crossed with Mr. Universe wanted *her*. "Let me up, you creep!"

He grabbed her shoulders. "Listen well. I did *not* drug you, Olivia. You were ill."

"With what?"

For a long moment, he paused. " 'Tis difficult to explain . . ."

"Some side-effect of the drug you gave me?"

"God's blood, wench, I gave you nothing! I vow it. Tell me the last thing you recall."

Quickly, a flood of memories seared her. "I remember being . . . um, in bed with you. Then there was just pain and weakness. It was like a nightmare. I came out of it and we were . . . um, here again."

"As you came out of the nightmare, what did you *feel?*"

Feel? "This weird . . . connection to you. It doesn't make sense—"

"It makes perfect sense. Do you recall speaking words to me before we first made love?"

"Yes, but I just blurted them. I don't know what they meant or why. You answered me. Then we, um . . . But you didn't . . ."

"Aye, we made love, and nay, I did not climax. 'Tis not a drug that compelled your surrender to me, but that connection brought on by those words, methinks."

She remembered it now. Even through the dizziness and the heady pleasure of his touch, that link to him inside her urged her to accept him, give all to him. Even when the pain had been at its worst, her entire being had cried out for him.

Great, so she wanted him. The male angles of his gorgeous face and shoulders that eclipsed the room made that a "duh" observation. What woman wouldn't want him? It was the reverse that scared her. She could not endure more one-sided devotion. Eating Mom's crap had given her plenty of that lousy taste. Okay, so he'd wanted her enough to sleep with her. Anything deeper? She wasn't holding her breath.

"Is that connection why you sought me out and brought me here?"

"I know not why we shared the dream of us naked and impassioned, of you holding Morganna's book."

That's right, they had. Did that mean they somehow formed a bond before they'd met?

"That dream led me to believe you were my enemy, so I

lured you here. I see now you are meant to help me end my immortal curse, but not in the way I first imagined."

Beneath him, Olivia stiffened. "You're still insisting that you're immortal?"

"I am not insisting. I am."

Olivia finally managed to push Marrok off her and threw on his bathrobe. "You don't need to make this stuff up to get laid—"

"Nor would I! Morganna used the book in our dream to curse me when Arthur was king."

Olivia looked for some logical explanation and drew a total blank. Marrok was beyond sexy, and his touch had been amazing. But clearly, he belonged in an institution. Boy, she knew how to pick 'em . . .

"I *am* immortal. I have tried to die over the centuries. Believe me."

"That's crazy."

Marrok opened his mouth, then stopped. When Bram had first taken him to meet Olivia, the wizard had said she had absolutely no idea that magic existed or that she had a drop of power in her veins.

"Do you know aught of magic?"

She frowned. "Hocus-pocus stuff, like David Copperfield?"

"Nay. Like . . . Merlin. Or Harry Potter. Not illusionists, people *born* with magic."

"They're fictional."

"Merlin was very real. Odd chap, too."

"Are you trying to convince me that you're both immortal and magical?"

"Nay, merely immortal. I was cursed by someone magical."

"That Morganna woman you accused me of being? Morgan le Fay?"

"Aye."

Dare he say more? She was newly recovered from an illness he understood not. To tell her they were mated and that she was a descendant of one of the most evil witches to litter history's pages would either engender more disbelief or send her into shock. She would have many questions, for which he had few answers and less proof. Caution also tickled his brain. What did he know of Olivia's true nature? What if, under her innocence, a true le Fay waited, coiled and ready to strike?

"Morgan le Fay wasn't real either."

"Unfortunately, she was."

"It's folklore. Come on . . ."

Marrok said nothing. What could he say that would not make her think him mad? Better to keep quiet until she was better rested—and more open-minded.

"Crap! What day is it?"

"Wednesday."

"Holy . . ." Olivia gasped, bounding off the bed.

He grabbed her arm. "Where do you think to go?"

"My shop. I've been out for a whole day. No one is manning it, and I need the money—"

Marrok pushed her until she sat down again. "You have been unwell, and the hour is now well before sunrise. Later, we will find someone to keep shop until you are recovered."

"I'm fine. Just let me go home so I can run my business. Now that you know I'm not Morganna and I know nothing about the book—"

"Nay. I alone can prevent you from falling ill again."

"I thought you knew nothing about it," she challenged.

"I know how to prevent it."

"What, you have a special tonic?"

"Nay. We must join our bodies. Frequently."

Olivia burst out laughing. "Give me a break. You don't have to go through the immortal-knight-we-have-a-connection routine to have sex. You're a gorgeous guy. Coffee and a chat would have gotten you a lot further. I don't know why you'd go to this much effort for me . . ."

Frustration flashed across his face. "I have fabricated naught. I want you. You need me, and I can protect you."

"From what?" She looked suspicious.

"If I mistook you for Morganna, others may. Ruthless killers who will hunt you if they believe you are the sorceress."

"I think the chance that anyone else will mistake me for an Arthurian witch is pretty slim." She rolled her eyes. "Do you have a phone so I can call Bram? I'm going home."

"I apologize for abducting you, but you must stay here."

"For . . . ? You know what, I don't even want to know. Good luck with all your curse breaking and whatever. I'm going home, and you're not stopping me. I need to open A Touch of Magic in a few hours—" She winced. "Um, I meant what I said earlier about your talent. And I need the money. You're going to consign your carvings with me, right?"

"If you will rest here another few days, aye."

She braced a hand on her hip. "That's coercion."

"Do not attempt to play on my sense of guilt. In this, I do not possess one."

With her, he would take no chances. He wanted naught more than to keep her safe . . . and lay her back and love her again, while reveling in the fact they could satisfy each other. That she might possibly free him from his immortal ball and chain.

Marrok stopped—moving, breathing. Did being finally able to spill his seed mean he'd thwarted Morganna's terrible curse?

He jumped from the bed, flipped on the bedside light,

rushed to the simple maple chest of drawers he'd carved decades ago, and rifled through drawers.

"What are you doing?"

As he felt his way through the socks, his fingers closed around something pointed and leather-bound. He pulled the object from its confines, gripped the handle, and tore the protective casing off with a cry of triumph.

Olivia blinked, hoping her eyes deceived her. But no, she saw a long, wickedly-sharp blade that gleamed in the artificial light, gripped tight in Marrok's fist. It was huge, imposing—like the man who wielded it.

He turned toward the bed and prowled back in her direction, looking like the Chippendale's version of a horror-film slasher.

She scrambled back to the opposite side of the mattress. "Are you doing this because I want to go? If I had known that would make you homicidal, I would have kept my mouth shut."

Now that he'd had his fun, would he kill her? She almost didn't believe it. Their connection had given her a sense of safety. And she had flashes of hazy memories as he cared for her gently while she'd been ill, but . . .

"Bloody hell, I mean you no harm, woman." He held up the knife. "This is for me."

Before she could say a word, Marrok hacked into his forearm. Blood splattered and gushed in a sickening torrent around jagged skin. Her knees nearly buckled. "Stop! Oh my God—"

He dropped the knife. Blood poured from the wound, down his arm, pooling in the crook of his elbow, drizzling on the hardwood floor in a metallic-scented rush. Olivia tried not to panic as she rushed to the bathroom and grabbed towels. She couldn't waste a moment in getting the bleeding stopped. Then they had to get to a hospital. Marrok needed stitches. They had to call Bram for a ride.

Thoughts turning, she rushed back into the bedroom and stopped dead. Marrok stood, examining his injured arm. The awful gash was gone. Completely. As if it had never been.

Is this for real?

Marrok grabbed a towel from her numb hands and wiped the lingering blood away. "Thank you."

Olivia swayed on her feet, still staring at his arm. What the hell had just happened? Not only did it look healed, but unblemished. No trauma, no scar. Nada.

"What . . . You . . ." She raised frantic, confused eyes to Marrok's face. "It's gone."

Furious disappointment slashed across his face. "Morganna still prevails. As always, I heal in moments."

Olivia blinked, taking in his smooth skin and bitter expression. She saw no smoke, no mirrors. But something was going on here that wasn't . . . normal.

Something magical?

As bizarre as it seemed, what other explanation was there? She tried to fit other scenarios, but none worked. *Holy unbelievable hell*! Now would be a good time to learn how *not* to hyperventilate.

"Are you really . . . immortal?"

Marrok set the knife and bloody towel on the dresser with a sigh. "I was born in the sixth century. Even with the longer life spans people enjoy today, I am unusual."

And then some. Did that mean he had told her the truth about everything? What else could it mean? Okay . . . so it appeared that he hadn't drugged and tricked her into sex. They *were* connected. She couldn't deny it when everything inside her wanted to reach out to him. And she had dreamed of the man before she'd even met him. Something here was . . . abnormal. Magical.

Wow!

Olivia sank to the bed. "How . . . oh, Morganna, you said. Why did she curse you?"

"Because . . ." He dropped his head, and his shoulders followed. "I was an arse. I served under King Arthur as his most decorated warrior. We fended off the Anglo-Saxons at the Battle of Mons Badonicus, killing nearly a thousand invaders. We felt invincible."

A thousand? That turned her stomach. But if Marrok was telling the truth—and she didn't see another alternative—knights of the Dark Ages had lived vastly different lives from today's men. Killing one's enemy hadn't been sport, but survival.

"Well-known warriors in those days had the equivalent of groupies, like rock stars today."

"You had them?"

"My fair share . . . and the share that should have belonged to half of Arthur's army."

Somehow that didn't shock her.

"I was young and randy. Women were disposable, to be used for pleasure, then sent on their way. All that changed after Mons Badonicus."

"Because you met Morganna?"

"I had known her for some while. Several weeks before the battle, I made the mistake of taking Morganna to my bed. I whispered sweet words and told her pretty lies. Afterward, I left and never looked back."

"Hell hath no fury like a woman scorned."

"Indeed. She told Arthur I had raped her, beaten her, left her to die. I doubt he believed her, but she brought 'witnesses' and made it sound most damning. Arthur knew his half sister to be capable of all manner of retribution if he did not assuage her. So he cast me out of the kingdom, took everything I'd fought for my entire life. Morganna found me weeks later, dirty and wandering, and bade me to come back to her. She vowed she would return me to Arthur's good graces and my old life."

"You refused?"

"I laughed. She was the source of my misfortune. It took me decades to see that my callous treatment played a role in my downfall. When she appeared, the last thing I wanted was to ever go near her again. When I told her as much, she cursed me with that damned book. In that instant, I became immortal and incapable of obtaining sexual satisfaction. Until tonight."

Olivia's jaw dropped. "This was the first orgasm you've had in . . . ?

"A millennium and a half, aye."

If this tale was remotely true . . . wow. And *she* had been the woman to satisfy him? The thought made her feel stupidly giddy. Little unwanted *her* had given the big warrior the ultimate pleasure. Maybe she wasn't defective.

"Why could you . . . um, achieve it tonight?"

" 'Twould be more accurate to ask why I could achieve it with you, methinks. The answer is, I know not. I suspect it's about our connection."

Yeah, that inexplicable connection. Everything he said was pretty fantastical, but she couldn't deny feeling that bizarre closeness, either.

"So after you realized that Morganna had cursed you, what happened?"

"I paid her serving wench to steal the book for me. Morganna cursed me by writing in it, so I believed I could un-curse myself thus. But no matter how I tried, nothing made me mortal."

The story just got weirder and weirder. "That's . . . wow. But you seem pretty detached. If she cursed you, aren't you furious?"

"Anger burned out long ago. Centuries of it is draining." He grunted. "After Merlin tricked Morganna into exile, I thought that might release me. But nay. She amused herself by tormenting me with dreams of whatever she thought would crush me.

"At first, it was of the warrior who moved up in Arthur's army and was given my lands. Then it was of all the ale he drank, the battles he won, the women he tupped—symbols of the power I no longer had. Eventually, she haunted my dreams by showing me the deaths of all those I'd cared for. Arthur's slaying. My sister's death in childbirth." He choked out the last words, then swallowed past rage. "I saw them as they happened—and I could do naught but hear them scream."

"Torture was Morganna's idea of fun?"

"Indeed. Years passed, decades . . . centuries. A whole millennium. I hated every day, so like the last, knowing tomorrow would be the same. I forgot how to feel, to care. Then she visited me in dreams and began tormenting me with the possibility that I might find a way to die. It amused her that I tried every suggestion she planted in my head."

"You seriously wanted to die?"

"What had I to live for? My castle, family, and friends had been gone so long, they were dust. I dared not form friendships. If I did, Morganna visited their dreams and filled their heads with my evil. People I had come to respect soon believed me to be all manner of villain—a grave robber, a child slayer . . . By the time she ceased such games, I was accustomed to solitude."

Yes, hell hath no fury, as the saying went, but wow. What

Morganna had done to Marrok went way beyond revenge and into psychotic bitch territory.

Olivia didn't know him well, but her heart went out to him. He seemed like a proud man. His carvings and the gentleness in his touch proved he was capable of feeling. "Marrok . . . That's awful. I'm sorry."

How had he endured being so alone century after century? Olivia understood isolation, being an outcast, pressing your nose to the glass. Even with her dying breaths, her mother hadn't told Olivia the truth about her father. Mom had never once let Olivia believe she was anything more than a duty. Now, she was thankful she'd only endured the torment for twenty-three years. Marrok had a lonely eternity with no end in sight.

Abduction hadn't been the brightest plan of action, but Olivia understood it now. She wanted to help the man. He'd cared for her during her mystery illness and given her, if briefly, the sensation of being held and desirable, which she'd always yearned for.

"You said that the book you showed me is the key to ending your curse. Can I see it again?"

He shot her a narrow-eyed gaze. "Why?"

"I have a degree in art, and history is one of my secret passions. I have connections in the art and antiques business, literary scholars and historians. Maybe one of them will know something about this book and how to uncurse you."

Marrok said nothing, clearly wondering if he could trust her. Olivia would have been hurt, but after everything he'd been through, she didn't blame him.

"It's up to you," she assured him. "I'm not Morganna, so I can't just sing a chant and solve your problem, but maybe I can do something."

"You would help me, even after I abducted you?"

"I'm not thrilled about that part, but you've been pushed to the brink of sanity by a curse that would have warped the average guy long ago. The fact you're still sane and fighting, yet put your quest on hold to care for me, is . . . nice. I *want* to help you. Maybe together, we can unlock the secret of the book."

He cupped her cheek. "You have given me light, hope. Thank you."

Oh, just that little touch made her tingle all over. The sensation was still with her when he dropped to one knee and lifted the floorboards. He stood a moment later with the familiar little book in hand and sat on the edge of the bed. After a brief hesitation, he handed it to her. As before, its energy hummed in her hands. Not bizarre, she supposed, since it was capable of cursing people for an eternity.

Given its age, it should look ancient. But the reddish leather was smooth, the gold leafing at the corners crisp. An odd symbol graced the front, along with a sturdy lock.

She picked at it with her fingernail. "Have you tried using anything to pry this open?"

Marrok sent her a mirthless laugh. "Brute strength, sledgehammer, paper clip, skeleton key, wire cutters, chain saw . . . every tool known to man. I once tied a pair of ropes to the lock, then secured each rope to horses bolting in opposite directions. It gave not an inch."

Interesting. A very powerful object. "What do you know about this symbol on the front?"

"Naught."

There was an odd, scripty symbol in the same delicate gold as the leafing. Like a giant M, but underlined with curlicues.

She didn't remember seeing it in school, but suspected it was meaningful.

"Does it mean aught to you?" Marrok's eyes were guarded but hopeful.

"No. Sorry."

He heaved a disappointed sigh that tore at her heart.

"But old books aren't my area of expertise. If I had a computer and a camera, I could ask people much more knowledgeable than I."

"Nonmagical people?" He sounded suspicious.

"Yes, scholars, curators, professors . . ."

He hesitated. "Pictures of the symbol only, not the book."

"*You* have a camera?"

"My mobile phone does."

"You have a *phone*?"

"My cooking is tragic. How else would I order takeaway?"

So the big, bad warrior could poke fun at himself. Olivia pressed her lips together to hold in a smile.

He handed her his cell phone. The cameras in these things didn't have the best resolution, but it would do.

Quickly, she took a picture, carefully avoiding the rest of the book, and e-mailed it to herself from his phone.

"Do you have a computer?"

With a sigh, he trudged to the back of the house and opened a small door. It housed a stacked washing machine and dryer. On a little table, wedged in the corner, sat a cardboard box with the lid flung open.

"This is it?"

Teeth gritted, he nodded.

From the look of the dusty box, it had been here for a few months. "It's not hooked up."

"Not for lack of trying," he groused.

Suddenly, the picture became clear. Mr. Big Bad Dark

Ages wasn't down with technology. Lord knows her mother had always hated computers, and she'd just been a baby boomer. Imagine the learning curve when adding hundreds of years between birth and booting up. Astonishing that he'd managed the microwave.

Olivia tried to hide a giggle behind her hand. But he saw.

"I skewered people for a living. This whole modem, RAM, operating system vocabulary is worse than Greek. *That* I understand."

For a man the size of a mammoth, he was kind of . . . cute when disgruntled. "What made you decide to buy a computer?"

His jaw couldn't look any harder if it had been set in concrete. "Online shopping. I do not like people or cities. Having things delivered to my doorstep appealed."

Hmm. Definitely not the life of the party.

"I can hook this up."

"Thank you."

After he carried it into the living room, she attacked the Styrofoam cradling the unit.

"Are you hungry? You have not eaten in days."

"Famished, actually."

"What can I get you?"

"You said your cooking was tragic."

"I have managed a few dishes over the centuries. Toast and omelets, macaroni and cheese, or a tin of soup?"

If it had taken him over a thousand years to master three easy meals, she didn't want to know how bad his cooking had been before. "Toast and omelet would be fine. Cheese, no onions. Mushrooms?"

Marrok nodded. "And tomatoes?"

She inserted the wireless Internet card into the laptop, booted up, and began to configure it. "Please. With coffee!"

Fifteen minutes later, she was surfing while devouring a

breakfast that wasn't half bad and coffee strong enough to kill
an ox. Trying not to choke, she accessed her e-mail. The picture of the symbol had arrived, along with a dozen other mes-
sages of virtually no importance. Skipping them, she drafted
a message to a half-dozen professors, historians, and museum
curators. She hoped one of them turned up something.

"Now, we wait."

Marrok didn't look any happier at that prospect. "Indeed."

"So what's it like, being alive for so long?"

She could hardly wrap her mind around it. She might act
calm, but inside, she was freaked out. He was *immortal*. One
of her favorite TV shows was about a gorgeous immortal,
but he was fanged.

"Wait! You're not a vampire, are you?" She covered her
throat with her hands.

"Indeed not! I spilled blood, not drank it."

"Whew! Good to know. So if you're immortal, that means
you've seen every major change to come civilization's way.
All the inventions . . ."

"Imagine my surprise to find out that the earth is, indeed,
round," he drawled.

Olivia laughed. "What do you think of TV?"

"Except for news, somewhat pointless."

Really? She loved it. "Cars?"

"Despise them."

Guess that meant he didn't drive. She hadn't really mastered driving on the left side of the road, so that made them
even. "Ever been on an airplane?"

"Bloody hell, God did not mean for us to fly!"

His answer gave her the giggles all over again. "Come on,
you must admit some things are better. Medicine? Running
water? Electricity?"

"As someone who lived through three centuries of the

plague, I can heartily say I wish medicine had advanced faster. Running water and electricity, I confess, are vast improvements."

"Strip clubs?" she challenged.

"Where women disrobe for strangers? Never bothered."

That made sense, she guessed. If he couldn't orgasm, why get all wound up?

Silence invaded the small room. Olivia fidgeted with the little computer, but Marrok's hyperaware stare distracted her. She could actually *feel* his desire for her. Did the connection force him to want her . . . or did he do that all on his own? Did he even know the difference?

Sighing, she opened a browser and Googled Morgan le Fay and any symbols associated with her. She'd found drawings of a long-haired woman wielding magical instruments, stuff about a Grail quest, but nothing about the symbol on the book. Olivia scanned the entries about the legendary woman— her vast power, her cruelty, her varying roles in the stories of Camelot, depending on who wrote them. And descriptions of a great beauty with white-blond hair and violet eyes.

"Marrok, all my life, I've been told my eyes are unusual. How often do you see violet eyes? Why would I have the eyes and birthmark of a woman born forever ago?"

He didn't say anything for long moments, just pinched the bridge of his nose. "It appears I did not give you enough credit for connecting the dots so quickly." He eased onto the table in front of her. "According to Bram's aunt, your eyes and that birthmark are throwback genes. You are Morganna's descendant. Distantly, of course."

"Seriously? I don't see how I could be related to anyone with magic in their veins, even a millennium-plus removed. My mother was as American as apple pie and refused anything even the slightest bit 'woo-woo'. I wasn't allowed vampire books or a Ouija board at sleepovers. I couldn't see movies based on myth or legend."

"What of your father's side of the family?"

That sent her thoughts spinning. "I don't know . . . My father is British. Until my mother's death, I never knew the man was alive. He lives in London, or he did twenty years ago. The detective I hired hit a dead end, but he sent an address for a man who claimed to be five hundred years old. I assumed it was a joke and had a laugh. But is it possible . . . ?"

"That he is a wizard with the accorded magical life span."

"How long is that?"

Marrok shrugged. "About a thousand years, I think. I cannot say for certain. I strived to avoid everything and everyone magical after Morganna."

No big shock there. If she'd been cursed so cruelly, she'd avoid magickind, too. But wait . . .

"If I'm related to Morganna, even distantly, does that mean I'm . . . magical?"

"According to Bram's aunt, you are, and your powers will be considerable."

His answer stunned Olivia. Wow . . . If her life had truly become much longer, that put a new, mind-boggling spin on thinking about her future.

"What you're saying . . . me, magical *and* powerful? Maybe she's mistaken."

"That is unlikely. They know their own kind. You come from a strong bloodline."

"That makes a difference?"

"As I understand magickind, it does."

That made sense, as surreal as it was. A descendant of *the* Morganna le Fay. If she had even a tenth of the woman's power, maybe there was another way she could help Marrok . . .

Olivia sprang to her feet and backtracked down the hall.

The book sat on the bed, looking innocuous. She steeled herself against flinching when she picked up the book and it vibrated in her hands as she strode back to Marrok. He watched curiously as she sat with the diary in her lap and grabbed opposite edges of the book. And pulled.

Nothing.

"What if . . . ?" Her idea sounded silly, but how much stupider would she feel if this was the answer and she never tried it? Olivia pointed her fingers at the book. "Open."

Apparently not.

"Stupid, huh? I just thought . . . if I'm really powerful, that maybe . . . But if I was, wouldn't I have done *something* amazing by now? I mean, I've occasionally had a dream that came true or a wish that happened moments later. But hasn't everyone?"

"You are not yet five and twenty, correct?"

"Not for about eighteen months."

"That is when you will . . . change, and come into the powers Fate has destined for you."

"Oh." The fantastic assertions just kept on coming, one more staggering than the next. Where was Ashton Kutcher? She'd lost her virginity to an immortal man and she might be a powerful witch? Forget *Punk'd*; this was *The Twilight Zone.*

"What kind of powers?"

Marrok shrugged. "I know not."

A small beep let her know a new e-mail had arrived for her. It was followed closely by two more. The first one, from a former art teacher, wished her luck but knew nothing. *Damn.*

The second message was from one of her history professors. Dr. Chastain had always been bookish and new-agey and hopelessly lost in "what if." But she loved solving academic mysteries. Today was no exception, Olivia discovered as she opened the e-mail.

"Well?" Marrok prompted.

"One of my history professors. The symbol means nothing to her, but I also asked her about Morganna and instruments of her magic. One of her secret passions is Arthurian lore and that, in some circles, there's talk about Morgan le Fay having created a book that allows the one who controls it to have nearly unlimited power. Do you think she means this book?"

Marrok blew out a deep breath. "Aye, and we cannot let her—or anyone else—know I have the Book of Doomsday. The danger we will be in if anyone discovers that is great, indeed."

"Sure." A magical book? It sounded impossible. Then again, she'd thought the same thing about Marrok's immortality, and that had bitten her in the ass.

Olivia scanned the professor's e-mail again. "She says something about it being an object of feminine reverence."

"Which means what?"

She shrugged. "The book must have enormous power. It hums every time I touch it. Something that awesome must be revered by someone, right?"

"At least by one person I know," he answered darkly. "And likely a lot more."

"It was created by a woman . . . Maybe that's what she means. I'll ask her to elaborate."

Olivia quickly crafted her follow-up question and dashed off the e-mail. Then she opened the final piece of correspondence, from Dr. Reynolds. A pompous ass with a sweating head who always insisted on being the smartest person in the room. But he definitely knew art history.

Scanning the e-mail, she gasped. "Dr. Reynolds has seen the symbol! According to him, it appears on writing believed to be by Morganna. The symbol also appeared in two paintings. The first in the fourteenth century of a young unnamed girl. She's wearing it around her neck. He sent me a scan." Olivia showed Marrok the open attachment.

The symbol dangling from her fragile neck matched the one on the book.

"For all we know, the girl saw the symbol and fancied it."

"Maybe." But she sounded unconvinced. "It's really unusual. You know, among the things my mother left was something similar. Different shape, but like it might have been made during the same time or by the same craftsman. Even in this painting, the pendant looks old, but fast forward four hundred years . . ." She opened the next attachment.

And gasped all over again. A man in Regency dress wore the symbol affixed to his lapel. Even more shocking, he had familiar violet eyes.

The caption stunned her. Richard Gray of London.

"That's my father's name! His face! Could he be . . . ?"

Marrok glanced at the man in the painting, then at her again. "I know someone who will give me an answer."

CHAPTER EIGHT

MARROK GRABBED HIS MOBILE phone off the table and flipped it open, glad Bram had left his number when he'd departed with his aunt. By God's blood, he had spoken to the wily wizard more in the last week than in the past century.

With gritted teeth, he punched in the wizard's number. Using the rock had been effective, but too magical for his tastes. He glanced at Olivia. She was magical and perhaps the means to end his curse. But against Olivia's potent lure and the bond between them, he was weak. That troubled him. Magickind was tricky. For all he knew, she might use his feelings against him, no matter how sweet she looked or felt in his arms.

Despite that, the thought of losing her terrified him. He liked being near her. Her bright smile hit him in the gut like a welcome burst of light after centuries of darkness.

And now he was a bloody poet.

When she had extended her offer of assistance in researching the symbols on the diary, he'd been stunned and warmed. But the fact she was a le Fay and suddenly being helpful . . . two plus two did not equal five. He would do well to remember that.

Bram finally answered in a groggy voice. "Marrok? It's the middle of the night. Is something wrong with Olivia? Are you calling to break your mate bond?"

The bloody cur. "Nay."

"Is she still alive?"

"Aye."

Alive and well and looking very fetching, in fact. Marrok could almost forget that he had found cataclysmic release a mere hour past, that she was new to sex, and that he should be avoiding further entanglement with her. Desire scalded his veins. His skin felt too tight as he peeked at the shadow of her cleavage and visually devoured her. She had the softest skin, and made the most enticing little moans when she—

"She's alive, really? You were finally able to—"

"None of your bloody business."

"You know, if you want a favor from me, you could be a tad more polite."

Marrok gritted his teeth again. At this rate, he'd be chewing with nubs.

"I do not seek your assistance; I ask it for Olivia. She is one of *your* kind. Help her."

"We're magical, not Martians. The way you talk about us, it's as if you think there's little difference."

Marrok didn't bother to answer that. "We've located a nineteenth-century painting of a man named Richard Gray. Know you if the rendering is of Olivia's father?"

"Is the man in the painting violet-eyed and wearing Regency dress with a lapel pin that matches the symbol on the front of the Book of Doomsday?"

Tricky bastard. "That sounds accurate, except I have not the faintest clue about the symbol, since I have not seen the book in question."

"Right." Sarcasm colored Bram's voice. "I don't know if he's Olivia's father. I spoke with Richard Gray just once. He rang me, inquiring about the Doomsday Diary, in fact. At the time, I knew nothing and I told him so. Since I know him only from that brief phone conversation and what I've read about the man, I don't know how to find him. But I'll bet he's her father and that he knows something about that symbol."

Marrok silently agreed.

"I've searched for Gray, but . . . he's not going to pop over for a visit," Bram said.

"Why not?"

He lowered his voice. "I haven't told Olivia this; she would only run into danger if I did. Richard Gray is hunted by the Anarki. He was once one of them and turned traitor. In fact, he was Mathias's second in command."

Damn! Marrok wasn't surprised in the least; Richard Gray was a le Fay.

Aware of Olivia's rapt gaze on him, Marrok turned his back to her, mind racing. There would be time to hear more about Gray later. Best to get the facts, then plan a strategy to keep Olivia from rushing into a search that could endanger her. Besides, he had already shocked her enough for one day.

"Should you hear more, advise me," Marrok requested. "Also, Olivia needs someone to run her shop while she recovers."

"I could ask my sister. Sabelle would be perfect. She's very knowledgeable about art. Tomorrow soon enough?"

A witch? Somebody was better than nobody. "Aye."

"There's a catch . . ."

"Naturally."

"I've been planning a gathering. Since Mathias is back, magickind must band together. Olivia should attend to meet, as you put it, her own kind."

"A party?"

"Of sorts."

Marrok's gut clenched at his mental picture of Olivia in a skimpy cocktail dress, leaning on Bram's every word as he introduced her to the magical world. "Nay."

"The poor girl has to put up with a dour mate. She knows little about her roots or magic, much less her coming transition. She'll need information. The fact she's a descendant of one of the most ancient and powerful bloodlines in history will make her an instant celebrity."

"Smashing for you, but she needs no strangers gawking at her. We send our regrets."

"Are you certain? I've been reading more of my grandfather's dusty tomes. How fortuitous that I've come across several passages about what the symbol means to the diary. I think you'll be *very* interested, and I would be willing to share the information if you and Olivia pop by on Friday, say about seven?"

"That is extortion."

"Yes." He sounded pleased. "I'm sure you both need appropriate clothes. I'll drive over in a bit and leave a car for you."

Click.

Squeezing the mobile phone, Marrok actually hoped the damn device would shatter.

But what if Bram truly had information about the symbols and what they meant? Something that could end his curse? Eternity, even if he did have a beautiful mate capable of giving him ecstasy, was not something Marrok wanted to endure.

"Bram has invited us to a party day after next." He sighed, swallowing a lump of fury that nearly choked him. "We will be attending."

Olivia looked puzzled, but shrugged. "Fine."

"Grant me a favor." He cut a hungry glance in her direction. "Do not wear anything skimpy and black."

Bram's car arrived shortly after the sun rose that morning. After quick showers, they approached the flashy black sedan. Earlier, they had loaded the boot with as many of Marrok's carvings as would fit. Now that he had to get into the car . . . He stared at it, trying to hide a shudder.

"Can you drive that contraption?"

"Me?" She pointed at herself. "Not well. You people drive on the wrong side of the road."

"Since I do not drive at all, you must take your argument up with the other louts who maneuver these infernal machines."

"You're going to make me drive?"

"Do you have a license?"

"Well . . . yes."

"That settles our disagreement, for I do not."

"You can skewer a thousand people in battle, but not steer one little car?"

"Aye."

"Have you ever learned to drive?"

He shook his head. "Would you care to take your life in your hands and have me start now?"

"Oh, hell no. Where are the keys?"

"Mayhap we should not go into the city today. You are barely recovered—"

"I'm a little tired," she admitted. "But I'll be fine. I want to see my gallery, put out your carvings. Pleeeaaaase?"

With a sigh, Marrok pointed to the keys in the ignition, then stalked to the passenger's side, dragging his feet like a man heading to the noose. Damn, he missed horses.

Inside the vehicle, Olivia gripped the wheel and started the car, backing out smoothly down the long dirt path to his cottage. With a competent, quick turn, she found the wider path to the main road. In moments, they were headed on the M23 highway to London.

He was impressed. "You drive much better than Bram."

"I'll bet he's reckless."

"As if human life has little value."

Olivia shook her head. "Terrified of cars, but willing to practically slice off your arm. That's pretty whacked."

"I am not terrified. Warriors are never terrified."

"Yeah?" She laughed. "The white knuckles on the dashboard are a dead giveaway."

He glared at her—his best warrior stare. She grinned.

"Let's go to the gallery first, I think. I want to set these carvings out before opening." She paused. "You know, Sabelle doesn't need to come watch the shop. I'm fine now. I can work—"

"That was not our bargain. I want you healthy and protected. Do you want the carvings?"

"Yes," she huffed. "Tyrant."

"Indeed. You will tire quickly, so you will take proper care."

"Meaning the frequent sex you talked about?"

"If that is what you require, I will care for you."

"Funny." Olivia groaned. "Has anyone ever told you you're bossy?"

"Arthur's entire army, including Arthur himself."

She turned to him with a rapt expression that he felt all the way to his cock. Would she never cease to fascinate him?

"What was he like?"

"Arthur? Noble. Genuinely good. Crushed by Guinevere's betrayal. Camelot's end was a tragedy, brought on largely by Morganna."

"You really hate her?"

"With everything inside me."

She frowned. "But without her curse, you'd be long buried and gone. Isn't there some part of you that's happy to still be alive? You've lived history, not just read about it."

The only reason he had to be glad for life now was her, Morganna's descendant.

Dear God, had he sunk that far already? He must take care. It was possible that Olivia could practice the kind of deceit Morganna and her father had. But then, why did she not simply steal the book? Why try to help him find the origin of the symbol?

"For centuries, I have sought nothing more than to break my curse and die. I believe you and that book are the keys to doing so."

Olivia gnawed on her bottom lip. It was clear she wanted to say something, but she apparently rejected it for something neutral.

"If that's what you really want, I'll help you."

Once, he had sought little else. Now, he wondered what would become of Olivia if he died?

He glanced at her, the soft drape of dark hair over delicate shoulders, the flashing violet eyes. She looked tired, a bit pale, but her cheeks glowed with pink life. By Bram's admission, the breaking of the bond Marrok shared with her would be temporarily painful, and she would carry a wound of grief. But their mating was new, the bond still tentative. She would survive. Even if the very thought made him seethe with a mad rage, she could mate again.

But who would protect her from Mathias?

They waded through London's traffic and arrived at A Touch of Magic, carrying in the carvings that represented nearly two centuries of his work. He'd carved them as a talisman against solitude. As she set them on the shelves, he found himself pleased that she wished to share them with others. Perhaps they would bring joy the way Olivia had brought it to him.

Smitten fool. Allowing himself such sentiment only opened himself for heartache later.

Olivia set his carvings all over the shop, making prime places for them, adjusting the lighting. She honestly believed in his work. What had started as a way to pass time had become meaningful, and her obvious care for his pieces touched him.

"Thank you," he said quietly.

She turned. "Thank *you*. These carvings will save my business."

He hoped for her sake that was so. Her faith humbled him.

Before he succumbed to the urge to make love to her on the floor in front of the big picture windows, he hurried her out the door and back to the hated car.

When they arrived at her flat, Marrok exited the vehicle, rolling his shoulders in his tight shirt, flexed and fisted his hands. He would rather crawl out of his skin than ride in it again. Olivia watched him fidget with a raised brow and a smile.

Once inside, Marrok looked around the small, older unit. Her space told him a great deal about her. Even in this limited area, she had added color to every wall and window. Each room displayed her bold, modern flair, so unlike his spartan cottage.

Eventually, he followed her to her bedroom, a modern fairy tale of pinks and creams, with splashes of chocolate and an absence of lace, which he mentally applauded. There was something fresh, feminine, and mysterious about the room. Something very like her.

"You know, I could just . . . stay here. You don't have to babysit me. I don't want to be in your way. I'm feeling much better, and no one else has mistaken me for Morganna, so it's all good. I'll drive you back to your cottage whenever you want and meet you at Bram's party—"

"Stop."

She was mad if she thought he was parting ways with her now. Lord knew he needed her. She needed him, sexually if nothing else. How to tell her about their mating? He could not until he knew she was well enough to handle the news. She would likely rebel against it—and him—making both ending his curse and keeping her out of danger more difficult.

"Until my demise, I want you safe and with me, beside me at night. Under me, taking me deep. Pack whatever items you need and bring them to the cottage, love."

Olivia flushed but looked like she thought she should refuse. Regret crossed her face. He softly covered her mouth with his own. "Please."

"I don't want to be a burden."

"Never. I want you with me." He smiled. "Who else will help me with my computer?"

A reluctant smile creased her face. "You make it hard to say no."

"Then do not."

The giddy joy on her face made him smile. She wanted to be with him. For now, that would do.

"I know you want me to rest, and I will. But while we're in the city, I want to do one more thing."

"Dare I ask?" he teased.

"I want to check out this last address the detective gave me for my father. I didn't look before because he's supposedly five hundred years old and I didn't think . . . But maybe we'll find him and he'll know something about the symbol. Maybe he could help end your curse."

If Richard Gray had once been Anarki, Marrok didn't want Olivia looking for the man by herself. He didn't want her looking for him at all. Too dangerous. But he had no good excuse to say no.

"Come with me?"

"Aye."

The smile that broke out across her face blinded him with its beauty. She rushed to a little desk in the corner of her room. Pulling the drawer open, she took out a folder. "Here's the detective's report with the address." With her back to him, she stuffed some clothes and personal items into a bag. "Ready?"

After a twenty-minute drive, they stopped in front of a run-down building in an east London industrial neighborhood. Gray soot and caked mud tinged the once pale walls. Black licks of charred brick were exposed around each window. Though Marrok was relieved to find no trace of Richard Gray, Olivia's crestfallen face tugged at him.

"It caught fire. No one lives here now."

Marrok nodded, easing his arm around her. Truly, no one lived here now. It looked to be barely standing. In fact, the whole block looked deserted. But was the blaze accident or arson?

"Does your detective have other information?"

"No. I'll keep trying myself. I wish I knew more about the fire and if anyone . . . survived."

If her father had been Anarki and turned traitor, he'd likely been burned out by the "friends" he had stabbed in the back. Marrok had no idea if her double-dealing sire had been inside, but he hoped so. Olivia had grown to a beautiful woman without him and had no need of a varlet who failed to honor his promises.

"Bram is looking as well. Mayhap he will find the man."

She nodded. "I hope."

He caressed her shoulder in a gesture of comfort. "Shall we return to the cottage, then? I want you back in bed."

"Do you?" she asked saucily.

Indeed. Need was beginning to make his cock ache. Even simply comforting her was giving his body wicked ideas.

"Aye. Consider your health, temptress. Mere hours ago, you were very unwell."

"Me, a temptress? Right . . ." She rolled her eyes.

"*You.* But now, you should rest."

She flushed. "Yeah, that was some weird flu or whatever."

"It could relapse if you do not take care."

"You take the fun out of everything. You may not look it, but under that stud-muffin exterior, you act like an old man."

Stud muffin? He smiled. "I am an old man."

"I know rest is important, but we should have, like, a date. We've, um . . . shared the sheets, but don't really know each other."

Fate and magic had already decided that mattered not. "I thought we got on well enough."

"In bed," she whispered. "I don't know that much about you. Brothers? Sisters?"

"A younger sister. Analise was always happy. I still miss her smile." Marrok hadn't talked about her in forever, and it felt good.

Olivia soothed him with a caress to his shoulder. "I always wanted a sister. You know stuff about my parents. What about yours?"

"My father was a warrior for his chieftain and died in battle my twelfth summer. He was rarely home, so I knew him not. My mother was sweet and even-tempered, but superstitious. She told me to avoid Morganna. Would that I had listened."

"We'll find answers and get you the closure you want." Olivia paused, bit her lip. "So fifteen hundred years is a long time. You must have married a few times."

"Never. When I was mortal, I was too busy making war."

"And making love to whomever you wanted."

"That, too," he admitted wryly.

"But in later centuries, you were never tempted to marry? Take a girlfriend?"

"Nay."

She looked shocked. "Certainly you had a relationship with *someone* . . ."

"I could give no one my body and chose not to give anyone my heart. Why bother?"

Olivia crossed her arms over her chest. Marrok knew she disliked his answer. "Then why bother with me?"

How could he put this into words? "You are different."

She raised a brow. "Because you can orgasm with me?"

"That is a plus, but not the sum of my reasoning." For

the first time in centuries, he cared about something, someone. And it scared the hell out of him.

"Or is it because I can supposedly end your curse?"

That had been her initial appeal, but now . . . she meant more. Did he dare tell her these new feelings he could scarcely understand? "I only know that we are connected."

"But it's bizarre to feel connected to someone I don't really know. I can't wrap my head around it."

Olivia would not be placated on this. He sighed. "How do you propose we become better acquainted?"

"I don't know. Most people date and talk and *then* decide if they're interested in more. Everything's happened backward for us."

"Indeed. So let us date. What shall we do?"

"It's a beautiful day. We could explore the city together. When was the last time you really saw London?"

Marrok paused. Before the Great Fire of 1666, for sure. Flames and Sir Christopher Wren had completely changed the cityscape. "A few years."

She shot him a leveling glare. "Which means centuries."

How did she know him so well already?

"Aye, London has changed. I hardly need to explore it to know it is polluted with more noise and people than ever."

She rolled her eyes. "There are so many wonderful landmarks. The Tower . . ."

"There I have been, and not under pleasant circumstances. You will forgive me if I wish to forgo that tour."

Olivia knew the Tower's reputation and laughed. "St. Paul's Cathedral?"

He shook his head. "I was never one for religion. I preferred war."

"The Victoria and Albert Museum?"

"You will be on your feet too much, it will take too long, and we will see little of the city."

She sent him a mulish stare. "The Tube."

He shuddered. "Never. I dislike cars, but that . . . I would rather burn in hell."

"I've got it!" She snapped. "The London Eye."

"The what?"

An hour later, Olivia settled into one of the observation cars of the giant Ferris wheel and watched Marrok sitting stiffly beside her. Amazing to think that, in fifteen hundred years, he'd never given his heart to anyone. What did that say about him? He didn't seem to fear intimacy, but she was no expert. Was he gun-shy, after Morganna?

The attendant closed the door. The big warrior turned green.

"You're claustrophobic."

"I am not."

"That's why you're restraining the urge to claw out of here with your bare hands."

"Silence. I must focus on not vomiting."

"Look out the windows. There's so much open space and air."

"And one locked door trapping me."

Olivia sighed. She didn't want to upset Marrok, just make him see what he was missing by hiding out in the forest. "The view is gorgeous."

It was. Fall nipped at the last of the summer greenery, giving London an austere face. But some of those flowers remained. A warm wind blew. People laughed. Tourists snapped pictures. She loved being in the middle of it.

The observation wheel took them up, up, up. Slowly.

Olivia grabbed Marrok's hand and squeezed reassuringly. He grabbed on to her like a lifeline, his breathing shallow and fast.

"Look." She pointed out the window to distract him. "Westminster Bridge."

He nodded. And gripped her hand tighter.

London spread out before them like a giant maze. The River Thames just north, south London filling the other half of their view. From here, the scope of the city amazed her.

"Wow," she breathed.

Marrok finally gazed out at the city. "It has grown . . . beyond belief."

"There was nothing here when you fought for Arthur?"

"Nothing like this. I am in awe. Though I could not live amongst all these souls."

"You will never be a modern man."

"Not if I can help it."

Olivia laughed and let him clutch her hand. It was crazy. She'd barely met the man twenty-four hours ago and by his own account, he wasn't into relationships. But somehow in that short time, he'd . . . filled her up. The bond between them kept growing, strengthening. First like a sturdy rope, then like a heavy-duty chain, now a mammoth steel rod reinforced with seven feet of concrete. The sense of attachment astounded her, like she belonged with him. *To* him.

Did it work both ways? He seemed in no hurry to let her go. He was immortal, difficult, had an ax to grind with one of her ancestors—and still, he *seemed* to care. True, he needed her to help break his curse, but it felt as if they shared more. Was she deluding herself? She hoped the feelings were mutual, because she feared she was falling hard and fast.

CHAPTER NINE

THE NIGHT OF BRAM'S GATHERING arrived. Olivia had honored Marrok's request . . . sort of. Her dress wasn't skimpy and black; it was minuscule and siren red, left over from a gallery showing back in her college days. She'd grabbed the flashy garment from her flat when he wasn't looking, and now couldn't wait to see the look on his face when she removed her coat. Or discover every wicked thought on his mind once they were alone. That he wanted her so feverishly and often amazed her. Yeah, he'd done without for a long time, but when he touched her, it felt as if she mattered to him.

It was more than sex. He was gruff, not a big talker, but his protective glances and constant touches were like buckets of golden sunshine after years of her mother's indifference.

He had no idea of the immense gift he'd given her.

But a nagging question persisted: What would happen if they managed to break his curse, he no longer needed her, and this fling ended? He sought death. If he found it . . . Olivia knew she should be pulling back, protecting her heart. But he was so damned hard to resist.

She shoved the thought aside and flipped a glance over her shoulder. Tucking her hand inside his callused palm, Olivia led Marrok to Bram's door. He knocked reluctantly.

The man *so* didn't want to be here. So why had he come? Marrok wasn't a people person, and Bram appeared to be one of his least favorite. What was the purpose of this gathering anyway? Every time she'd asked, Marrok muttered something about information and silenced her questions with a kiss . . . or more.

Olivia flushed just thinking about the delicious way he'd reduced her to moans a mere hour ago. For a man deprived of sexual satisfaction for a millennium and a half, he was making up for lost time fast. She wasn't getting much sleep. And she wasn't complaining.

Marrok turned to her. When their stares met, his mouth lifted in a wicked smile. "Your face tells me the thoughts on your mind."

"Proper party etiquette, of course. Is there an Emily Post of the magical world?"

"Liar." He leaned closer and whispered, "If you are not very careful, I will enjoy making you suffer later tonight."

She shivered. That was a promise she knew he could keep.

"Ditto in double for you," Olivia shot back.

The door opened then into a sleek, contemporary room. Small clusters of people sat about or stood in various corners. The middle of the room was filled with people of all ages dancing to a contemporary but unfamiliar tune. The sounds of children playing upstairs echoed in the high-ceilinged room during the pauses in the music.

As soon as they stepped inside, about forty strangers stopped and turned to stare. When she stripped off her coat, Marrok's eyes bulged. He swore under his breath.

"You will pay for that dress," he whispered.

For once, she wasn't listening. Everyone, young and old, male and female, was staring.

Marrok glowered at the partygoers—big surprise—as he escorted her farther into the chocolate brown and taupe room, brightened by splashes of terra cotta and turquoise. He made his way directly to the bar, ignoring the partygoers' gapes and gasps.

"Why are they staring?" she whispered.

"They are thinking how scrumptious you look in that

dress." He ripped his gaze away from the low neckline and scanned the room.

Not likely. They looked shocked. "Let's get lost in the crowd and dance."

His gaze zipped back to her. "What?"

"Dance. You must know how."

"As well as I cook."

"In fifteen hundred years, you never learned to dance?" Olivia wondered what else he'd skipped.

"Bawdy victory dances with an ale in one hand and a wench's backside in the other, aye."

Olivia glanced around the room. "Everyone is still staring. Please. I'll teach you."

"Is the goal for them to stare at me instead?"

"If we're in the middle of a crowd, I won't feel like an insect on a corkboard."

He frowned, clearly confused. She supposed he'd never taken tenth-grade biology.

"Come." He held out his hand and led her to the center of the room.

People gave them a wide berth as they found their place in the middle of the crowded floor. A sensual ballad drifted through the speakers. Just what she needed to take her mind off being the local freak show.

Olivia stopped Marrok and put her arms around his neck. He looked around, watching other men gather their women against them and did the same. Against him, she melted. And felt safe. He brushed his hand down her spine, to the small of her back. She filtered her hands through the silky strands of his dark hair that hung to his shoulders. That woodsy male scent went to her libido in seconds. She wished the crowd would go away and leave them alone. But she had one problem . . .

"You're not moving."

"I told you, I know not how to dance."

"When you fight, you have to move your body, for goodness' sake. It's the same sort of thing."

"Not exactly." Marrok glanced around again, then shuffled back and forth from one foot to the next. "Like this?"

She tried not to, but it couldn't be helped. Olivia burst out laughing.

"Few of these men dance differently."

It was true, but that's not what tickled her. "I guess it doesn't matter the century. Your average man doesn't like to dance."

"I am a warrior, not a fop on a stage."

Olivia soothed his ruffled feathers with a kiss on his neck, his jaw . . . oh, his tempting lips. Again. Once more, just in case he was still angry. She sighed when he took charge and captured her mouth. The man's touch truly was heaven.

The song ended, and they returned to the bar. People still stared, but now she was far more attuned to Marrok than a bunch of strangers she might never see again.

"An ale, please," Marrok said to the bartender. "I need one to pass this evening. Especially if there will be more dancing." He muttered the last so that only she could hear him.

"We all need a pint after hearing about the Anarki's attack on the MacKinnetts, mate." The bartender, an Irishman with curly auburn hair, set the beer in front of Marrok with a heavy sigh. "And now to hear that Craddock's youngest girl is missing, and the Anarki symbol burned into her bed . . . Poor thing. If she comes back at all, she'll wish she weren't alive."

Olivia gasped. "The Anarki? What is that? And what's being done to find this poor girl?"

The bartender suddenly zeroed in on her as if she were an idiot.

Marrok shot the man a warning growl. "Ask the lady if she would like a drink."

She should chastise him for being rude to the man, but the bartender had been rude first. And Marrok's chivalry was endearing.

"Forget it. I'm fine."

"The questions you ask about the Anarki and the girl, they are for magickind, love," Marrok soothed. "They do not want humans involved."

"True," Bram said as he snuck up on them. "But in this case, neither of you are exactly human, are you?"

Marrok turned, pulling at his white collar and tie. Bram, with his artfully-mussed hair, looked like he'd just stepped from a salon.

"We have arrived. Now keep your part of the bargain and tell me what you know of the diary and that bloody symbol."

"Soon." Bram grabbed a glass of champagne from a passing tray and handed it to Olivia with a smile. Then he took hold of her other hand and brought it to his lips. "You look incredible. Red is your color."

"If you wish to keep that hand, release her," Marrok's voice rumbled in warning.

Bram let go, wearing a sly grin. "Feeling possessive of a new mate is to be expected, especially one so lovely."

Mate? Did he mean in the British "we're friends" sense? Given her very intimate relationship with Marrok, she wondered. He couldn't mean in the wife sense, right?

"Thanks. If I look so lovely, why is everyone staring? They have been since we arrived."

"Besides the fact you're gorgeous, you're a le Fay, an incredible bloodline most believed to be long dead. Right now, they are wondering how powerful you'll be once you transition, and exactly where I found you."

Bram directed his blue stare back to her. Cunning swirled in his eyes. *Whoa!* She'd better not make the mistake of underestimating him, as she'd clearly been doing since she'd met him. Suddenly, she understood that he'd cultivated a friendship with her for reasons she could only guess at.

"She is not a conversation piece." Marrok sounded pissed.

"Not intentionally, but—"

"Transition?" she questioned. "Marrok says I'm going to be magical. Is that true?"

"Very much so, I believe."

"That's . . . incredible. What will I be able to do?"

Bram blew out a breath. "I can't say exactly. Magic depends on the individual. Everyone magical is born with a basic set of powers to perform small tasks. Increased ability usually starts to develop shortly before transition. The big stuff comes afterward."

"Basic powers? Like what?"

"The ability to bewitch and conjure small items, teleporting from one place to another—day-to-day stuff. After transition, your powers truly develop. Those vary widely, based on a few factors. The power you're born with is critical. And that comes from your bloodline. But performing magic also depends on your intent and passion. Even if you're an exceptionally gifted witch, you can think you might want to do something difficult, but unless you truly mean that and want it with everything in your body, it won't happen. The more difficult the spell, the more you must truly desire the outcome."

In a weird way, that was like real life. People who succeeded at anything persisted because it meant everything to them. Magic sounded similar. "You said the 'big stuff' comes later. What does that mean? Doesn't everyone have the same power?"

"No. Think of it this way: when you were in school, some kids were good at math, others good in sports, and yet others excelled at, say . . . dancing. Some kids might have been good at more than one skill, even, right?"

"Sure. Dancing and sports, I'm there. Math . . . not so much."

Bram laughed. "Magic is the same way. Some people have magic of the heart, like my aunt Millie. My sister, Sabelle, is good at many things. Manipulating people comes to mind," he groused good-naturedly. "She has good magical battle skills for a female. She's a walking Internet of magical knowledge. But she also possesses domestic magic. Food is always perfect. The house is always spotless. She can make anything, repair anything. Very handy."

"Marrok says I will transition at twenty-five. So I have to wait until then to know what kind of magic I have?"

"I'm afraid so. But after that you will learn the special magic you were born to wield."

"What's yours?"

He cleared his throat. "That's actually not a polite question in magical circles. Your special magic can often be your last line of defense if you're attacked. People confide only in those close, never someone they don't trust and never before the other has proven themselves. Asking someone about their particular magic is a bit like asking how much money one makes in the nonmagical world."

Magickind was a new and different place. She'd have to adapt.

"What *will* transition be like?"

"Arduous, overwhelming, possibly dangerous. You'll spend a hellish few days absorbing your full powers."

Olivia still had a tough time believing it all. Where was the laugh track? Certainly, it would sound at any moment . . .

Her thoughts must have shown on her face because Bram added, "Don't worry. Marrok will be with you."

Why would he think that? She and Marrok were having a . . . Well, it was more than a fling on her part. But that didn't mean those feelings were a two-way street. She was with a man who hadn't had a relationship *ever*. And the man wanted to die, for heaven's sake. He wasn't a good risk. And once he'd gone, she would hurt like hell.

As Bram escorted her across the room with Marrok in tow, they passed small groups of people, presumably all magical, who stared.

Bram paused when they reached a laughing couple. Scratch that. A *gorgeous* laughing couple. The man was striking, with the bronzed skin of an outdoorsman, sleek dark hair that brushed the tips of his shoulders, and blue, blue eyes. She was petite with a head full of golden curls that brushed baby-smooth cheeks and a centerfold's breasts. They held hands like teenagers, looking totally smitten with each other.

A bolt of envy pierced Olivia.

Next to them stood a goddess. There was no other way to describe her. The only thing average about her was her height. After that . . . the woman was all sumptuous and golden. Her shining hair fell in soft waves to her waist. Her blue eyes danced with humor and intelligence. Good genes had also blessed her with dimples, grace that would make ballerinas cry, and a damn near perfect body. Even her sparkling sheath dress was *Cosmo*-ready. Was it any wonder that virtually every man in the room was giving her the visual twice-over?

Next to her, Olivia felt like the old hag from *Snow White*, nose wart and all.

"Olivia, Marrok, these are my good friends Lucan MacTavish and his . . . wife, Anka." Bram gestured to the couple.

Lucan smiled and extended his hand. Marrok shook it as Anka greeted her.

"Do I need to brew you a remembrance potion, dear brother?" the goddess chimed in.

Bram laughed. "As if *anyone* could forget you. This is my sister, Sabelle."

"Oh! You've been manning my shop. I can't thank you enough. How has business been?"

Olivia missed A Touch of Magic, but with Sabelle watching the place for the past two days, she had no worries. After a phone conversation, Olivia knew the witch was more than qualified. Amazing how expansive nearly a hundred years' knowledge could be. If she had half of Bram's charm, there would be hordes of customers clamoring at the gallery's door.

"A small, fledgling gallery? Not anymore. Word of Marrok's carvings has spread like mad. People adore them."

Marrok shrugged his massive shoulders as if the compliment didn't matter. But Olivia caught a little flash of pride on his face and grabbed his hand.

"He's incredibly talented," she added.

"He is! Just today, I sold over thirty pieces," Sabelle added.

"Thirty?" She grabbed Marrok's sleeve. "I told you! I knew they would sell." She turned back to Sabelle. "I'm planning to come back in a day or two."

"A week or two," Marrok cut in.

Olivia elbowed him.

Tinkling laughter spilled from Sabelle. Gosh, even her laughter shimmered. "I've had a great time running the gallery. I love art and people. It's been so refreshing. Everything is fine at the shop. Really. Take as much time as you need."

"I'm not imposing?"

"Please. You're saving me from spending all day under his thumb." She pointed at Bram. "I should be paying you!"

"Very funny, little sister."

After quick nods and good-byes, Bram led them deeper into the crowd. Two men, opposites in every way, stood in the corner arguing in low tones.

"If this is some sort of outcast outreach program, you can sod off," grated out a scruffy giant.

"I merely suggested that in these troubled times, per-haps—"

Bram cleared his throat. The conversation stopped and the two men turned identical heavy stares—on Olivia.

Goody. Isn't this awkward?

The man on her right was smooth, urbane. Every pore of his unblemished skin and every thread in his clothing shouted money. Old money. A lot of it. He was incredibly good-looking in the male model sort of way, with his dark hair styled in some carefully artless, £200 haircut that ac-cented his sophisticated charm. Not staring at the man was impossible.

"Your Grace, this is Miss Olivia Gray and Marrok of Cadbury." Bram's lips twitched as he spoke. "Olivia, Simon Northam, the Duke of Hurstgrove."

A real live duke? Holy hell! She hated being so American about these things. What was the proper greeting here?

"How do you do?" He nodded at her, shook Marrok's hand, then turned to Bram. "Dispense with the formalities. You know I dislike them."

He sounded even more British than the average Lon-doner.

"Just call me Duke," Northam told her. "To me, it's a joke, not a title."

Olivia didn't get the joke, but whatever.

"Amazing." He stared as if she were a priceless work of art. "A walking, breathing le Fay. I had no idea—"

She gasped. "How can you tell?"

Duke shot her a startled stare. "Your magical signature, of course."

Before she could ask what that was, the leather-clad man on his left tried to sneak away. Bram caught the guy by his tattooed arm.

He looked like a cross between a biker and a marine, built and big. A khaki vest strained against mammoth shoulders. His biceps were ringed with various tattooed designs. His inky-dark hair hung to his shoulders. She had no idea what color his eyes were behind his black shades.

"You don't want to be rude to our guests, Shock," Bram chided the man.

"Why the hell not?"

Bram sighed. "Is 'polite' in your vocabulary?"

"No, but 'fuck yourself' is."

Then he tried to bolt again. Bram held tight.

Olivia wished he wouldn't force Shock to stay. The biker/marine clearly didn't want to be here, and it was somewhat embarrassing to have Bram push her on the guy.

Suddenly, Shock snarled, "You're making her uncomfortable and she thinks you should shove off."

Bram raised a golden brow. "How would you know that?"

"Besides the fact she's no poker player? She's blaring her thoughts."

Seriously? Olivia dropped her gaze.

"I'm finished socializing," Shock snarled at Bram. "I came to bounce Anarki, not make friends."

After yanking his arm free, Shock stalked to the other side of the room and propped up the wall with his sizable back.

Even behind those sunglasses, his watchful stare could have burned a hole in her.

"Well, that went swimmingly." No one could possibly miss Duke's sarcasm.

"Indeed." Bram sighed. "Let's move on."

"It was nice to meet you," Olivia tossed back to Duke as Bram led her even deeper into the room.

"Enough." Marrok wrapped his arm around her to stop them and leaned toward Bram. "I came about the diary. Tell me what you know."

"First, there's someone else Olivia should meet. Come with me."

Bram took her hand and extracted her from Marrok's embrace, then placed it on the crook of his elbow, drawing her near. He looked down at her with a calculating glance. There was something in this for him.

She wasn't at all unhappy when Marrok took her by the shoulders and nudged her to the side, inserting himself between her and Bram.

"Do not touch Olivia again, or I will tear off every protruding part of your body."

Despite the bloodthirsty warning, Marrok's possessive tone warmed her. She should pull back. He'd had centuries to experience romance—and had chosen to avoid it. Comparatively, she'd had ten minutes and didn't know jack. But she adored his protectiveness. He made her feel special. How was she supposed to ignore that?

Bram smiled. "I had no intention of stealing her from you. I merely intended to steady her. She may need it."

Suddenly, Bram stopped before a door and turned back to her with a dramatic pause. "You've been looking for someone . . ."

He opened the door to reveal a stranger. Yet his eyes told

her he wasn't a stranger at all. She recognized his face; it matched the painting of the man in Regency dress.

"Richard Gray?" she asked softly.

Salt-and-pepper hair dusted his temples. He dressed sleek, retro European. Very *GQ*. Besides violet eyes, they shared very fair skin and black hair. In fact, looking at him was like looking at a masculine version of herself in thirty years.

"I guess it's too soon for Dad." He sent her a smile of regret.

Oh. My. God. "It really *is* you?"

At his nod, elation bubbled inside her. Finally, the father she'd been waiting a lifetime to meet was here. With her! She tried not to tear up, but when everything turned blurry, she realized she'd failed miserably. She desperately wanted to hug him, but what kind of reception would she receive? Her own mother had never touched her willingly. She'd always hoped her dad would, but who knew? His rejection now would crush her.

"I'm happy to meet you." She held out her hand.

Richard grabbed it and pulled her in for a tight hug. Joy warmed every corner of her heart. Her search was finally over. This was her father, and he was holding her for the first time ever.

"How did you find him?" Marrok asked Bram, frowning.

"A few months past, I put the word out that I sought Richard on Olivia's behalf, but heard nothing, until tonight. He dropped in an hour ago."

"You might have warned us," Marrok growled.

"No time," Bram whispered.

Olivia frowned at the side conversation and turned back to her father. "I've been searching for you. I even moved to London to find you."

His eyes were tight with regret as he caressed her shoulder. "I'm so glad. I loved you from a distance for years and wanted so badly to see you. But your mother . . ."

Having a magical father probably explained why her mom had been antiparanormal. "I saw a letter you wrote to her, asking about me."

"She received it?"

Olivia nodded. "But she didn't open it, just stashed it in the back of her dresser. I never knew until she died."

"Her death saddened me very much. I'm sorry."

It seemed odd that this man she'd never met had been intimately acquainted with her mother. She wondered how he'd found out about her mother's death. Maybe it was a magic thing.

"Thank you. We weren't very close, actually."

Richard frowned at Marrok hovering near, then settled his gaze on her again. "You must have exhibited magic early. Barbara would have disliked that."

Olivia shook her head. "We just didn't . . . click."

"But you have abilities. Under the Gray name, we're le Fays. This blood comes with amazing magic. I had early tendencies. Certainly you've had something manifest."

Occasional snippets of dreams that came to fruition, but she'd heard average Americans talk on TV about having the same experience. "Very little. Except Marrok and I had the same dream."

"Of each other?"

Hoping like hell that no one could see her flushing cheeks, she nodded.

"When?" he asked.

"A few days ago. The night before we met."

Richard frowned again. "Sometimes, females call to their

mates through dreams. If you dreamed of him, your heart magic guided you to him."

Olivia blinked. There was that word again: mates. And the way he talked about it definitely sounded like a husband/wife thing.

"What do you mean by mates?"

Bram coughed. Olivia glanced over her shoulder. Marrok glowered.

"Heart mates," her father said, as if that explained everything.

She whirled back. "You mean like, 'until death do us part' sort of mates?"

"Yes." Given his sour tone, her father wasn't happy to be confirming that.

Did that mean magic compelled Marrok to be with her, that he wasn't with her of his own free will? Without this magical bond, would he even want her?

Dear God, if mere news was ever going to make her sick, now was the time.

She whipped her gaze to Marrok. His stony countenance revealed nothing, but the very absence of surprise was a bomb to her. He'd known they were mated. And he hadn't told her.

Anger, distress, and uncertainty blended to make a potent emotional cocktail that juiced her bloodstream. She felt like bouncing off the walls . . . or hitting an immortal warrior.

But she'd confront Marrok later. Alone. It was damn hard to hold in her fury and humiliation. But now wasn't the time, and here wasn't the place. After this party, they would have their first fight as a "married" couple. That was something to look forward to.

For now, she turned to Bram. "Did you suspect when you introduced us?"

"That you would be mates? No. I only knew you were a le Fay and that you might have some means of helping Marrok end his curse."

Of course. The reason Marrok began this "romance" with her. "Why would you care about helping Marrok?"

Bram merely smiled. "He knows what I want."

"You really should not yet have a mate," her father chimed in.

Olivia frowned. It wasn't as if she'd taken out a bridal registry the moment she'd met Marrok. "Meaning?"

Richard must have sensed her growing anger, because his voice dropped to a soothing level. "Parents usually recommend their younglings refrain from forming a mate bond until after attaining their powers. It can be very dangerous otherwise."

Dangerous? She mentally riffled through the moments before she and Marrok had first joined. She'd felt so weak, and he'd been her beacon of strength. Something inside had compelled her to speak words to him. Unfamiliar words. Words that had swirled around in her head—a jumble of confusion amid her hazy, scattered world. Shortly after Marrok touched her, the words formed and . . . she'd been unable to *not* say them.

Apparently those words had been the magical equivalent of wedding vows.

"I had no way of knowing that mating before getting my powers was dangerous. Mom certainly never warned me when *not* to get hitched, and since this is our first meeting, it's a little inappropriate for fatherly advice on the mating front."

Richard hung his head. "I haven't been a father to you. I'm sorry."

His dejection made her feel like a major bitch. And still she had a question. "If you knew about me, where have you been for the last twenty-three years?"

"Your mother . . ." he sighed. "Left me."

Olivia frowned. "Did she refuse to let you see me?"

Richard cast an uneasy glance at Bram, as if looking for privacy. The younger wizard clearly wasn't budging from the room. Behind her, Olivia felt Marrok's solid presence.

"Yes," her father murmured. "You were conceived during dangerous times for me and— No, I must go back further. You know nothing of magical history, I presume?"

"Good guess."

"Four hundred years ago, an evil wizard named Mathias d'Arc gathered followers with the idea of crushing the current order in the magical world. He named his minions the Anarki."

"Why would he want anarchy?"

He shot another careful gaze at Bram. "Magickind is divided into the Privileged and the Deprived. After some unfortunate deaths about five hundred years ago, the Council enacted the Social Order, which outlawed magicfolk with certain magical traits or diseases from professions in which they could influence crowds or harm younglings. What really happened is that anyone of a bloodline that had ever produced a witch or wizard with any tendency to violence was affected. Soon, once prosperous families no longer had their jobs and fell into poverty. Richer ones simply paid the Council's minions to dismiss transgressions. Anger, divisiveness and finger pointing become the norm. Magickind has been divided since."

Magical segregation?

"Mathias came along a hundred years after the Social Order. His philosophy made him the Karl Marx of the magical world, and his Anarki like the Bolsheviks. He wanted to balance the power structure and make magickind equal."

"That isn't the same thing as creating chaos."

"To the Privileged, it is. He didn't care how many wizards, witches, or younglings he had to kill to achieve his supposed utopia," Bram snarled.

Richard jumped in again. "Not everyone understood that about him right away. The oppressed were tired of being poor, of getting no respect, often for reasons completely beyond their control. They had no family fortunes to recommend them and wanted more opportunity for their children. Many said it was heartbreaking to look at your infant and know he or she was doomed to hundreds of years of prejudice and squalor."

"Which is why I've always advocated change within the system," Bram pointed out. "I agree that originally the Council did it badly. But matters will improve."

Her father sneered. "Rubbish. The Council does nothing but bicker. They are made up of Privileged like you who cannot possibly understand what the Deprived endure."

"Reshaping the beliefs of people steeped in tradition isn't quick."

"We've been 'patient' for hundreds of years."

"Was impatience the reason you sided with Mathias? You like the bloody ravages of war?"

Olivia's father ignored Bram and turned his attention back to her. "Two hundred years ago, I saw Mathias for what he was and helped bring about his demise, but that came at a terrible price. The Anarki were minus a leader, a rallying symbol for their cause. They wanted revenge and they pursued me. So I fled England."

"You went to America?" Olivia surmised.

He nodded. "I met your mother and persuaded her to

return with me to England. We were happy for a time until the Anarki found me shortly after you were conceived. When we were attacked, I was forced to reveal my powers to your mother to defend us."

"She didn't know?" Olivia felt her eyes go round. "She would have been terrified."

"Utterly. That was the beginning of the end. I tried to explain and begged her to stay." He shook his head. "She refused to hear a word of my explanations and ran. I did not know she was pregnant when she left. I didn't learn about you for three years, and only then because I had another run-in with the Anarki, who told me they'd tried to kill my daughter."

"The Anarki wanted to kill me?"

"The product of my bloodline? Yes. Using my power to bring down their leader was an act of war."

Olivia paused, taking in the fantastical information. Less than a week ago, she'd been a normal, if broke, American living in London. Now, she was the mate of a cursed immortal seeking death and the descendant of one of the most commanding bloodlines in magical history. Oh, and she apparently had a target on her back. Life was sure looking up.

How much of this had Marrok known?

She turned a questioning glance to him, but he didn't seem too shocked.

"That explains why we moved so often when I was a child. Mom would suddenly decide to pack up whatever rental house we were living in, load everything into her tiny car, and drive as far as a few tanks of gas would take us. I always thought she was insane."

"She was cautious," Richard corrected. "And she had a duty to protect you."

Oh, yes. If her mother had done anything by her, it was her duty. Barbara had reminded her daily of the difficulties and sacrifices of having a daughter. Olivia bet the woman had blamed her for each and every relocation—obligations to keep her daughter safe. No wonder she'd refused to tell Olivia about Richard Gray, even with her dying breath. To the end, she'd been performing her protective responsibility.

Olivia teared up again. "She resented me for ruining her life, and now I know why."

Richard clasped a soft hand around her shoulder. "Barbara wasn't a cold woman. I'm sure she wanted to love you, but was afraid both for you and of you. After she saw what sort of magic I was capable of, she would have feared you'd inherit that—almost as much as she feared the Anarki."

As hot tears spilled down her cheeks, running her mascara, Olivia suspected Richard was right. Forgiveness washed through her at the same time that anger poured back in. Why hadn't her mother ever said that she loved her daughter, just once?

"So Mom never told you about me and refused to answer your letters because she didn't want me in any additional danger."

"I'm certain of it. I vowed to do everything in my power to keep you both safe. I would have promised her the moon if I believed it would help. I wanted my mate back."

Olivia gasped. "You were mated?"

"Children are much easier to conceive in the magical world if you are."

Oh. Did that mean that she and Marrok could soon be . . . magical parents?

Bram whispered in her ear. "In case you were wondering, you cannot conceive before transition."

His answer was welcome. Maybe now wasn't the best time for motherhood.

Marrok frowned. "How is it possible her parents were apart with no . . . ill effects?"

"The illness Olivia experienced in being separated from you was the result of being a mated but untransitioned witch. This is a critical time in her life, and she needs a lot of power. Sort of like starving a teenager going through a growth spurt. Your vitality will sustain her. Olivia's mother, on the other hand, was human and suffered no such trial in her father's absence except to be irritable and unable to . . . ah, be intimate with another man, but she was otherwise healthy."

Her recent flu-like trauma had been because she was mated but not yet a witch? Again, Marrok didn't look surprised. So she needed Marrok to support her somehow. Had he been serious when he said she needed frequent sex? What the hell else hadn't he totally explained?

Richard glanced at Marrok, then took Olivia's hand in his. "Mathias is back. Your mate looks strong, but he is still only human."

"Sort of. He's immortal," she clarified. "He was cursed by Morganna—"

"*You* are the one? You're Marrok of Cadbury?"

Richard knew his name? Did he know anything else about Marrok's troubles?

"Aye," Marrok answered warily.

Olivia regained her father's attention with her next question. "What do you know of his curse? What is the symbol . . . ah, in the painting you posed for during the Regency?"

Her father cut a questioning gaze to Marrok, as if seeing him in a whole new light. "You saw the painting?"

Olivia nodded. Her father knew something; she could tell.

"The symbol is only meaningful if you've seen Morganna's Book of Doomsday. You *have* seen it, have you not?"

A picture of Marrok holding it, showing it to her, popped into her mind. She opened her mouth to whisper of it to her father alone, but Bram touched her cheek and closed his eyes. When he opened them, triumph glinted in those blue depths.

Marrok grabbed her shoulders and pulled her back. "She knows nothing."

"Of course not." But Bram's smile gloated.

With a shove, Marrok put her behind him and advanced on Bram with aggressive steps. "Keep your bloody hands off her."

Richard cleared his throat. "It doesn't matter. Bram's abilities in this area may require touch, but anyone with a true telepathic ability now knows that you have the Book of Doomsday. I suspected it anyway. Although legend says that the man who paid to have the book stolen vanished from this earth for his sins, I see that is untrue."

Marrok shot him a stone-cold glare but said nothing.

"Your secret is safe with me, but others out there . . . I can sense at least a dozen with the ability to hear thoughts who just received Olivia's information loud and clear."

With a curse, Marrok snapped his gaze to Bram. "Fix it."

"Impossible. The damage is done."

Her father curled a gentle hand around her shoulder. "My sweet, you're going to have to learn not to broadcast your feelings quite so clearly. Many in this house know you're furious with Marrok, happy to meet me, and are trying to break your mate's curse with the Doomsday Diary."

Olivia felt a flush spread from her eyebrows to her toes as she stepped up beside Marrok.

"No need to be embarrassed," Bram assured. "You're young and untrained. You will learn—"

"Not at your hand." With a roll of his massive shoulders,

Marrok edged closer. "You promised if we arrived that you would tell us what you have learned from your grandfather's journals. We have kept our end of the bargain; now keep yours."

Bram seemed to weigh his options. Beside her, Olivia could feel the wall of Marrok's fury. He didn't like being manipulated, and Bram didn't care as long as he got what he wanted.

Finally, Bram said, "According to Merlin's writings, the symbol is actually a key that opens the diary. Two keys, in fact. Somehow, the symbol comes apart, yet fits together again to latch into the Book of Doomsday and unlock it."

"Where are these keys?"

Bram shrugged. "Morganna gave them to her son before she was banished by Merlin. No one knows what he did with them. They've been absent for a thousand years."

Richard piped in. "We can explore this later, but we have a more pressing matter now." He turned to Marrok. "You were Arthur's greatest warrior. Some believe you may be the greatest warrior of all time. But Bram is telling the truth. Olivia needs protection from Mathias. You are not magical. You can stop no one."

Marrok's eyes narrowed. "I protect what is mine. I may not be magical, but thanks to your ancestor, I am invincible."

"Your curse may prevent you from being killed, but it will not stop the Anarki from storming your home, immobilizing you, and taking the diary and Olivia away. *If* you ever see her again, she won't be the same woman."

Marrok flinched and clenched his fists.

"What Mathias can do to a woman . . ." Richard shuddered.

"I am aware."

"Then let her come with me. I know how the Anarki works. I can protect—"

"Nay. Olivia *needs* me. Without me, she falls very ill. Before I understood that, she nearly died. She will not endure such hell again."

"We'll arrange safe visits for you. But let me hide her."

"Nay."

"You are risking her life to spare your pride," her father argued. "If I hadn't learned how to hide from the Anarki, I would have been dead long ago."

"Without me, she *will* be dead. Safe visits may be too difficult or come too late." Marrok was resolute; he would not stand aside.

"Are you listening, you stubborn warrior?" Richard snarled, "She is my daughter, and—"

"She is my *mate*. You failed to acknowledge her for twenty-three years. Why should either of us believe you now care?" Marrok removed her father's hand from her shoulder.

Olivia frowned. "Marrok, surely we can work something out? I've waited my whole life to meet my father. If he knows how to hide from the Anarki, shouldn't we at least listen to him?"

Her warrior paused, turning deadly still. "You waited because he did not come for you. What kind of father is that? You should not put your safety in the hands of someone who could not be troubled to even meet you."

"He was in hiding, trying to avoid bringing danger to our doorstep."

"Excuses."

"And what are yours, huh? You withheld the little fact that we're essentially married."

Marrok grasped her shoulders in his huge but surprisingly gentle grip. "You were unwell, and I feared your body could not endure such shock after you awoke."

"Yesterday, maybe. Today, I'm fine. *You* just gave me excuses. Why should I believe them?"

"Because I am your mate and I will protect you with every ounce of my strength and every breath in my body. This, you know."

"Do I?" Marrok wasn't with her because he cared. He was with her because his curse and their mating made it mandatory. He'd never once said he had feelings for her. God, how careless she'd been.

"You should." Marrok bristled, then pointed at her father. "What do you know of him?"

They arrived back at the cottage, and the silence was grating, even for Marrok. Olivia had not uttered a single word since they'd left the party.

Bram's driver let them off in front of the cottage, saving them the long walk. Marrok had actually looked forward to carrying Olivia the mile-plus up the road to spare her little feet in those ridiculously sexy high heels. At least he would have been touching her. As it was now, she stormed up the steps of the darkened house.

Given everything he'd heard tonight, Marrok thought better of it. "Wait!"

She didn't even face him as she reached for the door. "What?"

He grabbed her hands before she could touch the knob. "We must be cautious. Let me make certain the house is safe before you enter."

She glared at him over her shoulder. "If you were so damn worried that someone could find your place, maybe you should have at least listened to my father instead of being confrontational and rude. He knows how to evade the Anarki. But no, you had to be a proud jackass and assume you're powerful enough to fight anything."

Marrok gritted his teeth as he nudged her aside, unlocked the door, and stepped into the cottage. He sensed nothing. Doubtful that Mathias's ruffians could pass his line of magic protection, but just in case . . . His gut told him they were alone, and instinct had saved his life more than once when he'd been mortal. Still, better to look with his eyes, as well.

Silently, he eased into the house and flipped on the lights, quickly checking the little cottage, every room, every wardrobe. Nothing.

He returned to the entry where Olivia still waited, looking more than a trifle irritated.

"Are you even listening to me?" she groused when he returned to her side.

"Aye, and I heard plenty about Richard Gray tonight. He knows not only how to evade the Anarki, but how to twist the truth as well. It seems convenient that he should take such an interest in you now, when you know where to find the Doomsday Diary."

Olivia slammed the door. "Bram just found him. Richard couldn't have known that I know something about the diary."

"He contacted Bram once before looking for information about the diary. Then, lo and behold, he and Bram are suddenly chatting again just as you mentally blare to all and sundry that I have the book. Make no mistake, if that word reaches Mathias and the Anarki, we'll be in for one bloody fight."

"It was an accident! What do you want, an apology in blood?"

"Of course not. I understand you knew not about project-ing your thoughts. But I will not release you to a stranger, even if he shares your blood. You know naught of his past, his allegiances, or his character."

"But he's *proven* that he can ditch these monsters."

"Is that how you wish to spend your life, running?"

She hesitated. "No, but I want to live to see another day."

"I want that for you. I want to give that to you." He took her hands in his big, slightly rough ones. "I want a mate who trusts that I can take care of her."

Olivia shook off his touch. "Yeah? Well, I want a man I can trust, too. One who might have bothered to tell me we were mated in the first place. It would have been dandy if you'd also let me make a decision about where I'm safest, since I'm an adult, not a blow-up doll. If I'd made a list of the most at-tractive traits in a man, deceiving and controlling wouldn't have made the cut, pal."

"When you were weak and recovering, I dared not stun you with the truth. I could hardly believe the strength of our bond myself."

"Ten minutes after I woke up from my trance or what-ever, I can understand. But what stopped you for the last forty-eight hours? Did the truth just slip your mind?"

"No. It is . . . complicated."

"Yeah, I can see it would be hard for you to confess that you're only with me because you think I'm your ticket to the land of the uncursed."

"That is untrue."

She propped one hand on her hip. "Really? Then what exactly made you answer my Mating Call?"

"The same thing I assume that made you issue it: It was impossible to resist."

Olivia wondered if there was any truth to that. She wanted to believe him so badly, it was a physical pain. But she didn't dare. "Did you know what it meant when I said the words? I sure as hell didn't."

He hesitated. "Aye."

Her jaw dropped. "You weren't shocked?"

"I was."

"And you said nothing, asked no questions?" She frowned. "At the time, you thought I was Morganna. You believed you were binding yourself to the woman who cursed you? Despite your protests, you *did* answer my Mating Call because you intended to use it to somehow end your curse. I gave you—" she paused, choked. "Every bit of me. I was nothing to you but the means to an end."

He stared at her with solemn blue eyes. "Whatever this bond between us, it is one we share. I feel it too."

"Aww, such pretty words," she mocked. "The only thing you feel is that I'm the key to your freedom. Let me tell you, jackass, from now on, you can go to hell."

Olivia stomped out of the room, hardly able to believe the turn her life had taken.

"You will die without my touch," he said from behind her. "Because you are mated and untransitioned, you need sex with me to retain your energy."

Not a single word about their lovemaking being something his heart craved. Nothing about how he enjoyed being with her or that he cared. He didn't, and she'd been a fool to indulge in the fantasy that he did. No wonder he'd never had a relationship. He sucked in the sensitivity department.

She almost thanked him for opening her eyes; she wouldn't make that mistake a second time.

Stiffening her spine, Olivia told him, "I'd rather die than let you use me again."

CHAPTER TEN

A FEW HOURS SLIPPED BY, and Olivia wondered if she'd spoken too soon. At the moment, she wouldn't rather die than have Marrok touch her. Even if he was a tricky, lying bastard, her body ached for him. Her skin felt tight and itched for his touch, flesh prickly, insides fevered.

She rolled over and encountered a hard chest. When had he slipped into bed beside her? Instead of rolling away, she scooted closer and smoothed a hand over the sleek bulge of his shoulder, down the steely rise and fall of his pectorals, across his ridged abdomen.

He groaned in his sleep. She snatched her hand away.

Since he'd withheld the news of their mating, she shouldn't be tempted to drop her grip to the erection she suspected he'd have. But with his warrior's body under her hands and midnight scent around her, the temptation crept in.

All the time he had spent with her, given her incredible pleasure, acted as if he cared about her, none of that had been real.

Olivia looked at the clock. Not quite two in the morning. She was groggy but awake. Her body was on red alert, with gut clenched, nipples peaked and flesh swollen. Damn it.

She rolled away. Instantly, her energy dissipated, as if some vacuum sucked it from her. Dizziness swooped in, debilitating. But she throbbed, itching to cross the sheet and resume her exploration. She barely had the energy to move a muscle. Chill seeped in. Awareness bled out. The edges of her vision turned black.

God, she was going to pass out.

Pain set in, and Olivia moaned. She remembered nearly dying and *so* didn't want to experience that nightmare again.

Being dependent on Marrok sucked. She'd been a burden to her mother for years, and she'd be damned if she was going to repeat the experience with Marrok.

He thought himself cursed? Welcome to the party.

What had compelled her to seal their union with those nonsensical words? She'd tried a dozen times to recall whatever had driven her. But she could only remember the way every cell in her body had screamed to say those words and her euphoric joy when he'd accepted and touched her.

None of that helped now. She was trapped in a hell of her own making. She needed him or she would die, that simple. But Olivia refused to be a sacrificial lamb. She'd get what she needed on her terms, in her way.

She focused on that mantra. A twitch of fingers became a curling of knuckles, then a fist. She fought to reach Marrok, as if shifting her arm through thick water with the current raging against her. Trembling, she battled the fatigue using her anger.

The chasm across the bed may as well have been a continent.

Damn it, she refused to literally lie here and die now that she had a father to get to know . . . and love. A mate's ass to kick.

Heart mate? Yeah, right. She couldn't imagine two people more ill-suited than a Dark Ages immortal warrior and a twenty-first-century American girl.

After another increment of movement, Olivia felt a glimmer of Marrok's body heat. She twitched, grazing him with her pinkie. Relief poured into her as she touched hot skin, steel under silk and scars, dusted with hair. His forearm.

A spark of energy shot through her veins, followed by a hot wash of unbridled need.

Rolling across the mattress, Olivia couldn't miss his scent, spicy, clean, complicated. Just like Marrok. A rush of pleasure jolted her, fierce and sizzling.

Don't feel anything. Do what's necessary and get away. Don't fall for him.

Easier said than done.

Marrok wanted her here so she could break his curse. At best, he was using her. At worst, he pitied her.

That made her want to retch.

She was used to being an outcast—the new girl in town, the otherworldly-looking child with midnight hair and violet eyes. Occasionally someone tried to make her their sympathy case. Enduring pity from a man she desired so ferociously infuriated her. Her mother's unfeeling obligation had been painful enough. To bear the same from Marrok would crush her. Damn, she knew she should have been guarding her heart.

"Olivia?" he murmured sleepily.

She hesitated, wishing that merely touching him would keep her "charged" or whatever term magic had for this little inescapable clause. But kidding herself was pointless. Yes, she had more juice in her veins when she touched Marrok, but enough to leave the bed? No.

Before she could talk herself out of it, she flung off her T-shirt and panties, baring herself completely. Then she slung a leg over Marrok's thighs and climbed on top of him. Wow, he was like climbing a mountain, so huge in every way.

He came awake with a gasp. She ignored him.

After straddling his hips, she anchored herself, curling her fingers into his pectorals and lowering her chest to his. A blast of body heat nearly melted her.

He sucked in a quick breath. Stomach rippling beneath

her, he tensed. His erection went from promising to *bring it on* in a heartbeat.

Their eyes met in the moonlight sweeping through the bedroom window. He drilled her with his silvery stare.

"Olivia?" He wasn't asking what she was doing; he was asking if she was sure.

They both knew she didn't have a choice.

"My energy is waning."

He nodded. Wordlessly, he curled one hand around her neck, the other anchored on her hip, pressing her against his waiting mouth, his stiff arousal. In seconds, he nearly overwhelmed her with his fevered kiss and the want seeping from his skin. Olivia moaned before she remembered all the reasons she shouldn't.

In a restless sweep, his hands sought and found her hard nipple. There was no stopping her gasp. Her head fell back as pleasure bloomed. Energy zinged inside her. Every instinct screamed to resume the kiss, to open her mouth and her body wide and let him in.

She refused to be used and pitied again.

Still sitting atop him, she shoved the covers out of her way until nothing hindered skin-on-skin contact.

Olivia grabbed his erection beneath her and stroked him. Thick, smooth, it was almost too hot to touch. Gripping him barraged her with sensations. If there was even a remote chance he could love her, she'd delight in caressing him to the edge of his resistance. She'd love to know the taste of his taut belly under her lips, his arousal swelling on her tongue.

None of that could happen . . . or she'd lose her self-control.

"Olivia . . ." he groaned.

She tried to impale herself on his thick staff, wriggling and pushing until she managed to take half of him. She bit her lip against the discomfort of his sudden intrusion. She hadn't known that being on top would make him feel downright imposing.

"Slow down, love. Let me touch you."

He pressed a thumb to her clit, which always made her putty in his hands. Unacceptable. She shoved his hand out of the way, gritted her teeth and forced her body to take all of him.

Despite her efforts to hold it in, she whimpered, and he knew it wasn't in pleasure.

Marrok grabbed her hips, stilling her. "Stop. We have all night. There is no reason—"

"Do it. Now! Just . . ." She couldn't say it.

"Fuck you? Is that what you desire?"

He sounded pissed off, and she didn't care.

"Yes!" She swiveled her hips until he could go no deeper.

With a gasp, Marrok tossed his head back. So that lit his fire. Smiling, she did it again. He groaned long and loud.

He stared at her in the shadowed moonlight, eyes unmistakably intent and pleasure-filled.

She reached behind her and stroked his testicles. Beneath her, he bucked deeper into her and growled. A thrill thrummed through Olivia's veins as she lay across his chest. Desire tightened her nipples and flashed straight to her sex. She squeezed her eyes shut.

Damn, this was about getting what she needed from him, not what she wanted.

Marrok clasped strong arms around her, pumping up as he drew her down. The sensations burst between her legs and forced a high-pitched gasp from her. The man was good.

She had to be better.

Diverting to a new tactic, she nuzzled her face in his neck, dotting kisses and nipping her teeth on the tendons and veins bulging with effort. And all the while, she continued a hard, steady rhythm of her hips—and brought out the big guns.

"The feel of you deep inside me . . ." Olivia purred in his ear. "You fill me up. Every glide down." She demonstrated, lowering herself over him. "The pleasure is amazing." She moaned, wishing it were fake.

With a thrust up, Marrok glided over a sensitive spot that sent her reeling. Too much more of that and . . . *No!* Time to finish this.

She sat up and felt instant relief. Being near him, their faces so close, it was too . . . intimate. Now, they only joined in one place.

Wearing a kittenish smile, she toyed with her nipples. Instantly, he hissed in a breath.

"You like to watch me touch myself?"

"Aye. The sight of you . . ."

She did it again, thrust herself down on him harder and felt him swell, press tight against her slick, swollen walls. Time to turn up the heat—before this backfired on her.

Bracing herself on his shoulders, she propelled her hips faster, faster. Marrok was grabbing the sheets and gritting his teeth, his body taut beneath her.

"Olivia," he panted. "Come . . . with . . . me."

Not on your life. Unlike before, sex would be on her terms. Since, until her transition, she derived her vitality from the power of his pleasure and orgasm, that's all she would take from him.

She was tempted. The sensations were there. Only sheer willpower kept her from focusing on the tingles racing and blood burning. He was going to beat her to the finish line . . . but not by much.

"Now!" she shouted. It had to be or she would go over the cliff with him.

Marrok grabbed her hips and impaled her on his length in rapid-fire strokes. Clawing her thighs with her fingernails, she managed to focus on the pinpoints of pain, not the incredible feel of him as he powered into her.

With a massive roar, he let go. She did her best to block out the quivering of her womb as he splashed it with hot seed, ignore the heavy ache of unfulfilled desire in her weeping body.

Suddenly, one of his thumbs brushed across her clit. Fire streaked right between her legs. He did it again, and the fire grew hotter, flames licking at her self-control.

"Marrok, stop." Olivia tried to climb off his body.

He held her firmly impaled on him. What the . . . ? How was it possible he was still hard?

"I have no notion what game you play, but you will cease. Now."

Instead of feathering the pad of his thumb across her clit, this time he held her down on his cock and pressed in.

Pleasure burned her thighs, merging with the tingles in her belly and the swollen ache of her sex. Ecstasy poured across her, and there was no escape. Marrok was deep inside her, his scent all over her, his hands controlling her. Dimly, she wondered how the hunter had become the hunted. Then the thought was gone.

She was too busy screaming in pleasure.

Winter decided to roar with all its might and spit snow on everyone in and around London. Including Lucan.

He'd give anything to be at home with Anka. He'd left her deliciously naked and had not been able to spare the time for seconds. Duty called, damn it. Or rather, Bram had.

Lucan cursed the bloody blazes that Shock hadn't seen fit to stand the guard duty for which he'd volunteered. Instead,

Lucan sat deep in shadows, watching Marrok's little cottage in what Bram had aptly named the Creepified Forest. Alone, silent, the place seethed with something disquieting. Pain. Haunting loneliness.

The very things Lucan had seen in Marrok's eyes, until the immortal looked at Olivia. Even without their blended signatures, he would have known she was his mate. Idly, Lucan wondered if Marrok himself knew how besotted he was. His guess? The man had no clue.

Watching branches sway with the chilly night wind was dull. But after Olivia all but shouted that Marrok had the Book of Doomsday, they needed protecting. Marrok was mad if he thought that old magic circle would keep true evil out forever.

The mental tap on his shoulder made him smile. Apparently Duke, stationed somewhere on the other side of the house, was bored, too.

A *whoosh* a mere handful of feet away made Lucan pause. It wasn't Duke coming by to bitch about monotony.

Five figures materialized on the path to the front door. Gray capes and masks with the emblem he—and virtually all of magickind—dreaded. Those explosive bursts around the upside down M only meant one thing: the Anarki.

Bloody hell! With his mind, he sent a silent message to let Duke know they had uninvited guests.

Five was a small squad, and none of the signatures was powerful. Then again, why would Mathias imagine he'd need more muscle to capture a human and an untransitioned witch with no protection? The better question was, how had Mathias learned about the diary's location in barely five hours? Lucan had his suspicions, and he couldn't wait to beat the bloody hell out of the culprit.

In his head, he heard Duke's silent countdown to action.

Heart revving, Lucan leapt from the black shadows on *three* and, with a wave of his hand, stunned the nearest unsuspecting Anarki. With a silent spell, he tied the nearest fiend with invisible bonds and moved to the next.

He glanced up to find that Duke had already dispensed with one berobed freak and was doing his best to stun another.

The other two peered frantically into the treeline, their wands at the ready, indicating that playtime was over. Lucan dashed behind a sycamore and, for the heavy fighting to come, he drew his own wand. They wanted to play rough, did they? He'd indulge them.

Lucan waved his wand, making an Anarki's nose bleed before he slipped into unconsciousness. As the goon fell, he hit his head on the tree with a *thud*. Lucan checked quickly. The bastard was still alive. Not his first choice, but Bram would approve.

Death seemed a more fitting punishment for these Anarki dogs, since Lucan was certain they had a similar fate in mind for Marrok and Olivia. But Bram wanted at least one Anarki captured alive. Good sources of information, he'd said. Lucan thought they would make better sources of fertilizer.

A quick glance across the grounds revealed Duke wrapping up Anarki number four. The last looked ready to teleport away. Clearly, they hadn't expected resistance.

With a quick spell, Lucan whipped invisible bonds around the man's ankles and wrists. His wand fell to the ground, and his eyes grew wide. He searched around, trying to find his attackers, steeped in fear so cloying, Lucan could smell it.

Once Duke had the other Anarki out of commission, Lucan strolled from the shadows and to the attackers who were all bound or passed out—or both. They were all wizards gone bad, not soulless humans converted against their will.

"Good evening, gentlemen. What a shame you're wandering where you aren't welcome. Do I have to ask who sent you?"

The goon captured last glared at Lucan with gritted teeth and mutiny on his face. He wasn't saying a damn thing.

Lucan tucked his wand away and lifted off the man's mask, revealing a craggy face with bronzed skin, inky hair, jet eyes. Stupid sap.

Lucan pointed his finger down at the man's balls, made a wrapping motion, then yanked. The Anarki grunted, choked, reached down with his bound hands, but Lucan stopped him.

Perfect. Now that Mr. Silent's testicles were in a noose, he might prove more cooperative. If not . . . Lucan had no trouble pulling tighter.

"I take it you're not here for an evening stroll."

The Anarki tensed. "Fuck. You."

Lucan pulled tighter on the invisible rope, and the man made a satisfying gurgling sound. "England is home to some of the most accomplished poets and playwrights in history. Apparently none of their eloquence rubbed off on you."

"Release me, or I will make you pay." He thrashed fruitlessly in a mad dive for his wand.

Lucan kicked it away. "I'll keep that in mind. Answer my questions, and I'll let you keep your stones attached."

Under the bluish shadows of moonlight, the dark wizard visibly steeled himself. "Eat shit."

"No, thanks." Lucan knew he could make the man not just spill his information but sing it in three-part harmony. "Let's start simple. What was your mission here tonight?"

The man glanced at the other four hooded figures. "I have nothing to say."

With a jerk of his fist, Lucan yanked on the invisible

bonds—hard. "Do you really want to lose your family jewels over such a simple question?"

Even in the moonlight, Lucan could see his captive sweating. He glanced again at the other Anarki members. Looking for help?

Duke knelt beside the man. "You're keeping him from his mate, and that makes him cranky. Perhaps you could simply cooperate. We'll all be much happier."

"Go to . . . hell," he let out, despite his pain.

"We're not making progress," Lucan said in mock concern. "I have a knife. Since the bindings aren't getting his attention . . ."

"Good thinking." Duke watched Lucan extract a long blade. Wicked and serrated. About ten inches long. Unforgiving.

The Anarki's eyes threatened to pop from his skull.

Lucan smiled and began to clean under his nails with the blade's point. "Let's try again. What exactly was your mission tonight?"

The dark wizard cast wary glances at the other Anarki members. Some were staring back. Ah, if he talked he didn't want anyone squealing to Mathias. *Now* Lucan understood.

With a flick of his fingers, Lucan rendered the two nearest him unconscious. Duke followed suit with the last two, just to make certain all stayed out.

"Now answer the question," Lucan prompted.

Still, the wizard hesitated. Lucan yanked on the invisible rope around his balls again. They had to be blue and painful as hell. Stubborn bastard.

Their captive panted. "Break into the house and search it."

Lucan had a sinking feeling there was more. "And?"

Again, the man hesitated. "I can't say more."

"I'm afraid I'm going to insist."

Duke piped in again. "Mathias sent you?"

The wizard's gaze blazed with panic. "He'll kill me . . ."

True. Mathias was ruthless to those who had crossed him.

"We can always keep him captive until we defeat Mathias," Duke suggested to Lucan.

"Last time, vanquishing him took decades. And it was only temporary," the wizard pointed out.

"Your name?" Lucan prompted.

"Zain."

"If we make Mathias believe you're dead, he won't kill your family for betraying him."

"Are you planning to kill me?"

Lucan tried not to roll his eyes. "We're the good guys here, so no. But we'll make your death look convincing. Mathias will chalk it up to your ineptitude and you'll keep breathing. We'll keep you with us until this blows over. We'll try to step up the timetable, but mind you, there's only so much we can do. The Anarki is growing again, correct?"

Zain nodded. "You're not going to kill me?"

"Your information is more valuable to us than your running blood at the moment. So if you were a dead man, what would you be willing to divulge?"

Struggling against the bonds, Zain sneered. "Why should I trust you?"

"Listen up." Lucan leaned over Zain again. "We want to spare lives, especially innocents like the MacKinnetts. More blood will be shed if we fail to stop Mathias. Unless your idea of a bright future is pushing up daisies, he will not deliver on his promises. If you help us, we'll help you."

"The MacKinnetts were Privileged."

"What did they do to you? Did they really deserve their fate?"

Zain flinched and closed his eyes.

"Maybe you should pull tighter on those bonds 'round his balls," Duke suggested.

The supine wizard stiffened but remained mute.

"It hasn't worked well thus far. Are you any good with a knife?" Lucan asked.

"Terrible."

"Perfect." Lucan handed the blade to Duke.

"No. God no!" Zain pleaded.

"Then talk," Duke snarled, gripping the wicked blade by the handle. "What did Mathias plan to do with the man and woman inside? Why does he want the house searched?"

Zain looked in panic between the blade and Duke's face.

"Yes, I will cut you. And yes, it will hurt like the devil," Duke vowed. "You leave me little choice."

The guy was now clammy and sweating and looked half-ready to wet his pants. Good. They'd be in a bloody pickle if Zain called their bluff.

Their captive tensed, swallowed. His frenetic gaze bounced from Lucan to Duke, then back. "The man we were to kill."

Lucan snorted. "Kill an immortal who's been trying to off himself for centuries? Did Mathias fail to do his homework? How sloppy of him."

At his side, Duke merely raised a dark brow to acknowledge the irony.

With eyes narrowed, Zain glared at Lucan. "I would find some way to carry out my order."

"Unless your magic is stronger than Morgan le Fay's, your task is impossible," Duke pointed out. "I do not believe Mathias was unaware that he ordered you to kill an immortal. He's many things—"

"Manipulative, ruthless, evil—" Lucan cut in.

"Backstabbing, bloodthirsty, maniacal, and power-hungry. What Mathias is *not*, is stupid."

Lucan agreed. Did Zain see that he'd been set up to fail? Set up to die?

The dark wizard exhaled. His defiant expression collapsed. "I'll say no more until you take me someplace safe. More Anarki will arrive if we do not return soon."

The last thing they wanted was more Anarki all over Olivia and Marrok, who, Lucan supposed, were sleeping peacefully inside.

He quickly zapped the four unconscious Anarki back to their last location. Presumably, they would reach Mathias. With a quick swish, Lucan unwound the invisible rope around Zain's balls, removed his robes and puddled them next to his mask. Beneath, the wizard had on a pair of shorts and a T-shirt that said Can You Hear Me Now? and showed a picture of a Tibetan monk giving the one-fingered salute.

"Someone needs to give you wardrobe tips," Duke commented dryly.

Quickly, Lucan grabbed the knife from Duke and sliced into his own hand. Zain gasped as Lucan smeared a little blood on his robes before zapping them back to their last location.

Zain glared. "You were never going to cut me, were you?"

"Not unless you proved uncooperative." Lucan shrugged. "Now, we'd like that information."

"The woman we were supposed to abduct and take to Mathias."

Lucan winced. "You do know what he would have done to her?"

Zain shook his head violently. "Not her. He insisted she was valuable. Priceless. And was not to be touched."

Duke shot him a glance, and Lucan wondered if he was thinking the same thing: valuable in what way?

"And the house?"

"We were to secure and search it."

"For what?"

A lick of his lips, a shifting of his gaze. Zain hesitated for a long moment, as if he knew that whatever he said next could not be retracted. It would betray Mathias as nothing else had. Lucan's heart pounded as he waited for the guy to gather his courage.

He was about to give up and resort to empty threats again when Zain confessed, "Mathias received word last night that the Book of Doomsday is inside this cottage."

Bloody hell. "Who told him?"

"Don't know." At Lucan's skeptical stare, Zain added, "I swear!"

He shot a glance to Duke. "We must stash him somewhere out of sight immediately."

"And get Bram here, along with another guard detail."

Nodding, Lucan sent a grim stare at Marrok's cottage. "Before it's too late."

Olivia jolted fiercely with pleasure, contracting around Marrok's cock, filling his ears with her ecstasy. As it should be.

He stroked her skin, like sun-warmed silk, with one hand and pressed right against her clit with the other. Beneath her, he stroked into her deep and slow, prolonging the climax until she clawed at him. Until she moaned her throat raw.

Until she begged. Then he gave her what she wanted.

Now, he gathered her body against his and rolled her to her back, still buried deep inside her. Tears wet his shoulders. Sobs shook her body as he stroked her hair in silence, easing farther into her, covering her completely, trying to absorb more of her inside him.

With quiet words, he soothed her. How amazing to have a woman who felt so deeply. After being alive, yet dead inside for centuries, experiencing Olivia's emotions, even second-hand, was like basking in life again. He suddenly saw the world through her human sense of mortality, fear, wonder, and worry. He gloried in the gamut of feelings between her yearning and uncertainty that spilled over her barriers and into the connection between them.

That, along with their ever-growing bond, made his eternal life less hellish. At moments like this, she was a miracle.

At the realization, he held her tighter, adjusting her body to curl around his. He nuzzled her neck, kissed her cheek, whispered in her ear.

But her sobs did not stop. Or slow.

Marrok frowned. These tears, they weren't all from the pent-up power of release. They weren't due to being overwrought from pleasure. Now that he was paying attention to the sounds . . . they were fraught with despair.

What was happening? She'd felt desire but tried to deny her orgasm while forcing his. Her surrender seemed to be ripped from her soul. Yet it was clear she sought not just to refuse her own climax, but their very bond.

This was more than leftover anger from Bram's party.

"Love, do not cry."

A jagged inhalation led to a wail that pierced his chest like a claymore. Pain and remorse sliced his gut. What had he done to her?

In her eyes, he'd taken her from the parent she had waited a lifetime to meet. Marrok did not trust Richard Gray or his explanations, and his every protective instinct had risen when the wizard talked about parting him from Olivia. Marrok would fight her father on that for eternity.

That he had not been honest with Olivia about their mating was an enormous sin in her eyes. Did she now regret their union? Zounds, after seeing her in that small red dress, he had nearly begged to have her. She had been anything but eager. So why had she come to him tonight if not for pleasure?

Because she had to. Nothing more.

He winced as Olivia continued to sob as if she would never again find solace. The truth hurt—almost as much as her tears. How she must resent her dependence on him, a man she had met but a handful of days ago. Naturally, Olivia had tried to do what she must without giving in to her desire.

Marrok took her cheeks in his hands and looked down into her wet, reddened face. She squeezed her eyes shut, refusing to look at him. No matter, he thought, melding his lips against hers, taking her mouth in a long, slow penetration—exactly as he did with her body. He pressed inside her, gliding slowly over the spot that made her gasp.

In his arms, Olivia stiffened. Marrok eased back in, stroking her sensitive tissues as if he had no other purpose in life than to please her.

She whimpered, then softened in his embrace.

Marrok praised her with kisses across her jaw, down her neck—and unhurried thrusts that soon had her lifting her hips to him and clawing his back. He'd have scratches all over him. The thought made him smile, until he realized they would heal as quickly as she made them. Damn immortality! Her nail marks in his back was something he yearned to feel later as a reminder of their passion. Morganna had denied him that, as well.

"Aye, love. Feel me."

"No," she sobbed, her eyes tightly shut again. "I can't—"

He captured her mouth in a slow kiss saturated with his longing to reach her heart and claim her for always. God, who would have thought he, of all men, would become so infatuated with someone of Morganna's blood?

"You just want release from your curse."

"I want release with you." He shifted his hands beneath her, lifting her into the rhythm of his body melting with hers. "I want *you*."

"You're using me." Her accusation ended with a moan when he pushed deep inside her again.

"As you tried to use me?"

At that, her eyes flew open. Red-rimmed, bloodshot, and so full of emotions, he could hardly discern them all. Except pride.

"If I did, it would only make us even."

Marrok didn't answer. He used the silence to slide deep into her again, where he belonged, and dust fresh kisses onto the corner of her lips. God, she tasted so sweet. He felt as if he'd waited an eternity to have this with her.

In this moment, she had been worth it.

When he finally lifted his head, they were both panting. Marrok felt himself swelling inside her. This time, she would find satisfaction with him.

"I seek to pleasure you. To help you. To share a bond with you."

He cut off the rebuttal he saw gathering on her face by pushing inside her again, harder this time, right against a sensitive spot at the very end of her channel.

She gasped, grabbing fistfuls of his hair. Her sex began to flutter. Good. He was so bloody ready, the top of his head was about to explode.

Her teeth nipped at his shoulder. Her breathing went ragged. Hundreds of years ago, he should have held his own emotional funeral. Yet even he could feel her outpouring of confusion, need, fear, and desire.

"No. You pity me!" she sobbed out. "You merely do your *duty* by me."

Pity? Duty? Did she think pity made him hard? Or that mere duty made his heart ache when he saw her tears?

She was beyond beautiful, and the fact she'd remained untouched until their mating told him something had been desperately wrong with her life before they'd met.

In the back of his mind, he knew he should not care for her so. What if betrayal flowed in her veins?

Right now, as desire sizzled up his spine and emotion flooded his heart, none of that mattered.

"Pity and duty never crossed my mind, Olivia," he gritted out, withdrawing, then sinking deep once more. Every downward plunge into her body brushed her clit, too. She gasped and dug her heels into his thighs.

"I might have sought to use you at first. That changed when you Called to me as your mate. Fate, magic, Kismet, whatever you believe, put us together. You are mine."

Olivia's gaze locked onto his with his words. Shock reflected in those violet depths, confused and hopeful. Wary. But her body yielded, taking him deeper, closing around him more. As her cry rang in his ears, something in his chest twisted and roared.

Her sex clasped him fiercely in release. Everything inside him demanded that he let go again, cement this bond between them that was too strong to fight or deny. Make her his mate in word, deed, and truth.

He surrendered to the pleasure, to the need he sensed within her, and gave her everything inside him with one last push. The white-hot ecstasy shimmered inside him, seeming to last forever. He filled her with seed, with need, with everything he was.

This time, in the aftermath, she spilled no tears. Marrok was grateful. Listening to her cry was like pouring acid on an open canker in his chest.

Instead, she lay quietly in his arms. And for the first time, he felt an odd peace lying with a woman after a thorough loving. She belonged here.

Dangerous to feel such for a woman whose help he needed to be uncursed. What if this was another of magic's practical jokes, to be cursed by one le Fay and have his heart ripped asunder by another?

"Why?" she breathed, so quietly, Marrok almost missed it.

He reared back, looking down into her face. "Why keep you? Why make love to you again?"

Olivia's tortured gaze tore at him. So afraid and confused . . . Did she not share his lazy bliss? His sense of rightness?

"Why try to convince me I matter? We need each other. I must be with you to stay alive, and you can't—"

"Climax without you? Aye, but that is not the only reason—"

"You need me to break your curse." Her flushed face mottled as fresh tears threatened.

But that was not all he needed her for. This caring for her, it was reckless. Yet, he could not leave her in such pain.

"We require one another. Why does that frighten you?"

With a desperate push, she tried to wriggle out from under him. Marrok anchored his elbows to the bed, rendered her immobile by spreading her legs wider with his knees.

He had some suspicions about her past. Time to find out how true they were.

"Tell me about your mother," he asked softly.

"No." She looked at him as if he'd lost his mind. "You don't care."

"You have no notion how I feel, Olivia. I want to know. Please."

"You want to lay me bare? Fine." Anger screwed her expression. "When I was seven, I was picked to play the lead in our school play. Mom always browbeat me to be average, but I didn't want to be like everyone else. She loved the theater. I thought she'd be so proud to see me onstage. I practiced for days and days, giving up playtime, TV.

"After the first performance, all the other kids' mothers brought them roses and hugged them. I'd really hoped . . ." Olivia swallowed. "She told me I would have been better in a nonspeaking role and that I was making a spectacle of myself. I quit the next day, but even that didn't please her. She just nodded and went on."

Her words made Marrok's stomach churn for the young girl seeking her mother's approval and finding none. "You cried."

"It was nothing new. Mom took care of me, protected me. She was obligated to do it, and she never let me forget that. She was afraid of whatever magic I might hold, but at the time, I didn't understand."

The picture became clearer now. He ached for her. How could any woman with a heart treat her own daughter so coldly? "And you looked to her for love. When she did not provide it, you felt rejected. Lacking. Like a burden."

Olivia bit her lip. She said nothing, but her expression told him that his guess was accurate. That explained why she was so eager to embrace her long-absent father, despite knowing so little of the man.

Which only made his next words more difficult. "So meeting your father was a dream fulfilled."

She nodded. "He won't reject me because I'm magical and he won't feel obligated to care for me. He *understands*. And you rudely dismissed his every suggestion to keep me safe."

"Do you think me incapable of protecting you?"

"In the human world, no. There is no one I would trust

more. It's the magical one I'm not so sure of. What do either of us know about this Mathias and his Anarki?"

"This place has magical protection. The book is hidden, locked. And until we discover its secrets, it is useless. Believe me, I know."

"But my father—"

"While sharing blood ties to you, is someone you know not." When she opened her mouth to object, he laid a finger over her lush lips.

"He hid from the Anarki for a long while, I know. Do you not think it curious that he never once felt safe enough to seek you?"

She looked away as if such had occurred to her. Marrok did not wish to shatter her dreams of the perfect father, of finally finding parental love. But he could not bear to see her crushed, especially if the man was not genuine or only sought her because she shared a connection with the Doomsday Diary. And Bram's information about Richard Gray troubled him deeply.

"We don't know exactly what he's been through. How do you know that he wasn't concerned that, by visiting me, he would be bringing trouble to my door? I *need* these answers."

And Marrok did not have them. His gut told him to be cautious of Gray, but Olivia would hear none of it. She wanted to see the man again, hear his side of the story. But until she saw reason, trouble would keep brewing.

Soon, Marrok drifted off. The predawn gray was hours away, and still Olivia was unable to sleep. She slipped from bed and studied Marrok in the moonlight. At six-four, he consumed three-quarters of the massive bed. As sleep overtook him, his big, hot body had been wrapped around hers protectively.

He could be so intimidating yet gentle—when it suited his purpose.

Despite all his pretty words, she didn't dare trust him with her heart. He'd mated with her, then withheld that fact. He was insistent on keeping her here, even if it was no longer the safest place for her. And, despite his protestations, he surely pitied her. Ugh! The sex was mind-blowing, but he wouldn't stay with her simply for the orgasm. For freedom and death, though, he would bear anything.

Unless she guarded her heart, she would fall for all his staged concern and well-acted tenderness and fall in love. Already, she'd let him far closer than she should. He'd had fifteen centuries to hone his relationship-avoidance strategy. Olivia always led with her emotions.

If she wasn't careful, he was going to crush her.

Maybe her best defense was to give Marrok what he wanted: the means to end his curse. If he didn't need her anymore, he would leave. He'd take a piece of her heart with him, but she'd mend. As long as she didn't fall completely in love with him, she'd survive.

First, she had to see her father again and get answers. Find Richard and discern what he knew about the Doomsday Diary.

But Olivia admitted that wasn't the only reason she wanted to see her father. As a lonely girl, she'd spent hours devising tales about the man, who had, of course, died in some heroic way and would have loved her to pieces, had he lived. As a confused woman, she had to try to separate her fantasies from fact, her emotion from logic. She wanted to know the man from whom she'd received her powerful le Fay blood.

Last night, before they'd left the party, her father had pressed a piece of paper with his phone number into her hand. Now seemed like the perfect time to use it.

Vibrating with nerves, she rose from the chair and wandered into the bedroom. On the nightstand, she spotted Marrok's phone.

And enough weapons to defend a small country scattered on the floor by the bed.

An enormous broadsword leaned against the mattress, tucked between the bed frame and the nightstand. In a nod to contemporary warfare, he had something that looked suspiciously like a machine gun, two semiautomatic pistols, and a terrible-looking knife—for starters.

"I told you I would protect you," he murmured, rolling to face her, his voice morning rough in the grayish light.

Olivia dragged her gaze to him. His blue eyes were so focused, as if he pointed a laser at her.

"Will these weapons kill anyone magical?" She nodded to the guns.

"They will at least slow them down. In battle, winning isn't always possible. Sometimes, gaining the advantage to make a tactical retreat is enough to save you. You have yet to sleep. Come back to bed." Though he said the words softly, it was a demand.

"I'm going to call my father. I need to ask him some questions. I need to understand what's going on."

Marrok's jaw clenched, and he swore under his breath, but wisely did not argue. "Are you planning to call at five in the morning?"

She bit her lip. Put like that, the idea sounded stupid. But the longer she stood here dithering, the more she had a feeling that time was ticking away and she needed to act fast, get answers, and help Marrok gain his freedom—before he had the chance to rip out her heart.

"I'll leave a message."

Before Marrok could protest, she walked out the door,

down the hall, then to the farthest corner of the house—the kitchen. In the semidark corner, she punched in the number she had memorized by heart. Then she waited.

A man's voice, husky and slurred, answered on the third ring.

"I'm sorry to wake you. This is Olivia."

"Is something wrong?" Sleep cleared from his voice quickly, leaving the clear tones she remembered from Bram's party. "Did you change your mind about staying with Marrok?"

"No. I don't know. I . . ." She hesitated. She couldn't just jump ship and go with her father. Marrok's point was valid; she barely knew the man. She'd be stupid to trust him too quickly, no matter how kind or accepting he seemed. "I'd like to talk to you before I decide anything."

"I understand. Becoming mated, finding out you have magical blood, and so soon after losing your mother, is a great deal to cope with."

Exactly. "I have a few more questions about the past. About the diary and the symbol on the front, my mother . . . everything. Can you talk now?"

"Of course. I should come there. Some explanations are better in person. Where are you?"

Olivia hesitated. She didn't know him, but would the man who'd turned on the Anarki sell out his own daughter for the Doomsday Diary? She'd never know until they talked. Quickly, she gave him directions.

"I'm looking forward to seeing you," her father said.

She disconnected the call and folded the cell phone in half and waited for her father—and the answers she desperately needed.

Less than three minutes later, a soft tapping at the door alerted her. She whirled to answer it. But Marrok beat her.

Shirtless and barefoot, he yanked the door open with his

left hand. In his right, he held his enormous broadsword. Tucked into the back of his jeans, which were slung low over his hips, was one of those nasty semiautomatics.

He took one look at Richard, then whirled to glare at her. "You *invited* him here?"

"Yes. You don't want me to go, and I need to talk to my father. I figured here would be safe, right?"

"Unless he has been followed and brought some of his past along with him."

Olivia stormed across the room, charging at him like a bull. "Give the man a chance. He's here because I called and asked him to tell his side of the story."

"Start by asking him how he came to be close enough to lure Mathias to his doom."

What was Marrok insinuating? Confusion tangling her thoughts, she stared up at her father, who still stood in the doorway. "Richard?"

Her father did not meet her stare. Instead, he looked at Marrok, his violet eyes strained.

"Invite me in."

"Why should I?" Marrok leaned against the door, clearly in no hurry to get out of the way.

"I've waited nearly a quarter of a century to meet Olivia. I simply want to explain—"

"*All* of it. Not just the heroic bits."

Richard nodded earnestly. "Everything."

Still Marrok hesitated. "It is for Olivia I do this, not as any favor to you."

"She is your mate. You want what's best for her."

"Do not *ever* forget that," Marrok growled, then stepped back. "Enter."

Richard crossed the threshold with a shiver. "Interesting magic circle. Who drew it?"

"Merlin."

Richard raised a brow and looked around the cottage. Olivia stared too, trying to see it through his eyes.

"Electric lights, running water . . ." He sauntered in, then looked around the corner to the kitchen. "An oven, a microwave. Merlin was not alive to draw a magic circle around this structure."

"I have demolished and rebuilt several times in this exact spot."

"It's a good line, but not infallible. Fading. The Anarki can be very determined."

"You should know. Did you come here to discuss the protection of my dwelling or talk to your daughter?"

"We are beginning with a less than friendly relationship." Richard's words held a note of censure.

"You know precisely why."

Olivia had had enough. "You both are talking around me and it's really annoying."

Marrok turned to her with burning eyes. "You deserve the truth. Make him give it to you."

"You keep saying that. What truth?"

Her father sighed and sat on the sofa. "I knew exactly where Mathias was most vulnerable because . . ."

"Go on." Marrok's growl said he was quickly losing patience.

"I was once one of the Anarki."

"You are being modest," Marrok sneered.

Richard wrung his hands and sent Olivia an expression that implored her to understand. "I was Mathias's second in command."

Olivia's horrified gasp shattered the quiet. She backed away until her knees hit the sofa. She sank down onto it, before her Jell-O legs gave out.

Her father, in league with Mathias?

"You must understand," Richard rushed to his knees before her. "I was young and idealistic when I joined him. I was scarcely out of apron strings when his ideas of equality seduced me. He showed me the squalor of the Deprived. Their shanties, the discrimination they suffer, the vile hate they often endure for nothing more than having mixed blood. It horrified me. Mathias sounded so forward-thinking; at a time when humans here in England tore themselves apart in some stupid civil war, he spoke of fairness and tolerance, doing away with a cruel establishment."

"But he . . . killed people. He raped women and enslaved children."

"Eventually, I saw that. But when first presented with the evil he was capable of, he made rape and murder sound necessary, the ends justifying the means."

"And sometimes, for the mere sport of hearing innocent people scream," Marrok added.

Richard nodded, but said nothing.

Olivia looked back and forth between the two men. Neither had asked her to choose between them . . . yet.

Then something horrific occurred to her. "You participated in Mathias's cruelties?"

His face a mask of agony, Richard looked much older than he had yesterday. "Yes."

She recoiled, backing away until Marrok placed a soothing hand on her shoulder.

"You're wondering how I could do such a thing. In the centuries since, I have wondered that myself. Sometimes, I still hear the screams . . ." Richard choked. "I wanted to believe we were doing something that would change magickind for the better by opening opportunities for wizards and witches of all classes. I allowed myself to be led blindly. Youth and ignorance are no excuse . . . but they are the only ones I have to offer."

Well, she had wanted answers about her separation from her father. Now she had them. Bile crept up her throat. All the time she'd been building up a hero in her head, he'd been running from the fact he'd raped, murdered, and conscripted innocent people.

The rest of her questions—the symbol, the diary, the past—mattered, but not now. Not when she was this over-whelmed.

"I've alienated you."

Olivia wanted to reassure him, but was stunned to her very soul.

"I'm trying to . . . process all you've said."

"As you should. I'm hoping you can set it aside for a few minutes. There are more important things to discuss. Namely, your future. I have remained hidden and many think me dead. But by virtue of Bram displaying you at his party, now everyone knows you exist. Your magical signature tells them your bloodline. Through your untrained thoughts, some now know I am alive, and the Book of Doomsday is here in this cottage. It will be mere days, or hours, before Mathias learns all this as well. Then, I fear, your human mate will be unable to save you."

"We have had this conversation." Marrok's very tone warned him.

"I'm not certain she understood the full import. I have knowledge of the diary. I can evade the Anarki." He stared at Marrok, eyes pleading. "She is my only child, and I have just found her. Please, I beg you, let her come with me and bring the diary. With them, I can break your curse, keep Mathias at bay, provide you peace."

"Or harm my mate and turn one of the most powerful objects in existence against magickind. How am I to know which?" Marrok edged in front of her and casually fingered the handle of the broadsword.

The sting of shock and anger lashed at half of her. The other half . . . the foolish, romantic half, loved that Marrok was so willing to protect her.

A pounding on the door interrupted them. Olivia glanced at the time on Marrok's cell phone in her hand. Not yet five thirty in the morning.

Keeping Olivia behind him, Marrok edged to the door. "As busy as the bloody Oxford Circus Underground Station. Who is it?"

"It's Bram. You have grave problems."

"I do, indeed. Richard Gray is under my roof, and you are on my doorstep." He glanced at Olivia. "I could say more, but prudence begs me to stop there."

"Funny. But shove off and listen."

Olivia's heart beat faster. If Bram was arriving with the sun, it couldn't bode well.

"Since my party last night, I set a guard duty near your property, just in case—"

Marrok opened the door with his sword raised threateningly. "You have no right. It is my property to hold."

"Lower that, damn it." Bram raked his hand through his unusually mussed hair. "I set the guard duty because I suspected the Anarki would be at your door soon. I was right."

"We saw and heard nothing."

"Because Lucan and Duke stopped the five dark wizards before they came near your door. They were sent to kill you."

Marrok snorted at that.

"Agreed. But they were ordered to take Olivia to Mathias.

They were told she was 'valuable.' Do you want to learn why the hard way?"

Given the way thunder crossed Marrok's face, the very thought incited his rage.

"The Anarki were then told to secure the house and search for the book." With bloodshot eyes, Bram cast a bleak expression at the group. "Mathias *knows* where you are and what you have. And he will stop at nothing to obtain both. He means to hold the power of Doomsday in his hands."

"What do you suggest?" Marrok's eyes narrowed.

"Bring the Book of Doomsday and come with me. Now."

Marrok crossed his arms over his chest. "By your own admission, two of your kind dispatched them."

"This is Mathias and the Anarki, not some lone nutter brandishing a wand at you. He will return with an army to abduct Olivia and take the book. Other than the one time he was exiled, he has never been gainsaid."

"He cannot pass my magic circle."

"This one?" Bram crossed his arms and stepped over the line, into the house. "If I can breach this line, Mathias can do the same."

Marrok recoiled. "How long have you been able to breach that line?"

"Long enough to know it's shit. I let you believe it was strong so you could keep your sense of security, but the magic of the line has faded. Times being what they are, you need to know it."

"Magic fades?" Marrok looked skeptical. "I know a particular book that has not faded at all since the day it was used to curse me fifteen centuries ago."

Bram looked at Marrok as if he wasn't dipping both oars. "Morganna poured a bit of her soul into that diary and bound that book to this earth. To this day, her spirit keeps it humming with power so you will be sufficiently tormented. My grandfather drew the magic circle as a favor, I'm guessing, not with any real passion or power—both of which make magic strong. And why are we wasting time with this foolish discussion when Mathias and the Anarki will most likely be sweeping down on us at any minute?"

"You could draw another magic circle for protection."

"They will come with an army, and it won't hold."

"Why should I think your words are something other than swill?" Marrok sent him a pointed glare.

"Because if you don't, Mathias will strike—quickly and hard. And by now, he knows where you are vulnerable."

Three sets of male eyes fell on her. Were they insinuating that *she* was Marrok's weakness?

Marrok reached out, pulled her against the solid bulk of his body. "No one touches her."

Bram clenched his fists. Olivia had seen him laughing, always with a certain detachment, arrogance, and devil-may-care attitude. Today, he looked frantic to find something—anything—that would help Marrok see reason.

"Then get her out of here. Come with me. Bring the book. Stay at my home—"

"Or with me," Richard cut in. "I offered before you arrived to take Olivia with me into hiding and to bring the book. Together, I'm certain we can unlock the book's secrets and right Marrok's life."

"Nay."

"Marrok," Bram braved the sword and grabbed his shoulders. "Listen to me. You don't like or trust me. But Olivia is my friend. I care what happens to her and the book. We have that in common. I won't attempt to separate you from her or the book. If you don't come with me now, Mathias will get his hands on Olivia. You know the possibility then."

A heavy silence fell over the group. Marrok stared at Bram, who refused to back down. He might be a calculating bastard, but Olivia didn't think he was a liar.

"Marrok, I think he's right."

He snapped his gaze to her, fury blazing from his eyes.

She held up her hand to stay his anger. "I know you don't trust him or my father—"

"You know exactly where trusting magic has gotten me."

"Yes, but what if Bram is telling the truth and his friends thwarted the Anarki here recently? Then it won't be long before they're back. Can we afford to be stubborn?"

Marrok looked from Olivia, to Bram, then back again. "I would not risk you."

He spoke so softly, this huge mountain of a man, as he caressed her cheek. Did he say things like this because she meant something to him or because she was the means to an end he craved? She couldn't worry about it now.

"Staying here sounds like an unnecessary risk. I'm scared. Even if we don't go with my father, I think we should go somewhere."

"The book—"

"We'll take it with us." She grabbed the hand cupping her cheek to remove it. But he warmed her; his thick wrist, veined and solid, soothed her.

"As you wish." Marrok shot her father a dark look. "She stays with me. Period." Then he turned to Bram. "For Olivia, I will come to your house."

"There's plenty of room and a great deal of magical protection around it. It is the safest place against Mathias and the Anarki now. You are free to leave anytime you wish. You can hide the book wherever you like."

Marrok left the room and returned moments later with

the Doomsday Diary in his arms. As usual Olivia stumbled back against the blast of power it radiated.

"Bloody unbelievable." Bram stared at it reverently.

"It's been found!" cried her father.

"And so have we." Lucan ran up and braced himself in the open doorway. "The Anarki are here, hundreds of them! And they mean business."

CHAPTER ELEVEN

OLIVIA SLANTED A GLANCE past the men and out the cottage door, to find a sea of gray robes trimmed in blood red with an unfamiliar symbol on the front.

"Oh God," she uttered, shock and fear blending to stun her.

Bram cursed. "We must leave! Get Olivia and the Diary and I will transport us to my house."

"I will not forfeit my home without a fight." Marrok stood ready to defend all that was his.

"Give me the book, then. Let me protect it."

Marrok's glance answered Bram with a silent "hell no."

"Stubborn prat." Bram charged for the door, then shouted to the others, "Wands at the ready; this will be ugly. Fight!"

Duke jumped into the fray with his wand. Just outside, Lucan brandished his own wand furiously. Three of the Anarki dropped instantly. Others merely jolted when a spell hit them, then resumed, zombic-like, coming straight for the cottage door.

As they shuffled closer, Olivia gasped. Their skin looked

cadaver-pale. One reached the threshold, staring at her with colorless, malevolent eyes.

"What is *that*?" she cried out, recoiling.

"Former human," her father said. "Unlike Anarki wizards, these creatures have no soul."

"I don't understand."

"Mathias lacks enough wizards for his cause, so he converts humans to swell his ranks. He abducts capable men—often military. He rips out their souls, then commands their thoughts and actions. Nothing can break the link but death of the body."

Another of the eerie Anarki reached the door. Then another. Marrok and Richard shoved them back. One reached inside and swiped out at Olivia with rotting hands, its grip missing her shirt by a mere breath. Cold oozed from him, like a walking freezer. Gasping, she jumped back.

Her insides shook, washing her in terror, brutal and breath-stealing. That . . . thing had nearly touched her with its rotting flesh. But the eyes in the sagging face were alive—and ruthless.

Marrok shoved the book into her hands and grabbed his broadsword. With a mighty growl, he wielded the weapon, skewering all three zombies at once on his blade. Black blood oozed from noses and mouths. Though she was thrilled they'd been stopped, Olivia clutched the book in horror.

Nothing fazed Marrok. With a yank of his massive arm, he freed the sword, then lopped the head off another soulless demon headed in Olivia's direction.

Mathias had targeted her, and these beings were too big to fight off with self-defense techniques and a can of Mace, damn it. "Should I hide with the book in the back of the house?"

Without pausing, Marrok stepped over the bodies and into the fray. "Nay. They may sneak behind you."

Good point.

He charged another pair of half-dead Anarki and emerged victorious. Relief edged through her. It wasn't logical; he was immortal and healed instantly, but . . . what if something happened to him? Without Marrok, life would seem empty again.

When had she started falling for the hunky immortal?

Didn't matter right now. She wasn't giving him up until it was *her* choice, not some extra from *Night of the Living Dead.*

Whirling on one foot, she sprinted down the hall.

"Olivia!" Marrok's cry rang above the din of his sword.

Moments later, she returned with a pair of handguns. When she'd decided to move out of her mother's house and live on her own, she'd taken gun safety classes and purchased one for home protection. She might not be able to identify the weapon, but she knew how to unlock the safety, aim, and shoot.

Marrok stood in the doorway, fending off two of the half-dead creatures, one on his left, the other on his right. He backed up a step. Foolishly, they tried to follow. Marrok crouched down and swung the sword in a wide arc, almost like a baseball bat. He severed the beasts' torsos in half.

Olivia tried not to gag when the black liquid spurted from their bodies and puddled on the porch, running over the stones, into the wood and dirt below.

Still, Marrok charged forward. More of the awful creatures came. The determination stamping Marrok's face said that he would kill anyone who tried to harm her—or he'd sacrifice himself trying.

Bram, Lucan, and Duke scanned the crowd as they brandished their wands. Richard had perched himself on the sloped thatch roof and was zapping the members of the Anarki who didn't look as if they were rotting on their bones.

Soon, however, a pile of healthy-looking Anarki, all wizards gone bad, lay bound and stacked at Lucan's feet. Bram sighed and put away his wand.

Was he insane? There were hundreds of creatures left. Did he expect Marrok to slay them all? The odds were overwhelming, even for someone with Marrok's amazing prowess.

A moment later, Bram tried to punch one of the half-dead. The first time, he missed completely, nearly knocking himself off balance. The second time, the crack of knuckles on flesh sounded all the way across the yard. Bram grimaced in pain as he shook his hand, uttering a few choice words, which he repeated when the Anarki continued toward the cottage.

Marrok had been waylaid too far away to help Olivia. The half-dead beings marched for the door. Bram tried to punch another. The thing shoved him on his ass with a hearty push, then continued toward her.

"Olivia!" Marrok called to her.

"I've got it," she called.

She didn't want to die or become Mathias's personal plaything. And she'd be damned if the evil bastard wasn't getting his hands on the Doomsday Diary. Anyone who could create these soulless zombies wasn't someone who needed a book with such immense power.

Swallowing her fear, Olivia tucked the book between her knees, set one of the weapons on the table beside her, then fumbled to release the gun's safety. She raised it and aimed. Her arms shook as she stared at the nearest zombie closing in—with a veritable army behind it.

Former human. Once upon a time, it had been human with family, friends, people who would mourn it. How could she just kill it?

"Olivia, shoot!" Marrok shouted.

She bit her lip. Her finger curled around the trigger.

It's not really alive anymore, said her father's soothing voice in her head. *He can never be human again. You're doing him and yourself a favor by putting him out of his misery.*

Perhaps . . . but it felt a lot like murder.

Until several more of the terrible creatures stacked up behind the first, all trying to crowd into the doorway. A blast of arctic air chilled her. Suddenly, the cottage's furniture zoomed past her, and she looked up to find Bram brandishing his wand. The sofa and chairs, a few tables, all stacked up at the door to keep the rotting Anarki from entering the house.

The first one climbed the blockade and lunged for her, looking at her with rapacious eyes that told her he smelled a kill. No time for compassion now.

Olivia steadied the gun and pulled the trigger. The rotting freak jolted, spasmed. Smoke poured from him, and his blood ran black before he fell in a heap.

Despite her success, another Anarki stepped up behind the fallen one. He pushed at the furniture with evil glee. No time to wonder if she was doing the right thing. She fired again.

Bingo! Right in the head. Black liquid splattered everywhere, the walls, the floor, her shirt. The gag urge was strong, especially when she saw what was left of its head roll off its body.

"Give me a gun," Bram barked from the door. His knuckles were bleeding. He looked sweaty, his clothes in tatters, his hair a hurricane victim.

She tossed her spare across the room and watched Bram storm the barricade, firing without hitting much. He practically needed to be on top of one of the half-dead baddies to kill.

"Let me try," Lucan shouted from the other side of the barrier.

Bram tossed him the weapon. The results . . . the same. Until they ran out of bullets.

Her jaw dropped. Had these magical men never thrown a punch or used a gun?

Bram grumbled, "It looks easier on TV."

Then he reached out and grabbed her by the shoulder, shut his eyes and stood stock-still. Was he praying? That was all well and good, but right now, didn't he need to be fighting?

More Anarki have arrived, Bram's voice was a boom in her head. *Too many to fend off. The soulless humans are bloody impossible to kill with magic. We must leave!*

"Marrok." Bram motioned him into the cottage.

She looked out into the yard past Marrok, who was making his way to the door. The sun was edging toward the horizon, showing the slimy black liquid in a thick sludge on the ground.

Suddenly, Lucan vanished. Duke followed suit.

This must be that tactical retreat Marrok spoke of. She approved. The odds looked beyond overwhelming, judging by the sea of tattered robes, red symbols, and dead faces.

Bram wrapped an arm around her. A moment later, Marrok charged through the door and clambered over the barricade, three dozen Anarki behind him, all trying to get their hands on Olivia and the diary.

Bram shouted to her, "Hold tight to that book!"

Then he grabbed Marrok's forearm in his grip and muttered something.

Suddenly, Olivia saw nothing but black. She felt as if the ground beneath her had dropped away, she was falling, falling . . . her stomach pitching and rolling and hollow, like being on a roller coaster with a steep drop.

Just when she thought she might hurl, she landed on her

feet with a jarring thud, Bram's arm around her again, the book still clutched in her arms. Marrok appeared on the other side of the wizard, looking somewhere between furious and confused. Around them, the room had the gilded, expensive look of a palace.

"Where have you brought us?"

"My house."

Marrok set his jaw, clearly unhappy. He had agreed to come here . . . but not without reservations.

She gasped, looking around frantically. "My father?"

"Teleported away, likely back to his own place," Bram assured. "He was fine."

"Now what?" she asked.

"Are you hurt, either of you?"

The last few frantic minutes came rushing back, the battle, the black blood everywhere, the kickback of the gun in her hands as she'd blown a half-dead's head from its body.

"No fainting on me." Bram grabbed her by both shoulders. "Are you hurt?"

Marrok turned her into his own embrace, then rubbed grimy hands up and down her arms, as if testing her wellness himself. "Olivia?"

"I'm fine. You? You were so outnumbered. I worried—"

He hovered a gentle finger over her lips to quiet her. "I am unharmed. I have faced such odds in battle even before I was immortal and lived to tell. Do not fear for me."

Bram cut in. "We must get the book hidden immediately. I would ask that you give it to me so I can stow it someplace safe."

Marrok opened his mouth to protest, but Bram's next words stopped him.

"However, I know better. Spend a few hours here. Find a spot that is difficult to reach and damn near impossible to guess. Sabelle and I will put extra enchantments on the house to make it less likely the Anarki will be able to break in. For now, it's the best we can do."

Something about Bram's words—the way he'd phrased them—gave her pause. "What happens if the Anarki are able to invade your house?"

Bram sent her a hard stare. "We pray. Then fight like never before."

An hour later, Marrok paced the sumptuous room Bram's staff had readied for him and Olivia. Creams, golds, and taupes surrounded him, decorated with a Louis XIV flavor. Nothing over the top, but very posh and all the finest. Bram would insist, of course. *Spoiled cur.*

A huge bed dominated the room with a sitting area to the left. Ah, the ways he longed to worship Olivia on that bed . . . Marrok shook the thought away and continued cataloging the room in order to find a hiding place for the Book of Doomsday.

A bathroom was just beyond the couch and chairs—currently cut off from his sight by the closed door—with his mate inside naked and wet, soaping the bare silk of her skin . . . while he stood here, shaking with the need to feel her alive in his arms.

Stop!

The book. He must hide it well. Now. *Search the grounds,* Bram had said. Cheeky. But the wizard was no fool; he knew Marrok would not hide that book far from his own line of sight.

Glancing around the room again, Marrok looked for a hiding place. No opening floorboards here, as he'd done at the cottage. The wall-to-wall carpet made that impossible, but it was so thick that if he could not wait to carry Olivia to the bed, making love to her on the floor would be no hardship. He could spread her wide, sliding her legs over the crooks of his arms as he felt her very life pulse around him . . .

Concentrate! The furniture, while ornate, provided no obvious hiding places. Marrok had a knife and could rip out a hole in the mattress—but that would be too easily guessed. And might lessen the pleasure he and Olivia had in both sleeping and sex.

Think! For contrary to what Bram said, the Anarki would not be the only ones searching for the Book of Doomsday. Marrok had no doubt that Bram would use its presence under his roof as an opportunity to try to seize the book himself.

The battle today had shocked and worried Marrok, in both its scale and timing. At last night's party, Olivia had mentally blurted out the fact that he possessed the book to many people in the room. If Bram was to be believed, two of his friends had warded off a small Anarki attack scant hours later. Not long thereafter, Olivia called her father, who had come to the cottage—with the Anarki army virtually on his heels. Coincidence?

Marrok closed his eyes. He wanted to believe so, but happenstance damned Richard Gray. Traitors could be relied upon for one thing only: to switch sides when doing so would most benefit themselves. The question was, did he include Olivia in that traitorous picture?

He didn't want to believe Olivia capable of betrayal. Such duplicity . . . even pondering it hurt. But what if she had been angrier after their fight than he had thought?

Olivia was no lover of the Anarki, and her surprise at her father's involvement with them in the past had been genuine, but how far was she willing to go to please her long-lost sire? Olivia had moved to a new country and begun a new life, simply to find parental love. He hated to believe she would cast aside her ideals to win her father's affection . . . but it was possible.

Despite his doubts, when Olivia opened the bathroom door wrapped in naught but a towel, her skin steamy, a part of him wished he could write off their connection purely to magic meddling in his life again. But deep down he knew it was about Olivia. She, with her shy bravery and sassy attitude, touched something in him he had believed long dead. *So sweet.* Could she actually be poison? He wanted her beyond desire, needed her beyond sustenance. Did their mating affect her feelings in the same way?

Dripping wet, she clutched the towel to her bare body. "Marrok, are you okay?"

A compelling need to reaffirm her safety, to restake his claim, overcame him.

Must. Have. Her. Now!

Marrok dropped his towel from about his waist and stalked toward her. Wide-eyed, Olivia watched him approach with an intent stare and ready erection. Was he serious? She was still shaking, her mind seething with fury and terror from the battle, and foreboding for what was to come. And he wanted sex?

She muttered the first excuse that came to mind. "Marrok, I'm all wet."

"Not as wet as you will be."

He cut off more talk with a kiss. Fisting a desperate hand through the wet tresses at her nape, Marrok angled her face under his and devoured her.

The aggression in his touch put her more on edge, and right now, she wanted peace, perspective, to be able to think, figure out what the hell had happened and why. She didn't want to surrender so utterly again to a man who only wanted her because she could help end his curse.

She wriggled free. "I don't need energy right now."

"I need to touch you." He stroked her hip with a rough caress.

"I'm not answering your booty call just because you're in the mood to get laid."

His entire body tensed. His eyes narrowed. "You cheapen what we share. I do not want to simply fuck. I want *you*."

"Why would you want me now? The really bad guys are after us, and before that you and I fought—"

"I cannot *not* touch you after seeing the Anarki pursue you so cruelly." He clutched her nape in his grip. "And you, foolish, brave woman, did what was necessary by shooting them. It pleased me to see your fighting spirit. But had I been mortal, you would have taken ten years off my life."

"I'm here. I'm fine."

"Thank God." He cupped her face in his big, rough palm. "As soon as the battle ended, I craved you. I want to know that you are alive and whole and mine."

She bit her lip. Her belly fluttered at his possessive words. How wonderful that sounded, to belong, to be cherished. But everything he said could be just a lure to keep her close so she could help uncurse him. He had never, in fifteen hundred years, been committed to a woman. He gave new meaning to the term "eternal bachelor." He had never been in love, and hoping she could be the one to change that would be incredibly reckless.

"We don't have time for sex. We need to hide the book and figure out what to do next."

"You are right." Marrok sighed at length and donned his towel again. Then he leaned in, nearly touching her. "But hear me: Aye, we argued before the attack. You were angry with me. But that changes naught. We are mated. Once the book is hidden and we are certain we are safe for the moment, I *will* have you."

Olivia swallowed. Her pulse leapt. Reckless or not, she believed—and responded to—him. The utter determination on his face, in his grip, said that somehow she mattered to him . . . even if she didn't understand why.

"Is that a threat?"

"A vow. I will keep and protect what is mine."

"Regardless of what I want?"

"Say you that you want me not?"

She couldn't say that, not without being a liar. She yearned for him, and it wasn't just the bond. He was stubborn and difficult . . . and he might be using her, but that didn't change the fact that he was quickly working his way into her heart.

"Aren't you being a little medieval?"

His grip tightened. "You can take the man out of the Dark Ages, but—"

"Yeah, yeah, you can't take the Dark Ages out of the man. Nice. Let's focus on hiding the book now. The rest, we'll deal with later. Agreed?"

Marrok gritted his teeth, looking less than happy. "Aye."

"We can't go back to your cottage. I'll bet the Anarki did a lot of damage to it looking for the book." Olivia grimaced. "I'm sorry."

He tensed. "Why, because you rang your father?"

"Why would that matter?" She glared at Marrok. "You can't think my call to him brought the Anarki down on us. According to Bram, they'd already located us, remember?"

"Aye." But he didn't look like he appreciated the reminder. "But Richard brought more."

"We don't know that. I apologized because Mathias found

out you had the book when I accidentally blasted the thought to everyone at Bram's party."

"You knew not that others could hear your thoughts. Nor did you know what your father would do with the information."

She pulled away. "I don't think my father had *anything* to do with that attack. Richard may have been with them once, but he saw the error of his ways and helped capture Mathias."

"How do you know that, in two hundred years, Richard Gray has not changed his mind again?" He took her shoulders in his hands. "Olivia, he likely has friends on both sides. With his past associations, he has divided loyalties at best. You want so desperately to please the father you have never known to compensate for the mother who did not show you her love. I understand—"

She shook free of his touch. "Who are you now, Dr. Freud?"

"If I must be to make you see the possibility that he may not be the father of your girlhood dreams, then aye."

"This is why you've never been in a relationship. You wouldn't know someone else's feelings if they slapped you upside the head." She turned away with a stomp.

Marrok grabbed her arm and hauled her back. "Have you not wondered exactly from whom Mathias learned I had the book?"

She hesitated. Damn it, it was a fair question. Still, why would her father risk his life to do away with Mathias, only to go back to the dark side? "Bram said a lot of people heard my thoughts last night."

"But your father once worked hand in hand with Mathias."

"I don't think he would betray us—me—like that. Shock could read my mind, too. H——he did it as we were introduced."

"Shock is no saint, I grant you. But your father has the

motive, the connections, and the history. Deceit runs in le Fay blood."

Olivia scowled. "That's my blood, too. Do you think *I'm* guilty?"

CHAPTER TWELVE

"I DID NOT SAY SUCH. I merely point out that you know Richard not," he dodged the question. " 'Tis also possible that Mathias coerced your father into compliance. He is evil in a way you can scarcely fathom."

She frowned. "Forced. I suppose it's possible . . ."

"Aye, and if he procured the book for Mathias, the wizard might well forgive your father his past transgressions. He could regain his life. No more dodging death, always watching his back. I know you dislike thinking that the fantasy father you have built in your mind may not exist, but consider that to save his hide, Richard Gray might have been willing to forfeit the daughter he hardly knew."

"I won't believe that without proof. Where I come from, people are innocent until proven guilty."

Frustration roiled inside him. Every instinct screamed at him to keep her safe, yet how could he if she refused to see danger lurking in her family tree? "You have no proof he did not."

The fury on her face reminded him that arguing was only likely to get him pushed at arm's length and kicked out of her bed, where he could neither protect nor claim her.

"I merely ask you to consider the possibility," he placated.

"You speak true; we know not his intentions. If I knew for certain who had divulged the book's whereabouts to Mathias, I would know better how to protect it."

She reached for a dressing gown that Sabelle had brought earlier and tossed it on. She secured it around her, then pulled her wet towel loose, and Marrok lamented that he'd seen not one bit of her smooth, pale skin.

"True." With her fingers, she combed the wet strands of her long, midnight hair. He yearned to help her. "But we don't know, and we have to hide the book now."

We. An interesting concept. Did she ask because she wished to help her mate? Would she keep the information strictly between them? Marrok hoped Olivia could see her father's intent—whatever it was—before her desire for his acceptance put everything at risk. At least she acknowledged that Gray had potentially been coerced into betraying her. Marrok hoped that would keep her cautious.

"Indeed."

She glanced around at the little red volume on the table. "Where? I don't think it's wise to hide it where we can't guard it. Otherwise, Bram could easily find it himself."

"I thought as much."

Including her in the task of keeping the book hidden served multiple purposes. It kept them together. With some instruction, she could conceal the book in magical ways. And if the hiding place made it back to Richard Gray, it would tell Marrok how willing she was to please her father. That was key. Protecting and needing her, yet wondering if she would choose Gray over him would weaken Marrok. He wanted to believe in the honesty shining from her eyes. If she betrayed him . . . well, he would know. And the eternal misery he'd endure would be more hellish than anything he'd suffered thus far.

A brief knock sounded on the door. Marrok wrenched it open. A servant handed him clothes that Sabelle had altered to fit them. Olivia changed in the bathroom, and as he donned the trousers, he acknowledged that Bram's sister had mastered magical domesticity.

"They fit perfectly," Olivia said, emerging from the bathroom in a pair of jeans and a simple black V-neck T-shirt that clung to her breasts in a most enticing way.

He was doing his utmost to respect the fact that she didn't want sex now. Wanting to hold her near and wondering if she wore a bra was making his new jeans uncomfortable. "Have you ideas where to hide the book?"

"There aren't many places here."

"I reached the same conclusion."

"But I was thinking . . ."

Marrok braced against a repeat of her suggestion that he give the diary to Richard for "safekeeping."

Before she could say a word, another knock on the door sounded. Marrok tugged it open with rising impatience. If Bram and his staff were going to be down his bloody throat this much, he and Olivia would have to go elsewhere just to get some damn peace.

In the threshold, Bram's sister stood with a hesitant smile. Likely the most beautiful female he—or any other man— would ever set eyes on. She seemed the soul of kindness and gentle temper, but intelligence and cunning lay behind those lovely blue eyes.

"Oh, splendid. The clothes fit." She smiled.

"Indeed. We thank you."

"My pleasure. So, anyone hungry? The Anarki were very rude to pop in before you could eat breakfast."

Olivia nodded. "Famished."

"Breakfast will be served in a quarter hour in the dining

room. Down the stairs and to your left. Follow the scent of eggs and sausage."

"Thank you." Olivia smiled at Marrok. "We're grateful to you and your brother."

"It's our pleasure."

Naturally, Marrok thought. Bram was now one step closer to the Book of Doomsday.

Sabelle turned away, then whirled back. "Oh, I almost forgot—" She snapped, and into her hands a small leather volume appeared. "This is for you, Olivia. It's a simple book of spells to get you started. My brother says you were not raised with magic?"

"Not at all."

"Then this will help catch you up so you can perform a bit of magic before transition. You'll hardly be setting lakes on fire, but with practice, you'll master the basics . . . like hiding the diary from my brother." She winked and turned away.

The moment Marrok shut the door, Olivia frowned. "Wouldn't she want her brother to have the book?"

"One would think, but . . ." He shrugged.

Olivia opened the little volume. "This might help us. What if I got you a hunk of wood? You could carve a hiding place for the diary, maybe something that would . . . I don't know, attach to the furniture or mount to the ceiling somehow? And maybe we could find a way to make it lock."

He stared at her. Naught about Richard. Simply the two of them, working together.

With rising hope, he peered at the furniture, and all sorts of possibilities leapt out at him. Attaching it inside the armoire beside the door or the credenza near the airy windows might do. Or under the massive bed. He could carve something to the book's dimension to blend beneath the existing furniture.

Marrok smiled. Her solution was simple but brilliant.

"You like that idea?" she asked.

"Love it." He couldn't resist kissing her.

Olivia beamed. Mayhap he had been foolish to judge her with so cynical an eye and that growing up apart from magic had kept her spirit less tainted? Perhaps he had misjudged her excitement to meet her father as a foolhardy, impetuous devotion?

Or perhaps she lets you grow complacent before helping Richard once more to earn his favor.

As much as Marrok hated to think it, ignoring the possibility only endangered her and the book more.

Blood will tell. If Olivia was indeed a typical le Fay, hers would soon be screaming.

"You high-handed prick! What's this bloody summons about? I was cozy with a blonde and a pint."

Bram stared at the wizard. At nearly six and a half feet tall with blazing green eyes, Isdernus Rykard wasn't someone anyone intelligent trifled with. Bram didn't count himself as stupid. But desperate times . . . Having Ice under his roof was definitely a desperate measure.

The Rykards were a crafty lot—and distrusted because of it. Through the centuries, they had lied and cheated their way into a great deal of property, some of it Rion lands. Despite the fact their rightful owners had enchanted it to be fallow and dead until it passed back into proper hands, they refused to return it. Bastards—the lot of them. And that was little compared to the personal history between them.

But at the moment, Bram didn't have the luxury of hate.

"If I demanded you appear tonight, Rykard, it's because Mathias is back and magickind is in a dire situation. You've heard that, right?"

"Yes."

Lucan crossed the room to stand beside Bram. "The events of the past three days are alarming. And will grow worse."

Bram nodded. "Indeed. The Doomsday Diary has been found. It—"

"Bloody hell, man! Did you grab it? Hide it?" Ice demanded.

"No."

Ice's expression was both incredulous and appalled. At this point, Bram could only hope that Olivia would help break Marrok's curse soon. He had to get that damn diary, before Mathias found a way to steal it.

"When the time is right, we'll secure it," Bram assured. "At the moment, Marrok of Cadbury holds it. He is currently upstairs with his mate."

"The Anarki attacked him this morning," Lucan added. "We all fought and barely escaped with the book and our lives."

Ice swore. His face, like well-carved stone, tightened, his narrow eyes glowing a furious green.

"We need your help. Unless you want more abducted women to suffer your sister's fate—"

"Don't you *dare* use Gailene as some rallying cry for me!"

"It's not my intent to offend, just to help you understand the urgency," Bram gritted out and turned to address the rest of the men. Lucan silently provided support with a nod. Duke looked on with a studied air of boredom, but Bram wasn't fooled.

Bram went on. "What of the frightened children forced to perform unspeakable magic? If we hurry—"

"Hurry?" Ice cut in, grinding his teeth so hard it was a wonder he had any molars left. "He's already got those kids' souls. We can't help them now."

"Do you suggest we wait for Mathias to grow more confident? For the Anarki's numbers to swell with more magical children and humans they've managed to bewitch? When do we take action? When Mathias is knocking down our doors and threatens all we hold dear?"

Like magickind did last time. Bram didn't say it; he didn't have to. Everyone in the room knew their people had been slow to act during Mathias's last ascent to power. No one had wanted to believe someone so evil walked among them. Only a handful of brave wizards had acted, managing to defeat Mathias and rid magickind of such a cancer.

"We all know who brought Mathias down last time."

"The Brethren," Duke murmured.

"Shock, you're late. Do you know about the Brethren?"

They all turned to the man entering the room.

The incoming wizard glared hatchets at Lucan behind black sunglasses, then shifted his gaze back to Bram. "I *am* capable of reading. I know magical history."

That wasn't all he was rumored to be capable of—but everything was just rumor. Shock, like the rest of his clan, kept to himself. His long hair added to his unsavory appearance. Built big for strength and stamina, Shock was a scary bastard on the best of days. On the worst . . . no one wanted to push the man's limits. People in his tainted bloodline tended to go mad. Bram wondered how close to that edge Shock was.

The furious wizard was scowling at Lucan as if he'd like to help the man with a one-way trip to his own funeral. Of course he would, given their history.

"I wasn't insinuating that you're not learned about magical history. But you were barely alive when Mathias was last in power."

"I know what happened."

"After the Brethren defeated Mathias nearly two hundred years ago," Bram went on. "They disbanded, vowing that if magickind ever saw dark times again, they would reunite."

"They've all moved on to their nextlife," Ice protested.

"I'm not suggesting we find the old members of the Brethren; I'm suggesting we *replace* them."

"Become Brethren warriors to take down Mathias and the Anarki?" Ice no longer sounded annoyed.

"Exactly. But unlike the last Brethren, this group has another task. We have the Book of Doomsday under this roof. It's imperative we keep it out of Mathias's hands. So I suggest we pair the old purpose with the new."

Ice asked, "We protect the book and we defeat Mathias?"

Bram nodded. "Who's with me? Several of you have helped protect the diary already, but who will officially join the cause?"

"You know I will," Lucan answered immediately.

Bram acknowledged his friend with a grateful nod.

"I'll join. Vastly more entertaining than watching my parents plan my brother's wedding to a human girl," Duke murmured.

Relief chugged through Bram. With Duke came his powerful connections and a sizable fortune.

That left Ice and Shock—the two hardest sells. Shock had claimed after Mathias's first attack that he would help, but he'd been largely absent since. The wizard was big and struck fear in others . . . when he showed up. But in coming here, he was defying his family. That had to mean something.

Shock turned, angling his body away from Lucan. "Look, I have no quarrel with you. As long as I don't have to work with the bloody mate thief, I'll—"

"Mate thief?" Lucan snarled. "You and I both issued the Mating Call. She chose me. I did *not* steal."

"You waited to ask her until you knew I had, until you knew she was thinking of saying yes. That's stealing in my book."

"I didn't steal anything that didn't want to be stolen, you bast—"

"Gentlemen," Bram cut in, his tone a friendly warning. Lucan was his friend, but Bram felt a twinge of sympathy for Shock. "I'll keep the two of you as far apart as possible," Bram promised. When Lucan cursed, he went on, "We need Shock, so whatever bad blood lies between you, put it aside for now. Saving magickind is bigger." Then he turned to Shock. "Thank you."

Shock shrugged, straightened his sunglasses, then sought a solitary corner again.

"What about you, Ice?"

"What, fall in with a bunch of rich pricks and a madman?" Ice's harsh laugh could have scraped the paint off the walls. "Hell, no."

"You want Mathias tearing through magickind?"

"I want to protect what's left of my family."

"Then help us stop Mathias."

"Who'll stay and protect our loved ones? You've got a sister. Imagine knowing that a sick freak like Mathias had taken her, then forced her to subm—"

"Leave Sabelle out of this."

"Why? Mathias didn't leave Gailene out of his evil schemes. We just got heartbreak and a mangled body scorched with his brand."

"Then do something."

Ice hesitated. "I don't need a bored rich boy on a Good Samaritan trip for that. I'll do it myself."

With a turn, Ice made for the door, his long, economical strides eating up the Italian slate floor. Bram knew the cause needed him. He had to bring out the big guns—now.

"Alone, he'd just kill you, too. Is that what Gailene would have wanted?"

Just then a pop and a puff of white smoke burst in front of Bram's face. *Thank God*. He'd been waiting for this: a photo of the body of Auropha MacKinnett, the girl in his vision. Magickind knew of the attack on the family, but seeing the horror and tragedy in the picture made a much bigger impact. Bram hated having to use the girl's dreadful death to make a point, but he was out of more polite options.

After the smoke dissipated, the image floated in the air. What he saw would scare the hell out of anyone who had a heart—or a brain in their head. "Do you want more innocent women winding up like this?"

He sent the picture across the room, right into Ice's face. The rest of the men crowded around.

Arms and legs sprawled wide, the young witch looked up from the picture with silent terror in her sightless eyes. Once, she'd been pretty. Now, she looked horrified, violated, desecrated. Blood soaked her thighs and the ground between. Her pubic hair had been removed and the Anarki symbol, Mathias's signature, had been branded red into the soft skin there.

"Dear God," murmured Duke as he cast his eyes down.

Lucan grimaced and turned away.

Shock recoiled. "The sick bastard."

"This will happen again and again if we fail to band together," Bram stated. "Ice?"

The man's eyes glowed—fury, retribution, terrible sadness—though he was doing his damnedest to look unmoved. Finally, Ice swallowed and closed his eyes. Then he sighed.

"I'm in."

In the bathroom, Olivia stared in the mirror and sighed with frustration.

From around the corner, Marrok peeked in on her. "Is something amiss?"

"No makeup, no hair clip, no brush . . ."

"You had no makeup until we dropped by your flat the other day."

"But I had your hairbrush to borrow."

"Is that why there are long hairs in my brush?" he teased.

Her heart jerked at his smile. She really was going to have to watch herself . . . though part of her feared the warning was futile. She already cared, way more than she should. But why was he teasing her? To smooth over their recent arguments about his lies, placate her after his suspicions about her father?

"I have nothing here," she groused. "I look—"

"Gorgeous?"

God, the man could be so sweet, it was hard not to fall for him. "Like a refugee."

"You were unconcerned about your looks at my cottage."

"Well, it was just us, and you were a horny kidnapper. Of course I didn't want to look good."

He laughed. "I will see about obtaining a few common items for us after breakfast."

"Thank you."

"I want to take care of you. That is what a mate does. Remember, I will protect you from *any* threat."

Including her father. Before she could respond, he laid a brief, fierce kiss on her lips, then took her hand, grabbed the Doomsday Diary, and led her from the bedroom.

They descended the stairs and drifted down the wide, airy hallway, made stunning by exquisite tile floors and rows of marble pillars flanking both sides.

As they approached the breakfast room, Olivia saw Bram awaiting them outside an open door to their left.

"Breakfast will be ready shortly. May I have a word with you first?" Bram asked Marrok. "Olivia, you're welcome to come, if you like."

Beside her, Marrok tensed, as if gearing up to be battle ready. "Rion, we appreciate the hospitality. We will not trouble you for long. I doubt you would stage an inquisition to ask about the length of our visit, so I will assume this involves the Book of Doomsday and decline your 'gracious' invitation."

Olivia saw his hands tighten around the book. He would guard it with everything inside him. Would he go so far as to pretend devotion for her, too?

"Actually, it has little to do with the book and everything to do with this morning's battle. Please." Bram gestured into the sitting room again.

With a sigh, Marrok placed his hand at the small of Olivia's back and led her into the room.

Room? It was like a museum. A gilt fireplace, heirloom rugs. Traditional mixed with modern to create an eclectic but expensive effect. And the art? She wanted to cry at how beautiful it was. As she studied each piece, she felt her jaw drop. Was that an original Pollock on his wall? Nearby was a statue that reminded her very much of a . . .

"Is that a Bernini?"

Bram frowned absently. "Art would be Sabelle's department, but I believe so. Please sit."

They dropped down onto a small velvet sofa facing a huge picture window that showed off the bright sun of a cheerful morning. Hard to believe that a mere two hours ago they'd been fighting for their lives.

She'd been so dazzled by the art, she hadn't paid attention to the other four men in the room. Three she remembered from Bram's party. One she didn't know at all.

In the far corner, the marine/biker guy she recalled, Shock, was decked out in leather and badass, complete with sunglasses and killer attitude. Lucan all but growled at the man, a good indication that he had no problem challenging

Shock, despite the fact he had four inches of height and forty pounds on Lucan. Near the door, the real-life duke hovered, shrewd, pedigreed, and gorgeous. His designer khakis, crisp shirt, and impeccably expressionless stare belonged in Bram's palace.

But the unfamiliar man . . . He was a mountain, almost as tall as Marrok, but rather than being good-looking in a stark, masculine way, he was flat-out scary. His dark hair was merely stubble inching up from his scalp. Intense green eyes pinned her in place. A model's cheekbones slashed across his strong face. Below the neck was all Conan the Barbarian-style: enormous shoulders, biceps, and pectorals. He wore a black T-shirt, camouflage pants, and dirt-crusted combat boots.

Beside her, Marrok clutched the diary in a death grip. "What the devil is this, an ambush? I will not surrender the diary."

"Think of this as a mass plea."

Olivia had seen the wizard teasing, calculating, but never quite this determined.

Pure fury narrowed Marrok's eyes—and no surprise. Olivia was feeling a little ganged up on, too. "I will not give you the book."

"I won't ask for it. I know better. What we need now is your help."

"*My* help?"

Bram nodded. "First, thank you for jumping into the battle today. If not for you, Lucan, Duke, and I would have been completely overrun by the Anarki."

"Do not thank me for protecting my mate. It is her I sought to rescue, not you."

"Of course. I'm sure, however, that you did not fail to notice that the rest of the Doomsday Brethren and I—"

"Doomsday Brethren?" Marrok cut in.

Bram nodded. "We're wizards banding together to defeat Mathias and help you protect the book. Lucan and Duke, whom you met at my party, captured the Anarki in front of your house early this morning." They nodded at Marrok. "Along with Shock, whom you also met at my party." The dude in leather sneered. "And Ice, whom you did not."

"Is five enough wizards to fight an army the size of Mathias's?" Olivia asked.

"No, especially not after what we saw this morning. The Anarki is comprised of more former humans than wizards. Wizards we can fight with magic. The half-dead . . ." Bram shrugged. "They deflect magic. I'm not certain why, perhaps because they have no soul."

She shivered. It sounded awful. They looked horrific. And she knew there were many more out there. "How do they come to be half-dead?"

"Dark magic. The soul cannot be removed from the body without the individual's consent. He or she has to release it. After Mathias captures them, he uses his well-honed skills to make people beg. The promise to wipe away the shattering memories or unbearable pain will prompt virtually anyone to surrender their soul to him. Then, with a powerful bit of dark magic . . . Well, you saw."

"How is it possible to fight someone so insane?"

Bram answered with a grim smile. "I believe it's crucial to reduce the number of nonmagical Anarki. Mathias has made them impervious to magic, so the Doomsday Brethren cannot fight them." Bram turned his solemn stare back to Marrok. "That is why we need you. We must learn human combat, what's needed to dispense with the half-dead. You skewered several at once. I saw you punch them. Olivia shot two. These methods work. And we are clueless. Mathias will slaughter us unless we learn to fight as you do."

Marrok sat back in his chair. "You want me to teach you guns, knives, fist fighting?"

"Yes. Anything that can be used against the human Anarki. Wands were useless against them. All the Doomsday Brethren are warriors to the core. I know casualties are a part of war, but I cannot abide sending them into battle unless they know how to defeat their opponents."

Marrok said nothing into the long silence, and Olivia wondered what he was thinking.

Finally, Bram stepped into the quiet. "You are likely wondering what's in it for you, why you should throw your lot in with us. In exchange for teaching us human combat, we vow to provide magical protection for the Doomsday Diary and your mate."

With a swish of his fingers, Bram produced a trio of images. "This is the aftermath of an Anarki attack."

Immediately, the pictures had her clapping her hands over her mouth, to contain both her scream and her bile. Blood everywhere. Chaos. Sightless eyes. Naked, abused bodies. Men, women, babies. The pictures reeked of pain. Her stomach churning, Olivia looked away.

Beside her, Marrok clenched his jaw. He wanted to be unmoved by the photos, but he wasn't.

"This could be any of us," Bram went on. "All of us, if we don't band together to stop Mathias. He won't rest until he has the book in his power. And you," he swung his gaze back to Olivia, "are particularly at risk. According to our prisoner, Mathias believes you're critical to his plan. He will kill anyone he must to get his hands on you. God help you if he does."

Olivia swallowed, fear stabbing her. Having seen these pictures, she didn't want to be one of Mathias's victims, stripped and tied, used up and bled out, branded and left to die.

"What else has Mathias done since his return?" Marrok's voice was just above a hush.

"Odd disappearances. Missing reports among the male human population in England are up threefold in the last month, I just discovered. There have been two full-scale attacks on magical families, one on a member of the ruling Council. The other on a family with two breedable daughters. One of the girls is dead, the other missing."

Olivia singled out one of the images. "This picture shows what Mathias did to the dead woman?"

"It's called *Terriforz*," called the scary one by the door.

"Tell them, Ice," Bram suggested.

Menace rolled over Ice as he prowled between her chair and Marrok's. "It's a magical rape. Mathias gets off on torture." Ice's voice trembled. "*Terriforz* kills slowly. He makes her beg for it, but leaves her fully aware that she's being raped over and over. After Mathias got tired of the victim in the picture, he gave her to his army. She bled to death. He's already moved on to the next victim."

Olivia gasped, and Ice turned those green eyes on her. She felt the instant chill. To say he stared at her as if she were an insect under a microscope would be an understatement. "You're the le Fay woman."

"Olivia." Should she offer her hand? In the end, she didn't. He just looked too scary.

"It seems like you're in the shit or you wouldn't be here."

"The Anarki have my mate's address."

Ice glanced at Marrok and greeted him with a short nod. Marrok returned the gesture.

"As I said before," Bram went on. "We have no training in mortal combat. Mathias's army is filled with beings resistant to magic. How can we keep the balance for magickind if we're unable to fight them?"

"How much can the five of you accomplish?" she asked.

"Likely not enough," Bram acknowledged. "But it's better than not trying at all."

Marrok hesitated, then set his jaw. "I want no part of this. Staying here places Olivia in greater danger." Marrok still clutched the book with white knuckles. "I will take her elsewhere and—"

"And if they follow you? Find you?"

"They will not."

"Bullshit!" Bram thundered. "Now that they know who has the book, they will hunt you down, no matter where you hide. They already have."

Marrok dismissed Bram with a wave of his hand. "Mathias had help locating me."

"Agreed. Someone at the party overheard Olivia's thoughts and came after you, but we don't know for certain who betrayed us. And that doesn't change the fact that Mathias—"

"I have an idea who betrayed us," Lucan said suddenly.

"Who?" Marrok whipped around to face the wizard.

Olivia tensed, hoping like hell Lucan had a better theory than Marrok's. It couldn't be her father. It couldn't. Granted, she didn't know him well, and he had been Mathias's second in command, but it didn't make sense to her to take the guy out once, then help him gain power again. She was going to get to the bottom of it all—soon.

Lucan's burning blue gaze suddenly snapped across the room. "Shock can read others' thoughts. He must have heard Olivia's last night. His family is crawling with Mathias sympathizers. How many of your brothers turned Anarki, Shock? Zain, the one we captured, for sure."

At the sound of his brother's name, Shock jolted. "He's barely more than a kid, damn it."

"Old enough to don Anarki robes and kill people. You'd

stand to gain a lot if Mathias's high-minded ideals about equality were adopted."

Shock lunged over the sofa to leap at Lucan's throat. "Bastard! I don't piss about to get what I want. I leave that to you."

Lucan held off Shock's attack—barely—with a raised hand that seemed to create some invisible force field. But the effort was costing him. Sweat broke out across his forehead. He tensed, the tendons standing out in his neck as he strained to maintain control. And still, Shock kept charging, cursing Lucan in creative ways that made Olivia's jaw drop.

Finally, Shock flung a hand in Lucan's direction. A buzzing sound filled the room. Lucan gasped as if a thousand-pound weight had settled on his chest, then jolted. He dropped his hand, and Shock invaded his personal space with a growl, wrapping his hand around Lucan's neck.

"Listen, you holier-than-thou wanker, I—"

"What is your magical blood mixed with?" Lucan croaked. "Your whole family is known for evil tempers. Did your tainted blood win out after Bram's get-together? Did you get cozy with Mathias?"

Shock's fingers tightened around Lucan's neck. "Your mate's too good for you."

Lucan leaned into Shock's face. "Are the rumors true? Are you part vamp? Or are you infected with darklust? Is that the reason for the sunglasses, to hide those lust-filled stares you can't control?"

"The sunglasses are to stop you from seeing the exact moment I'm going to rip you apart with my bare hands."

"Stop, both of you!" Bram barked.

Evidently, he'd had enough of this argument, and Olivia couldn't blame him. Lucan enjoyed baiting Shock. And Shock . . . Was there really such a thing as being part vampire?

Bram, though not the biggest badass in the room, carried the mantle of a leader, cool most of the time, but in your face when he had to be—like now.

"Lucan, I know you and Shock have . . . issues. But I do not believe he betrayed us. By helping us in the first place, I have no doubt he has put himself at odds with much of his family, and still he remains."

"As a spy!" Lucan insisted.

Olivia agreed. She had to—or face the thought that her father had betrayed her.

"You're way off, dickhead," Shock spat.

Olivia had no doubt that, behind Shock's sunglasses, the wizard glared out a death wish.

"Enough," Bram said to Lucan before he addressed the group. "The truth is, we don't know exactly who our Judas is. I won't believe it's someone in this room." He cast a hard glare to Lucan. "Nor will you. Anyone telepathic at the party had the information. Any of them could have told Mathias, and we will likely never know who. Fighting the Anarki and learning to eliminate the half-dead is our priority. So, Marrok, will you train and join us?"

CHAPTER THIRTEEN

MARROK SAT BACK in his chair. Six pairs of eyes burned into him, none more than Olivia's.

Being denied the chance to replenish their bond and her strength was playing havoc with his head. But that would have to wait. The possibility that she was conspiring with her father to earn the man's affection disturbed him. But ignoring the possibility that she distanced herself from her mate because she had sided with her sire only placed her and the book in more danger. He could not afford to make decisions based on fear, denial, or ignorance of the magical world.

He needed an ally. Though he hated to admit it, the job of protecting both the book and Olivia while fighting the Anarki and Mathias was too big for him alone. Part of being a good warrior was knowing when to align with someone.

He knew of only one person in the room, who, without a doubt, would never take Mathias's side.

Marrok tore his gaze from Olivia's worried one and focused on Bram. "I must speak to you. Alone."

Surprise flickered across Bram's face, but Marrok could read men. His request was not unwelcome.

"Right. Out with you," Bram said to the other men. "Let me talk to the warrior."

With a mixture of shrugs and disgruntled stares, the others filed out the office door, all except Olivia, who hadn't moved an inch. She, more than anyone, could not hear this.

He turned to her. "I'm sorry, love. Can you leave us for just a minute?"

His request clearly hurt her. Marrok watched emotion churn in those dazzling violet eyes, but didn't apologize. If he could prove his worries false, he would find a million ways to make it up to her. If not . . .

Stiffly, she rose and left.

Bram shut the door softly behind her. "What's on your mind?"

"I would not say we have been friends."

"I've tried. You seem not to appreciate my finer qualities."

"After my experience with Morganna, you will understand why I distrust those who wield magic."

"And here I hoped you'd come to understand that we're not all evil freaks."

Marrok smiled faintly. "After the attack this morning, I have reevaluated my position. I trust no one except—and I never believed I would say this—you. When you crossed the magic circle at my cottage, it was clear you could have entered and stolen the book anytime you wished."

Bram nodded.

"Why did you restrain yourself?"

"To build your trust. I didn't know exactly where you'd hidden the diary. Stealing it does no good because I don't know if any dark magic comes with it. Some objects can be cursed so that if they're taken from their makers, bad things happen."

"Like the book locking and never opening again?"

"Or worse. Illness, death, tragedy . . ."

"So you restrained yourself?"

"I continued to hope that if I helped you get free of your curse, you'd pass the diary into my hands for safekeeping. Such a powerfully magical object should be well protected from Mathias. So until your curse is ended and your connection to the book severed, stealing it could do more harm than good."

Logical, Marrok supposed, in a magical sort of way. "Had you ever met Richard Gray before your party?"

"No. He rang me once, years ago. I'd read up on him, of course. After Olivia said the man was her father, I floated word 'round the magical underground types that I had information Gray might want. When he showed up at my party, I asked if he had any children. He supplied me with Olivia's name, age, and London address."

Why would the man know so much about Olivia, yet never take the time to meet her? "You let him in simply to reunite father and daughter? I doubt your motives were that touching."

"Olivia is your mate and a le Fay. I don't think it's a co-incidence that one le Fay woman created the instrument of your torture, while another completes you. Somehow, Olivia is the key to ending your curse."

"And if you help me find peace, then you obtain the Doomsday Diary more quickly."

Bram shot him a self-deprecating smile. "Yes, but Richard Gray likely knows more about the diary than anyone."

Marrok sighed and sat back, steepling his fingers. "My cooperation, if I give it, does not come without a price."

"Naturally."

Bram had nerves of steel. Though he looked calm, Marrok knew that the future of Bram's Brethren—indeed, magickind—rested on the man's ability to persuade a warrior who loathed magic to teach wizards to fight like mortals.

His and Olivia's lives depended on evading Mathias, something Marrok was uncertain he could do without magical help. If Bram's forefather could defeat a bitch like Morganna, Bram himself likely had the skills to deal with Mathias.

"Olivia is protected—no matter who threatens her, what it costs, or how many die."

"That is a given. She is critical to both sides. We questioned Zain, the Anarki Lucan and Duke captured. His mission was to take Olivia unharmed to Mathias, along with the book. Mathias called her 'valuable' to his cause."

Thoughts raced through Marrok's brain even as his blood turned to ice. He resisted the urge to swear—something too telling while negotiating. Instead, he crossed his ankles, acting as if he had not a care.

"So my hunch about Olivia being critical to the book is correct. Which leads me to his former comrade. I do not trust

Richard Gray. Should he come here, I want him watched. He must never be alone with Olivia."

Suddenly, Bram burst out laughing. "You have balls of steel. At the thought of their mates in danger, most magical men would have a panic level somewhere near atomic. Yet you sit there like a stone. No wonder history recorded you as a great tactician."

Except when it came to his cock. Likely, Olivia was a mistake he should not have made, but he still could not regret her—even knowing that, because of her, he sat squarely in the middle of a war he cared little for and that the very woman he tried to protect might ultimately stab him in the back to please a parent who had never troubled himself to find her.

"Let us bypass the pleasantries. You want me to teach you and your men how to fight like warriors in . . . weeks? Days?"

Suddenly sober, Bram nodded. "Wizards have abilities that will allow us to master skills faster than humans, but we still haven't a moment to lose. Mathias will do anything to obtain the diary or Olivia. He can't succeed."

"Indeed not. This place must become a fortress, guarded with everything possible."

"We have spells and enchantments on it, some placed here by Merlin himself. It's tight."

"Call me old-fashioned, but I want eyes in the very topmost tower scanning the land every direction, every moment of every day." He'd love to have high-powered rifles or rocket launchers, but they were bloody difficult to obtain and would be useless in the hands of the untrained. "And only by those you trust, who have a vested interest in our success."

"Done. Olivia and the book will be safe as long as the Doomsday Brethren are well trained."

"They will be. What you suggest will require eighteen

hours each day of sweating dedication. You will hurt as you never have in your life. You will cry and beg for mercy, and I will have none."

"You will find us up to the challenge."

"Shock, perhaps. Maybe Ice, too. If Lucan can channel his anger . . ." Marrok shrugged. "Duke looks far too privileged to sweat for hours on end. Tell him to leave his designer clothes at home."

Bram cracked a smile. "Yes, sir. And what is your assessment of me?"

"When I am done with you, you will no longer look like magic's pretty boy. But you will be ready to fight."

"That's what's important." Bram stood and extended his hand across the desk. "Do we have a deal?"

Marrok took Bram's hand in a firm grip and gave it a decisive shake. "Deal."

After breakfast, Marrok journeyed upstairs to find Olivia lounging on the bed, reading her new spellbook, apparently in a snit, since she refused to look at him. So she hadn't liked being asked to leave Bram's office. It had been for the best. Insulting her father within earshot would only rile her again.

Olivia closed her eyes, mumbled something to herself, then opened her eyes wide.

"Damn it!"

"What are you doing?"

She arched a dark brow at him. "Oh, I'm supposed to let you in on stuff, but you don't have to tell me anything."

"Forgive me for protecting you from what I sense will be a terrible war."

She glared at him and turned away. Marrok was tempted then and there to cover her mouth with his own, stretch her out on the bed and take her until she cried his name, until she acknowledged their bond again.

But the wizards were waiting to begin their training now. Their assistance in Olivia's protection must start immediately, no matter how badly he wanted otherwise.

"I'm not a hothouse flower. You can't protect me from everything."

"Protecting is in a warrior's nature. I am too old to change."

"And I'm too independent to be cosseted."

It was one of the things that both attracted and infuriated him. "I will do my best to remember such. Now, tell me why you are cursing."

"Well, I'm guessing you're going to be training all the guys to fight, right?"

"Aye."

"We need to hide the diary before you leave."

Excellent notion. Hopefully, it would be temporarily safe, since all the men would be with him . . . unless Olivia contacted her father and told the man where to find it.

"What has that to do with your cursing?"

She cast him an impatient glance. "We talked before breakfast about you carving something to affix to the furniture to hide the book. So I was trying to conjure up the wood for you to carve."

"Is it not working?"

"Not worth a damn. While you shoveled down your third helping of eggs, I was trying to figure this out. I'm focusing, picturing what I want, pouring my energy into it. I know I'm not going to learn magic overnight, but . . . argh!"

He sat beside her on the bed and forced himself to cup her cheek—and nothing more. "Can I help?"

She shrugged. "I don't see how."

"Magic requires concentration and desire for the outcome?"

"Yeah, but maybe since I haven't transitioned yet, I'm trying to do too much."

He wondered if he were an imbecile to encourage her magic; but he hated to see her glum. "Sabelle said these spells were simple. You have powerful blood. Believe in yourself."

Olivia turned a soft gaze to him that hit him in the chest . . . and below the belt. In days, the woman had wrapped herself around him, and no matter how often he told himself to disengage, he could not.

"Thanks. Maybe this will help." She took his hand and squeezed it. Closing her eyes, Olivia concentrated. "How big do you need the wood?"

"Just enough to hide the diary. I will devise a way to affix it to the furniture."

She nodded and started mumbling again, squeezing his hand tighter and tighter. Zounds, who knew his woman was so strong?

Suddenly, a hunk of smooth cherry, the same color as the furniture, appeared in the middle of the bed.

Her eyes popped open again, and she squealed. "I did it! My very first bit of real magic!"

"You did." He couldn't resist the chance to plant a congratulatory kiss on her mouth. She had used magic for the first time to help him, no one else.

Had he been too suspicious of her and her heritage for naught?

"It was easier this time. It was like I had more energy because you were here. Now you can carve a hiding place for the book."

Quickly, he whittled the hunk of wood, kneeling at the head of the bed periodically to measure the fit of the piece in a niche beneath. With rapid hands, he carved until the wood fit in the corner, behind the support for one of the bed legs. He placed the book inside and affixed it to the bottom of the bed, beside the post nearest his head. As Marrok held her hand again, Olivia managed to conjure a lock and enclosed it with a spell. If she genuinely wished to help him, that should adequately hide the blasted book. If not . . . He stifled the thought. She had helped him. Mayhap he should try to put the past behind him and judge Olivia on her actions, not her family.

Satisfied for now, Marrok switched his morning clothes for a T-shirt, jog pants and trainers. Now he was ready to teach the wizards to fight like men.

Within a few hours, Olivia had finished reading the book of simple spells, she'd practiced conjuring a bit more, and also managed to move a picture frame, turn on a faucet, and close a door, all with her mind. She was miserable at teleporting, so far, not moving even an inch. She tried not to be impatient; magic wouldn't come overnight. But she wanted it to.

In a way, being magical was a relief. All her life, everyone—even her own mother—had treated her as if she were different. Turns out, she was. Now that she knew how and why, it was almost cool. Except Marrok loathed magic.

She had so many questions, especially about her heritage.

Restless, Olivia wandered downstairs. She couldn't shake the feeling that something was wrong, beyond Marrok shutting her out of Bram's study. The fact her father had once been Mathias's right-hand man definitely ate at her. And her mate was clearly determined to dislike her father, based on his past alone. She didn't blame him exactly. The possibility that she might have uprooted her life to find a man capable of terrible crimes was almost too much to bear. Had his actions left scars on his soul? Likely, or he would never have ultimately chosen the right path. Didn't everyone deserve a second chance? Yes . . . but Marrok had a point. She should check out all the details. And while she was at it, maybe she could find out something more about Marrok's curse and the diary.

In the grand entry hall, she stood and looked around at the gorgeous, expansive house. Surely a place like this had a library.

"Second door on your right," Sabelle provided helpfully from behind.

With a start, Olivia turned to face her. "How did you know—? Oh . . ." The truth hit her. "I thought too loud, didn't I?"

Sabelle sent her a kind smile. "Masking your thoughts takes some getting used to. I try to keep a song in my head if I become upset in public. A very mundane one. People tune you out very quickly if you're mentally singing the alphabet. Off-key works even faster."

Olivia laughed at her hostess's mischievous streak. "I'll keep that in mind."

The witch crossed the floor and offered, "Want help with the library? I don't have to bother with dinner for a bit, and the family collection of books is a bit imposing."

"Sure."

Together, the two women made their way to the open door. Once Olivia peeked inside, her jaw dropped. "Holy cow! You weren't kidding."

"My brother sometimes seems a bit of a cavalier playboy, but he's actually read nearly every book here and brings new ones home all the time."

Wow, Bram a hardcore reader? "How many books are in here?"

"I stopped counting after eight thousand."

And why not? There had to be double that and then some. How was she ever going to find what she wanted? Uneasiness and a ticking clock in her head told her that she needed to start right away.

"Don't panic. What do you need to find?"

Damn, Sabelle was reading her thoughts again. She started humming one of her favorite songs in her head, then wondered if it would really mask her curiosities about her father's past, Marrok's curse, and the diary itself.

"Not yet," Sabelle supplied. "Your thoughts *were* harder to hear this time. Keep practicing. Which subject do you wish to learn about first? I can probably help you quickly with the diary. Bram has already set aside some books he intends to read soon."

Despite the woman's nosiness—and breathtaking beauty—Olivia liked Sabelle. She was friendly, smart, funny, and seemed genuinely nice. Easy to talk to. Olivia didn't have many friends, so this was nice.

"That would be great."

Sabelle crossed the room to retrieve a stack of books on an enormous table. "Curses . . . You want to know about Marrok's?"

"If we get this diary open, how do we end it?"

"I'm not certain." Sabelle plopped the books on the sofa between them. "Let's read."

The pair skimmed books for a good hour. Olivia was about to sigh in frustration until she found something that made her eyes pop. "Here! Here's an account of someone who saw Morganna use the diary. She wrote in it. Which fits. Marrok talked about her writing a curse in it. This also says she could uncurse someone with a stroke of her pen."

"Great. But she's not here."

"Yeah." Olivia sighed. "That's a problem. Unless . . . maybe I could do it?"

"You're a le Fay. Perhaps so."

Olivia read a bit further, hoping to find more information. "This says that she often set the curse with conditions, so it would be broken once her terms were met. Marrok's is that way. He told me that his curse has an out-clause. But he has no idea what it is."

A few minutes later, Sabelle spoke up. "A man Morganna once cursed with the diary tried to steal it. He swore it dissolved in his hands and materialized back in Morganna's."

"What does that mean?"

"Some objects cannot be stolen."

"But Marrok told me that he had one of Morganna's serving maids steal it for him."

"Really? Morganna was known for liking men as bed partners, and disliking them in all other ways. Perhaps she blocked the book from belonging to men or performing magic for men."

Olivia gasped. "One of my professors called it an object of feminine reverence. Do you think that's what it means?"

"It's possible."

"Until we can get it open, we can't test the theory that it responds only to women."

"True, but if Mathias has reached the same conclusion, it explains why he wants to capture you, along with the book, so badly. You're female *and* Morganna's descendant, which would likely make the book more potent."

That scared the hell out of her. The attack at Marrok's

just proved that Mathias was going to great lengths to get what he wanted. "But maybe any woman would do."

"It's possible, but from what we've read, no other woman has ever tested it. You're the most likely to be able to use the book. Mathias knows that."

That was bad. Worse was wondering if the psycho could coerce her father into winning her trust. Or if he already had. "If Mathias can make humans into Anarki, can he mind-control a wizard, too?"

"He can't control anyone without taking their soul. You could tell if that were the case by looking at him."

"Because they'll look like the soulless humans, all rotting and stuff?"

"Exactly. Wizard or human alike, when you remove the soul from the body, they start dying from the inside out."

Olivia breathed a sigh of relief. But that still didn't mean Richard wasn't being coerced in nonmagical ways.

She needed to find something that would tell her exactly what kind of man her father was.

"What is his name?"

"My father? Richard Gray. He's played a role in history, but I don't understand it all. Do you have a book that might explain what happened?"

"Absolutely. He helped bring down Mathias, right? I wasn't alive then, but I think I remember your father's name from school."

"Is he remembered as a hero?" She held her breath.

"To most, I believe. He's definitely been written that way. I'll show you."

Sabelle led her across the room to a musty corner, then pulled a few books free. "These were written after Mathias's exile and contain information on how it happened."

Olivia took them greedily, sank back to the buttery leather sofa. Within a few minutes, she slapped the book closed with a smile and picked up another. Then another. Each time, her grin got wider.

"Well?" Sabelle finally asked. "Great rendition of 'Old MacDonald', by the way."

"Thank you. You didn't hear my thoughts?"

"Snippets only. You sounded pleased."

Nodding, she rose. "This book, like the others, said that when Mathias began abducting the children of Council members, my father secretly contacted their parents and promised the children's safety. The previous Brethren were gunning for Mathias, and my father gave them the location of Mathias's hideaway, led them past the magical protections, pretending he had captured them. Then, together, the Brethren and my father ambushed Mathias and exiled him. The Brethren cheered him, the parents revered him, and the wizards of the Anarki began to hunt him. But many of the new friends he'd made concealed him, some for years. According to these sources, he came to the party late, but he was a hero."

If these accounts of his life were true, then she understood his absence during her childhood and could be at peace with the fact he hadn't wanted to bring death to her door.

But if magickind was anything like mankind, history was always written by the victors. "Is there anything else about him? Anything . . . not so flattering?"

"Yes, but most of it was written by Anarki-sympathizing trash grumbling that your father had cost them their leader. The versions you've read is what they taught in school."

So now she had the truth, and she was ready to help him. Maybe that would help Marrok, too.

But what would happen to him when his curse ended?

"What do you mean?" Sabelle asked, reading Olivia's question.

"He's been immortal. If that's no longer true, will he . . ." She couldn't bring herself to say it, to even think about Marrok dying.

"I don't know. Usually mate-bonds are stronger, since mating is the most powerful magic of all. But then, I've never seen a curse as potent as Morganna's."

Which meant Marrok may or may not survive the end of his curse. Even if he did, he wanted to die anyway. The pain that shafted her at the thought told her how dangerously close she was to loving him.

Olivia wanted to call her father, talk to him, try to figure out whose side he was really on, see what he knew about Marrok's curse. A restless urgency to hear his voice swelled inside her.

"May I use your phone?"

Sabelle snapped her fingers and produced one a moment later, then handed it to Olivia.

Richard answered on the third ring, sounding winded. "Who is this?"

Dad? Richard? "It's me, Olivia. Are you all right?"

"I've been running from the Anarki since leaving your cottage. They were awaiting me when I returned."

Olivia's heart stopped. "But you got away?"

"I'm fine."

"Do you have anywhere to go?"

He hesitated. "No worries. I'll find a place."

Biting her lip, Olivia turned to Sabelle. "My father needs help. I have to go to him."

"I heard him—with my ears. You can't go. It's too dangerous."

Going out alone was like a neon sign to Mathias to abduct

her. And if her father was being coerced or did have any lingering allegiance to the creep, she was playing into his hands.

"Now what? He needs help—"

"Invite your father here. I'll let him past our protections for the day. He can hide for a bit and hopefully dodge the Anarki."

She squeezed Sabelle's hand. "Thank you. You don't know how much this means to me."

"I can hear it. You forgot to sing."

Within minutes of commencing training, Marrok was worried as hell. The wizards were terrible. Their fisticuff skills were deplorable, their sword fighting laughable. Firearms . . . he was afraid to try. No telling what—or who—they would shoot. Clearly, anything as complex as martial arts, much less explosives or modified weaponry, would have to wait. But as Marrok doffed his sweaty shirt and the surprisingly strong November sun beat down on his back, he found himself surrounded by men sworn to become great fighters, and felt a certain kinship.

He had enjoyed moments of brotherhood with Arthur and his army. In some ways, Bram reminded him of Arthur: shrewd, fair . . . deceitful when it suited him. Marrok suspected Bram had a grand plan beyond their alliance that he kept secret, but that had often been Arthur's way. Marrok hated to admit it, but his opinion of Bram had increased today. The spoiled, attention-seeking coxcomb had become a leader.

Oh, he still didn't trust the bastard completely. He was magical and used to manipulation to win his way. But at the moment, he knew Bram's priorities matched his own.

Afternoon rolled into early evening. After dark, the dragging, sweating men headed inside for a break. Massive amounts of food were consumed in moments.

"You poor nonmagical bastards." Ice rolled his shoulders, working through the soreness. "You did this every day for years to master this rubbish?"

Duke groaned. "This makes waving a wand look damn easy."

"Hell. I don't know if I've got legs anymore," Shock complained.

"You will feel them tomorrow," Marrok supplied helpfully. "The lot of you is pitifully out of shape. You *look* fit . . ."

"We aren't meant to lift fifty-pound swords for five hours or knock off one another's heads with our fists." Lucan grimaced, stretching his tightening shoulders.

"Think of how much better prepared you will be to meet the Anarki," Marrok replied.

"It's the only thought that has kept me moving for the past two hours."

Shock snorted. "Precisely. I'm quite motivated by not allowing some soulless, flesh-rotting bastard to whip my arse."

"More, gentlemen?" called a husky female voice from the far end of the obscenely long dining hall. Sabelle lifted a platter still laden with food.

Duke and Lucan both thanked her and declined. Shock followed suit, rising to his feet very slowly—with a vicious curse.

"No more for me," Marrok added. "My thanks for a wonderful dinner."

"Just a wave of my wand . . ." She shrugged. "I have it pretty easy."

Bram merely shook his head and tried to shoo her out of the room. Instead, she looked at Ice, who stared back with the intensity of a laser beam.

Sabelle approached him. "We haven't met. I'm Sabelle."

He rose to his feet, and his green eyes burned. "Isdernus Rykard."

The smile fell from her face.

"Most people call me Ice." He tried to gentle his tone, Marrok could tell. Even so, his voice rattled with a growl.

She took a step back. But Ice just kept coming for her and stuck out his hand.

Glancing between his outstretched palm and his bright, fixated eyes, Sabelle slowly held out her hand.

Before they could shake, Bram stood, huge footsteps eating up the distance between them in a blur of speed until his big body shadowed his sister's. "Sabelle, you have done your duty as hostess. Go."

At her brother's words, she glared at Bram. "I am a woman, not an obedient dog."

"You are still my sister and my ward. *I* decide whose hand you shake. Out. Now."

"You are straining my affection," she warned.

"And you're pushing your luck."

Bram's expression morphed into unbendable fury. Sabelle heaved a sigh of frustration, then stomped out of the room.

As soon as the door closed behind her, Bram turned to Ice. "I need you as a fighter. I will provide instruction and feed you at my table. Do not *ever* touch my sister."

"I'm not trying to shag the perfect princess." Hatred spit from Ice's cold eyes.

Bram ground his teeth together and got right up in Ice's face. "You will not use my sister and 'shag' in the same sentence or I will kill you. Are we clear?"

Ice snorted as he sat again and dug into the last of the food on his plate. "Hold your shotgun. I have no designs on Sabelle. Talk about nightmare in-laws."

Marrok watched the exchange end. Whatever feud lay between Bram and Ice, it was bad.

"This cannot go on," he warned. "You *must* work together,

build trust, know that every man has the other's back—at least on the battlefield. Or you will fail to vanquish Mathias."

Ice and Bram shared a quick glance but nodded. And mercifully shut up.

As a unit they left the dining hall. Night spilled in through the manor's huge windows. At the end of a surprisingly long hallway, Bram threw open some double doors. What had once been a ballroom had been converted into their evening training facility. Every light in the expansive room burned brightly. Someone—servants?—had moved all of their equipment inside. Weapons and protective padding littered the elegant carpet.

And in the center of it all, Olivia stood talking to her father.

How had the sneaky bastard known where to find them? Who had invited him inside?

The older man held her hand, patted it, but there was an urgency to his carriage. Even at a distance, Marrok discerned a rush of mumbled words. Then Richard saw him. And fell silent, his face closing up.

Ah, guilt. It was so strong, he could almost smell it. Acrid. Annoying.

Every protective instinct rumbled to the surface, as Marrok tore across the room in long-legged strides. When he reached Olivia, he wrapped an arm around her and brought her close. Marrok glared at the unwelcome intruder. "Richard Gray, you were not invited here."

"Actually, he was," Olivia cut in. "By Sabelle and me."

So she let Judas into their lair. Was this indicative of a deeper betrayal designed to win the bastard's approval?

"Olivia called me to make certain I had survived the Anarki attack. I was glad to be assured that my daughter was unharmed."

Marrok's eyes narrowed at his mate. "As you see, I protected my mate. While you . . . what? Disappeared? Were you
simply willing to let the Anarki capture your daughter?"

"Stop it! He helped thwart the Anarki by tricking Mathias
into exile—at great personal risk—because it was the right
thing to do," Olivia protested. "I read about it." She grabbed
a book off a nearby table that had been shoved against the
wall. "Why don't you do the same?"

"I know how events must look to you," Richard began.
"But I swear, I have no alliance with Mathias. Do you realize
how badly he wants me dead?"

Marrok grunted. "I suspect they would keep you alive
long enough to lead them to the Doomsday Diary."

"I deeply regret that I was ever a part of the Anarki. All I
want now is to know my daughter. Please see reason. Mathias
will look for her here. He knows exactly who fought beside
you, so he will deduce where you hide."

Bram snorted. "I would love to see him try to invade."

"He knows better," Richard assured. "He'll find a more
subtle way in. But rest assured, he *will* find it. He needs the
book and believes that he must have Olivia to open it. Let
her come with me. I know how to protect her. She should
not be—"

"*No!*" Rage roared through Marrok. As long as Gray was
determined to separate Marrok from his mate, he didn't owe
Olivia's father any modicum of politeness.

Marrok grabbed Richard by the throat and carried him
across the room, slamming him to the wall, then snarled,
"You dare come here when your very presence is a threat?
When the Anarki could be right behind you? You are a fool
if you think I would let her leave with you, even for a second."

"She's my daughter."

"She is my mate. Try to separate us again, and I will break every bone in your body and smile while doing so."

"If Gray wanted to," Bram whispered, "he could rip out your entrails with a spell."

"Not before I knocked a few screws loose in his head."

Not too far to his right, Shock laughed. "Pound him. I know all about Mr. Gray from my brothers. Smarmy bastard who tossed the Anarki over when the shit got too deep. After betraying his boss, the coward ran and hid like a rat in a hole."

That sounded accurate to Marrok. He had disliked Richard Gray on sight.

"Let go of my father's throat, Marrok," Olivia insisted. "Right *now.*"

She was one furious mate. The fact that she refused to see the potential threat the man presented infuriated him all over again. Still, Marrok sighed and let up on her father's neck.

Gray cleared his throat and rubbed his neck, milking the injury for all it was worth.

"He's trying to protect me in his way, just like you are," Olivia shouted. "And this is *my* choice."

Surprise at her words scalded him. "Do you wish to leave with him?"

"No, we're safer here. I know that. I just want you to *listen.*"

"As soon as he stops trying to part us."

"He's talking to me about the diary. He knows stuff that might be helpful, and you dismissing him isn't helping your cause."

Marrok turned a furious glance to Gray.

Richard said, "The diary is locked, yes?"

He considered the shifty wizard. His gut told him the

man had information. If he wanted it, he was going to have to play Gray's game. "It is."

"Because, according to my great-grandmother's writings, the diary has keys and requires someone special to open it."

"Who?"

Gray shrugged. "As with all things, Morganna was mysterious."

"One of my history professors called the diary an object of feminine reverence. I read something today that made me think it's more powerful in a woman's hands," Olivia said to her sire. "Is that right?"

"Morganna's writings never say explicitly, but it would be like her to create a powerful object only for the fairer sex. And it's possible it might be more powerful for a le Fay woman."

"Like me?"

"Indeed."

"Are there any other le Fay women?"

Richard shook his head.

Olivia whistled. "That explains a lot."

"Tell me about the keys," Marrok barked at Richard. "Do you have them?"

"When I was a young man, my mother died. You saw her painting?"

Marrok knew when Olivia's eyes went wide that she recalled the painting of the woman with the symbol around her neck, which was echoed on the Doomsday Diary.

She nodded. "That was your mother?"

"The painting was done before her mating, long before my birth. But upon her death, she left me that thing around her neck. As I said before, it's actually in two parts. Together, they comprise the key that unlocks the diary."

Just as Bram had said Merlin's writings indicated.

Olivia frowned. "Where are the keys now?"

Gray swallowed. "One half I—I gave to Mathias." At the collective gasps and growls, he explained, "It was years ago. He demanded a show of fidelity and—"

"And like the sniveling yes-man you are, you gave him half the key to the end of the world," Ice cut in.

"I believed in equality. At the time, I didn't think he'd actually hurt people—"

Marrok sneered. "Rubbish! How did you think Mathias was going to enforce his will, if not with blood?"

"I was young and idealistic and—"

"Incredibly daft." He itched to put Richard Gray out of everyone's misery. The man smelled like a stinking heap of trouble. "What happened to the other half of the key?"

Again, Gray turned his gaze to Olivia. "I left half with your mother for your protection. I told her why it was important and that if the Anarki knocked on her door, she should give it to them to save you."

"Wh—what does it look like?"

Olivia's voice shook, and Marrok turned to her. She'd gone impossibly white. He dashed from Gray's side to Olivia, in case she sank to the floor.

To his surprise, Ice came behind him, lifted the older wizard by his shirt front and shoved him against the wall again.

"You might be able to zap our immortal friend if the mood struck, but no such luck with me. I'm an Anarki-hating bastard from way back."

Bram might not like Ice, but at the moment, Marrok appreciated the hell out of him. Menace rolled off the green-eyed wizard. Only someone suicidal would cross him. If Gray was smart, he would heed Ice. Marrok hoped Gray remained daft.

"All right?" Marrok wrapped his arms around Olivia and supported her.

"Let him answer." She looked to her father in expectation.

Drawing her closer to his warmth, Marrok glared at Gray.

"The piece hangs from a chain of twined silver and gold." His voice wobbled, violet eyes latched onto Ice with all the fear of someone looking at an ax murderer. "It—it's half of the symbol. The top half. It's an ornately scripted L with rubies."

If anything, Olivia blanched even paler.

Marrok's guess was that his mate had seen the key, perhaps even had it among her possessions. Was she broadcasting that very thought? If so, the last thing he needed was for Richard Gray to "hear" it.

If Gray did, Marrok had a terrible suspicion the Anarki would know it. Within seconds.

"This conversation is over." He picked Olivia up, tossed her over his shoulder and ran for the ballroom's door.

"Wait!" Gray called from across the room. "Do you have it, Olivia?"

"Get him gone now," Marrok snarled as he ran for the exit, hoping he could make it through the door before Olivia mentally or verbally answered.

Before he could escape, she cried, "Yes!"

Marrok carried Olivia down the long gallery and up the stairs. The hard chunk of his shoulder pressed into her belly, his hot hand wrapped around her thigh. Blood rushed to her head—and not just from being upside down.

"Put me down!" She squirmed, fury racing like lava through her veins. "Damn you, now!"

Marrok didn't say a word as his sneakers stamped across the marble floor. He smelled like sweat and man and hard work forged in steel. Olivia tried to ignore his scent and her great view of his ass. Better to focus on the fact she was pissed off.

"How *dare* you drag me out of there like some—some child in need of correction!"

"Did you think before you spoke?" he grunted as he mounted the stairs. "Before you blurted out something that might help Mathias?"

"Mathias?" she shouted to his back, despite the fact the impact of his every step on the stairs jolted her stomach. "Richard isn't the dirtbag's right-hand man anymore. He assured me."

"So of course you believe him?"

"I've been reading magical history books. Three of them. He became a hero! And he's concerned about me. I don't think he's going to sell me out to evil. And he knows more about the diary than anyone. Before you barged in and nearly strangled him, he promised to help us. He may have more information about the book's secrets that might free you from your curse. How the hell can we learn anything if you won't talk to him?"

"We will discern what we must."

"Really? You've had fifteen hundred years and haven't made a lick of progress. Maybe we should try it my way. My father has apologized for the past. You have nothing but circumstantial evidence. I have actual proof that he did the right thing, yet you're determined to believe the worst. Why can't you give him a chance?"

Marrok paused halfway up the stairs. "We know little about him, except he was once Anarki and he never bothered himself to meet you until recently. That does not inspire trust, and I will not risk you."

Olivia saw Marrok's point, but without proof, she wouldn't believe that her own father was lying to her or still had ties to Mathias. "Those books described my father as Anarki enemy number one."

"Deceit is in his blood. I can smell it."

"Um . . . his blood is my blood. Does your little statement include me? I've asked you this before and, you know, I never got an answer."

"Because only you can answer that question. I cannot prove or disprove that you and your father are hatching a scheme to steal the diary."

Pain ripped through her that he could believe that possible. "Hatching? *Hatching?* Unbelievable! You don't trust anyone. You blow suspicions out of proportion. You abducted me, just because I had violet eyes and reminded you of Morganna."

"You *are* le Fay."

"Which doesn't make me an evil, lying bitch, but you don't believe that either. Let me go!"

He began climbing the stairs again. "Never."

Now he was pissing her off. "You threw me out of Bram's office and are trying to keep me apart from my father because you're afraid of what I'll tell him. Admit it."

"All right. Aye. I understand you want your father's affection, but it cannot be at the expense of your safety."

"And the diary's. Isn't that the *real* issue? Your 'protection' is to keep me away from Richard so I don't tell him what I know. And your tenderness is a lie to keep me with you because you probably need me to open the book. But you don't give a shit about *me*."

Marrok simply snorted. He might be bigger than her, but she wasn't taking this crap and certainly not while hanging upside down.

She shoved her hands into his sweatpants, groping around for a waistband to boxers, briefs—whatever. She might not be able to fight him with her fists, but a really vicious wedgie would bring him to his knees.

When her hands slid over smooth, well-muscled cheeks, she realized the problem: he'd gone commando.

"You're not wearing underwear?"

"Never wore them in the Dark Ages. Why start now?"

Argh! This was *not* happening. "You aren't taking me into the bedroom for 'time out' or whatever. It's *my* emblem, *my* father, *my* decision."

"You are *my* mate talking to someone who wishes to steal *my* book."

Impasse. Left with few choices, Olivia took one of her few remaining options: She shoved her hands under his shirt and dug her fingernails into the hard flesh of his back.

Marrok tensed, but kept walking down the looming hall to their bedroom door.

"Is that meant to hurt?" he taunted.

Oh, the jackass! She dug harder into his skin.

No response.

Desperate times were upon her. She dragged out the desperate measures.

Olivia slid farther down his back, until he had to grab on to her knees to keep her on his shoulder. With a smile, she reached around his hips for his balls. If she could just reach low enough to twist them, no doubt he'd fall to his knees. Yeah, he was a tough warrior, but he was still a man with a man's vulnerabilities, right?

She maneuvered herself to one side of his back, and bracing herself with her knee, reached to his front.

And felt his massive erection.

Oh, hell.

She gasped. "This drag-me-to-the-cave stuff has you all torqued up?"

"You hold the answer," he quipped.

And then some. She might as well use his arousal to her advantage.

She nipped at his lower back in an erotic lick and stroked his hard flesh in her palm.

Beneath her, his entire body tensed. "You are playing with fire, woman."

Maybe, but his steps slowed. He faltered. She hoped her touch was setting him on fire, because coiling her fingers around his erection was making her uncomfortably damp.

Suddenly, Marrok stopped, turned. He swatted her ass with a broad palm. A sting fired its way across her butt as he jerked her down, against his body—her back unexpectedly against the wall. Her shirt crept up her torso. Her bra was no match for his determined fingers, and soon he flung both on the floor.

"I warned you."

He growled the words, eyes narrowed. Olivia swallowed, aware that she was half-naked in a hallway that anyone could wander down.

Always, Marrok had been a tender lover. Considerate. Gently thorough. She'd never seen this sexual beast rising to his surface. A hungry predator.

Marrok took her wrists in his hand and pinned them to the wall. His eyes burned into her with a fire so consuming, they looked damn near iridescent. Her belly flipped over. A dam burst between her legs. She shivered.

"Shouldn't you be training Bram and the others?"

His eyes narrowed. "Right after you and I . . . talk."

As his mouth crashed into hers, flattening her against the wall, Olivia sucked in a breath. There wasn't going to be a lot of conversation.

He was ravenous, as if he hadn't had a taste of her for a year, a decade. He sank into her mouth, an insistent male determined to take—and to give—undeniable pleasure designed to make her whimper with need.

"Marrok—" She tore away and whispered in protest. "You said talk."

He stripped off his shirt, then braced his elbows against the wall and panted, his hot breath steaming across her skin. "We are. Eloquently."

Maybe, but they weren't communicating. "You think my father is helping Mathias and that I'm conspiring with him, don't you?"

His fingers tightened. "He is your blood and you have longed to meet him, but we do not know him or his motives well. Be careful."

"Answer the question, damn it. Do you think I'm conspiring with my father?"

CHAPTER FOURTEEN

MARROK HESITATED.

"I deserve a goddamn answer!" Torn between fury and tears, Olivia shoved against the mountain of hard muscle trapping her in place, heating her breasts with his naked chest.

"As do I! You meet the man one night, ring him the next morning, which brings an Anarki army to my door. Now I discover you possess some emblem that unlocks the diary and you said not a word to me, but told him straightaway. What else are you hiding?"

"The Anarki coming to your place had nothing to do with me calling my father, since they already knew how to find you. Whoever read my mind also betrayed the location of the diary to Mathias. My father fought against the Anarki at the cottage, if you'll recall. And the emblem? I didn't know what it was or what it meant until now. It never occurred to me— Never mind, asshole." She struggled against him. "You don't believe me."

"Why tell him?"

"Because the only way we're going to get the book unlocked and get you uncursed is to work with him. Don't you get that?"

Marrok just sent her a stony stare.

"Let me go."

Against her, Marrok tensed. "Nay."

"Your social skills haven't grown during the last fifteen centuries. You can't just accuse me of stabbing you in the back. I'm not Morganna."

"Honesty from her is something I neither needed nor wasted my breath asking for. You . . ." he swallowed, pain shadowing his face. He buried his fists in her hair and stared at her with stark blue eyes. "Do not betray me. You will rip out my heart."

His voice was a whisper, his words a plea. And they melted her like butter.

Was he telling her that she, a woman who had never been wanted, could bring this fierce warrior to his knees? How often had she fantasized about being wanted, having someone who would touch her freely, with affection? Marrok knew it. He could be feigning all this emotion to keep her close until he discovered how to open the diary and end his curse. When he'd met her, he hadn't been hoping for a wife.

When he'd mated with her, it hadn't been for love.

But when he touched her, she swore that nothing—no one—mattered as much to him.

Tears pricked her eyes as Olivia grabbed the hard line of his jaw and looked into his icy-hot eyes. "I know what rejection feels like. Why would I purposely hurt you?"

"Mayhap you resent your abduction, our mating. Or simply because you can."

He'd given her power over him . . . but all she wanted was his touch, his affection. Marrok pressed against her, chest, belly, hips, thighs, as close as he could without being inside her. Then his lips followed, consuming hers in one greedy stroke.

She should stop him, sort out this tangle of thoughts, hopes, and desires before jumping into the fire. But her nipples burned into his chest, and he pulled her deeper into the kiss. Everything inside her incinerated. Letting him go was impossible.

Panting, he pulled back and drilled her with a hot stare. Without words, Olivia knew he wanted to be deep inside her. That look siphoned off her anger and inhibitions. She forgot everything but the moment as he pressed passionate kisses to her neck, his hands drifting to her breasts. His cock pushed between her legs as if begging for entry.

She burned up, itchy and hot, smoldering inside for something only he could give her. Leaning into him, Olivia opened herself to him—her kiss, her need, her heart. He took them, hungry and unrelenting. The contrast of his soft lips and rough stubble mesmerized her.

"Mine," he growled against her mouth, challenging her to deny it.

"For now."

"Forever."

He sounded so determined. Marrok was looking to break his curse and die. Did it really matter to him? Did she?

He kissed her like she did, now at her mouth again, sliding deep. His callused palms burned her breasts, pinched her tight nipples. The pleasure-pain made her gasp. As Marrok unsnapped her jeans and shoved them down her legs and off, he took sensitive nipples in his mouth, one after the other, back and forth. Until she trembled. Arched. Gushed.

Olivia couldn't believe she stood completely naked in Bram's hallway, her back against the wall, panting for Marrok to make love to her. Worse, she didn't want it to stop.

Marrok nipped at her breast with his teeth, then licked softly. As he repeated the process on her other, he shoved his sweatpants past his hips.

"Open for me."

The need to feel him deep rose hard and fast. Olivia complied, and he kissed his way down until he kneeled between her spread feet. When he latched on to her wet folds with his mouth, tongue toying with her, she cried out, grabbing the dark silk of his hair as his lips spread desire all through her.

He lapped at her and her need soared. As she whimpered his name, he nibbled at her thigh, rose to kiss her belly, suckle a breast, breathe against her lips. "Release all your need unto me."

Then Marrok lifted her, wrapped her thighs around his hips, and thrust deep. At the sudden intrusion, pleasure shot past any pain, washing through her. She opened her mouth to scream, and Marrok covered it, driving her higher with his hungry demands.

His kiss claimed her, never-ending. He swallowed all her cries, as if he refused to share the sounds with anyone. Her body devoured every inch of his erection and squeezed, craving more. The ache inside skyrocketed, burning hot, threatening to incinerate her. Blood rushed to her swollen clit. Olivia convulsed as pleasure climbed, spiked, and overtook her.

He opened his eyes. Hard, bright, rapacious. A sizzling blue that threatened her sanity—her soul.

"Again," he demanded.

The warrior in him compelled her surrender; he'd settle for nothing less than a proverbial white flag. But with one relentless thrust after another into her weeping core, the tightening tension and the perfect friction only strengthened their bond. It expanded outward, filling everything inside her, cocooning and disintegrating her at once.

"Feel me," he whispered. "Tell me who you belong to."

"No one."

"Wrong! You belong to *me*."

His determined growl resounded with passion and filled an empty place in her heart. Did she dare believe him?

"Say it," he demanded. "Tell me."

Inside her, he swelled, eased back, then pressed inside her again with a molasses-slow stroke that had her clawing his back.

"You!" Pleasure ripped the word from her.

"Only me. There will be no other."

"Never!" She threw her head back to the wall.

With her neck exposed, Marrok planted his lips just beneath her ear.

"Come for me, love. Give everything to me."

At his words, she released again in a cataclysm of sensation. Tingles poured over her, with a dash of hot ache and boneless satisfaction.

Marrok bit into her shoulder as his body tensed, jerked. He smothered his cry of ecstasy with her flesh as hot blasts of semen jetted inside her.

All between them was complete again . . . even if she didn't understand his insistence. Was she more than the means to an end for him? Did he care?

Halfway down the stairs, clapping shattered the silence.

* * *

With a snap of his head, Marrok jerked around and stared over his shoulder. Bram. Olivia gasped in his ear. Covering his mate's nudity with his own body, Marrok growled at the wizard, "What the hell do you want?"

"The way you dragged Olivia from the ballroom, I wanted to be sure you hadn't strangled her. I see you had entirely something else in mind."

A dazzling smile, a flash of white teeth. That rubbish worked on the ladies, but infuriated the piss out of Marrok.

"This was not for your eyes." Every muscle in his body tightened. He wanted to charge Bram and beat him to a bloody pulp for witnessing even a moment of Olivia's stunning pleasure.

Bram backed down a stair with raised palms in a gesture of surrender until he could no longer see them. "I heard more than I saw. Sorry. I actually came to tell you that Gray left."

"Left?" Olivia whispered. "The Anarki are after him again. He has nowhere to hide."

"He has hidden for over two hundred years," Marrok said. "He will manage again."

"Do you plan to continue training tonight? I believe Shock has had enough for today, since he disappeared after we ate. Should I send the others home?"

Bloody hell! Marrok wanted to stay with Olivia, protect her, feel her body writhe against his again, make certain she knew she was his. But Gray knew exactly where he and the Doomsday Brethren were training. Coupled with the staggering information about the keys, Marrok feared they had not a moment of training time to lose.

"In five minutes, I will meet the lot of you in the ballroom. We must continue. I've seen young girls wield a sword with more acumen."

"Sod off," Bram called, descending the stairs with a laugh.

Marrok turned back to Olivia. Her bare breasts still pressed into his chest, and reluctantly he slid from her sex as something vulnerable stole across her face.

Had he hurt her in his haze of fury and need? He was three times her size. Fear seized him as he forced his hands to gently curl around her shoulders. "Olivia?"

"That was humiliating," she muttered into his shoulder.

"I lost my temper and my control. I never meant for anyone to find us. The responsibility is mine."

"I care a lot less that Bram saw your bare ass pinning me to the wall than I do you carrying me out like a child in front of my father and everyone else. You accused him—to his face—of still being involved with the Anarki."

"You make me . . . insane," Marrok confessed. "I worry deeply, for I know what Mathias would do if he caught you. If I were cavalier with my trust and simply embraced Mathias's former underling, you could pay with your life. My body might still walk because Morganna decreed it, but everything inside me would die with you."

How could she not be moved by that? "Marrok." Her face softened, and tears trembled at the corners of her eyes. "You say these things . . ."

"I mean them."

She drew in a shuddering breath. "I would never help my father by betraying you, but I doubt you'll ever believe me."

Before he could say a word, Olivia wriggled herself out of his embrace, disappeared into their room and slammed the door.

Damn it.

With a heavy sigh, he righted his clothing and headed downstairs. This wasn't over yet, not by half. Olivia had waited all her life to meet her father and resisted seeing the miscreant's dishonesty. Richard Gray would put a wedge between himself and Olivia, should he fail to tread carefully.

At the bottom of the stairs, Bram waited.

"Is everyone ready?" Marrok asked.

"They are."

The two walked toward the ballroom. Marrok wouldn't call the wizard a friend exactly. Far too crafty and magical. A temporary ally, aye. But something troubled him.

"You seem to accept Gray. Why do you trust him?"

Bram sent him a cunning glance. "Who said I did? His past concerns me, obviously. But I've no specific reason to distrust him now. He gives every appearance of being a decent wizard and concerned father."

Frustration clawed at Marrok. Did no one understand? "He has given us no reason to trust him, either."

"Indeed, which is why I'm giving the man enough rope to hang himself. If he's conspiring with Mathias, accusing him will only make him cling to his facade more tightly."

Marrok closed his eyes. Bram was right, and he had allowed his temper and protective instincts to mangle his common sense. He had ignored simple tactics and revealed his suspicions to Gray too early. Stupid fool!

"How will you make amends if Richard Gray is guilty of nothing more than a terrible past? The same could be said of you."

"I never plotted to make war with the enemy."

"No, you did the horizontal mambo with her."

With his fingers over his eyes, Marrok rubbed at them, suddenly exhausted. Why did Bram have to be right again?

"Let's pretend," the wizard continued, "that Gray actually is trying to make amends and is the only person who knows a damn thing about the diary. Reverse your positions. If you were he, what would you tell yourself?"

Get stuffed. Sod off. Fuck you . . . He could really go on with that list.

"I see you're getting it," Bram murmured. "Personally, I don't trust the prick. But until he gives me a reason to *dis*trust him, I must give him a bit of leeway."

Normally, Marrok wouldn't care a whit what Bram thought. But the bond between Gray and Olivia must be addressed, and he had handled it poorly tonight, alienating the father and infuriating the daughter . . . making it more likely he'd be immortal forever.

"We'll write your behavior off to the excitability of a new mating," Bram said. "It makes newly mated men overprotective for a time. Hopefully, Gray will accept your apology."

Marrok would choke saying it, but say it he would. Would Olivia accept it?

Just then, Lucan came darting around the corner. "Zain is gone."

"Gone?" Bram snapped.

"Unless you moved him, he escaped."

Bram shook his head. "I left him below after the questioning. Bollocks!" Bram clenched his fists. "How?"

"Someone freed him."

"*What?*"

"The wall was blasted from the outside," Lucan explained.

"When?"

"In the last hour. There was no hole in the wall while we practiced outside."

"No one can step foot on my property uninvited without warnings triggering all over."

"Richard Gray was here an hour past," Marrok pointed out.

Olivia's father seemed guilty, indeed. But he could not tell his mate of this new suspicion about her father. They would only argue again, and as delicious as the last spat had been, he did not wish to upset her. He must remember strategy.

"Do we give chase?" Lucan asked.

"Zain is long gone. To think, I actually began to feel sorry for the sad bastard." Bram shook his head. "What he said was total crap, of course."

"Was anyone here who might have been persuaded to help Zain besides Richard Gray?" Marrok doubted it, but for Olivia, he asked the question.

"Shock," Lucan spat.

Bram warned, "Don't start that."

"Zain is his brother!"

"Shock has been here all day and never asked about the git once."

"Because he was waiting until the perfect opportunity— now! Shock also failed to show the night we captured Zain," Lucan pointed out. "It's possible he didn't stand his guard duty because he was telling Mathias that Marrok had the book and where to find him. Shock was here an hour ago. And now he's gone."

Bram paused. "I don't think he's our villain."

"You're my friend; I know your shortcomings. Your worst is that you always want to be right, and you're dead wrong about Shock."

"The crap between you and Shock over Anka? Bury it. You're as bitter as he. Why? You've got a mate, while he's endured a century of celibacy. He's had to steal energy or skim off half-encounters to survive. He must be starved for a full charge. What's your excuse?"

Eyes narrowed, Lucan looked pissed. "You know his blood-line. If the rumors are true, he doesn't have a right mind to be in. Whole families tend to join the Anarki, and Zain has followed in his parents' footsteps. How do you know Shock hasn't as well?"

"Without a doubt? I don't. But I'll send Duke after Shock and see if he's harboring Zain."

"My gut tells me this is Gray," Marrok added.

"Of course you think he's guilty. You hate the dodgy prat," Lucan piped in.

"The same way you hate Shock?"

"Touché." Lucan shook his head.

"You need training, but perhaps it is more imperative to retrieve Olivia's diary key." Marrok clenched his fists. "If Gray is Mathias's man, he will hoodwink or force Olivia into surrendering her emblem and going with him. If she and that key fall into the wrong hands . . ."

"Exactly. The three of us together should provide her sufficient protection while she retrieves it. I hope."

"Olivia?" The short knock on the door made her tense.

Marrok. God, the man confused her, accusing her of be-traying him to please her father one minute, then telling her she was his life the next. He didn't trust the father she'd waited her whole life to meet. He didn't really even trust her. Yet she couldn't deny Marrok anything. *Stupid. Spineless.* She rolled her eyes, trying to hold back tears.

Where did that leave them? She needed his touch to sur-vive. But more and more she ached for him in a way that had nothing to do with magical bonds and everything to do with her heart.

"Olivia?" he repeated softly.

He opened the door. Since their encounter against the

wall, she'd showered and donned the clothes she'd been wearing previously. Pinned under his gaze, she felt half-naked.

"What do you want?" she asked.

He eased onto the bed beside her and took her hand in his. "I am sorry we had an audience. It was thoughtless and wrong. No matter how badly I wanted you—"

"I'm angrier that you were so rude to my father and that you think I might betray you. You accused us of the worst treason."

"If your father is not the man you believe, it will hurt you deeply. I wish to spare you pain if he's not all you wished or imagined him to be. Though he is your sire, he seeks to separate me from the woman I view as mine and mine alone. Adjusting to our bond takes time."

Olivia turned his words over in her mind. He could be telling the truth, and if so, it made him guilty of nothing more than a bit of overprotectiveness and poor judgment.

He took her hand in his. "Love, time is ticking against us. Regardless of whether your father is in league with Mathias, we must secure the second half of the diary's key. Opening that book can change the world, and not for the better. Can we afford to take a chance?"

"Opening the book helps you, too. Don't deny that."

"I would never try."

Biting her lip, Olivia looked away. Though their alliance was uncertain, what needed to be done was crystal clear: secure something that opened a weapon of frightening intensity . . . and something that would bring him one step closer to being uncursed.

"Okay."

"Where is the emblem? Your flat?"

She shook her head. "The shop."

"We should go now. If Mathias learns you have the emblem, he will invade—"

"I can help," Bram said from the hall, peering past the slightly ajar door. "In case we run into Mathias or the Anarki. Marrok can handle the half-dead. Lucan and I can dispense with any magical tossers."

Marrok hesitated, then nodded. "Olivia?"

She sighed. Stress weighed on her like a hundred pounds in each arm and leg. When had her life become so complicated?

A glance beside her answered the question. Marrok. From the moment he'd walked into her life, everything had been, as the British said, topsy-turvy. She was damned sick of it all.

"Let's go," she said finally.

Within a few minutes, they had piled into one of Bram's fifteen cars, this one a Hummer. Sleek, black, looking as if it could hold a dozen people. But somehow when Marrok and the two other testosterone-oozing guys poured themselves inside, the interior became cramped.

"Keys to your shop?" Bram prompted.

She shrugged. "They were in my purse the night Marrok took me to his cottage, and I never retrieved them before the Anarki— Wait, how has Sabelle been getting in?" She turned to Marrok. "I assumed you gave Bram the keys to pass on to his sister."

"No," Bram refuted. "You had no magical protection around the shop, so it was easy to break in."

"Nice." She shook her head.

"Sabelle locked the door behind her."

Yeah, he was totally not getting the point. Then she frowned. "I *had* no magical protection around the shop?"

"You didn't think Sabelle would leave it wide open, did you?"

Honestly, she hadn't pondered the question at all. "So how can you just break in?"

"Being Sabelle's trusted relative, she shared the spell with me."

Wasn't that great news? "While we're here in the city, do you think we could stop by my flat and pick up my clothes? I'd like to have something of my own to change into."

Bram turned to the side and shot Lucan a stare, then he glanced at Marrok in the rearview mirror. "I would rather find you new clothes tomorrow."

"I'm partial to my things. I'd like to have my own tooth-brush, a damn bra—"

"I can guess what happened to your last one." Bram laughed.

Crossing her arms over her chest, Olivia sulked. Everyone knew *way* too much about her undergarments and sex life. But that wasn't the biggest problem. Cruising the streets of London in the dead of night with three hulking men—one of whom was her "husband"—running from a band of evil wizards, knowing that a trinket she possessed might be the key to saving the world from doom . . . It was all just a little too bizarre.

Mile after mile slid past the tinted windows of the monster vehicle, the interior occasionally illuminated by a streetlight. Sliding her eyes shut, she struggled to tune everything—especially Marrok—out. How could she feel so much for a guy who'd done the horizontal bop with her great-great-grandmother and mated with her for some way to end his curse? They couldn't get along for a whole day, so even if he wasn't set on dying, she didn't see this lasting for an eternity. Where did that leave her?

"Nearly there," Bram murmured.

Within a few minutes, they piled out of the vehicle, Marrok watchful on her left, palming a Glock. A wicked blade

with serrated teeth was strapped to his other thigh. Good
thing there were no metal detectors in her shop.

On her right, Lucan was no less focused, wand at the
ready, his entire body tense. She swallowed. They expected
trouble. This wasn't just a precaution.

In front of her, Bram approached the door cautiously, his
gaze darting all around. He laid his palms over the glass of
the door and drew in a deep breath. Olivia opened her mouth
to ask what the hell he was doing, but Lucan warned her
with a shake of his head.

"It's undisturbed."

Bram eased the lock on the door, broke his sister's enchantments with a quick whisper, and they entered.

"Could anyone concentrate like that and get past Sabelle's protection?"

"No," Bram assured. "I only knew how because she told
me the specific spell she used and how to end it. If not for
that, I'd still be scratching my head. Sabelle is a particularly
powerful witch."

The rest of the "mission" was uneventful. She retrieved
the emblem in quick silence, the sharp edges and heavy rubies cutting into her palm.

They filed out, and Bram secured the doors and muttered
a quick few words. Olivia couldn't discern them, but after he
finished speaking, she absolutely felt the invisible iron bars
around the building preventing her from even getting close.
Even though this was her place of business, she felt as if she
were trespassing and should move down the walk immediately.

"Neat trick."

Bram winked. "Next, I'll bounce a ball on my nose."

"Will you bark like a seal, too?"

Lucan laughed.

"If anyone can make me, it's you, gorgeous." Bram flirted like he was born doing it.

Marrok gripped his Glock tighter. "Stop trying to charm my mate. You would dislike seeing me angry when weapons are so close at hand."

Bram backed away from Olivia. "Indeed."

They piled into the Hummer and, at her urging, made a quick stop by her flat. Again, the guys flanked her as they walked in. As soon as she opened the door to the dark flat, Olivia sensed that her place had been disturbed since she and Marrok had stopped by two days ago to pick up her red dress.

As she flipped the switch, she second-guessed herself. Nothing looked out of place. A stack of mail still sat unopened on the kitchen counter. The remote control was still half-buried between the cushions of her brown cast-off sofa. The plate she'd munched toast on the last morning she'd been home still littered the kitchen table as if life here had been put on pause.

But the vibe in the flat screamed that her space had been violated.

"Does anyone feel the weird atmosphere but me?"

"Weird how?" Marrok demanded.

"Like someone's been here."

Lucan shook his head. "My magic doesn't work that way."

Bram nodded. "My magic does. I feel it, too."

Marrok hovered beside her as they strode down the hall to her little bedroom. The bed was still unmade, her laundry still folded in the basket, but not hung in her postage-stamp closet. The sense that the room had been invaded was stronger here.

"Damn," Bram swore. "Mathias is working fast."

"Do you think? Maybe the landlord came to fix my leaky sink."

"Maybe." But Bram didn't sound convinced.

If the Anarki had been here, were they looking for her or the emblem? If the latter, how could Mathias possibly know . . . unless her father had told him. The possibility ripped at her heart.

Olivia shoved the last of her needed belongings into a small bag. As a group, they made their way back down the hall and out the door. Bram magically sealed the flat with a wave. She'd worry about how to get back in later, after Marrok's curse was broken.

Outside, cold prevailed. Fog, leafless trees, an odd stillness. The night was eerie. They'd piled into the Hummer and pulled away from the curb, Bram's metal/alternative music making the vehicle throb and thump.

Mid-chorus, Lucan crashed back against the plush leather seat, curled his fingers around his thighs in a crushing grip and let out a piercing scream of pain.

CHAPTER FIFTEEN

BRAM FLIPPED THE MUSIC OFF and shot Lucan a glance. "Oh, dear God!"

Olivia leaned forward from the backseat. Lucan clutched his chest as if agony burned a brand right through his heart, stabbing over and over. "What? What is it?"

Clutching the steering wheel, Bram guided the tanklike vehicle through London's dark streets. Horror splashed across his face, a gasping disbelief.

"The yellow and pink in his signature," Bram blurted,

checked the road, then turned back to Lucan. "It's fading fast."

Lucan screamed again, clawing his chest viciously, as if trying to dig into it with his bare fingers. "Anka . . . No!"

"Deep breath, friend. We'll get you—"

"Home!"

"Probably not a good idea." Bram seemed to mutter the words almost to himself.

Olivia caught a glance at the wizard driving. He looked grim as he pressed his foot to the accelerator and hurtled the Hummer faster through the night. The engine's sounds were drowned out by Lucan's cries of pain.

"What the hell is going on?" Marrok demanded.

Bram glanced toward the passenger's seat once more where Lucan was thrashing, gasping, shouting. "He's losing the light from his magical signature."

"What does that mean? What does that have to do with Anka?" Olivia asked.

"She was his light."

Horror dawned, curling like an acrid ball of bile in her stomach, roiling. "Are you saying . . . she's dead?"

"That or she's broken with him. Either will cause him agony."

"Broken with him?"

"The mate bond. If that's severed, he would lose his light, which would alter his signature."

"She can break their bond voluntarily? Like divorce?"

Bram sent her a curt nod. "It doesn't happen often with magickind, but it's possible."

Shock tripped through her brain as ramifications, one after the other, burst into being. Olivia turned to Marrok. He didn't look surprised. "You knew this?"

If ever a man looked as if he wanted to lie, it was Marrok. He hesitated, caught Bram's reflection in the rearview mirror.

"Aye," he admitted finally.

Her blood began to boil. "When?"

"At the time you fell ill."

"And you neglected to tell me this . . . because?" Because he'd wanted to bind her to him, keep her to himself, until he managed to end his curse. All his tenderness and caring, lies? The possibility was like a sword to the chest. She'd always feared that he was simply using her, but had hoped . . . *Stupid!*

Marrok cast an uneasy glance at Lucan. "Now is not the time."

Oh, she so wanted to argue that with him. But Lucan screamed again, his elbows thudding on the door, his knees on the dash. It didn't slow him at all, as if he felt only the internal pain that tore at him.

"Damn," Bram cursed. "His signature is nearly black."

"I can't see it."

"You won't before transition. You may not afterward, though most do." Another glance at Lucan, another shake of Bram's head. "We've got to restrain him."

With a wretched howl, Lucan tore at his shirt, ripping it from the taut muscles of his torso. He clawed at his face, his chest, the cries so furious and anguished, it made the hair on Olivia's arms stand up straight.

"Restrain him?"

"Before he kills himself. If his signature turns totally black, his soul may be lost."

Olivia sucked in a breath. Sabelle had said magical mating was powerful; she hadn't been kidding. "Can we help him?"

"Try talking to him. Soothe him in your female voice."

With a nod, Olivia learned forward. Bram grabbed her wrist in a harsh grip.

"Don't touch him. If you do, he may try to ravish or kill you."

"Why?"

"If he's not too far gone, he will deduce that you're female, assume you're Anka, and try to reestablish the bond. If he's gone primal, he will smell you and know you're not his mate. Then he may perceive you as a threat and try to kill you."

Holy shit. Slowly, she nodded.

Marrok took her hand from Bram's grip and held it in his own. "Careful."

With halting words, Olivia began to whisper to Lucan, words of comfort and reassurance, quiet, soothing syllables, crooning sounds. For a few moments he paused, listened, craned his head toward her. When he opened his eyes, she gasped.

His usually electric blue eyes were nearly black. With a gasp, she pulled back.

"Stop!" Bram urged. "Stay away. He's too far gone. The light has nearly left him, and God knows what he'll do. We're almost to my place."

Marrok hooked an arm around Olivia's waist and pulled her deeper into the backseat, against him.

"Was he like this before Anka?" she asked Bram.

He shook his head. "This can happen when a deeply-bonded magical man loses his mate. The stronger the bond, the heavier the loss. Whatever darkness and instability was in his soul before the mating rushes to the fore and is multiplied by the pain. After a time, it usually retreats. But if it takes over . . ."

"Anka?" Lucan demanded. His voice rasped as if he'd been

possessed by something akin to evil. Then he grabbed Bram by the neck. And squeezed.

Marrok lunged forward.

"No!" Bram managed to get out. "Not here. Olivia . . .."

With her mind racing, she pieced it together. "Bram has a hand crushing his throat while he's driving and he's worried about *me*?"

With a grim nod, Marrok repositioned his massive shoulders between Lucan and her.

"We can't just leave Bram to be strangled." Olivia reached for Lucan.

"Do you wish to die?" he challenged, shoving her against the backseat.

"You want to crash?"

Olivia reached around Marrok for Lucan, who released Bram and turned those dark-as-hell-pits eyes on her. "Female? My Anka?"

Olivia froze. Tell the truth? Lie? Which was least likely to get her killed?

In the rearview mirror, Bram shot her a warning glance.

"Friend," she murmured.

His eerie eyes widened. He sniffed her, and his eyes narrowed.

"Stop!" Bram warned. "His signature has gone completely dark."

Lucan lunged for her, looking determined to tear her throat out with his bare hands, just as Bram stopped the Hummer in front of the manor and darted out.

Marrok tried to pull her away from Lucan and tuck her behind his broad back. But the whacked-out wizard had a death grip on her arm. His fingers bit into her cruelly. She'd have bruises tomorrow.

Lucan hurled his big body between the vehicle's seats to

reach her, his free hand outstretched toward her neck. Then
he was on her. Marrok punched and pushed, drawing Lucan's
attention.

"Go!" Marrok urged her as Bram opened the back door.

Olivia hesitated, then realized the two men were having
a difficult enough time containing the insane wizard without
worrying about her safety, too. She darted out into the crisp
evening air. "Help!"

Ice darted out of the manor a moment later. "What the
hell? Why are they beating the piss out of MacTavish?"

She babbled a frantic description of their trip home, then
turned pleading eyes to him. She barely knew him, and Bram
didn't trust him, but they were losing the battle to contain
a crazed Lucan. A face hit the back window. Bram. He jerked
away a moment before Lucan's fist smashed through the
glass.

Blood ran down the clear pane. Olivia gasped. Ice cursed
and tore the Hummer's door off. Bram struggled to pin
Lucan to the backseat. Marrok sat behind him now and held
his arms. But Lucan escaped their hold, let loose a spine-
chilling war cry, and kicked Bram in the gut.

"My female!"

Ice peeled Bram off Lucan. Shaking his head, the bloodied
wizard protested. But it was in vain. Ice cold-cocked Lucan
with a mean right hook. Lucan's head snapped back.

He went limp.

Ice looked up at Marrok with a grin. "Good thing I learn
fast."

A moment later, Ice and Marrok carried Lucan out of the
Hummer.

As Ice trudged past with the unconscious wizard, Bram
clapped a hand around his arm. Ice looked up with murder
in his eyes.

"Don't touch me!"

Bram let go. "Just wanted to say . . . thanks."

"I didn't dive in to rescue your sorry arse. If it were up to me, I would let Lucan tear you limb from limb while I made popcorn for the show. But Marrok is too important to our cause to let your git of a friend dismember him."

Olivia swallowed her gasp as Ice and Marrok carried their burden into the house. No love lost there.

"What's that about?" she asked.

Bram dabbed the blood away from his mouth, then winced. "Ancient history."

Maybe, but time wasn't healing the wound, and it clearly wasn't open for discussion.

Beside her, Bram shoved a hand into his pocket, tossed a white rock into the air, then muttered, "Aunt Millie."

A few moments later, a sprightly little woman with a hundred pounds of pale hair in a bun appeared in the driveway and walked with spry steps in their direction.

"Again, boy?" She stood on tiptoes to receive a very dutiful kiss from Bram on the cheek. Then she turned to Olivia. "Oh, hello, dear. I see you're feeling better. Lovely."

As Millie walked into the house, she turned to Bram. "She came when I was ill?"

"Yes. She told Marrok why you were unwell and gave him the choice of breaking your bond or keeping it and . . . serving you as needed. I should—" He gestured toward the manor house rising with stately glory in the moonlight.

"Of course. See to Lucan."

Mind awhirl, Olivia followed him to the house. Marrok had chosen to stay with her rather than break their bond. She wanted to believe it was because he felt affection for her. But given his curse, she wondered if he'd done it for purely selfish reasons.

Inside, they followed the screams. Lucan had come around again. His wailing echoed through the house. She shuddered.

By the time she and Bram found the group, they'd commandeered one of the guest rooms. Someone had located or conjured up a set of restraints that looked right out of a BDSM club. Ice and Marrok were working to shove Lucan's arms into the cuffs. Duke had joined the party and had one of his ankles. Lucan's free leg was flailing everywhere. Bram dodged a lashing kick, grabbed the ankle and forced it to the bed.

Lucan snarled, a sound that threatened murder. But with a lot of grunting and straining of muscles and cursing, they got the rabid wizard restrained.

Bram swiped a hand across his tired face. "Go on, Aunt Millie."

The little woman stepped from the shadows and approached the bed. She put a hand to Lucan's brow. He howled, but she ignored him and made quick work of the buttons down the front his shirt. Her little hands roamed his chest with eyes closed. She breathed in and out.

"His mate is not dead. Distantly, I feel her alive in the bond."

"Injured?" Bram asked, puzzled.

Millie paused. Frowned. "No. She's broken with him."

Astonishment reverberated through the room.

Duke broke the silence. "Do you think Shock somehow convinced her to break with Lucan and accept him?"

"No. Shock wants that above all else, no doubt. But Anka had been devoted to Lucan for nearly a hundred years."

"Then, who . . . ?" Olivia gasped. "Oh, God. Do you think Mathias captured her and forced her . . . ?"

Bram clenched his fists. "That's precisely what I think."

"We have to find her now!" she insisted.

"Impossible."

Marrok cut in. "You know what he will do to Anka. You have seen it."

Trying—and failing—to resist the urge to flinch, Bram simply said, "I know."

"Good God, man! We cannot leave her to suffer such a cruel fate."

"And if you bring her back, maybe Lucan will be whole again," Olivia argued.

Bram turned to Marrok. "If you were Mathias and the three things you needed most, Olivia, the book, and her key, were in one well-protected place, what would you do?"

Marrok paused for a long moment, then swore. "Stage a distraction."

"Exactly. Marrok, you said yourself that Olivia must be protected, no matter what happens, no matter how many die." He sighed. "I just never expected that statement to be tested so quickly or terribly."

Hours passed. Aunt Millie left, proclaiming there was nothing more she could do. Lucan's raw screams bounced off the elegant walls, the marble flooring. Tempers flared and nerves ran thin. Marrok took Ice and Duke outside to resume training. Beating the crap out of each other had soothing qualities.

From a chair in the corner, Olivia watched Bram, looking tense and pale, bend over Lucan's still form. His brow knit into a frown.

"Is he going to make it?" she asked.

"My mate? Anka?" Lucan scratched out in that voice that made her shiver. Then he sniffed, and his eyes flew open, crazed and black. "Bitch! Where's Anka?"

Olivia feared she knew the answer to her question.

"I doubt it, but what's to be done is not my decision. We must call his next of kin."

Stunned mute, Olivia nodded. She didn't know Lucan well, but a vivid memory of him and Anka at Bram's party—had that been a mere two days ago?—still haunted her. They'd looked so in love.

"Are you sure Mathias forced Anka to break their bond? Maybe . . . Lucan cheated on her."

"Never. Once mated, a magical man relies on his mate for everything. Especially his energy. He will reject all others. Lucan will run out of energy soon, and if his family has not arrived . . ." He sighed.

"Energy? Doesn't he eat for that?"

"For his body, yes. But to power their magic, witches and wizards need to connect with another, exchange strong emotion. We store up the energy gleaned during sex. But for the unmated, if the experience is not a powerful one, we must recharge this way often. With a mate, the sex is more meaningful, so the energy charge is stronger and will last longer. If anyone magical goes too long without repowering, they die."

So Bram and Duke and all the unmated guys were frequently doing the wild thing with random women? "Oh. I—I thought . . ."

"That you and Marrok had cornered the market on needing sex? No, you need it more often because you're storing up energy for your transition. Anyone about to enter transition needs extra, but because you are mated you require even more. After you grow into your powers, you still need to . . . um, be plugged in occasionally."

"How much energy do you think he has?"

Bram shrugged massive shoulders, worry for both a warrior and his friend dragging at his noble features. "If he had a good charge recently, perhaps a few days, a week at most. But the darkness inside him will drain him fast."

"What will he do without a mate for energy? You can't turn him loose on another woman."

"Indeed. It's possible to get a charge in other ways. Engaging in anything that brings extreme anger or joy."

"Fear?"

"Another possibility. But none lasts as long as a sexual connection." Bram sighed. "If his family can't get here in time, I'll have to find someone to serve him and hope he doesn't kill her for trying."

Olivia was very glad she wouldn't be that woman.

Bram closed his eyes, obviously focusing inward. A few moments later, Sabelle appeared in the doorway.

"Is Lucan coming around?"

"No. Can you go to his house, see if you can find anything that would suggest what happened to Anka? Take Duke with you. And see if you can find any way to contact his brother. No unnecessary risks, Sabelle. Go there and come directly back."

She nodded. "Lucan's parents are too frail to handle this. But his brother . . . isn't he very young?"

"Caden is nearing transition. But he'd be a damn sight stronger than magic folks in their nine hundreds."

On that grim note, Sabelle disappeared.

Olivia looked at Lucan, still thrashing on the bed.

"Can he heal?"

"With extreme will, perhaps. I have only theoretical knowledge of this, you understand. It happens so rarely."

"Are there people who sell energy exchanges? Like magical . . . prostitutes?"

Bram cracked a smile. "We think of them as nurses.

Such women would tend him without intercourse. It's what unmated men who have extended a vow and been rejected must do."

"Why?" She was completely lost now. "If their offer is rejected, they aren't married."

"Magic works a bit differently. If someone extends the vow, they have mated in their heart, regardless of whether the vow is accepted. If they're refused, they must rely on these alternate forms of energy to survive. Shock would know more about this than I."

At that moment, Sabelle poked her head into the room. She was so pale, chalk couldn't compete. And her hair . . . She looked as if she'd survived a tornado. "Lucan's house? Utter chaos. Anka put up a valiant struggle."

Bram closed his eyes, and Olivia knew he was wondering if this was going to literally kill his best friend. She hurt for them both.

"Find anything about Caden?" he finally asked.

"He's untransitioned, as you suspected."

Bram's eyes narrowed. "Did you teleport to the States and bring him here?"

"Texas, yes. What else was I to do?"

"Did you take Duke with you?"

She sighed. "I am perfectly capable—"

"We know nothing of Caden. He could be dangerous. Or in transition frenzy."

"No, thank God. Your sister is lovely, but at the moment, I'm worried for my brother. May I?"

Olivia whirled at the sound of a new voice. Waves of light brown hair framed blue eyes so like Lucan's they broke her heart. Oh my . . . Mr. Drool-inducing was Lucan's brother?

"I'm Caden MacTavish. How do you do?" He thrust his hand toward her.

"Olivia Gray." She shook it.

"An American girl, here? Magical?"

"Not yet."

"I say keep it that way. Nasty business, magic. I'm hoping I escaped the gene." He turned back to Sabelle. "Thank you for the escort."

She nodded tiredly, her golden hair hanging limply at her shoulders. Teleporting across the pond and back must have taken a lot of her energy.

"Sabelle has to find a partner to recharge now, right?" Olivia whispered to Bram after the other two went to Lucan's bedside.

Bram turned horrified eyes on her and covered his ears. "I am *not* hearing this!"

Sabelle laughed. Olivia took that to mean yes, and Bram's big-brother horror was typical stuff. Shaking her head, she wandered to Lucan's side. Caden followed.

"Hiya, Lucan," he murmured close to his ear.

Lucan thrashed anew, flipped open those wild black eyes. And howled until the ceiling rattled.

The horror in Caden's expression spoke volumes. "Where the bloody hell is Anka?"

"We don't know."

"What has been done to find her? Sabelle said you know she is neither injured nor dead. She must have been coerced into breaking the bond. She and my brother were inseparable—"

"Except by Mathias, I fear," Bram answered. "Do you know who that is?"

Caden's jaw dropped. "That monster? We must recover her immediately before—"

"It may already be too late. I'd like to send someone after her, but we've discussed it and realized that's impossible.

Mathias and the Anarki are an imminent threat to all of magickind, especially if he gets his hands on Olivia. We need trained soldiers now, while Lucan . . . may be lost forever. I cannot spare a moment—"

"Blast trained soldiers! My brother is a man, not simply part of your little war!" Caden snarled.

"And he's my best friend, but that changes nothing. We fight a foe and an army much larger than us. Lucan may not come back from this. If I stop preparing for this 'little' war, there will be more deaths among magickind. Hundreds. Perhaps thousands."

Caden fisted his hands at his sides. "Another reason I hate magic. Humans can end a relationship, drown their sorrows in whiskey for a few weeks, then carry on. Lucan . . ."

Bram shrugged. "We brought you here to decide what's to be done with him. We can't keep him restrained to a bed forever."

"Are you suggesting I put him down, like a diseased animal?"

"That's your decision. I'm merely stating that you may never get back the brother you know."

"You pompous git. He *will* recover. I'll make certain of it. Do you know if Anka is dead?"

"Not yet."

"Good. Then I'll look for her. Where does Mathias live?"

"We don't know. If you want him, you'll have to hunt him. But I don't advise it. He's one of the most powerful wizards of all time. If you go it alone, your parents will only have your life and your brother's sanity to mourn at once."

"I refuse to sit here with my thumb up my arse and do nothing."

"Then help your brother by fighting with us. Together, we stand a better chance of finding Anka. Lucan said that you've had human combat training in the American military."

"I was a marine."

"You can be useful to both the cause and your brother. A huge portion of the Anarki is not susceptible to magic. We must fight them with guns, fists, and swords, which the rest of the wizards know little about."

"I practice shooting at a range in Texas. I box regularly. I've taken up karate. I learned to fence years ago."

"Perfect. Join us. We need all the sword arms we can get if we're going to save Anka and others like her."

Caden glanced at his writhing, snarling brother restrained to the bed, then back at Bram. He stuck out his hand. "As long as we continue to search for Anka, you have a deal."

Minutes later, Bram, Ice, Duke, and Marrok were again meeting. Caden was introduced to the lot of them. Bram attempted to contact Shock again. Nothing. On more than one face was the suspicion that perhaps Lucan had been right about Shock's loyalties to his family . . . and Mathias.

Despite the fact it was after midnight, training commenced with grim purpose.

Olivia watched them half the night, checking on Lucan periodically. She never got too close to the man-turned-beast strapped to the bed, but she worried for him—and Marrok. Would this be his fate if they ever ended his curse and broke their mate bond? Maybe not. Their bond wasn't the century-old union Lucan and Anka had shared. Marrok wasn't magical. And he would gladly embrace death.

The thought nearly crushed Olivia. Selfishly, she wanted Marrok to stay, but of his own free will, not out of obligation or necessity or to avoid Lucan's fate. In a handful of days, the bond had bloomed with real emotion and filled her heart. She wanted his love and feared it was because she loved him, too. Yes, she'd been craving someone—her mother, her father—to love her whole life. Her yearning for their devotion paled in comparison to her need for Marrok's.

Watching Lucan's pain became too heartrending, and Olivia left his room. Bram and Marrok climbed the nearby stairs, deep in conversation. Despite their obvious exhaustion, they made a solid wall of testosterone. At the top, they both looked up.

"Why are you not in bed?" Marrok asked.

Acutely aware of Bram watching, she swallowed all the worries in her heart. "Not tired. Training go well?"

"The lot of them are improving much faster, I daresay, than the average human."

"Praise?" Bram gasped mockingly.

Marrok snorted. "Do not accustom yourself to it."

"Wouldn't dream of it." Bram turned away and strode down the hall toward his room.

With a hand at the small of her back, Marrok led her to their room. Olivia resisted the urge to lean into him. How bad would it hurt when he broke his curse and died? She didn't want to know.

When they pushed the door to their room wide, pandemonium awaited. Their clothes had been scattered, ripped to shreds. Drawers were pulled from the nightstand and dresser, furniture overturned. Blankets and sheets were puddled at the end of the bed, the mattress hacked into. The ticking was scattered everywhere. The window had been thrown open, and a brisk breeze whipped in.

"What the bloody— Did you have a fit or something?"

The room's only mirror was shattered, but she didn't need to see it to know incredulity was etched on her face. "Of course not."

"Then someone has been here. The book!" He raced across the room, sliding into the carpet, groping under the bed.

His arm tightened, and his look of relief said it all.

"The carving still there?"

He nodded. She undid her simple spell, then he pried the hunk of wood free and clutched the book.

She closed her eyes and felt the lingering presence. "Someone *was* here not long ago. Look, the window is wide open! Whoever did this escaped through there."

"What happened? I heard Olivia gasp." Bram barged in, staring at the room in shock. "What the devil—"

Marrok filled Bram in as he approached the window slowly and looked down. "That is a long drop."

"For most magical people," Bram answered, "that's a hop."

"Bloody hell."

Olivia heard the frustration and fear in Marrok's voice as she turned away and began righting the room. As Marrok joined in, she tried to block out the sense of being hunted, of having her space violated yet again. Mathias was coming hard and fast for her, and for the first time she was truly afraid there'd be no outrunning the bastard.

Bram waved his hand through the air, which fixed the majority of the mess in the room. It wasn't perfect, but close enough.

Olivia skimmed the magical spell book Sabelle had loaned her. She located a simple repair spell, which worked well enough. The mattress was in one piece, if the seams a bit jagged. She put the sheets and blankets back on, trying to push down her anxiety. If Marrok could see it, he would only worry more. As it was, he watched her, arms crossed, with an unrelenting stare.

"We must ask ourselves who did this?" Bram said. "It

must be someone Sabelle or I extended an invitation to enter the grounds. I can feel my protections; none have been breached."

"It cannot be Lucan, obviously," Marrok pointed out. "Nor Caden, Ice, or Duke. They were all training with us."

Olivia swung her gaze to him. "You think my father did this."

Marrok paused. "Consider, he *was* here earlier tonight. And we do not know if he left the manor's grounds, only that he left our sight."

"The same could be said of Shock—and his escaped brother!"

"True," Marrok agreed smoothly.

But Olivia wasn't buying it. "What if Lucan is right, and Shock is Mathias's spy?"

"And what if he is not? I ask you only to be cautious. Certainly, you see now how desperate Mathias is to reach you and the diary."

Yeah, it was like a big neon sign. God, what could possibly happen next?

A day passed, then another, a third, a fourth. . . . Every night she went to bed alone. Every morning, she woke up beside Marrok's still-warm pillow. The man himself was gone.

No one could locate Anka—or Shock. Lucan slipped further into black madness, as his frenzied thrashing and piercing howls faded to heartrending whimpers.

Bram acceded to Caden's demands that they find an energy source for Lucan. Given the horrified screaming on the other side of the door, Olivia guessed there wasn't much sexual healing going on. Bram and Duke remained just inside, in case Lucan attacked the poor woman. They escorted her out in less than ten minutes. When Olivia peeked in on him, he looked marginally revived, but as crazed as ever. No one wanted to say that, if Anka wasn't found, Lucan should be taken down, but Olivia suspected that nearly everyone had thought it.

Adding to the tense mood at the manor, ever since someone had broken into their room, Marrok had acted like a demented drill sergeant, piling hour after hour of physical rigor onto the men. Near midnight, Marrok showered, ate a mountain of food, curled his body around hers in their bed, then collapsed like a coma victim.

They'd barely spoken since that night. Olivia knew Marrok still suspected her father was somehow behind all this. In her head, she knew it wasn't impossible. In her heart . . . she didn't want to believe it.

Everyone was on edge, Olivia most of all.

Tonight, she'd waited up for Marrok. His touch sustained her energy, and Olivia couldn't deny she was losing hers fast. But she needed him for way more than that. She missed him. Dare she say she even . . . loved him?

Had he told her the truth when he'd held her fiercely against the wall, that she had his heart? Or were his words another ploy, like not breaking their mate bond, to hold her at his side? Olivia had no experience with love—of any kind. How was she to know if he cared, or if she was just the means to his freedom? How could she ask a man who might not love her to make love to her? Pain spiked her when she thought of being a burden to him, as she'd been to her mother.

When Marrok slid between the sheets, Olivia ached to touch, feel his embrace. They were mates in magic, but she connected with him in many ways. He was protective, brooding, quick, fierce, stubborn. She loved all that about him, adored that he'd retained his humor through the centuries. She flushed thinking of the way he possessed her so completely. She craved the sense of belonging she found in his arms.

But what did he *really* feel?

She hated being between her mate and her father. Olivia still hoped Shock—who could hear mental broadcasts, who had failed to show up to guard Marrok's cottage when the Anarki found their door, who disappeared at the same time as Lucan's mate—was the guilty party. It fit and it wasn't hard to imagine the huge, scary wizard was a bad dude. The man's family had Anarki ties. He'd been invited into Bram's home and could have broken into her bedroom looking for the diary.

Why couldn't Marrok at least consider those clues?

"You are shivering, love. Cold?" Marrok muttered suddenly.

"Sorry." She rolled away—and instantly felt the energy drain from her.

She closed her eyes against a dizzy rush. Damn, she was going to have to reach out to him soon. Maybe tomorrow. She just couldn't endure his dutiful touch—not when she wanted his heart too. As a child, she would have been grateful for her mother's embrace, whatever the reason. Now she knew that touch without affection hurt all the way down to her soul.

Another dizzy wave assailed her. She dug her fists into the sheets. Suddenly, Marrok was poised over her, hard thighs spreading hers wide.

"You need me and you did not say so," he chided as soft hands soothed her face. "Come to me when you need, anytime you need. I will care for you."

Such tenderness. *Please let it be real.*

Olivia closed her eyes so he wouldn't see the tears shimmering there. "I'm fine."

"You are lying."

He smoothed the hair from her face and kissed her in gentle atonement. Her emotions were up, down, inside out. She wished she had the courage to ask if he actually cared about her, but wasn't in a hurry to break her own heart.

Instead, she asked with her kiss, nudging his lips apart with her own. Marrok grunted in surprise, then barged in and settled deep, as if he planned to stay all night. Long, languorous slides of his tongue, soft brushes of his lips, a melding of breaths and mouths and needs.

Something was different. He'd always been gentle, even tender, that one time in the hall aside. This . . . She couldn't put her finger on it.

"Olivia," he murmured softly. "I have been busy, and we have been at odds of late. I dislike that."

She hated it too, along with the feeling that she'd left her heart exposed, and he could either embrace or trample it as he pleased. But that didn't stop her from responding when he again sank deep into her mouth with a soft kiss, spreading the sizzle of pleasure throughout her.

"If I am cynical or have hurt you, forgive me."

He could never apologize for what hurt her most: not loving her. Nor should he. The foolishness had all been hers. Olivia had known better than to fall in love with a man whose heart had been untouched for a millennium and a half. She wasn't lovable or a beauty—even if she felt that way in his arms.

Instead, Marrok had apologized for the fact he could not be swayed from suspecting her father. And Olivia couldn't bear the thought that he was right.

Even if she let go of her anger now, a confrontation about her father or her le Fay blood was bound to come up again. Maybe they were just doomed to be at odds.

She'd barely finished that thought when Marrok kissed her so sweetly, her toes curled. Her belly tightened with heat. Maybe their end was near, but right now she could melt into him, take another memory.

Long, slow strokes of his tongue imitated what he would do to her body. The fire blazed between her thighs; Olivia surrendered. He wended his way down her body, pushing up her T-shirt until he stripped it off, then tossed it onto the floor. As soon as her torso was bare, he latched on to her sensitive nipples, one after the other. She hissed in a breath and grabbed his hair, hanging on while sensations roiled inside her.

Down lower, his hands went, divesting her of her panties A tug and a rip, and they were gone.

His hand covered her mound, then thoroughly explored her every crevice and fold. She gasped and nearly climbed out of her skin as need burned. She grew slick. Marrok murmured his approval. Stupid or not, she wanted him, even if this meant nothing to him.

Almost there . . . So incredibly close she could weep. But he was clever and patient, dancing away from her sensitive spots, allowing her to cool down before he revved her up again.

Then she was begging. The words fell out of her mouth, and she didn't care how they sounded. She wanted him inside her. She needed him. Now.

His expression ranged from possessive to determined when he took her in one controlled thrust. Pleasure spiraled instantly, sending her over the edge, into a morass of sensation that nearly drowned her. But he wasn't done.

Marrok held her firmly, thighs wide. Deep, measured thrusts came one after the other. Suddenly, the pleasure was ramping up again. Pleas rolled off her tongue as he overwhelmed her with ecstasy, even as she forced herself to bottle up her words of love.

Abruptly, he withdrew, flipped her over, and lifted her to her hands and knees. Before she could say anything, Marrok was back inside her, sinking deep, his chest draping her back, his fingers driving her wild. In this position, she felt every vein and ridge of his sex. The friction of every thrust enflamed her even more.

"Come for me again," he growled. "We will release together."

His hot breath hit her neck, sending shivers down her back that blended with the tingles he generated. Sensations converged in her belly, sliding down her legs. Pressure built, then a huge explosion rendered her breathless. Her vision faded for a moment. She sank to the bed in a heap as Marrok pumped inside her once more, then shouted her name in a cry of ecstasy.

His arms gave out, and he covered her body with his. "God, woman. What you do to me . . ."

Olivia resisted the urge to cry. The pleasure was amazing, but more and more, she didn't care about energy. She cared about his feelings, about having his love. But yearning for a man who had loved no one for fifteen centuries was hopeless.

She tried to tell herself that it didn't matter. He wanted to be uncursed and he wanted to die. For that, he needed her. She had pledged to help Marrok end his misery and didn't want the man she loved to suffer or be unhappy. If the curse was broken, his torment would be over.

But her own would just begin.

Marrok withdrew and padded to the bathroom. The door closed, then water ran from the sink. Olivia sank into the bed and sobbed. God, why hadn't she listened to her own warning before her feelings deepened? Because she'd wanted and needed him so badly.

Chirp, chirp.

The odd sound came from directly above her. She opened her eyes to the sight of a little white bird. Freaky. How did a bird get into the room?

"Olivia."

Now it was talking. In her father's voice. Even freakier.

"Yes."

"Quick! I'm outside. Can you invite me in? I've got something to share with you that will help Marrok. I want you to know you can trust me."

She glanced at the closed bathroom door. The shower began to run. And her father was outside, waiting to show her something that would prove that her faith in him hadn't been misplaced. Still, she must be careful.

"I don't have the power to invite you in."

"I understand. I'm just outside. This will only take a moment."

Tossing on a T-shirt and a pair of jeans, she crept downstairs and, at the front door, hesitated. But if her father had something that would help Marrok, she couldn't just stay here and hide.

Opening the door, Olivia saw Richard Gray in the distance, breathing hard, as if the hounds of hell had been chasing him. Cautiously, she drew near, comforted that help was likely just a scream away if she needed it.

He grabbed her arm and pulled her close. "Are you alone?"

He was jumpy, jittery. What had gotten into him?

"Yes." She rubbed her hands over her suddenly chilled arms.

"Look!"

As he extracted something from the pocket of his slacks, Olivia leaned in to glimpse the glinting thing in the moonlight.

The other half of the key!

Ruby-encrusted, this half was shaped most like an M. And suddenly, Olivia understood the symbol on the front of the diary. ML overlapping—Morganna le Fay.

"How . . . I thought Mathias had this? What did you do?"

"I stole it back." His smile stretched from ear to ear. "I waited until I knew most of the Anarki would be gone and snuck in. I knew where Mathias once hid it. I feared he had moved it, but no!"

"You know where Mathias's lair is?"

He nodded. "It hadn't changed and he hadn't put protections up against me."

"Where was Mathias while you took the emblem?"

"I don't know. I simply snatched it from its hiding place and ran."

Olivia didn't know what to say. "That was incredibly risky. Were you seen? Did they chase you?"

"No problems at all. I'd planned it for some days now, knowing how badly we need this piece. I couldn't let you down. I want to prove that you can trust me. I want Marrok to know it, as well."

Richard suddenly enveloped her in a big hug. Wrapped in his embrace, her heart stuttered with something bittersweet. He cared about her, her happiness. With his arms wrapped around her, she felt his acceptance. Yet . . . she no longer wanted it the way she craved Marrok's.

When he pulled away, she smiled. "You risked so much, but now we can do anything."

"Exactly. Now, what do you say we get the diary open and end your mate's curse?"

CHAPTER SIXTEEN

"You know how to end his curse?" Olivia asked.

"I believe so. Bring me the book and your half of the key. We'll do it together."

Marrok's warnings about her father whipped through her mind. As much as she wanted to believe the best, the man *was* a relative stranger. What she'd read in the history books reassured her. He'd realized his mistakes and turned against Mathias at great personal risk. And her father had tried to show he cared, despite Marrok's interference, since their first meeting.

Her father, with his le Fay roots and knowledge of the Doomsday Diary, could make Marrok's freedom a reality. Even if pain wrenched her heart at the thought of spending the rest of her life without him.

"Olivia, don't frown. This is cause for joy!"

Marrok would be happier finally leaving this life. And if the man didn't love her, she was better off without him. It just didn't feel that way now. She'd be alone again, since her father would still be running from the Anarki. But she was stronger now. Knowing she had been more than a burden to one of her parents and that she had helped Marrok achieve his deepest wish would sustain her in the coming years.

Pasting on a plastic smile, she nodded. "I'll go get Marrok."

She darted up the stairs, then slowed as she approached their bedroom door and pushed it wide.

Marrok stood tall, damp from his shower. Her breath caught.

He looked so vital. His Roman nose cast a bold statement

above sensual lips, edged by his goatee and sun-bronzed skin. His body rippled after spending all day training wizards he didn't like, so they would be victorious against the villain who would do anything to acquire her and the diary.

Long black lashes framed blue eyes smudged with purplish dark circles. Moonlight shadows fanned down his slash of a cheek. The man needed rest, and if all went well tonight, he'd have it—eternally.

She wished she had the courage to tell him that she loved him. But he probably didn't care about his enemy's great-great granddaughter, beyond using her to get free from his hex and getting an occasional lay. All his caring and seeming tenderness had been to keep the person he needed to help break his curse happy. Blurting it out would only put him on the spot.

He wasn't trying to stay in this life; he'd told her almost from the beginning that he was trying to leave it. Which meant he would leave her.

Fighting the prickling of tears that stabbed her eyes, Olivia retrieved her half of the diary's key from the pocket of the jeans she'd been wearing earlier and slung it around her neck. Dread multiplied in her gut.

"What are you doing?" He watched her every move.

"My father is outside. He has the means to open the diary and end your curse."

Marrok froze. "He told you that?"

"I know you don't trust him, but he's put himself at great personal risk to help you."

"Have you asked yourself why he would do such a thing?"

She hesitated. "Because you're my mate. I'm his daughter."

"That latter fact meant precious little to him for twenty-three years. The only reason to free me of this curse is to end my need for the diary. After which he assumes I shall give it to him. And what do you imagine he plans to do with it?"

That thought had actually crossed her mind, but Marrok's tart tone intimated something more sinister than keeping it out of Mathias's reach. "It belongs in our family, and I don't believe he's any fan of the Anarki anymore. Maybe he wants to hide it or destroy it. Ask him."

"Of course, he will tell me naught but the truth."

Frustration welled inside her, its level rising, resting on the trigger of her temper. "If you want to end this curse, you're going to have to talk to him. What can that hurt?"

"Olivia, neither of us are experts on magic. We know not what your father is capable of or if he has chosen to stand with Mathias."

"I read the books that Sabelle gave me. He chose good and right. I know a little something about magic—"

"Based on a spell book of basic magic. What your father and Mathias can do will be extraordinary." He caressed her shoulder. "Love, it's not my wish to crush your faith in him, but we must be cautious."

Olivia pulled away, wishing he wouldn't call her love if he didn't mean it. "Cautious isn't going to end your curse. If you want a normal life—and death—you're going to have to let my father perform his magic. One of my ancestors hurt you, and I'm trying to give you what you want, but I can't if you won't help yourself."

She stormed toward the door. Stubborn, difficult man.

As she reached for the door knob, Marrok was behind her, one palm flat against the door, holding it shut. The other curled around her waist. His agitated breath fanned across her neck.

"Shh. I know."

As Olivia sucked in a ragged breath, she realized that she

was crying. She swiped away the hot tears drizzling down her cheeks. Marrok squeezed her to him, drawing her into his heat and comfort. So perfect, his soft words and touches. So insidious, since he didn't really mean them.

"Together. We will go together. And you will be very careful."

When he held her like this, with such concern, it was tempting to believe. But he needed her to achieve his mortality. It behooved him to keep her happy. That fact flooded her with emotion. Her love for him, yes, but more. Sadness. Dread.

Opening this book would be the beginning of their end. If the curse didn't kill him, he'd likely do the job himself. And after a millennium and a half, he deserved peace.

Olivia turned and threw her arms around Marrok, hugging him so tightly, her arms ached.

I love you. It was on the tip of her tongue. But she held it in and held on as if the world would end once she let him go.

Before she got even more attached, she pulled back. But Marrok wound those two strong arms around her and brought her close again.

"All will be well. I will do everything in my power to make it so. No more tears."

She pulled away, swiping at wetness on her face. "Let's go."

Quickly, he tossed on his clothes, grabbed the diary from its hiding place, then turned to her. "What is amiss?"

"Why should anything be wrong?" she misdirected, looking deep into those gray-blue eyes and memorizing the sight of him.

"Tell me, what is it you fear?" he whispered, cupping her cheek.

"Nothing." *Being without you.* "Opening the diary is a big step."

"Indeed." He pressed his lips to hers softly. A reassurance?

It felt like a good-bye.

Marrok followed Olivia out of their borrowed bedroom, guiding her with a hand at the small of her back.

This might be it, the end of his accursed immortality. And it might be another ploy on Gray's part to get his hands on the book. Either way, change was afoot. He hoped it was for the better.

But he refused to go to Gray unprepared. Marrok was not privy to all a wizard of his stature could perform. Aye, he had learned much in the few days he'd been at Bram's estate, but Marrok knew he had but scratched the surface of the feats magickind was capable of.

His host, however, was a bloody expert.

"Wait here," he said at the top of the stairs.

At Olivia's reluctant nod, Marrok made the long trek down the hall. When he stepped into the shadows, he looked back at her, catching her unguarded expression. And he saw it squarely: sadness, grief.

Would she mourn him if was no longer in her life? He wished he knew. But as he had concealed his growing feelings because he knew so little of her heart, she had done the same.

Heaven help him, he was the consummate idiot, falling for the descendant of the very woman who had sentenced him to a horrific fate. And yet . . . Olivia's innocence and pluck, her belief in everyone's innate goodness, was like breathing fresh air for the first time in centuries.

He had been dead inside until he met her. And if his life ended tonight, he would be grateful for the precious days he had spent with her.

God's teeth, he sounded like a sap in . . . love?

Disquieted by the turn of his own thoughts, he hurried down the darkened hall to Bram's quarters. Time to play this drama to its end. If Richard's claim were another hoax, he would deal with her father and whatever he had up his sleeve, for good or ill. And if Marrok still lived—even if he never broke his curse—he would stay with Olivia until she understood they were meant for each other.

Finally at Bram's door, Marrok raised his hand to knock. Before he could, the wizard opened it. He was dressed and freshly showered. Odd, given that it was barely four in the morning.

"I saw that you were coming for me."

"In the shadows?"

"In a vision."

That took Marrok aback. "Do you know Richard Gray is here?"

Bram walked into the hall with a nod. He looked about as happy as someone who'd had their home bulldozed.

Marrok grabbed his shoulder, forcing Bram to face him. "What else?"

"I contacted one of the Council elders, who had the misfortune of meeting Mathias in battle before he was exiled. The elder warned me that Mathias can perform magic no one has ever seen."

"What does that mean?"

Bram shook his head. "Let's hope we don't encounter that—or anything in my vision."

Dread settled into Marrok's gut. "Tell me what you saw."

"I can't see details, damn it, just the result."

"Which is . . . ?"

"Very bad. I'm going to do what I can to prevent disaster. Tonight, do what I say; don't argue."

Marrok found himself nodding. Once, he had disliked and distrusted Bram. Now . . . he wasn't a half-bad bloke. For a wizard, anyway.

When they reached the top of the stairs, Bram greeted Olivia. The longing and grief he'd seen earlier in her expression was hidden. But it was seared in his memory, reminding him how much he had at stake. What if these were his last moments with Olivia?

Marrok scooped her up in his embrace. "We are not bound to do this. If you wish, I will send Bram to discuss Gray's plans for opening the diary and perhaps finding a way to dispose of it somehow. We can consider the information—"

"No. You deserve to be uncursed. You've wanted nothing more for centuries." She cupped his cheek, and he opened his mouth. "Don't argue. Mathias will soon realize my father has stolen his half of the key, and the Anarki will be here. It's now or never."

Surprise lanced through Marrok. Based on his expression, to Bram as well.

As much as Marrok disliked it, Olivia was right. "We need a strategy."

Bram nodded immediately. "Watch Olivia. Do *not* let her go. I will be responsible for ensuring that nothing peculiar happens with the Doomsday Diary."

They walked down the stairs in unison and crossed the expansive foyer. Bram brought the wizard inside and escorted him to the library. Richard clasped his pendant key in his hand. A large, ornate M encrusted with rubies, except where Olivia's L would lie on top of it.

So Richard actually had the other piece to open the diary. Perhaps he could now open the book.

Still, Marrok did not trust Gray. His gut churned, sour.

That feeling had served him well in battle. Something was afoot.

"Marrok. And Bram." Gray seemed surprised to see the wizard. And not a little unhappy.

"Richard." Bram sent the other wizard a false smile, but looked otherwise relaxed. "How do you plan to proceed with the book? Do you know what will happen if it's unlocked?"

Slowly, he shook his head. "I have some ideas, but nothing precise."

"Perhaps rushing in is unwise. I can guard your key here," Bram offered. "Without an invitation to enter, these grounds are a veritable fortress."

"I can't let this out of my sight. If I'm captured, surrendering it again may be the only thing that saves me. In fact, my plan was to open the diary, uncurse Marrok, and *return* this to Mathias before he's aware it's gone."

Olivia gasped. "Please, Marrok. There's no reason to drag out your misery. Just . . . I know you would prefer to study and strategize and ponder and . . . whatever, but my father risked so much to bring his half of the key to us."

"I still wonder why."

Richard turned solemn eyes on him. "She is my daughter. I failed her for twenty-three years, abandoning her to a mother who was ill-equipped to care for and comfort Olivia. It's too late to step in and parent, as you've pointed out. Perhaps I can offer her a future with a mate free of a curse he should never have been forced to endure."

Was Richard now vying for parent of the year?

"Will I live if this curse is broken?"

Olivia nodded. "Sabelle said that mating was the most powerful magic of all, so does that mean . . . ?"

"It's possible he will live. A human who mates someone

magical adopts their life span. The curse likely preserved Marrok's body. Reversing this hex should allow you to begin a normal—well, normal for magickind—aging process," Richard explained.

"Bram?" Marrok asked.

The wizard shrugged. "A curse of this nature is beyond most magical knowledge. When riled, Morganna was capable of great, terrible feats we've not seen before or since."

Olivia turned to Marrok with pleading eyes. Bloody hell, when she looked at him like that, he wanted to do anything in his power to please her.

"You want to be free of this curse," she whispered, clearly fighting tears. "*I* want you to be free to live or die as you wish, not as Morganna commanded," she implored. "Knowing that she used you so cruelly will always lie between us if you do not break this curse. Please . . ."

Marrok was not convinced and reached for the book.

"Wait! With an open book we have far more sway over Mathias," Bram explained.

"Meaning?" He should not care about magickind, but the thought of harm coming to the dedicated wizards he'd been training disturbed him.

"Once we open the book and learn to use it, we can banish Mathias forever. He will never target you or Olivia for revenge. If you fail to do this, he will hunt you. Neither of you will be safe—ever. No one will be."

The words turned over in his head. Marrok scraped at them hard, looking for a flaw in Bram's logic, and finding only one.

"With the book open, every magical megalomaniac will pursue us, since there would be no impediment to using it."

"Not exactly," Olivia said. "The diary is an object of feminine reverence, remember? In the research I uncovered that seems to mean it's more powerful in the hands of a woman. It's possible a man might not be able to use it at all."

"Very good," Richard praised. "And correct."

"And as a le Fay, Olivia—and perhaps only Olivia—will have the ability to destroy the diary once she comes into her powers," Bram argued. "If it no longer exists, the book will cease to be the cause of murders and wars. Until that day, we will tell magickind the book is in cinders or some such and guard it with our lives."

"Why not wait to open it until Olivia has the power to destroy it?" Marrok asked.

Her father shook his head. "It's been over a millennium since we've had all the necessary components to open the diary together. Consider, we may never have this opportunity again."

Marrok glanced at the little red book—so innocuous looking—then stared down at Olivia.

"It's better for us, for magickind."

Outside, thunder clapped. Inside, his gut roiled.

But he saw the logic. With an open book, he had the power. With a closed book, he and Olivia had a dangerous life on the run.

Marrok gritted his teeth and sent the group a sharp nod. "What next?"

"This is how it will work, Gray. You will hold your key in your right hand. Olivia will hold hers in her own. Marrok will stand between you. I will lay the book on the table. No one is to touch it except when necessary. We will discuss next steps once the diary is open. Are we clear?"

"Indeed." Richard nodded eagerly.

Dread gnawed at Marrok's gut. Richard was saying and doing all the right things. He saw the logic of acting before they were attacked by the Anarki. But that did not ease his worry.

He blew out a steadying breath and stood between Richard and Olivia. He wrapped a tight arm around her waist, pulling her close to him. He would have liked to do more to ensure Gray could do them no wrong. His stare met Olivia's, and the fearful sadness there wrenched him.

Outside, rain began to fall, wind lashing branches against the window. During his boyhood, the weather would have been perceived as a bad omen. The old superstitions were not always wrong.

Bram looked at Richard. "On the count of three, you will latch your emblem onto the front of the book, into the fitted grooves. Olivia, once he's finished, you will lay yours on top. She—and no one else—will open the book. And I will stun anyone who breaks protocol."

"Indeed," Richard said. "But we must hurry. I feel Mathias breathing down my neck."

"If you really did steal that from him," Bram began with a grimace, "I'm surprised he's not already trying to beat down my door. One . . ." Bram began.

Marrok tightened his arm around Olivia.

"Two . . ."

Out of the corner of his eye, he spotted Richard lean forward, emblem in hand, reaching for the book. With one hand on his mate, Marrok gripped the book even tighter with the other.

"Three."

Richard laid the emblem down into the sunken track. With a *click*, the key fell into place.

Lips pursed in concentration, Olivia repeated the process, latching her half of the key into place. With a soft *smick*, it fastened over Richard's M.

Suddenly, the book seemed to lurch into Olivia's hand, as if pulsing with a life of its own. It beat in a rhythm, like a heartbeat. Beside her, Marrok felt every bit of the power that had cursed him. It scalded his skin as his mate held tight and pulled the book open.

It cracked with age, yet hummed with an undeniable vibrancy. A sudden chill blasted the room. Page after page—most of them blank—whipped past in an inexplicable gust.

"Unreal," breathed Bram.

"I feel a rush of energy inside me," Olivia added, still gripping it as if afraid to let go.

Marrok stared, mesmerized. He'd always known the Doomsday Diary had awesome power. He'd always had a healthy respect for it, but now . . . Bloody hell!

A blast of light flashed to his right. Then a fireball of pain hit him between the shoulder blades. He staggered under the agony ripping at his skin, tearing joints. His next breath became almost impossible to draw in. His hold on Olivia began to slip.

Was this Morganna's way of punishing him for daring to open the book and trying to crush his curse?

The pain kept multiplying, unrelenting, slashing through muscles, gouging into his bones. His neck no longer supported his head, and his chin fell to his chest, as he strained to control his body and find his balance, to stay upright.

What magical treachery was this?

"Gray?" Bram shouted in question.

Must . . . protect . . . Olivia.

A second blast came, this time in the back of Marrok's skull. His head jerked back. His muscles froze. He sank to his knees, clinging to his mate's waist. He could not let her go, but never had he felt such excruciating pain. The torture infected him quickly, like a snake's venom, burning his veins, making his heart and lungs stutter and—for a few agonizing moments—stop.

He remained conscious by sheer force of will. Vaguely, he heard Olivia gasp at his side. Marrok forced himself to look up, lurch to his feet.

Richard came into view then, teeth bared, fury distorting his face. His violet eyes flashed with hate as he leveled his wand at Bram.

"Nay!" Marrok ground out.

Olivia's father turned and raised his wand. The bolt of light burst forth again and a fresh wave of agony slashed through Marrok's senses. He tried to brace himself for the spread of torment, reminded himself that he was immortal. But his consciousness was slipping . . . draining. He wondered if having a le Fay strike him with magic was enough to end the curse and kill him, all in one fell swoop.

Could he actually die?

He lost his hold on Olivia and slumped against the table.

She let go of the book and grabbed his shoulders, screaming his name, but she sounded far away. He couldn't possibly tell her that he was well. Such a blatant lie.

Bram growled something, and a *ping* of magic sounded to his left where Bram tried to stun Gray.

Still Olivia's touch gave him the will to fight on. He would not leave her to her father's evil whims.

With a battle cry, Marrok shoved away from the table, sweating, bleary-eyed. He pushed Olivia behind him and swung a mighty arm at Richard Gray. Before the punch connected, Gray leapt aside, grabbed Olivia, and pointed his wand at Bram.

A burst of energy flashed, this time directed across the table. Bram feinted and lurched forward, slamming his hands on the surface in front of him.

A snarl, a vicious curse, another ball of dark power flared

around them, killing the lights in the room. Marrok reached for his mate.

He felt nothing but air.

CHAPTER SEVENTEEN

"OLIVIA!" MARROK SHOUTED, terrified to the bottom of his soul.

In the room's pitch blackness, Bram snapped his fingers. That instant, the lights blazed back on. The book lay on the table under the wizard's palm, saved from Richard's desperate grab. But frantically scanning the room only confirmed what Marrok felt in every corner of his heart: Richard was gone.

And he had taken Olivia with him.

Marrok whirled to Bram, anxiety clawing his belly. "Where are they?"

The wizard winced, regret crossing his face. "Disappeared."

"Is there no way to trace their location?"

"I'm not a GPS tracker. Listen," Bram tried to calm Marrok with his voice, "It's no secret that Richard wanted you and Olivia apart."

"You suggested giving the knave enough rope to hang himself. He has."

"Indeed. I don't think he'll hurt Olivia, since he likely needs her to use the diary."

"And after that?" Marrok stared at him with growing horror and frustration. "Olivia, will begin losing energy quickly. That will kill her, if Richard does not. And if he is in league with Mathias, you know what that monster will do to her."

The very thought shredded his guts.

"We will find her before then." Bram paused. "You love this woman."

He flinched. Marrok had fought this feeling, but almost from the moment he had realized Olivia was not Morganna, he'd begun seeing not a le Fay, but *her*. Her compassion and willingness to help, both her strength and neediness, drew him. He had shown her reluctance and distrust in return. Oh, he'd wanted her and taken her as often as she allowed. But he'd been too cowardly to tell her of the feelings growing in his heart. And now it might be too late. *Dolt!*

Scrubbing a hand across his face, he stared back at Bram's concerned expression. "We must find Olivia."

Bram clapped him on the shoulder. "We will. We have something Richard desperately wants, badly enough to deliver a trio of killing spells right at you."

"Those blasts of pain were killing spells?"

"Puts a new spin on terrible in-laws, doesn't it? His treachery is unforgivable, and he'll pay for it. He's either a coldhearted bastard who would manipulate his daughter in order to acquire a weapon to be used against his own kind, or he's in bed with Mathias, who has the same wish and is ten times more powerful."

"What good does having the diary do us, unless we ransom it? We still must discover where they are."

"There is . . . another way, perhaps."

At Bram's pause, Marrok tossed up his hands in impatience. "On with it, man! Every moment she is gone, I feel the bond straining and twisting. It's painful, like dull razors gouging into my soul."

Bram nodded, brow furrowed. The wizard was clearly pondering something—but too slowly.

Though Marrok hated magic at the moment he wished he was filled with it. If it would bring back Olivia, he wanted magical power so strong, he glowed.

"Do something!" he demanded, knowing he was all but giving the diary to Bram.

Picking up the book, Bram flipped through the pages at the beginning, whipping from one page to the next—and whipped past the page that held Morganna's curse on Marrok.

Slapping his hand over the book, Marrok stopped Bram's perusal and flipped back to Morganna's damning scrawl. He expected a wisecrack from Bram, an arched brow—something—upon reading Morganna's words. Nothing prepared him for what the wizard said next.

"Let go. I've looked for the page where Morganna cursed you. But so far the damn thing is empty. Why?"

"What nonsense do you speak? Can you not see the words before you?"

"What words?" Bram stared at him as if he'd lost all sense.

Marrok sighed. "I know not what game you play. Stop messing about."

Bram glanced up and leveled him with an eerie blue stare. "We should try to use the book to find Olivia."

"Is it wise to toy with something so powerful?"

"It's worth a try. Can you think of another way to find your mate quickly, before anyone gets hurt?"

"We know not how the book works."

"Legend says that whatever the possessor of the book writes in it will come true. You said you saw Morganna write in it. I've read accounts of such. Perhaps it's that simple."

Nothing about Morganna had ever been simple, but if Bram's idea worked and he could have Olivia back in the few strokes of a pen, it was worth a try.

Sweat dripping and fear thumping, Marrok nodded.

Bram clapped him on the back and reached to his desk for a pen. He grabbed the book and paused. "You know of no special pen?"

"None. The night she cursed me, she used something of Arthur's."

"Splendid." Bram's voice filled with acid. "Magical experiments are always . . . interesting."

Interesting and magic were not two words Marrok wanted in the same sentence. But he was desperate to have Olivia back.

"Do it."

With a quick intake of breath, Bram took the pen to the page beside the one on which he was cursed and wrote, *Bring Olivia back to her mate. Banish those who took her and think to change her fate.*

After Bram dotted the last period with a flourish, Marrok held his breath, anticipation clenching his stomach. This *must* work. As his gaze darted around the room, out the windows, he saw no sign of Olivia. Worry replaced hope, and he swore.

When he looked down at the book, he swore again. All of Bram's writing had disappeared.

"Does that page appear blank to you?"

Bram stared at it—hard. "Yes. What the bloody hell happened?"

Marrok had no clue. "And you cannot see Morganna's words on the next page?"

Bringing the book toward his face, Bram peered at it, then brought it closer still. "Nothing."

"This diary has more secrets than we imagined." Like Morganna herself.

Still staring at the page, Bram nodded. Then he looked up with deep regret etched in his face. "You try."

Startled, Marrok took the book in hand. The wizard was giving it back to him with the slim hope he could use it to save Olivia?

"Go on," Bram urged.

The thought of his mate in danger, feeling fear, sent a fresh jolt of urgency deep inside him. Gripping the book by the spine, he wrote words similar to Bram's.

With the same results.

Once the words faded from the page again, Marrok closed the book, gripped it to his chest. "What does this mean?"

"Perhaps Olivia was right and that the book responds more to witches than wizards. But I fear Sabelle is still too weak from her journey to help us."

Marrok tossed the book on the table without a backward glance. The thing had been the source of his torture for centuries. Why had he expected it to save the only person he cared for—and thus his soul?

Terror crawled through him. The bond with Olivia . . . he could feel her far away, sense her confusion and weakness already setting in. And something else, some growing sense of disbelief. In the next instant, a splash of shock blanched him like a jump into an icy winter lake. Then suddenly, the echo of fear—Olivia's fear—burned down his nerve endings.

"Would you like to try anything else with the book? Other words?"

Sweating, terrified, Marrok shook his head. "No time. We must find her now."

Or, dear God, it would be too late.

* * *

Olivia saw a blur of light, heard a whir of noise. She was tossed end over end; her stomach turned.

Then she landed in a heap on the floor in a completely unfamiliar place. The room was dark with heavy curtains. A dim light illuminated an aging room with a beige sofa colored with mystery stains. She doubted even Goodwill would take anything in the room. A narrow bed with a gray spread she'd bet had once been white sprawled haphazardly, tangling with equally dingy sheets. An open pizza box with a half-eaten pie inside littered the table. Styrofoam cups of cold coffee lay everywhere. And cigarette butts filled ashtrays every few feet.

The smells, combined with whatever means they had just traveled, made her stomach pitch as if she were in a freefall. She nearly heaved.

Swallowing down the nausea, Olivia picked herself up and stared at her father.

"Where are we?" *Besides someplace that looks like a Motel 6 reject?*

"My rooms. At least for now."

She supposed he changed them often to outrun the Anarki. "What happened? Where is Marrok? What was happening to him before we . . . poofed out of Bram's house? Where is the book?"

"Full of questions," her father chided, then paused to pace. Finally, he leveled her with the oddest stare, almost an angry one. "That will cease. The book, blast Bram Rion, is still clutched in his fist, no doubt. And your mate isn't coming. If he had not been immortal, he would be conveniently dead by now."

She stepped back as dread slid through her. "I—I don't understand."

"Of course not. I perform magic that no one has even conceived of, breathed about, so you can't possibly understand."

Suddenly, his head snapped back. His face lost all color and animation. He turned an otherworldly shade of gray, while his eyes lost their luster and life, graying out like the rest of him. A ghostly leg kicked out from the side of his calf, almost as if another being was emerging from her father's body. But that was impossible.

Or so she thought until an arm protruded from her father's shoulder. Another head seemed to come out from his ear. Then a whole separate body emerged and stepped forward. Her father fell to the floor, lifeless, like a marionette with its strings cut.

Olivia's jaw dropped. Terror iced its way though her veins. With a frantic stare, she looked between her father's slumped form on the dingy floor and the new man in front of her.

He looked younger than Richard by twenty years. Dark hair brushed the bronzed tops of his bulging shoulders. His top half was bare except for a thin coat of sweat that accentuated every ripped muscle. Biceps bunched and flexed as he hooked his thumb into the waistband of his leather pants, hanging so low she could see his hip bones and follow the treasure trail leading down.

Who the hell was he?

"Olivia?"

She'd been so distracted by the fact that a half-naked hunk had emerged from her father's body, she hadn't looked into his eyes. What she saw there made her recoil.

An icy blue so chilling, she shivered from ten feet away. Rimmed in black, they threatened and seduced at once. He embodied compelling menace, with his slashing cheekbones, strong jaw, and sensual mouth. The man was completely sexual, impossible to ignore, and utterly without warmth in his soul.

She was repulsed.

"Wh—what have you done with my father?"

"I made sure he will rest." He smiled benignly as he stepped closer. "In peace."

Olivia felt her eyes widen, her pulse jump. She stepped back. "You ki—killed him?"

"He had served his purpose and was becoming tiresome. Suddenly, he sprouted morals and fatherly concern." The man pretended to yawn. "What use have I for those?"

God, his words . . . the man had no heart. The closer he came, the more her skin crawled.

"You may be happy to know that his dying words were about you. He never pleaded for his own life, but he begged quite convincingly for yours."

Dead? The father she'd barely had a chance to know had been murdered defending her to this . . . creature? "When?"

"Directly after he helped you fight off the Anarki at your mate's cottage. I had him followed—and his mind read—prior to that. As soon as he teleported away from you and back here, well, your father had been a smashing source of information, but I no longer needed him. So I provided him everlasting slumber."

Olivia trembled. It was all happening so fast, she couldn't wrap her head around the rapid-fire events. "Why kill him?"

"He was going to ruin my plan." He ran the backs of his fingers down her cheek in a soft caress that, for all its gentleness, scared the crap out of her. "I couldn't have that."

Olivia jerked away from his touch. "Who are you?"

"Mathias d'Arc, of course." He made a great show of executing a very courtly bow.

His name ricocheted around her head. *The* Mathias? Oh, dear God!

She stumbled back, only to encounter a wall. He laughed softly, the sound every bit as chilly as his eyes.

Mathias reached toward her and curled his fists around her hair, letting it slide between his palms before he grabbed her cruelly. "My fiery American witch. So lovely."

"Leave me the hell alone!" She struggled to get away.

Mathias held her against the wall. "To touch you, I could break your mate bond, which you might not survive. Or I could simply take you and disregard your pain, but you might not live through that either, and I have no use for a dead le Fay witch. You're quite lovely. More's the pity."

Yanking on her hair, Mathias pulled her closer. Olivia stumbled against him until her mouth was just beneath his.

"I would enjoy fucking you," he whispered against her lips. "Your moans and pleas would provide me so much energy and pleasure."

Olivia tried to shake her head, but he held her too tightly.

"But you reek of that immortal human," Mathias growled. "And I'm in no mood to smell him while you scream in pleasure."

Pleasure? How could he imagine that she would for a moment enjoy his touch?

"Your mind is deliciously easy to hear. You would feel pleasure because I would will it so. Watch."

Suddenly, he released her and stepped into the middle of the room. With a wave of his hands and a snap of his fingers, a woman appeared, looking mussed and dirty and naked. Head down, her pale curls shielded her face, her shoulders, part of her breasts, flirted with her navel. But Olivia could see she was a beauty.

"Come," he called to her.

Without looking up, she walked toward him.

"Kneel."

She did as she was told. Knees apart, hands clasped behind her back, pose submissive.

Behind the woman, Olivia's jaw dropped. Why would the beauty subjugate herself to a monster? God, she was going to be sick.

Absently, Mathias brushed the woman's hair from her face, then moved lower, fondling her breast. He grabbed her nipple and gave his wrist a slow, hard twist. The woman gasped, then began to pant.

Time to run. Maybe Mathias would be so distracted she would have the opportunity to get away. He'd probably kill her for it.

Olivia ran two steps toward the door when she felt something loop around her neck and give a vicious yank. She pulled and scratched, looking for the something choking her, but her nails gouged only her own skin.

Then suddenly, her hands were forced to her sides and she was turned to face Mathias and his slave once more.

"I insist you stay for the fun. This one gives me a great deal of energy. So full of anger I can translate into such juicy enthusiasm for my cock. Isn't that right, lovely?"

Grimacing, Olivia felt moments from losing her last meal.

"Rise," Mathias demanded of the woman, then dropped his voice. "You're a minx. I'll bet you liked it rough with your former mate as well."

The woman had once had a mate?

"Turn," he said to the woman, who obeyed without hesitation.

The sight of her face made Olivia draw in a sharp, shocked breath. "Anka?"

"Ah, is that her name? I've been too busy shagging her to ask." Mathias ran his palm up her stomach, over her distended nipples, then back down into the nest of pale curls. She looked swollen and smelled of sex.

"Spread your legs."

Anka trembled but complied without pause.

But her eyes, full of despair and horror, caused Olivia's heart to reach out to the woman in understanding and grief. Her body was being forced to endure this, even as her mind rebelled.

Mathias's fingers disappeared into Anka's sex. She winced, but in moments was struggling to catch her breath, flushing with arousal, slick with desire.

With a depraved smile, he slanted Olivia a stare. "Isn't she—no, I must rephrase this—wasn't she the mate of one of the Doomsday Brethren?"

Shocked, Olivia nodded. It wasn't a good sign that Mathias knew the Doomsday Brethren existed. Had he gotten the information out of her father's head?

"You forced Anka to break her bond?"

"I can be *very* persuasive."

Anka's red-rimmed eyes looked traumatized, terrorized, even as her thighs began to tremble with impending release under Mathias's lazy-fingered caress.

"Stop. She does not want this!"

The evil wizard held up his two very wet fingers. "Here is your proof otherwise."

"You're forcing her to respond."

He shrugged. "Pleasure is pleasure." He circled his free hand around her head. "There. She cannot hear us now. Don't want pesky memories getting in the way. I never bothered to ask her mate's name. Who was he?"

Olivia refused to tell. Lord knew what the psycho freak would do with the information.

"Tell me." He inched his hand lower, right back over

Anka's rosy sex. "Or she spends the entire night coming against her will and not just for me. I'm sure the wizards of the Anarki would love this pussy."

As Olivia recoiled, a silent tear rolled down Anka's cheek unchecked. The woman couldn't endure another rape from Mathias. She had already been forced to break her vows and been repeatedly violated. Mathias would only raise the level of hell if she didn't tell him.

"Her mate is—"

"Was," Mathias corrected.

"*Was* Lucan."

At that, Mathias's awful smile widened. "Splendid. One of the strong ones. No reason to go to the trouble of abducting a warrior's mate and forcing her to break their bond if it's not going to cripple Bram Rion's little rebellion."

That explained everything. Mathias not only knew of the Doomsday Brethren, but since he'd been impersonating her father when he'd interrupted one of their training sessions, he had a good idea who was in it, who had been mated, and figured out a shortcut to making them one key member smaller with Lucan's insanity.

He looked at Anka with such evil amusement, it sent chills up Olivia's spine. "I know just what to do with you."

Whatever he had in store, Olivia already felt sorry for the other woman.

With another wave and snap of his fingers, Anka was gone.

Olivia searched the room in vain. "Where is she? What did you do with her?"

"As much fun as I've had with her, I sent her to a place where she can be far more . . . interesting."

Did that mean he'd turned her over to the Anarki for

some sort of gangbang? "Send her back to her mate. Now! He's suffering and—"

"Good." He smiled. "Then my plan to both distract and weaken Bram's little group is working. Anka no longer has a mate, and she'll be very much appreciated where I've sent her."

"Damn you! Don't do this to her or Lucan. Don't—"

"I would not worry so much about their problems when you have ones of your own. Now, you may either cooperate with me . . . or I may change my mind and let you come to understand Anka's experience firsthand."

The very thought made her skin crawl. Mathias touching her, forcing her body to crave what her mind rejected. Breaking her bond with Marrok, severing their connection. She shivered and hugged herself.

"I see you understand me. What will it be?"

CHAPTER EIGHTEEN

NEARLY TWELVE HAZY, panic-filled hours had passed. Dusk would soon be upon them.

And still, Marrok had neither word nor sign of Olivia.

"Duke and Caden left a few minutes ago to search again. Ice left on his second outing. I'll continue to research. You stay here in case the Anarki come. You'll know what to do."

Marrok nodded grimly at Bram. He prayed they would find Olivia, but icy fear consumed him. No one knew where her father might have taken her, or where Richard hid. He wasn't answering his phone or rocks. But Richard had managed to evade the Anarki for several hundred years. Chances were, he could avoid the Doomsday Brethren as well.

Worse, if Richard had thrice leveled killing blasts, the man was not on the side of good.

"What of Shock?" Marrok asked.

"I've seen no sign of him since before Anka's disappearance. I pray to God he had nothing to do with Anka breaking her mate bond and causing my friend to be strapped to a bed while he loses his humanity and his soul."

For the first time, Marrok empathized. If someone had taken his mate, persuaded her to break their bond . . . A handful of hours without Olivia, and already he felt as if he were about to lose his mind. The bone-deep anxiety would not stop. For the millionth time since Olivia's disappearance, he paced the room.

And the failure to keep her safe had been incredibly painful. "Bastard! I wish I knew where Richard has taken Olivia and what he plans. I could happily rip his entrails out with my bare hands."

"There may be several reasons he didn't reply."

None of them good. Bram didn't say that, but Marrok knew.

Right now, he should prepare for battle, try to use logic to discern where her father might have taken her, and remember every moment he'd shared with her.

A few moments later, a little white bird whisked in, chirping, and appeared beside Marrok.

"Come alone and bring the Doomsday Diary to a tunnel on the south bank of the Thames at two a.m."

Marrok stilled. "That is not Richard Gray's voice."

"Or Olivia will die," the bird continued.

Bram grimaced, his face pained. "No. That is Mathias."

The words struck Marrok like a stake to the heart. Fear unlike any he'd ever felt swarmed him, thick and choking. "The bastard was in league with Mathias. Bloody hell! I knew it."

"Either Richard is plotting with Mathias or his past finally caught up with him after he tried to steal Olivia away."

Marrok sank to Bram's stylish sofa, dread charring out his belly. "Jesu, Mathias has my mate."

"Indeed," Bram whispered.

Aye, he knew exactly what Mathias enjoyed. He'd heard it in Bram's vision, seen enough pictures of the maggot's torment of women to haunt him. The thought of him doing the same to his mate, *his* Olivia . . . It was a battering ram, shattering and painful. Murderous didn't begin to cover how Marrok felt.

He dropped his head to his hands.

"I must save her." He looked at Bram with bleak eyes. Marrok hated showing anyone his weakness, but now, at this moment, the only thing that mattered was having Olivia returned to him safe and whole.

"We'll try."

Marrok shook his head. "*Try* will not do. I am willing to give the bastard the book. Tell the damn bird that."

Bram grabbed his arm. "You can't."

"The bloody hell I can't! If I wish to surrender it to save the woman I love—" Marrok realized what he had just admitted aloud and fell silent.

If Bram knew his feelings, chances were Richard did as well. Olivia was being used against him.

"Giving Mathias the book is no guarantee he'll spare Olivia. Surrendering the book puts magickind in the utmost jeopardy. This is the very event I sought to avoid when I formed the Doomsday Brethren. Innocents will die. Chaos will rule. Humans will be slaughtered for sport. Please . . ."

Every word Bram uttered raked at Marrok's insides. Once upon a time, he would have rejoiced at the thought of magical beings suffering, but after spending time with Bram and the others, training them to be warriors in the most human sense of the word, he could not stomach being the one to ensure their deaths.

"Those things are happening already," Marrok choked.

"Yes. I just don't know what kind of license this would give Mathias to kill. He may know more about the diary than we do. If so, there's every chance he could bring about Doomsday."

"But what can I do? I will not simply let my mate die at the hands of an evil butcher. Can you magically bind the book, make it impossible for him to use it?"

Bram froze, then his eyes widened. "That's it!"

"You *can*?"

"Not exactly. But we couldn't write in the diary. Doubtful Mathias will be able to."

"Aye, but he likely knows he will be unable to write in it."

"Perhaps, but . . ." Bram raced across the room. A moment later, a door emerged. Bram climbed in. Before Marrok could follow, the wall solidified again.

"Bram?"

Less than a minute later, the wizard appeared again, this time holding an ancient tome.

"What is that?" Marrok asked.

"Dear old Merlin's writings. They're more cryptic than helpful, so I didn't give them much credence, but . . ." Bram flipped pages, then stopped near the middle of the book. "Ah, here Merlin says something about him being too much of a man to use the book. All along, I believed he was being a bit of a macho sod, But given what Olivia learned about the diary as an object of feminine reverence and that we failed to wield it, I began thinking. Morganna's writings are loaded with rants about men and their ferocious desire for power."

"She wanted to be a man's sole focus. She hated that I had more desire to make war than to make love to her again."

"Exactly." Bram smiled. "Merlin said that she sought to create something more powerful than men. Again, I interpreted this to mean that she planned to make the book awe-inspiring in every way, but I think she meant something else."

Marrok paused, his mind racing. "She made it impossible for a man to use?"

"Yes. Neither of us could write in it."

"Why would Mathias seek what he cannot use?"

"At the moment, he has your mate. I'm sure, in his head, if he can trick us into giving him the book, too, he'll have the world at his fingertips. If not, the Anarki have enough female followers. He'll find someone whose magic connects with it."

"How will he know who?"

Bram shrugged. "Sabelle!"

She appeared a few moments later looking disheveled, her swollen mouth sultry and smiling. Bram grimaced, but he managed to maintain the peace and say nothing.

"Write in this."

Sabelle picked up the pen from the table slowly. "*This* book? The Doomsday Diary? Are you mad?"

Bram nodded. "Go on."

Sabelle hesitated. Swallowed. "All right, then. Write what?"

"A wish. A simple one."

Wearing an expression that clearly said she thought both of them were mental, Sabelle wrote a quick wish that the missing button on her blouse was repaired. A moment later, the button appeared exactly where it should have been and the words on the page disappeared.

She blinked. "Amazing!"

"Write there that you'd like Olivia back with her mate," Bram pressed.

"Please," Marrok pressed. "She is in Mathias's hands."

"Oh my God," she gasped, then quickly pressed the pen to the page.

Long moments later, she laid the book on the table between them again. The page was blank, but Olivia was nowhere to be found.

"What happened?" she asked.

"I don't know."

"The wish is too big for my magic," Sabelle said. "I'm likely just not powerful enough."

"It makes sense. Like casting any enormous spell, it must be your heart's deepest desire."

Sabelle sent a guilty glance to Marrok. "I'm sorry. I adore Olivia. I want her back with you."

"But it is not the most earnest wish in your heart. I understand." Even if he was bitterly disappointed.

"But Marrok, you must see what I mean? Even without Olivia, Mathias can find some way to use this book."

"But with someone who's both female and le Fay, it would be stronger."

"Yes." Bram was solemn once again. "For her, I suspect, the book's power would have no limit."

"We must keep her separated from the book."

Bram nodded. "Mathias isn't daft. He suspects that Olivia plays a role in using the diary."

"I cannot leave her to him. If the book is useless to him without her . . . I can give up the book, not the woman. Not my mate."

With a somber expression, Bram clapped him on the

shoulder. "If you give up the book, you surrender all hope of ending your hellish immortality."

"If something happens to Olivia, I will be in a hell worse than I've ever experienced. I can live forever, knowing I had her heart. She is worth any sacrifice."

As soon as he uttered the words, Marrok realized they were true.

"I think we *pretend* to give the diary to Mathias. The rest of the Doomsday Brethren will ensure that we get both the book and the woman back."

"I would not ask you to risk yourselves for me. I'm immortal; I cannot die no matter how badly I've wished to. She is my woman, and this is my fight."

"Uniting to defeat Mathias and protecting the book, regardless of the risk, are the reasons I created this group. You joined, so that includes you. Your mate isn't immortal, and you know that what Mathias can do to a woman will rip your heart out and haunt you forever."

Unfortunately, he did. All he could hope now was that he and the Doomsday Brethren could save her before it was too late.

Two a.m. Marrok entered the low-ceilinged tunnel. Dim lights shone overhead, so ineffectual he could not see his feet. In the middle of the tunnel, the lights simply stopped. Beyond lay complete darkness. With a pounding heart and the Doomsday Diary tucked in a pack strapped over his leather jacket, he put one foot in front of the other.

His boot heels echoed as they struck the brick floor. He could feel that he wasn't alone.

The smell inside the tunnel, dank with an awful mixture of dirt and sewage, nearly made him choke. The thought of

Olivia being here twisted his guts. He, who had felt virtually nothing for centuries, was nearly consumed with the anxiety and fury scalding his veins. In order to win, he would have to channel his energy and decimate his enemy.

He had to finish this. Presumably, Bram, Ice, Caden, and Duke had his back both figuratively and literally. None was more than a few feet behind him, concealed outside the tunnel. Of course, they were bound to protect the book at all costs.

"Stop there," a voice in the darkness beyond commanded.

Marrok halted and felt a strong invisible presence barge into his brain, overbearing, destructive, evil. The intruder tried to scan his thoughts. Marrok blanked his mind and gave a hard mental shove to the intruder.

The voice laughed, and Marrok could feel the icy drips of his amusement.

"I could push my way into your thoughts if I wished."

Marrok wasn't here to play. "You want the book more. Show me my mate."

To his right, one of the soulless Anarki ambled from the darkness, clutching Olivia in his decaying grip. She looked pale and disheveled and, with dilated violet eyes, frightened out of her head. But she was alive.

"*Tsk*, Marrok of Cadbury. Of course she is alive. I do not make a habit of killing women—at least not right away. There are far better uses for them."

He'd kill the evil prick if he'd touched or hurt Olivia. He'd hunt that voice down to the ends of the earth and find some way to destroy him. But not now. It took all he had to control his temper and stand mute. For Olivia's sake, he did.

"How touching, your desire to defend your mate. Don't

you think it's ironic that you should fall in love with a woman from the very line who cursed you?"

"Olivia is not Morganna."

"If it pleases you to believe one le Fay isn't like the next . . ." Mathias mocked. "Then we'll get on with business. Hand me the book."

"Give me my mate."

The voice hesitated. "A classic impasse."

Suddenly, the disembodied voice stepped into the light. Younger than expected. Darkness and power rolled off him, a calling card that would flatten most. Marrok towered a good ten centimeters above the man, and likely outweighed him by more than three stone.

But this man was deeply magical, down to his marrow. It vibrated from his very skin, sending chills down Marrok's spine.

Immortality would help him, Marrok knew, but this enemy held his Achilles' heel—Olivia—in an evil grip.

"I am outnumbered," Marrok pointed out. "Nor am I magical. We will have to leave here on foot. While you could zap me away the moment I surrendered the diary."

"True. Are you alone?"

Before he could answer, Marrok felt a stealthy tiptoe into his mind. Slick. Barely detectable. He purposely pictured Bram back in his office and Ice and Duke squaring off on the training field, foils in sweat-drenched hands. And he thought of absolutely nothing else.

"Of course," he lied.

"I'm not certain I believe you."

Marrok shrugged. "Bram saved me when the Anarki called upon my house uninvited. I repaid the favor by teaching his men to fight. We are not friends, but now we are even."

Mathias appeared to mull that over, then glanced over his shoulder. "Is this true?"

A second figure walked from the shadows, into the dim buzz of light drizzling down. Black hair brushing his shoulders, leather all around, dark sunglasses concealing his eyes to all.

"Shock," Marrok growled.

He dismissed Marrok with a tight smile. "He and Bram are not friends. About that, he does not lie."

"Still, Bram wants the book for his own."

With a nod, Shock confirmed Mathias's suspicions.

"You snake," Marrok hurled at him.

Shock shrugged as if completely bored by the conversation. "My family has ties to Mathias and his cause. I'm making Mummy and Daddy very proud. Besides, I owe Mathias a great thanks for a recent favor. It was simple enough to repay him with a bit of information and the agreement to fight you on his behalf. Nothing personal."

Marrok took it very personally. He might have been able to outwit the wizard since Mathias did not know him. Shock, the traitor, knew enough to make that improbable. Lucan had tried to tell Bram, tell them all.

"Escort our guest to her mate's side and hold her there until he brings the book to me."

"Nay," Marrok protested. "I give you the book once she leaves the tunnel unharmed."

"I've given you my terms. Take them or watch her die."

Though he could ill afford it, Marrok diverted his attention to Olivia for a moment. She was doing her best to escape the half-dead minion and the stink of his rotting flesh.

Then the evil wizard waved his hand. A moment later, Olivia stiffened in the Anarki's arms, clawing at her throat, mouth open, face turning red. Gasping.

"Give her some bloody air!"

With a smirk that made Marrok want to punch him into the next century, Mathias waved his hand again. Olivia gasped audibly, then let it out, shuddering.

Mathias would pay for that—and any other harm he'd done to Olivia.

"Cooperate, or your mate will lose her ability to breathe permanently."

Shock crossed the graying floor and grabbed Olivia by the arm, dragging her forward. Marrok would have protested—and taken Shock's head off—if he hadn't feared what the wizard would do to Olivia in retaliation.

Marrok raced toward his mate. In two steps, he was in front of her, bringing her against him, holding her in his arms.

"Are you well, love?"

She nodded, then sobbed. "He killed my father right after your cottage was attacked. Mathias was pretending to be him for days."

So, he had been right—and wrong—about Richard, but that brought him no comfort.

He tucked those thoughts away and focused on stroking Olivia's back, caressing her hair, offering her comfort with a brush of his lips against hers. Sweet and in one piece. Nothing else mattered.

"As touching as this is," Mathias cut in, "I require the book. Now. Bring it to me."

"Let Olivia leave the tunnel. All else is between you and me, and I have not the magic to fight you."

Mathias paused, considering. "She may walk to the end of the tunnel, but stays inside where I can see her . . . just in case."

Marrok hated it, but the concession did get Olivia a good

six meters from the fight he knew was about to happen. Slowly, he nodded.

Releasing Olivia was the hardest thing he'd ever done, but he unwound his arms from around her and tried to set her away.

"No," she protested, grasping at his shoulders. "He isn't to be trusted. He will take the book and do something dreadful."

"I will not let him harm you."

"It's not me I'm worried about!" She gripped him harder. "He's dangerous, unscrupulous. Please . . . Don't give up the book. You will never be free of the curse if you do."

"That is not important. Go!" he urged, shoving her toward the tunnel's opening. At least standing there, the others could watch her. She was one of their own. If all hell broke loose, they would save her.

Still, she wasn't budging.

From across the distance, Shock raised his hand. Marrok protested and lunged—too late. He blasted Olivia to the end of the tunnel. She tumbled on her backside on the bricks, just at the place where moonlight crept into the underground structure.

"You were given an order, witch. Obey," Shock snarled. "Or do you think yourself too important because you're a le Fay?"

Marrok grabbed a blade from the sheath strapped to his thigh and raised it threateningly at Shock. He'd dearly love to sink this blade into the man's flesh. Repeatedly, if needed.

But Shock wasn't his primary enemy. He'd be dealt with later. For now, Mathias and his considerable half-dead army deserved all of Marrok's attention.

"Now," Mathias tsked. "I want the book. Let us conclude this business, shall we?"

"Give me the damn book, human," Shock growled.

The wizard was begging to have his gut slashed open.

Taking a deep breath, Marrok took two steps toward Mathias and Shock, nearly to the edge of the light. Then he stopped.

"Meet me halfway."

"I am in no mood to compromise. Give it over!"

Marrok's mind raced. What happened in the next few moments would determine the outcome of this whole event—and the rest of his eternity. He must keep his wits about him.

Deep breath. *Three, two, one* . . .

Suddenly, Marrok leapt at Mathias. He flung the book in his face, hitting him square in the nose. Warm blood spurted across his forearms, and Mathias howled. Marrok followed the assault by sticking the knife in the evil wizard's gut and twisting hard.

"Run, Olivia!"

He didn't dare look behind him to see if his mate complied, not when the book fell to the ground with a thud. Marrok saw Shock lunge for it at the same time he did. Marrok dove at it, but Shock already had it in his grasp.

"Stupid human," Mathias spat. "I'd planned no more than light torture for you, since I cannot kill you outright. Now . . ."

Mathias raised his hands above his head, his expression more than fearsome; it was terrifying. Those blue eyes turned red, and Marrok swore he was seeing the devil in the flesh.

Quickly, he drew his Glock from the waistband of his trousers and fired a shot at Mathias, right between the eyes. He shot again, this time hitting the evil bastard right in the heart. The wizard fell to the bricks, limp.

Then he turned to confront Shock, only to find the traitor—and the book—gone. Bloody hell, the bastard had zapped out of here to God knew where. But losing the book to gain Olivia's freedom was worth every day of immortality. He'd endure anything for her. Everything.

He turned to the end of the tunnel, hoping he'd find it empty. Instead, Olivia stood there, wide eyes growing wider with each passing moment. She gasped, pointing to something just beyond him. Marrok whirled on the balls of his feet, expecting to see Shock challenging him.

Instead, Mathias stood. Blood dripped down his face, into his eyes, onto his white shirt, saturating it. Marrok could see the bullet lodged in his forehead. It would have killed any human.

Mathias definitely was not human. That was clear when he blinked and the bullet oozed out, falling to the ground with a *clink*. The wound healed itself instantly.

"You've ruined one of my favorite shirts, along with my evening, and given me an enormous headache."

Mathias made a quick whip of his arm, then a flick of his wrist, and Marrok felt something puncture his chest. Enormous. Ragged. Burning as it sliced down, threatening to gut him.

He dropped to his knees, and Mathias laughed, the maniacal sound bouncing off the walls, closing in on him. Marrok placed his hands over his belly and came away with a fistful of blood. He choked, and looked at Mathias in horror. Had the wizard somehow found a way to kill him? Because he could swear that he was rapidly losing his life.

"No!" Olivia shouted, running to his rescue. "Stop it."

"Go!" Marrok told her. "Be safe."

"I won't leave you!"

The fiery slice of his flesh was nearly to his pubic bone now. Certainly, his guts would fall out soon. Blood seeped everywhere. He was going to die. Mathias was apparently more magical than Morganna's curse. But damn it, he wanted to die in peace, knowing that Olivia was safe and well.

"Go. Please," he begged as he fell to the ground in a hot pool of his own blood. "For me. Love you." Marrok couldn't leave her and this life without saying those words.

Then everything went black.

CHAPTER NINETEEN

OLIVIA STOOD TOE TO TOE with Mathias. Before, she'd been terrified of the dark wizard, doing anything and everything not to draw his ire.

Now she was just pissed off.

"Perhaps your mate wasn't so immortal after all," Mathias drawled, his hands dripping blood.

He looked like an extra from a horror flick. Though wounded, he did a damn good job of hiding it.

Timidity had gotten her nowhere with the wizard. She'd played by his rules. He'd gravely injured her mate, whose possibly dying words had been that he loved her.

She loved him, too. It gouged her soul to think of him dying like this. Why wasn't he spontaneously healing, as before? Whatever the reason, she wasn't giving up.

Mathias was going down.

"Down? Hardly, witchling. You haven't yet learned to master your thoughts, much less me." Mathias cocked his head to the side, looking amused. "Are you getting angry?"

"I'm already there," she snapped.

Energy collected inside her, growing, glowing. Her fury melded with her determination. Fear fused with her love for Marrok. It coalesced in her head, racing through her body, a lightning-fast lava sizzling down her arms, into her fingertips.

Before she could let it fly, a commotion behind her disrupted the stream of energy.

Bram, Duke, and Ice ran down the tunnel, three abreast. Caden followed, his charming smile replaced by a feral battle snarl, backed up by the automatic weapon in his hand and wicked blades strapped to his hard thighs.

With a wave of his hand, Bram flooded the tunnel with light. Olivia gasped. Behind Mathias, at least two hundred of the half-dead Anarki waited, their eerie hooded faces gray and menacing.

Oh God. This would be a difficult and deadly fight for the Doomsday Brethren.

Mathias reached out, palms down, gathering his own flash of energy. Olivia shook at the red-eyed fury on his face, but refused to cower. She'd fight to the death.

Then sparks flew from Mathias's fingertips, red and orange and black, like something out of the bowels of hell. The Anarki rushed forward, charging right for her.

"Duck!" Caden screamed as he shoved her to the ground.

The *rat-tat-tat* of machine-gun fire resounded off the ungiving walls of the tunnel. The first row of Anarki fell. Another cropped up to take their place.

Mathias staggered against another bullet, but when Olivia looked up, he'd already healed the wound in his thigh as he had the gunshot to his head, with a wave of his hand. Though paler, he stood tall, looking down at Olivia huddled on the ground where Caden had shoved her.

"This battle is pointless. You cannot win. Already, you're in the position you'll occupy for the rest of your days, witch: kneeling at my feet."

"Never."

"Saving yourself for your mate?" He glanced at Marrok. "You needn't bother. He's not yet dead. But soon, he will be."

"Bastard!" Caden shouted. "Where the hell is my brother's wife?"

Mathias simply smiled.

Bram and Ice both drew nasty-looking guns and began firing at will into the crowd. Duke hacked his way in with a blunt sword, dripping sweat and black blood as he stepped over decaying bodies resolutely. Olivia scarcely noticed. All the fury and energy that had been coiling in her before the Doomsday Brethren's appearance made another surge.

Bram fought his way to her side quickly and stood between her and Mathias. "Go!"

"I'm not leaving Marrok."

After the barest glance down, Bram fixed his gaze on the enemy. "He wanted to die."

"Not like this," she argued.

"I have no doubt that his last wish was for your safety. Go! Don't make his death in vain."

Damn it, Olivia hated it, but Bram was right. Marrok had surrendered both his chance to break the curse and his life to save hers.

With a sob, she darted toward the end of the tunnel, the chill of Anarki right behind her. Adrenaline charged her veins, mixing with a potent rush of energy.

Before she could dash out of the tunnel and into the moonlight, a figure stepped out, blocking her. Leather, sunglasses, and bad attitude. Shock.

Olivia skidded, trying to change direction, but Shock

snaked out a beefy arm and caught her against his chest, then turned her to face the battle inside the tunnel.

"Release it!"

"Let me go, traitor!" she screamed, struggling for escape.

His grip remained painfully tight. "That energy inside you. Can't you feel it? Mask your goddamn thoughts and release it!"

A few feet away, Bram and Mathias faced off. Like gunfighters in the Old West, they stared and waited for the other to twitch first. Power sparked the air, clashing and crashing.

"Do it!" Shock insisted.

"Go to hell! You betrayed us—"

"Shut up." Losing patience, he brought her hands to her sides. "Marrok is enduring agony after excruciating centuries alone. You'll know the same once your mate is gone, if you let Mathias take him from you. You want that?"

No!

Would her despair somehow help Mathias? She struggled to hold the feelings back, but couldn't. Fury and anguish swarmed her as the half-dead Anarki ran her way. The energy wound up inside her like a screeching crescendo, tight and keening inside her. *Mathias, the bastard. The mate thief. The cruel monster.* It blasted her with power, yanked away the fear.

"When I tell you, take all that energy ramping up inside you and let it fly," Shock growled in her ear.

"Bite me!"

"You want to rescue your mate or not?"

Olivia did, and everyone knew it. She had to start masking her thoughts better. In her head, she chanted one of her favorite songs, *How many people want to kick some ass? I do! I do!* Shock chuckled.

Bram and Mathias raised their hands and blasted one another. Their energies collided head-on, like two high-speed trains traveling in opposite directions on the same track. The resulting crash was terrible and awesome. Fire roared at the ceiling, then flamed out toward Bram.

He ducked and, with a grunt, hoisted Marrok up from the ground.

Then Shock raised her arms and shouted, "Now!"

As if his words were the match on a tinderbox, a spark jolted inside Olivia like lightning. Thunder followed when she shuddered. The energy that had been gathering shot from her fingertips, sizzling her skin. As it jetted from her, she saw it, white, gold, and violet mixing in an odd laser— headed for the wrong person.

"Bram!" she screamed.

He couldn't hear, didn't move out of the way at all. Instead, he reached for Marrok, lying so frightfully still in the pool of blood on the brick floor. Oh, dear God. She was going to hurt Bram when this blast of energy hit him square in the back. She might even kill him, all because she'd let Shock crawl inside her head and used her magic for violence.

But as the energy hit Bram, the stream flowed around him like water around a rock. It hit Mathias in the dead center of his chest.

He staggered, tripped, gasping for air. His evil eyes opened wide in shock. Then he crumpled to the ground, blood oozing from his nose, mouth, eyes, and pores.

"Bloody hell, witch!" Shock growled in her ear.

Everyone stopped dead. Collective amazement sucked the air out of the tunnel. Incredulity was written all over Ice's face.

Duke whistled. "Amazing!"

What the hell had she done? "Is he dead?"

No one answered. She looked over at Duke, who was now closest to Mathias. "Devastating injury. It would kill most wizards."

"But this is Mathias," Shock pointed out.

Right. The man had healed his own bullet wound, so it was possible that she hadn't finished him for good. On the other hand, he wasn't getting up. Or moving—at all.

Still . . . "We ought to finish him off now," she suggested.

She struggled against Shock's hold so she could help out. He refused to release her.

"Get your bloody hands off her," Duke demanded.

"Piss off!"

Ice ignored the drama, and with broadsword in hand, stalked toward Mathias.

"She's right. The only good evil wizard is a headless one." He paused, peering closer. "What the— His signature is nearly blank, almost like he has no magic. Bloody hell!"

"Is it possible she eradicated his?" Caden asked.

"Normally, I'd say no. But she's a le Fay."

They all turned a glance on her that was part awe, part fear. Was she that powerful?

Suddenly, the Anarki swarmed around Mathias protectively, resuming the fight with Ice and the others. They also blocked Olivia's view of the psycho wizard.

The Doomsday Brethren jumped back in the melee. Bram ran, clutching Marrok's bloodied form against him. Before he could escape, the half-dead reached after him, seizing, grasping, fists ready.

Carrying Marrok's superior weight, Bram stumbled to his knees. Immediately, he took a blow to the face from one of the half-dead. Another grabbed him by the hair with a skeletal hand and yanked back. Still clutching Marrok to his chest, Bram couldn't defend himself against the brutal punch that pounded the right side of his jaw and sent his head snapping into the kick of another Anarki.

She had to fight!

Olivia struggled against Shock's hold, but he wasn't budging.

"Stay," he growled.

"I swear I'm going to kick you in the balls the first chance I get!"

No matter how she flailed her arms or kicked out with her legs, she could not dislodge the incredible strength of his hold.

"Don't be daft. If you charge in there, the Anarki will kill you."

"Why the hell do you care?"

Shock cursed. "Here, hold this."

Reflexively, she grabbed the item he thrust at her as he stalked off toward the battle. She looked down at the small-ish, leather-bound thing in her hands.

The Doomsday Diary?

"Is this . . ." Shock was already gone, shoulders deep in the melee. But doing what?

Why had he given her the book?

Caden emptied bullets into the Anarki, expertly avoiding the other Doomsday Brethren. Slowly, Bram crawled to the edge of the tunnel, Marrok clutched against him. The Anarki tried to claw him back.

Olivia tucked the book inside her blouse and raced forward. She didn't know much about fighting, but she'd played a little soccer in school. She had a mean kick.

She reached the first half-dead soldier camped on Bram's back, who was beating Bram brutally. The wizard's gorgeous face was swollen. Blood dripped from his nose and mouth, matted his hair, covered his shirt.

And still, he did not leave Marrok to the whims of Mathias's army.

Olivia kicked the half-dead Anarki on Bram's back. The decomposing body's head snapped back, then fell off. She grimaced and fought the urge to retch as black goo spewed. Instead, she locked her fingers together, and with a battle cry, struck the ribs of another Anarki attacking Bram. The zombie's rib cage collapsed under her fist. She shuddered.

"Get yourself safe!" Bram panted.

He was rescuing a man who might already be dead and was halfway there himself, and he worried about *her*?

"You two get somewhere safe. I'm fine."

Olivia charged into the battle as Caden flattened another four Anarki with bullets. She sidled closer to him, grabbed one of the blades strapped to his thigh, and plunged it into the half-dead soldier headed for her. It crumpled to the ground.

"Damn it!" Caden swore, shaking the gun.

He had run out of bullets. Very bad news. Anarki still fought everywhere, and Olivia knew they needed all the firepower they could muster.

At least she didn't see Mathias up and fighting.

Caden tossed the gun down. "Give me the knife."

"Don't you have another?" she asked as another zombie closed in on them.

"Shock has it."

He'd given Shock, the traitor, a weapon to help the Anarki defeat them? Well, hell.

Suddenly, the lights flickered, then blanked out entirely. She held in a scream. In the dark, someone grabbed her, but she knew instantly it wasn't Anarki.

"Be still," a voice whispered in her ear.

Shock. He'd tried to capture her for Mathias's personal

use earlier. What did he want now, in the middle of the darkened tunnel, in the heat of battle? She stomped down on his instep, and he hissed in her ear, hopping away.

Eerie silence fell, making her shiver.

Someone snapped then, and the lights illuminated the tunnel again. Bodies of the dead Anarki zombies littered the charred tunnel, oozing black slime. To her stunned surprise, Shock and the Anarki who hadn't been felled by the Doomsday Brethren were gone.

So was Mathias.

The Doomsday Diary was still resting against her chest, close to her heart.

Exactly where she wanted Marrok to be.

"What happened?" she murmured.

Duke scanned the tunnel. "We won the battle. Time will tell if we won the war."

Back at Bram's estate, Olivia paced beside her bed, across which Marrok lay, frighteningly pale and still. On the other side, Duke, Ice, and Caden had gathered near with grim faces. Olivia knew by their expressions that her mate's condition was grave. Bram, standing at the foot of the bed, had called for a wizened old wizard, magickind's answer to a doctor. The old man mixed a poultice, said a few words, and waved his hands.

Earlier, she'd washed Marrok clean of blood and Sabelle had helped her dress him in fresh clothes. He was mending, and faster than the average human, but not at the pace he had mere days ago. Why wasn't he healing into his protective, pushy self?

Bram watched the healer intently. Olivia held in a scream. The not knowing killed her. Would her mate, the man who held her heart in his hands, die for saving her?

"Damn it, what's going on?" she asked.

Still bloody and ragged, Bram looked like he'd fought a pack of bears and lost. To his credit, he hadn't once mentioned cleaning up . . . or asked about the diary.

"He will live," the old healer said finally. "Many others would have gone on. Something holds him here."

Yeah, cursed immortality. She sighed as the healer left, explaining there was nothing more he could do.

Bram's eyes narrowed in a scheming expression that meant he was up to something. "I have an idea for healing him." Bram took her by the hand, guiding her to Marrok's side. "Put your hands on his chest."

She frowned quizzically, but did as she was told. Marrok's hard flesh felt so alive under her touch, his warmth, the ripple of muscle. So . . . normal. Olivia could almost believe he was sleeping, if it weren't for the angry jagged cut bisecting him and his shallow breaths.

Puzzled, she frowned at Bram. "Won't I infect his wounds with my germs? Maybe he needs a hospital."

"Imagine filling out that form." He cleared his throat and mimicked a female nurse's voice. "Age of the patient, madam?"

Good point.

"Just put your hands on him, close to his heart, and close your eyes. Remember that burst of energy you had in the tunnel? How did you know to do that?"

"Shock grabbed me as I was trying to escape. He barked at me to gather and focus the energy, then encouraged me to blast it." The memory of the event rolled over her, and she cast an apologetic glance at Bram. "When I first released it, I thought it might hit you. Thank God, it ran right around you."

Bram sent her a stunned stare. "How did you do that?"

"I don't know. I just kept hoping it wouldn't touch you and it didn't." Bram's expression made her pause. "That's not normal, is it?"

"By all rights, your blast should have hit me, perhaps killed me. Shock had nothing to do with your energy missing me?"

"He made me madder and madder, taunted me into blasting out all my anger. And I was furious! Mathias was hurting you, and he'd already—" Olivia dropped her gaze to Marrok. Fear climbed inside her belly again, gouging at her composure. She fought tears as she curled her fingers around his arm. "What will happen to him?"

"You're going to cure him by focusing on healing thoughts instead of anger, then pouring that power into Marrok."

With a gasp, Olivia jerked her hands from Marrok. "No! I either killed Mathias or ripped out all his magic with that blast. I couldn't—"

"You seriously wounded him, but the bloody sod is still alive and had at least enough magic to teleport out and take the Anarki with him."

"Maybe Shock did that."

"We don't know which side Shock truly supports, but only Mathias could control the Anarki and make them disappear. So unfortunately, he's alive and well. But you reduced him a great deal. That in itself is a victory."

Olivia didn't know if not having killed Mathias made her feel worse or better. Power had surged through her, and she had wished him dead when she blasted him. She'd stunned him enough to flatten him to the ground and make him bleed.

"But it didn't really help."

"I wouldn't say that. Mathias was down, even as he left. His signature was nearly blank. That indicates very weak magic. It's likely you damaged his power a great deal, maybe even permanently. That is very helpful. Mathias without power is just another cheesed-off man."

Which made him a heck of a lot less dangerous. "Isn't it odd that I can do magic before transition?"

Bram hesitated. "Yes and no. Most can perform simple spells before reaching maturity. The key, however, is simple. The magic you performed was both strong and complex beyond what an untransitioned witch should be capable of. Beyond what many fully transitioned can do. You'll be extraordinarily powerful someday. And everyone in that tunnel took notice."

"Are my powers strong enough to heal Marrok?" She glanced at her pale, fading mate, her heart squeezing in fear all over again.

"At the very least, your concern and need for him should carry through your bond and give him strength."

"W—what if I accidentally hurt him?"

Impatience crossed his face. "Do you love Marrok?"

"Yes."

"Your love will reach him. Magic isn't merely about spells. You can learn them—and must. But casting magic revolves around the power of the witch or wizard. Power you clearly have. It's also about passion and intent. You *intended* earlier tonight to hurt Mathias and you violently wanted it. You did. Right now, you intend to heal Marrok and yearn for his recovery. I don't know if you have healing magic, but as I said, at worst, your touch will reaffirm your bond and strengthen his will to live."

Olivia stared at her mate, lying so still. His breathing had grown more ragged. His skin now rivaled a winter snow. No more time to argue or worry. Though Marrok had said that he wanted to die, she knew he would never want to die at evil's hand. She had to do everything possible to enable him to choose life . . . or death.

Closing her eyes, she placed her hands on his chest. Before that touch, she'd begun to feel weak. But the power of the bond came to her rescue, infusing her with new vitality. That power circled back to him, providing a seemingly endless loop of emotional fuel.

Focusing, she gathered her healing thoughts. They swirled, warming and growing, gentle yet strong. Her chest sucked it up from the rest of her body, like a vacuum cleaner. It rolled together, begging for freedom. Then suddenly, it reached critical mass and rolled down her arms and into her fingertips. That same sizzle and burn that happened in the tunnel accompanied this exchange of energy. It hit Marrok. He jerked, bucked, groaned.

She sagged against him, spent.

Suddenly, Marrok clamped a huge hand around her wrist. Gasping, he jackknifed up and opened disconcertingly blue eyes, aiming a startled stare at her.

Olivia pushed him back to the bed, scanning his chest. The jagged cut bisecting him had completely healed. No gaping wound, no puckered flesh, no scar. Nothing.

A miracle!

"Oh my . . . You're all right!" Olivia threw her arms around Marrok as joy suffused her. "I was so worried!"

He caught her in a fierce hug. "I felt your essence, our bond. You healed me."

She smiled through her tears. He was whole and well. In that shining moment, she felt complete. "How is this possible?"

"Your power," Bram supplied. "Once transitioned, you'll be a great witch."

"But I am no longer invincible," Marrok cut in. "I feel pain again. I bleed. I no longer feel immortal."

Olivia gasped. No longer immortal? No longer cursed?

Then he no longer needed her. The reality hit her like an avalanche.

"You're certain?" Bram asked.

"Aye."

"Marrok, Olivia is an amazing witch, but she only healed you, my friend. She couldn't have ended your curse."

"Nay." The harsh syllable came from Marrok. "Olivia did not uncurse me. I felt it end sooner. 'Twas something Mathias performed, I think. What did he do to me?"

"You're truly certain?" Bram sounded skeptical. "I've never heard of casting a spell to end a curse." Bram looked to Duke and Ice for confirmation. "Do you know of any such spell?"

Caden said, "I have no idea. This bloody business of magic is not one I'm eager to fall into. Once my brother is well and Anka is found, I'll be returning to Texas."

"Transition is hard on your heels," Bram pointed out.

Caden shrugged as if to say *So what?*

Duke answered Bram next. "I've never heard of magic stronger than the curse Morganna laid on Marrok. But my family is steeped more in the human than magical, so . . ."

Ice drew in a breath. "I've never heard of such magic, either."

Bram cursed. "Shock would know, given the dark magic in his family." He cut a glance over to Olivia. "You saw him last. Do you know where he went?"

She shook her head. Even if she did know, she wouldn't ask someone who might be cozying up to Mathias.

"Was anyone able to retrieve the book?" Marrok asked.

Olivia moved around Bram, then opened a drawer in the dresser behind him. Snatching it up, she handed the book to Marrok. "Shock gave it to me before the tunnel went dark and he disappeared."

"He put it right in your hands?" Bram asked.

"Yes."

Every magical warrior's jaw dropped.

Marrok's hands dwarfed the little red volume. Olivia wondered how such a small thing could have caused one man so much agony. But she knew it was because her great-great-grandmother had wished it so.

He yanked the book open, thumbing through blank page after blank page. Until he stopped suddenly, his attention riveted on yet another blank page. Puzzled, she frowned.

"Does it say something?" Bram asked.

Slowly, Marrok nodded. "On the very page which Morganna once cursed me."

"Well? Out with it!"

Marrok's frown deepened. " 'For not loving me, I cursed you and your cruel black heart. To live alone forever, despondent, unsatisfied, apart. Only true love for another, given freely, would uncurse you. Your heart fully shared until you were one, not two. Now you truly love, as my diary can see. Your sacrifice and caring have not gone unnoticed. As such, I release thee.' "

The silence around the room was deafening, and Olivia stared at the gleaming hardwood floor beneath her feet.

He loved her?

"It was your sacrifice," Bram said to Marrok. "Your willingness to surrender the book—and your only known means of ending your curse—in order to save Olivia."

Slowly, Marrok nodded. "I threw the book at Mathias, and a wave overcame me. A cold sweat and dizziness I chalked up to nerves. It was the end of my torment." He closed his eyes. "Now I can die."

Olivia swallowed a sob that crushed her momentary happiness. After a millennium and a half of loneliness, anyone would seek peace. He'd said all along that he sought death. Now that he could achieve it, Marrok's serenity was overpowering—and painful. She wanted to touch him, love him, beg him to live, but she wouldn't cling to him now, no matter how badly she wanted to. If dying would finally make him happy, she could not stand in his way, either as a le Fay or a woman. His death would break their bond. Then, she'd figure out what to do with her life. She was strong; his love had made her that way. She would survive, thrive even.

For him.

"If you wish to die, yes," Bram said quietly.

Olivia stared at Marrok, anguish tearing at her. He watched her, his face veiled.

No one had ever loved her. Until now. Until him. But his life was his choice, and she couldn't beg him to stay.

But she'd always miss him.

Before she said good-bye to Marrok she had one last unhappy duty.

"Caden, I found Anka with Mathias." She bit her lip. "She was naked, and . . . he fondled her, forced her to respond. She was protesting on the inside."

"Dear God," Ice muttered, looking pale and grim.

"Knowing she's endured *Terriforz* will kill Lucan," Caden breathed.

"*If* he survives the mate mourning," Bram supplied. "With Mathias weakened, we need to direct our energy to finding Anka, now that we know who she's with."

Olivia shook her head. "Mathias waved a hand, and she disappeared. I don't know if he sent her to be used by the rest of the Anarki or . . ." She touched a gentle hand to Caden's shoulder. "I'm sorry I couldn't help her."

Caden's jaw clenched, but he managed to shake his head.

"You were in your own danger. Thank you for the information."

She hoped it helped, but based on what she'd seen, she wasn't sure if the couple could ever be the same.

"I hope you find her," she murmured.

Bram nodded. "We'll split into teams. Ice and Duke, see if you can return to the tunnel. Take Caden with you. Lucan mentioned that you're good with a camera?"

At the younger MacTavish's nod, Bram instructed, "Take one and shoot photos. Maybe there will be some clue there."

"I'm going to track Shock down. He might be playing for Mathias's team now, but I know he'd never want any harm to come to Anka. We'll find her," Bram promised.

"I'd like to help if I can," Olivia offered.

"Nay," Marrok barked.

"Too dangerous," Bram said.

"I'm not the only one risking myself. You risked today, too."

"Indeed," Marrok said to Bram, looking puzzled. "I was wounded, and you raced into the battle to pull me from the thick of it."

"Olivia is the hero. She provided the magic that allowed us to escape."

"But you carried me at great risk to yourself." He stuck out his hand. "Thank you."

The handshake lasted moments, but seemed to cement a bond between them. Marrok turned his gaze to her, and Olivia's heart raced triple time. His stare said nothing and everything. Her heart wrenched. He loved her.

But it wasn't enough to hold him to a life that had given him such pain.

"After everything my family put you through, I'm glad I could help you be free. I know you have to . . . go. That you want to. I understand. I will always love you." Olivia got the words out before she choked on tears. She placed a soft kiss on his mouth.

Before she could get out the door, the Doomsday Diary caught her eyes. She snatched up the book and put it in Bram's hands. "This has caused Marrok enough misery. And I don't want it. You and the Doomsday Brethren guard it. I know you will keep it safe."

Bram accepted it with, not the smile she would have expected, but a solemn nod. "With our lives."

"I'll rest easier knowing that." She sent him a sad smile, then took a last, lingering glance at Marrok, memorizing the strong angles of his beloved face before tears blurred the image. "Excuse me."

The door closed behind her with a soft *snick*.

Marrok watched Olivia leave. Resignation hung off her. And pain. Damn, he couldn't stand to see her hurt.

He sat up and swung his legs off the bed, conscious of four sets of eyes on him—the rest of the Doomsday Brethren. The men he had trained, fought beside, in whose hands he had put his life. After all that, they were something like friends. The first he'd had in over a millennium. He could leave them all, cast aside all the connections he'd made since Bram had interrupted his dream of Olivia and forced him to her little shop. He was now free to embrace death.

But he wanted nothing less.

Jumping off the bed, he stared at the book in Bram's hands. "My mate is right. Keep the diary. I am ill-equipped to guard such a valuable relic against magical evil by myself. But together, you are." His gaze touched on Duke, Caden, and Ice.

Then he strode to the door.

"Are you going to die now?" Bram asked.

Hand on the latch, he paused. "Nay."

Bram released the breath he'd been holding. "Then we need you. We cannot properly trounce the Anarki without you. You fit well with us. Stay. Fight by our side. Be one of us."

Marrok turned, struck nearly speechless by the show of not just camaraderie, but friendship. "It would be my honor and my preference, if that is what my mate wishes."

Duke cleared his throat. "I hear quite well. Olivia just arranged a ride to London."

The thought of Olivia gone was a stake in the heart. He wasn't letting her go without a fight, without telling her that he no longer wanted death or solitude, just her.

"Rest today, men. Tomorrow, be prepared to train until you can barely stand upright. You *will* be sweating."

Marrok shut the door on their collective groans with a smile.

He caught up with Olivia in the hall, very near where he'd once made love to her against the wall. The memory alone twisted his guts into knots. He could not reconcile having someone so wonderful and losing her so completely.

"Wait! Olivia . . ."

She whirled, and the tears glistening in her violet eyes reached right into his chest and ripped out his heart.

Marrok grabbed her shoulders and pulled her closer. "My love . . ."

She closed her eyes for a moment, then seemed to compose herself. "I'm glad you came to say good-bye. You're finally able to seek peace. I'm happy for you. Since my family was responsible for your misery, I'm glad I was part of the remedy." She cupped his cheek, her eyes overflowing with tears. "I will miss you every day of my life and I will never forget that you taught me to love. Or that I am loved."

Olivia stood on tiptoe, eyes closed, and leaned in. Excitement jumped within him. Need pressed at him so hard, Marrok nearly imploded. Blood rushed through his body, engorging his cock. *Take her, claim her. She needs you.*

But he wanted her decision to stay to be of her own free will.

"You were not a mere part of the remedy, but the key. Always, I believed you were the necessary ingredient to break my curse. I was right . . . and wrong. The answer was not about forcing you to use your le Fay power to reverse the hex, but about letting go of my bitterness long enough to fall in love with you, le Fay or no. You taught me that I wanted to be uncursed, not because I wanted to die, but because I finally want to live. You have no reason to stay with me, I know. What does a modern twentysomething woman want with a man old enough to be dust? If you desire freedom, I will not fight if *you* wish to break our bond. But I will not end it. Ever. I want you as my love and my mate."

Her breath caught in her throat, and fresh tears floated down her face. "You don't want to die?"

"Not when I have so much to live for. Not when I have you to cherish." He frowned. "I believe men still do this." He dropped to one knee and took her hands in his. "Stay with me. Be my wife."

Olivia gasped, and fresh tears fell in earnest. "Seriously?"

"I have old knees. Would I be upon them if I did not mean it?"

She laughed through her tears, and happiness glowed on her face, reminding him of just one of the many reasons he needed her. She was his light. His future.

"I love you. I'm sorry I believed my father above you," she murmured.

"You were seeking the parental approval your mother denied you and you most desired. You are entitled to seek happiness. I cannot change what she did to you, but I can give you every bit of my heart and hope you find the joy you seek with me."

She nodded. "I never thought you would genuinely return my feelings. I was afraid to hope—"

"Do you say aye?"

"Yes!"

"Thank God. I can wait no longer to touch you." Marrok pinned her to the wall.

Then he kissed her senseless, breaking away once they were both panting and aching.

"Are you going to make a habit of ravishing me against walls?"

"Do you like it?" He pressed his erection against her, dotting her soft, scented neck with sweet kisses.

She purred. "Love it."

"Then aye. I will love you in any way you wish me to show you."

Olivia pressed her soft mouth to his. "Promise?"

"Always. Care to start now?"

Enjoy this excerpt from Shayla Black's
next steamy Doomsday Brethren tale,

Seduce Me in Shadow

Coming in Fall 2009

CHAPTER ONE

"We have problems."

If that was supposed to be news, Bram Rion's statement came about two weeks too late.

Hovering on the edge of a plush bottle green armchair, Caden MacTavish watched the wizard slam the door as he stormed into his palatial home office, locking the members of the Doomsday Brethren into the edgy silence with him. As the tension ratcheted up, he thought again of his brother. *Please God, let this end soon.*

A loud crash upstairs thumped the ceiling, shook the walls. A woman screamed, terror bleeding from her voice. On the floor above, a door crashed open, the shrieking grew louder, and footsteps pounded. She was running. For the door. To leave. Bloody hell!

Darting out of his seat, Caden raced for the stairs she flew down, ignoring Bram's shout calling him back.

At the foot of the stairs, he grabbed the frantic, fleeing witch by her shoulders. She was lovely, blonde, deceptively young looking. Her wide green eyes were frightened, as if she'd been playing a game of chicken with a barreling freight train—and was on the verge of losing.

"Wait. Please," he pleaded, trying to catch her gaze. "My brother—"

"I can't." Her voice quivered. "He's big and feral and . . . snarled that I smell like another man. He—he ripped away his chains." Her words broke with new tears. "Then he lunged for my throat."

Caden closed his eyes. The fifth energy surrogate Lucan had frightened away in two weeks. Now what?

At the top of the stairs, Bram's sister Sabelle appeared. Her clothes and hair were askew, but her demeanor was calm. "I have Lucan under control again. Let her go."

Instead, he clasped the witch tighter. "He needs her. Without her energy…" Caden couldn't finish the sentence. The thought.

"He'll die, yes. His mate mourning is strong. My Aunt Millie says she's never seen a case this severe." Sabelle sighed. " Lucan has refused to let any of the surrogates near him. Maybe . . . it's time to consider that he wants death."

"No! My brother will *not* die like this. I *will* find Anka and bring her back."

"It may be too late," Bram said from behind him. "Let the woman go."

"Please," the scared witch pleaded.

Caden shook with rage. He wanted to crush something, hit a wall—any means to rail in fury at fate. At magic. But the witch in his grasp with her broken sobs shrank back in fear. Like he, too, was a monster.

For about the two hundredth time since being dragged into this misadventure, he cursed magic and its power. The loss of a beloved wife to a human male could be emotionally devastating, true. But Lucan's loss of the bond he'd shared with Anka had driven a perfectly sane man completely mad, reduced him to a rabid frenzy.

Caden prayed again that his sleepless agitation was merely concern—and not a harbinger of his own coming transition into magic.

With a curse, Caden tore his grasp away from the blonde witch. "Go."

A few footsteps later, the door opened. Closed. Silence reverberated.

"Come back to my office," Bram said.

Caden whirled on him in low-voiced fury. "It isn't too late for my brother, damn you."

With a twitch of Bram's finger, magic grabbed Caden by the arm and hauled him into the office again. Bram followed, slamming the door behind them. Caden whirled on the wizard to give him a furious earful. Bram held up a hand.

"Don't. I understand why you feel frustrated. But this isn't merely about you and your family. Our problems affect everyone here." He gestured to the other three men in the room. "And all of magickind."

"My brother is chained to an upstairs bed like a lunatic, my sister-in-law is still missing and we have not a single clue where she's gone. Whatever your other problems, nothing could be more important than that."

"That's where you're wrong. Our other problems are, unfortunately, grave."

"You called me here to tell me a fact I already bloody know?" Annoyance stamped Ice Rykard's face. He rubbed the dark stubble covering his head. "I have other things to do."

As he rose to leave, Bram blocked his path. "Something new has arisen. Prudence requires that we attend to it. All of us. Immediately."

"I've come to help my brother, not to solve your problems," Caden insisted.

The gravity of Bram's expression took Caden aback. "Lucan is my best friend, and I want more than anything to make him whole again. But doing so is a mission of mercy. The other issues are matters of life and death."

"If you do not help me find Anka, he will die! Your sister admitted as much."

Bram hung his head, then looked up again, weary and slumped. "But if we fail to take care of this new problem, thousands, maybe millions, *will* die. Including Lucan."

The mentality of sacrificing one for many. Bram had shoved this strategy down Caden's throat before, and he still hated it. His patience was wearing thin. Exhaling, he rubbed gritty eyes. Every day, worrying. Every night, not sleeping—caught up in the electrical surges and odd urges racing through his body. He often paced, Lucan's mad countenance swimming in his mind. Yet his brother's friends worried about everyone else.

"Please." Bram grabbed Caden's shoulders. "We need you. Lucan needs you, and the sooner we tend to these issues, the sooner we can help him."

Caden felt four pairs of eyes drilling into him. He owed these men nothing. He'd known them a mere fortnight, wanted nothing to do with their world and their problems. But their stares accused him of abandoning them, and guilt twisted in his gut.

"The Doomsday Brethren meant a great deal to Lucan," Bram reminded.

The manipulative bastard.

"Besides, you may soon need us. Your magic is coming . . ."

"Not if I can bloody help it."

Marrok, the big human warrior, frowned at Bram, dark brows slashing down. "This new problem, does it concern Shock? Have we yet heard from the varlet?"

Good question. The shadiest member of the Doomsday Brethren had been MIA since their battle with Mathias and the Anarki two weeks ago—in which Shock had suddenly appeared to switch his loyalties to the other side. No surprise there, given the man's dark background. Because Shock was both Anka's previous suitor and in the back pocket of the very man who had abducted her, he might know something of his sister-in-law's whereabouts.

Bram, Ice, and Duke all shook their heads in reply.

"That is damn vexing," Marrok snarled. "Surely he has told Mathias much about us."

Indeed, the conniving prick had likely told Mathias everything necessary to sink the group of magical warriors. But that wasn't Caden's issue.

Bram blew out a breath. "That is a serious problem, but—"

"Mathias is the worst of it," Ice cut in. "Two weeks of silence from him . . . it's right dodgy. Makes me itch."

If Caden cared about magickind, he wouldn't disagree. But he worried only about discerning what Mathias had done with his sister-in-law after abducting her. His focus was bringing Anka back. That alone had the possibility of returning Lucan's sanity.

"During our last battle, Olivia laid a bolt of power on Mathias that should have flattened the bastard," Duke said. "It appeared to deplete his magic and should prevent him from rising again, but..."

"This *is* Mathias," Ice finished. "I would put no feat beyond him."

"Indeed."

If Mathias regained even half his power, the Doomsday Brethren were screwed, and every man in the room knew it. How could they kill the wizard intent on enslaving magickind who had already returned from the dead once? He had an army at his disposal. The number of Doomsday Brethren...Caden could count them on one hand. But not his problem. As soon as his brother recovered, he'd be gone.

Bram winced. "I'm afraid, gentlemen, it's worse than that."

"So you've seen this, then?" Duke slid a newspaper in the middle of Bram's desk. The bold black headline screamed "Supernatural Forces Battle in South London Tunnel."

Bram glanced at the paper. "*Out of This Realm*? It's a rag. No one takes that rubbish seriously."

"That may change after the article. The byline belongs to a reporter named Sydney Blair. She's disturbingly close to the truth. Most news outlets wrote off the battle with Mathias as a foiled terrorist act, a gang initiation, or a madman's haphazard attempt at chaos. Ms. Blair calls it 'an ongoing clash between powerful factions within magickind.'"

Bram's jaw dropped. "If she's human, how the bloody hell does she even know there's a magickind, much less an ongoing battle? Is she some wizard's mouthy human mate?"

"I consulted *Peers and People of Magickind* before coming here. I found no mention of her." Duke turned back to the newspaper. "The rest of the article is worse. 'The bodies discovered in the tunnel are decomposed far beyond expected, given their very recent deaths.'"

"Everyone knows that. The media has been scratching their head over that, like a mongrel with fleas."

"Listen further," Duke barked. "'*Out of This Realm* has learned the bodies bear new wounds and fresh traces of gunpowder, suggesting they somehow fought in the battle, rather than merely being left behind as a macabre message. Were they actually more dead than alive prior to the battle, but able to fight due to evil magic? We think so.'"

"She must be guessing," said Bram.

But even he didn't sound convinced.

Duke shook his head, dark length of hair curling against his collar. "Here's more: 'According to my source, there's a certain wizard on the loose again, allegedly fighting social injustice in the magical world. He'll stop at nothing to tear down the establishment and replace it with his version of anarchy. His name starts with an M and very nearly rhymes with Tobias.'"

Duke's words detonated in the room like a bomb.

"Fuck," Ice muttered.

Poor magical bastards, Caden thought. They did have problems.

"Who *is* this source?" Bram demanded.

"Ms. Blair only says that it's 'a witch who recently found herself tangled in this magical war.'"

Caden's heart stuttered. He slashed his stare over to Bram. "That could be Anka."

"Or any other of the dozen women missing, like Craddock's daughter," Ice pointed out.

"Whoever her source, Sydney Blair knows there's a magickind, that we're at war, and that Mathias is supposedly fighting the bloody Social Order," Duke insisted. "The moment anyone actually listens, she'll expose us to humankind. Then the Inquisition will seem like a bloody holiday. And if Mathias reads this, her life may well be in danger."

"We need to handle this situation." Bram raked a hand through his disheveled golden hair and continued to pace. "Soon."

"Would that we knew from whence Mathias found so many disposable recruits," Marrok muttered.

"That is yet another problem," Bram conceded. "But I called you here to discuss something more critical, if you'll all shut up."

Ice cast him a cutting stare. "The fact that your magical signature tells me that you took a human mate last night?"

Caden barely held in a gasp. Bram, the most pedigreed wizard of this generation, had taken a *human* mate?

"Wouldn't your grandfather be proud?" Ice sneered. "Merlin prized that pure bloodline. Pity."

Bram charged around his desk, directly at Ice. "Shut your bloody mouth, you fu—"

Marrok grabbed the Doomsday Brethren's quasi-leader and held him back. "Stop!"

"Piss off!"

Marrok rolled his eyes. "You have mated? Is this the problem?"

"Let me go," Bram snapped. "Or I'll break your arm."

Snorting, Marrok released him. "Were you to try, it would amuse me. Remember, we can fight no enemy if we are too busy fighting one another."

"Beating in the tosser's skull would make me feel better."

"What has you so on edge?" Duke asked.

Caden wondered the same thing. Not that he really cared, since this had nothing to do with Lucan. Though it was a puzzle. Bram was usually the voice of sanity amidst all this magical muck. At the moment, he seemed to be crawling out of his skin, as if he was one step away from needing a bed in the mental ward beside Lucan.

"Where is your mate?" Ice added fuel to the fire. "I'd like to offer her my condolences."

"*My* mate is none of your concern. What is, however, is the Book of Doomsday." Bram hesitated, then rolled his shoulders. "Last night, while I slept, she found it."

"Found it? Lying about?" Duke demanded.

"No. It was well hidden." Bram hung his head. "She must have searched for it."

"She cozied up to you in order to find the book?" Ice looked ready to laugh any moment.

"Enough!" Marrok glared at the stubble-headed wizard.

But Bram didn't have to answer; the humiliation on his face did it for him. The human woman had used the wizard's cock and the magical mate bond against him.

"And? Out with it, man," Duke demanded. "What happened?"

"She took the book and disappeared."

The silence in the room was a roar.

"Double fuck," muttered Ice.

If Mathias got his hands on that book and figured out how

to use it to bring about his evil wishes, including the commencement of doomsday—well, Bram was right; that could be his problem.

"You had no magical protections on the bloody book?" Duke's jaw dropped to his chest.

"Of course, against anyone *magical*. I never imagined a human would know of the book's existence. I have no notion how any human possibly could, and that I had it, unless she's a pawn of Mathias. What if he has the diary now? What do you think he will do to her?" Bram paced, raking a frantic hand through his golden hair.

Marrok planted a friendly hand on Bram's shoulder. "Can you use your bond to find her?"

"After one night, it's not strong enough."

"You touched her, aye?" Marrok asked. "Did you not use your powers to read her mind?"

"She is the only woman I have ever encountered whose mind I cannot read with a touch."

Duke sighed. "What the devil should we do now?"

Panic, perhaps? Caden kept the thought to himself.

Bram leaned back against his desk. The morning sun slanted through the office's open shutters, showing just how little sleep and how much strain the wizard was enduring. He swallowed, then pinned a wily gaze on Caden that made his blood freeze. "I have an idea . . ."

"So, have we gotten to the part yet where I spank you?"

Sydney Blair closed her eyes as the last notes of "Happy Birthday to You" echoed through the small conference room. This could *not* be happening. Had Jamie actually suggested a little light S&M with the entire staff of *Out of This Realm* looking on? *Bugger!*

A dozen of the newspaper's employees twittered with nervous laughter, except her yummy new freelance photographer, Caden MacTavish. Mortified, Sydney risked a glance at him. The taut arms bunched over his wide chest and the chilly blue of his watchful eyes made her wince. He looked like the poster boy for the unamused.

Sydney slowly turned to her on-again, off-again boyfriend with a glare that let him know she appreciated his comment as much as someone shouting the F-word in a nursery school class. He just shrugged and grinned from ear to ear. While Sydney wanted to believe Jamie was smart enough to realize his faux pas, she knew her chances of marrying Prince William were better.

"So, have we gotten to the part yet where you leave?" Caden countered.

The words somehow sounded polite. Caden had that upper crust thing going for him. He could say nearly anything and sound civilized. He didn't appear civilized, however. His current expression rivaled Attila the Hun's on a bad day.

"You think you should be first to spank her." Jamie challenged Caden, stroking several days' worth of dark stubble on his chin. "You've thought of it, haven't you? I've seen how you look at her."

Avoiding eye contact with Caden, Sydney went hot all over—from more than simple embarrassment. Caden lit her up like a millennium fireworks show. She'd be thrilled if the man had sexual thoughts of her. But in the two days she'd been working with him, he had not appeared to notice her in any capacity beyond work, despite Jamie's delusions to the contrary. The possibility that Caden secretly wanted her ranked as unlikely as a month without rain in London.

"Bad Karma!" Aquarius, her flower-child assistant, scolded. "Mellow!"

Neither spared a glance for the little waif. Silver bracelets tinkling, Aquarius reached out to Caden. Whether she intended to soothe him or test his aura, Sydney didn't know. She shot a warning glance to her assistant. Now was not a good time for a healing-crystal/save-the-world remark.

"You may find this concept hard to grasp," Caden asserted, "but some men are capable of admiring more about a woman than what's in her knickers."

Jamie scoffed. "Only if he's a total Nancy boy."

Sydney smothered a snort. Caden was definitely not gay. Despite that, she felt certain he'd never considered what went in her knickers.

"Both of you, stop it!" Sydney huffed. "This is a birthday party, not a brawl."

"What's your wish?" asked Leslie from Circulation, trying to smooth the tension.

A romping shag with Caden, but since that wasn't likely to happen... head reporter had a good ring. Yes, she worked for a paranormal tabloid that no one took seriously, but it paid well enough. Soon, she hoped to feature the stories, the *real* ones that traditional journalists rejected, when she found proof of the supernatural. Besides, *Out of This Realm* was a scream to work at. Where else could she collect a salary for chasing Ripper ghosts and conducting serious interviews at the London Psychic Centre?

Her personal life, however? Disaster. How did one manage to become a sad spinster at twenty-eight? The endless string of dates from her uni days had been replaced with deadlines and staff meetings. She'd begun dating Jamie to avoid being alone. A decision as smart as microwaving tin foil. His pretty face could not make up for the fact that he had the IQ of a dead houseplant and the emotional range of a frozen pea. Perhaps she *should* wish for a man.

For Caden.

Yummy waves of chocolate hair with caramel streaks, endlessly blue eyes, a body that belonged in magazines—and a reserved nature that made her curiosity claw to know the real him. He pulled at her like a magnet—but since Caden rarely looked at her, Sydney surmised the attraction didn't work both ways. She sighed. Sometimes the loo smelled sweeter than reality.

"She can't tell us her wish or it won't come true," Holly, her editor, pointed out, then faced Sydney. "Now stop fannying about and open your gifts."

Sydney looked at the gifts on the table. Very sweet . . . but Caden and Jamie continued to stare at one another like a pair of junkyard dogs.

What was the matter with these two? Jamie was brassed off; Sydney hadn't rung him lately, made a lot of excuses that she was too busy. No doubt, his rampant insecurity had seized his modicum of sense. But Caden . . . he was a puzzle, that one.

From the moment he'd walked in the door, he'd been focused on the battle in that Southark tunnel. Period. Yes, he'd called her story utter rubbish, eschewed the notion of a magical war . . . but he'd asked a load of questions, especially about her information source. Not that Sydney would tell him—or anyone else—the woman's identity.

So his argument with Jamie stunned Sydney. She wasn't sure why he bothered, but it was potentially a good sign. Maybe he was at least a bit interested.

Aquarius distracted the tense crowd by shoving a bright pink floral-wrapped box in her hands. From the number of packages stacked on the small round table in the conference room, it looked as if everyone had brought her something.

"You didn't have to go to this trouble."

"We wanted to show you how much we appreciate you," said Leslie.

Aquarius started pouring cups of her infamous home-blended herbal tea, so Sydney began unwrapping gifts. A pair of delicate silver earrings, a relaxing massage at a local day spa, and a sumptuous Italian silk scarf, trimmed in midnight blue crushed velvet. Jamie gave her a gift certificate for a large pizza and a Blockbuster card, good for a free rental—both of which he'd likely insist on sharing. Caden had given her a somewhat impersonal card and a small box of nice chocolates. She would have preferred a hungry kiss.

Wrapping paper and greeting cards littered the table like a refuse rainbow when Harry from Accounting asked, "Time to cut the cake?"

"You want Aquarius's carob cake? She's made it with prunes," his cohort muttered.

Harry flinched.

Aquarius ignored the usual digs at her unusual cooking and thrust a smallish, square package into her hand. Her friend vibrated with excitement. "Don't forget this! It's from me."

"You baked and organized and still got me something. You shouldn't have."

"Leslie is right; we all appreciate you." A smile brightened Aquarius's elfin features as she absently rubbed the butterfly tattoo on her shoulder, visible just outside the spaghetti strap of her tank top. "Me more than most."

Aquarius didn't dress like a *normal* assistant and refused to make coffee—too full of chemicals and caffeine. She wasn't good with a computer . . . yet. But Aquarius had a knack for stories, for juggling Sydney's hectic schedule, fielding the editor-in-chief, soothing paranoid readers and keeping internal chaos at a minimum. And despite being total opposites, she and Aquarius had become good friends.

"I appreciate you, too." Sydney smiled.

"Are you two going to start snogging or are you going to open that?" Jamie hollered.

After tossing another glare at Jamie—the subtlety of which was likely lost on him—Sydney turned to the final gift. It was square and slightly heavy. Aquarius had wrapped it in buttery yellow linen and an over layer of white lace—different from her usual recycled choice.

"Open it," she whispered.

An odd anticipation revved through Sydney as she plucked at the silky white bow around the wrapping. Holding her breath, she tore at the feminine trappings. She turned it over to reveal . . . a book. An old-fashioned-looking book. A red leather cover with gilt framing and some sort of scripty-looking symbol on the front. *Hmm* . . . the inside revealed an empty book with ever-so-slightly yellowed pages. Sydney tried to hide her confusion.

Caden elbowed in and stared at the book, looking somewhat stunned. Apparently, he thought it an odd gift as well.

Aquarius laughed and urged her, "Read the card inside."

To humor Aquarius, she opened the soft cover to reveal a little white square decorated with a formal script writing that said:

> *On these magical pages, spill your sensual fantasy,*
> *In a mere day's time, your wishes will become reality.*
> *A kiss, a touch, a whisper, whatever you most desire,*
> *In the arms of your lover, pleasure will burn hotter than fire.*